THE
LONDON
STONE

THE LONDON STONE

The Nowhere Chronicles
BOOK III

SARAH SILVERWOOD

Indigo

The right of Sarah Silverwood to be identified as the author of
this work has been asserted by her in accordance with the
Copyright, Designs and Patents Act 1988.

First published in Great Britain in 2012 by Indigo
An imprint of the Orion Publishing Group
Orion House, 5 Upper St Martin's Lane, London WC2H 9EA
An Hachette UK Company

A CIP catalogue record for this book
is available from the British Library

ISBN 978 1 78062 067 1

1 3 5 7 9 10 8 6 4 2

Typeset by Deltatype Ltd, Birkenhead, Merseyside

Printed in Great Britain by Clays Ltd, St Ives plc

The Orion Publishing Group's policy is to use papers that are natural,
renewable and recyclable products and made from wood grown in sustainable
forests. The logging and manufacturing processes are expected to conform
to the environmental regulations of the country of origin.

YA

www.sarah-silverwood.com
www.orionbooks.co.uk

For Baby Fin,
Happy adventuring in the world and make this
living business fun above all else!

THE MAGI'S PROPHECY

Nine there are, and standing side by side
Linked by Love, Truth, Freedom, Hatred, Pride –
Their blood, it is the river's ebb and tide.

Here are two reflections of the same,
The dead bones of the one, the other's frame –
The Magi see the unravelling of the game:

This, their Prophecy.

The dark man comes to rule the new Dark Age.
His door admits those too who come to save.

Travellers from without, within
Bring honour, valour, hate and sin.
Light and dark and shades of each,
Will move through voids, the worlds to breach.

When life and death are bound in one,
The balance of all will come undone,
And love, the greatest damage cause
And forge the war to end all wars.

Eternal stories held unready shall bring
Black tempest, madness, and a battle for King.

The Magi cannot see the Prophecy's end,
Perhaps the Order of Travellers will defend.
Perhaps the stories will hold strong and clear,
The damaged keep us from the abyss of fear.

Don't fight these tellings: their passing must come,
But prepare, both worlds, for that which must be done.

When one plus one plus one is four.
All the worlds shall wait no more.

THE STORY SO FAR...

After their first adventure in the Nowhere, Finmere Tingewick-Smith and his friends have been separated. Joe is in the Nowhere with the Storyholder, where the Knights hope to restore the stories to her, while Fin and Christopher have been sent back to their respective schools. But they have all been changed by recent events. Christopher carries the secret that his father, Justin Arnold-Mather, was in league with the treacherous Alexander Golden. Joe's personality is becoming darker, the longer he holds the red and black stories for the Storyholder. Fin can't shake the feeling that the Prophecy is still coming for them. With a tiny crack discovered in the table in the Oval room, that feeling spreads to the old Knights as well. The worlds are still uncertain. Perhaps nothing has been saved at all.

The Christmas holidays arrive, and Fin and Christopher are united back at Orrery House in time to witness the induction of the new Knights of Nowhere, under Fowkes' command, before going to visit Joe in the Nowhere. The three boys go out in the early morning to find Mona, but instead they come across the victim of a horrible attack – a woman whose hair and tongue have turned black while her eyes have turned red and filled with madness. Mona, now the head of the Borough Guard, reveals this attack is not a one off. There have been others. Something is stalking the streets of the Nowhere's London, and it's *changing* people. Tova, the Storyholder, has even had visions of it. Something unnatural is amongst them, and the boys return to talk to Fowkes.

As Arnold-Mather makes plans to lure Joe and the Stories to his side, the Prince Regent enlists the Knights to uncover whatever is attacking his people and turning them into 'the mad'. At the White Tower they realise the boys knew the first victim and, combining their information with Tova's visions, the Regent comes to believe the attacks are somehow linked to the Knights, to the Traders, or even to the Prophecy itself.

Their visit to the White Tower is cut short when a fire breaks out at the Storyholder Academy; a fire started deliberately as part of Arnold-Mather's plan. His henchman, Levi Dodge, murders the boys who truly set it and, despite Fin and Christopher's protests, suspicion falls on Joe. Even though he's proved innocent, his sense of isolation from the Knights deepens. And the stakes have been raised too: now there are no novices capable of becoming Storyholders – there's just Joe and Tova, with the Stories torn between them.

With the Knights, the Traders and the Gypsy Traders enlisted to help track down the sinister attacker, Fin, Christopher, Mona and Anaïs, a Gypsy Trader girl, begin their own investigation. At the moment Fin realises that the man they're looking for is George Porter – the Knight they threw down Clerke's well and into exile – thunder rumbles ominously across the sky. Acting on Arnold-Mather's instructions, Joe has stolen the remaining stories from Tova and escaped to the Somewhere using Baxter's sword.

In both worlds strange weather heralds the Black Tempest and the night of Rage, when everyone must choose their sides … and in the Somewhere's London a Seer who's been missing for decades, Arthur Mulligan, reappears demanding to return to the Nowhere to fulfill a vision he's been unable to block – that of his own death.

As Fin races to the Storyholder's apartments to tell about George Porter, he sees Tova throw herself from the roof of the House of Real Truths. Stricken by grief, Fowkes carries her body in the Chamber of Real Truths and, inside, Fin learns his true origins. Tova used her magic to create him from Baxter's dead body. He is Baxter re-born, and yet not.

As the Rage sweeps through the night, Arnold-Mather and Joe take charge of the Palace, switching Joe's clothes for the Regent's ... and sending the Regent to an execution that Mona and her father can't stop. The mad free themselves from the White Tower and start to seek Joe out, and in a Nowhere full of anger and fighting, the four friends are completely separated. Anaïs falls victim to George Porter, who is being drawn to West Minster by a small magical stone he possesses, and Christopher and Lucas Blake are captured by the Gypsy Traders. In the grip of the Rage, the Gypsy Traders blame them for Anaïs' fate.

The Knights and Jack Ditch join forces to defend the Knights' base in the Nowhere, leaving Fin and Mona the task of saving Christopher. But they arrive too late: the Knight and the teenager have already been pinned out at Traitor's Gate and lost to the river.

With George Porter captured by Arnold-Mather – after taking another piece of magical white stone from the spire at West Minster – the ex-Minister begins his procession to the Future Blocks. When Joe touches the stones, a surge of power rushes through him and cracks appears in the skies of both worlds. It's tiny in the Somewhere, but huge and dark in the Nowhere.

There can be no doubt now. They are all in the grip of the Prophecy and they must fight to save the fates of all the worlds. As Fin stares out at the black snow, grieving for Christopher, something dawns on him. Someone had been giving Arnold-Mather information. And he thinks he knows who. Taking new Knight Alex Currie-Clark with him, he cuts a doorway back through to Orrery House to unmask the traitor in their midst ...

PROLOGUE

They met in the swirling sands far from the citadels of the South, in the place of the Elders where the past was held for time immemorial. At dawn the sky was clear and the air was cold. The steadily growing wind whipped around their robes and drove wrinkles deeper into their dark skins as they walked the miles from the boundaries of civilisation towards the Temple of Nowhere, hidden in the middle of Nothing.

The desert was empty this far into the dust, although even those who scavenged for flesh close to the citadel gates would stay away from the Magi. The only sound on the wind was the jangle of jewellery as the Magi walked, each one coming alone from the cities and towns that had so long been their homes, to this building that held the treasures of a land none of them had ever known – London and the bustling North. As they drew closer together, the steady clink of metal from heavy loop earrings and chains and bracelets became the sound of a flock returning home. The citadels of the South would be short of the Magi's guidance for today, and maybe tomorrow. Everyone would wait for their return. No one had summoned them, and yet these leaders of the tribes had heard the call anyway. It came to them in many ways.

In the sleepless night they had heard the beating of drums from the North. They had seen the black snow falling. They had felt a shift in the ground beneath their feet, the same ground that ran beneath the river and linked the South and North whatever else divided them. They had all looked up into that cold dawn light and known that it was time to walk. To don the ceremonial robes. To find the Elders. They had known even before one amongst them saw the Trader ship dock from the North with tales of stories split

1

and held unready. No one fought their leaving. Even in cities of magic and wonder like those of the South, there was an air of disturbance. Time had changed again. This dawn was early. The mist that came from the river stank of betrayals untold, and those early risers amongst the ordinary folk stared out into it, their eyes narrowed with care and worry. So the Magi walked into the sand, just as their forefathers had so many years before when they had crossed West Minster Bridge for the final time.

It was quiet as they gathered in the temple. They took their places and worried at their beads and let their minds empty of the simple magic that ruled their days. They drank and ate and let their tired, cold bodies warm. It did not take long. The metal panels that ran around the building glinted and shimmered like mother-of-pearl, hints of pinks and purples flickering in the glow of the large candles that lit the sand coloured walls. Heat pulsed from them like a fire, defying the wind that tore around the exterior. As the night slowly fell that wind would build into a frenzy, making it impossible to leave the temple without the sand blasting your skin from your body. Only when dawn broke again would the air fall still once more.

The Elders of old had chosen their retreat wisely after the betrayal of the North. They would never be so open to attack again. The temple and the network of dwellings beneath could keep the Magi safe if needed. It would take a lot of anger and hatred to make the people of the Southern cities come this far into the middle of Nothing to fight them, if that day ever arose.

The Magi waited until the air shimmered and the thrum of an echoing gong filled the temple as the Elders appeared, their purple robes clashing with the crimson of the visiting Magi and the pale yellow of those who would one day become Elders themselves. The Elders wore amulets around their necks that glowed like the metal on the walls. The gathered Magi knew what that meant before the Elders spoke of it.

A Seer had died.

A Seer was being born.

This was known. They could feel it in their blood. They could hear it in the murmurs of the river. They talked of other things. The North. The stories 'held unready'. The boy made from the spirit of a dead man. The Knights. The events that carried across the mist from one side of the broken city to the other. They knew the Prince of the North was dead, ending the terrible curse forged by their forefathers and placed with so much hatred that none of the Magi who followed could undo its power. They had each felt the moment; a slight weight gone from their shoulders, a burden of ages lifted. They spoke of the black snow that drifted over the cities of the South, starting at the water's edge but which would no doubt spread further. There was dark magic there – old magic of nature. The magic of the worlds.

They talked of the novice who had gone North, who had helped put these wheels in motion and who had never returned. They talked of their sacred vows to shun power and politics and live peacefully amongst the people of the South and wondered if that decision had been running away, or whether it had become the nature of their people to keep their power bound.

They talked all through the long night that beat sand against the temple walls; and finally, they talked about the Prophecy.

PART ONE

—◆—

The Change

ONE

It felt as if the space between the worlds held Fin for a second. Perhaps it did, or maybe it was just that his head was still reeling. It was Christmas. It should have been a time to celebrate with friends, but instead the Prophecy was coming true and he and the Knights were in a battle to save the worlds. What was left of the Knights anyway. Lucas Blake was dead, and how many more would be lost? It was surreal. Worse, thinking of Lucas forced him to think of Christopher. How he had been choked by the mist and then drowned in the awful river water. Had he expected Fin and Fowkes to save him? That's what happened in adventure stories, wasn't it, the last minute rescue? But Fin and Mona hadn't been fast enough and this wasn't the sort of adventure you read about in books.

He hated himself. He'd been so wrapped up in self-pity after discovering the truth about him and Baxter – Baxter anyway, there was no *Fin*, not really – that he'd forgotten the others were all in danger too. And he'd let Christopher die. He'd let Joe down too, he should have been there more for him. He should have insisted on staying in the Nowhere with him once he had the stories, rather than going back to Eastfields for the rest of the term. He hadn't insisted, he'd just done as he was told, the way he always had in his strange one year here, one year there existence.

The moment in the doorway between worlds passed and finally his feet found solid ground. There was no one in the

Oval Room when Fin stumbled through, his sword still firm in his hand, ready to be used as a weapon if he needed it. After the cold air and icy black snow of the Nowhere the heat in Orrery House hit him like a wave, knocking his breath from his lungs. He was back in the Somewhere, but this time there was no sense of relief or of excitement to see Ted and the other old men that lived here. Too much had happened that night and he was carrying too much pent-up grief inside.

The lights were off and the Prophecy table was covered but the room was lit by the pale glow from the display cases that held the Orreries that gave the house its name. They twinkled like lost universes in space, beautiful and mysterious. For some reason they made Fin's heart ache even more. The beautiful things in life were fragile and could be taken from you so quickly; he'd learned that in the past few hours. He thought of blonde hair that was almost white. He thought of Christopher's smile. He gritted his teeth. That kind of thinking was pointless. The only way to prevent their losses – Christopher, Tova, Anaïs and the Regent amongst them – being in vain was to make sure they won this battle. Christopher's father, Mr Arnold-Mather, had to be taken down, and the first step was to uncover the spy who had been helping him all this time. Once again, Fin was annoyed with himself. Why hadn't he thought of it sooner? Everything was moving too fast, there was no time to think. Maybe right now, with everything he'd learned about himself, that might not be a bad thing.

'We need to find Ted,' he whispered to Alex Currie-Clark, the Knight behind him. 'He'll know what to do.' His first thought had been just grabbing the traitor, confronting him, and hauling him back to Fowkes in the Nowhere, and the temptation was still great, but he knew Ted and Freddie Wise might think differently. They might want to keep it quiet and feed false information to Arnold-Mather; who knew how this battle would be best fought? Certainly not a sixteen-year-old kid. His stomach turned in on itself. Not even one made out of the spirit of a dead man. Maybe it was Baxter who was making him think sensibly. Maybe Baxter was doing *all* the thinking. How much of Fin was him and how much was the Knight? It made his head swim. Fin's only certainty was that neither of them would let Arnold-Mather win – they'd beat him for Tova, and the Prince Regent and Christopher. His thoughts hitched slightly over his friend's name, but he pushed his pain aside.

'Come on.' He jogged towards the door. 'If you see anyone, just tell them Fowkes sent us and we need to see Ted.' He got no answer and, suddenly aware of the empty room around him, realised Alex Currie-Clarke wasn't there. Confused, he turned around. He froze, his mouth half open as if he'd been about to say something that was now lost for ever.

'Alex?' he finally whispered, aghast.

The old man curled up against the wall wasn't recognisable as the young red-haired Knight of a few moments before. Thin wisps of grey hair coated a liver-spotted scalp and his clothes hung loosely on his scrawny frame. Milky eyes peered sadly at him from behind the familiar black-framed spectacles.

'You're right,' Alex Currie-Clarke's voice was reedy. 'You better had get Ted.' His sword toppled onto the carpet with a dull thud and the old man stared at it. 'And just when I was starting to get the hang of all this.' He rested his head back against the wall. Finmere crouched beside him.

'We can make you better ...' he said, hopelessly, his heart thumping. This wasn't fair. Not on top of everything else that had happened. Not this too. 'Ted will be able to ... Ted can ...' The words drifted away as a gnarled, dry hand gripped his. There was such desperation in it that for a moment Fin was transported back to Judge Harlequin Brown's office, when the dying man had grabbed him and told him to pull the sword he now carried out of his chest. The grip had been the same. Doomed.

'Ted can't do anything about this. It's the Ageing.' Although his voice was still relatively firm, a tear rolled out from behind the thick glasses and ran down the now unfamiliar cheek.

Fin said nothing, but he squeezed Currie-Clark's hand tightly. All thoughts of the traitor were gone. He could wait.

'How bad is it?' Currie-Clark asked. For a moment Fin almost lied, but then realised that the Knight deserved better than that. If he lied, it would just be to make this moment easier for himself, and the moment when Currie-Clark finally looked into a mirror would be so much worse.

'It's pretty bad,' he said softly.

Alex Currie-Clark, all of twenty-two, sighed, and the air came out of his lungs like a death rattle. 'I thought as much.' He tried to smile. 'Merry bloody Christmas.'

Finmere was so absorbed in the moment that he didn't hear the door behind them slide quietly open and when the lights came on he jumped slightly and spun round.

'Mr Smith?' Jarvis asked. 'What on earth is going on?' The butler's eyes widened as he saw the elderly husk of a man sitting against the wall, black-framed glasses sliding down his shrunken head. The spectacles were recognisable even if their owner no longer was. 'Mr Currie-Clark? Oh, I am sorry.' He paused for a moment and then spoke again. 'I think perhaps we'd better fetch Mr Merryweather.'

Fin stared at Jarvis for a long second. 'Yes,' he said eventually, not taking his eyes from the butler's prim and unreadable expression. 'I think we'd better had. Is he here?'

'No,' the butler said, coming towards them. 'He's gone to the London Library with Cardrew Cutler and Freddie Wise.' He glanced down at the Prophecy table. 'They're researching what might have caused that.' Fin followed his gaze. A dark crack, jagged like black lightning, stretched about ten centimetres inwards from one corner of the cover. Only a few days before that crack had been a barely visible, tiny thread of trouble that the Knights could scarcely see. Not any more.

'Does it go through to the map?' Finmere asked. The crack filled him with dread but it didn't surprise him. Not with everything that was happening in the Nowhere. The Black Tempest was upon them. One plus one plus one equalled four.

'So it would seem. It sounded like an explosion, when the crack expanded. It happened just before dawn. An hour or so ago.' Jarvis moved past Fin as he spoke and then crouched by Alex Currie-Clark, primly pulling up the knees of his pressed trousers as he did. 'I know you feel frightened,' he said to the Aged Knight. Finmere was surprised by the kindness in his voice. 'Try not to be,' Jarvis continued. 'We will take care of you. Now, let's get you to your feet and somewhere more comfortable. Your legs will probably feel a little strange' – he draped Currie-Clarke's arm around his neck – 'but you'll get used to them.' He strained slightly on the last two words as he pulled the man to his feet, but the movement was swift and steady. Jarvis was stronger than he looked.

'I'll get Mr Currie-Clark settled. You go to Ted Merryweather,' Jarvis said. 'He'll want to know about this immediately.' Fin looked at the shrunken old man who leaned so helplessly on the butler. A fresh wound of guilt opened up inside him. If he had just come alone this wouldn't have happened. Maybe if he'd brought one of the Wakley twins with him instead ... he let the thought evaporate. There were so many 'if only's that he couldn't keep track of them all and he had a more pressing problem to deal with.

'It's all right,' Alex Currie-Clark wheezed. 'You go. I might be old, but I'm not dying. I'll still be here when you get back.' His left eye dropped in a tired wink. Fin looked from him to Jarvis, his stomach tying in knots. He didn't have a choice. He had to get Ted. He held the door open and followed the two men out into the brightly lit hallway. 'Where's the Library?' he asked.

'St James' Square. There's a black cab outside. He'll take you there.'

11

Fin nodded.

'And take care, Master Smith,' Jarvis added. 'It's dangerous out there.'

Fin looked at him for a long moment and nodded again. 'I will, Jarvis. You can be sure of that.' He felt the butler's eyes on his back until he'd rounded the lower landing. For the first time, leaving Orrery House felt like a relief.

Fin sat on the edge of his seat in the taxi and stared out at the city. His city. His London. Even after he'd realised that there were secret doorways and secret worlds and cab drivers with strange small stickers in their window, London still always felt like home. He loved the city. During his one year here, one year there school life, London had been the solid foundation of his uncertain existence. He'd hidden his most precious object, the blanket he'd been found in, behind a plaque in Postman's Park. Safely tucked away in the heart of the city. As it turned out, the blanket wasn't just precious to him, but to all the worlds as the Storyholder had woven into it the five eternal stories.

His nerves jangled, his muscles tightened in his shoulders, and Fin wished for the time when the blanket had been his alone and life was merely confusing, a time when all he and Christopher and Joe had to worry about were detentions and homework. He wished his two best friends had never met. He wished he'd never dragged them into all this. He blinked back the tears that stung behind his eyes when he thought that he would never again laugh until he cried at one of his friend's wry impersonations of their teachers. Christopher had a devil-may-care attitude that was so the opposite of his father's dour and humourless personality. The thought of Arnold-Mather made Fin feel less to blame. He might have got Joe involved, but because of his father's plans Christopher had always been a part of all this, just like Fin had. Maybe none of them had

12

ever had a choice. Not Baxter, Joe, Christopher or him. They were all in the Prophecy.

There was no black snow falling in the streets of the Somewhere's London, but they still suddenly seemed alien to Fin. It was Christmas morning, and although the shop fronts were filled with displays of Santas and reindeer and presents, there was something tired about them. The lights strung along the streets and in the trees in the squares were only half-flickering, as if many of the light bulbs had died during the night. The sky, too, was strange; the morning grey coloured with terrible bruises of forbidding pinks and purples. The worlds were linked and what happened in one was echoed in another. Fin looked more closely. Here and there sharp eyes peered out from the edges of buildings as the taxi purred past.

In another corner, three tramps made a pretence of drinking from a bottle in a paper bag, but their eyes were clear as they met Fin's gaze. Who were these people? Had the Rage happened here too, but in a quieter way? Had sides been drawn? Was this the event Ted and the old boys had been preparing for, when he'd arrived after discovering the truth at The Old Bailey House of Real Truths? He hadn't been paying attention, but the old nightwatchman and Fowkes had been organising the cabbies to do something. Central London was always quiet on Christmas morning, but this eerie stillness was not normal. Fin wondered if ordinary people opening their presents could feel it too. The sense that things weren't quite right. Or that they were in fact, quite, quite wrong.

Every half a mile or so they passed a black taxi parked somewhere, tucked into the mouth of one side street or another, almost invisible with its yellow light turned off. As Fin's cab drove by each of them they flashed their headlights, twice in quick succession. The cabs weren't as empty as they looked. Fin wondered if his own driver flashed his lights back at them. More than likely. The world, whichever one he was in, was full of secret signs and unspoken alliances. He tried to catch a glimpse of the driver as they passed one taxi, but he could only make out a hunched-over shadowy figure. They were keeping watch. But what for?

As they drew closer to Piccadilly and then to Westminster beyond, the frequency of the headlight signals grew. Strange as it was, Fin decided that even after everything he'd been through in the past few days there was a comfort in knowing that a fleet of solid black London cabs was watching out for him and Ted and the Knights. London cabs had something unbreakable about them. He didn't care if it wasn't entirely true, he still liked the idea of it.

'Here you go, son.' The driver pulled up at the far corner of St James' Square. 'That's the library there.' Fin looked at the white stone building, which didn't look very much like a library at all. The number fourteen was stamped into the stone that arched above the doorway. 'The London Library' was printed in gold on the wood above the door itself, declaring its purpose despite the subtle exterior.

'Thanks,' Fin muttered as he climbed out into the cold morning air. There was a pressure in the atmosphere that belonged in the humidity before a summer storm rather than an icy December day and it made his head throb slightly. *A storm. A tempest. Black snow.* He turned away and the cabbie whistled him back.

'Don't knock on the door. They won't let you in that way. You see that bronze plaque on the wall?'

'Yes.'

'If you run your fingers under the bottom, you'll feel a tiny button. Press it twice. You got that?'

Fin nodded again. Of course. Wherever the Knights of Nowhere conducted their business there were always secret passageways and entrances. Why would the library be any different? The cabbie dropped him a wink and drove away, leaving Fin standing alone in the quiet as if he were the last person alive in the world. He stared at the library and then climbed the steps to the door and ran his fingers under the cold metal of the plaque. On his first attempt he didn't feel anything, and then he found it, a tiny circle under his fingertip. He pressed twice and waited.

TWO

'Is he all right? He hasn't said a word.'

Two men stood in front of him, one stocky, the other tall, but he didn't look up. Their words were dull in his blocked ears. Everything was a haze of nothing.

'He's breathing. That's something.' One of them shoved a cup of something at his face. It steamed and smelled of citrus and honey. He felt weighed down on the wooden bench, his limbs like lead under the blanket.

'Take it.' The voice was naturally commanding, and he looked up into the swarthy face, seeing it for the first time. A thick scar ran like white lightning down the length of the man's face, cutting across his nose and disappearing into his stubble. His troubled eyes were green. 'I said take it,' the man repeated. *Curran Tugg.* He was Curran Tugg, leader of the Traders.

He followed the order and forced one heavy arm to lift, reaching for the wooden cup. Only when it was fully extended did he see he already held something in his hand, something he was gripping tightly. A necklace. Beads and a silver pendant. His mouth dropped open with a surprise that was mirrored in Curran Tugg's green eyes.

Green like the water.

Christopher's breath hitched as the past crashed back into him.

*

'Let us be ready,' Lucas Blake said with a wink, but Christopher had no time to answer it as the water rose over his mouth. His heart was racing and although the dark mist-induced madness willed him to breathe it in, he took a long, deep last lungful of air as the water began to lap at his nostrils and held it. At school he could swim three lengths of the pool without coming up for air. He was the champion. At school. A lifetime ago. A lifetime that was ending.

He squeezed his eyes shut and the numbness in his trapped wrists spread out through his body as the cold of the river gripped him. He was vaguely aware of Lucas Blake thrashing beside him, struggling to stay alive, even as part of Christopher wondered what they were trying to live for. His lungs were starting to burn but although his mind despaired, his body fought to live, straining at the cuffs that held him down, but there was no escape from this. He opened his eyes as the first few bubbles burst out between his lips. The river had risen fast and he could no longer see the surface through the grainy green. He looked to his right. Lucas Blake's bruised body was still and relaxed. His hair drifted upwards and his mouth was open. The Knight was dead. His struggle was done. Christopher struggled harder, thrashing in the water even as his heart ached for the Knight. He wished he hadn't been so cowardly and held his breath because now he was truly going to have to die alone here in the awful river ...

... more bubbles slipped free and as the pressure in his lungs became almost unbearable he strained at the cuffs that held him down. The dark, murky swirls of the water encouraged him to let go and sink into the black depths. It would only be moments before his lungs filled with water. He had to get out ... he had to get ...

... and then there was a glow. Pinks and silvery purples reached out to him from the inky depths of the water. He lifted his head and looked into the heart of the Times. Where there had been only a terrible blackness there was now a swirl of colour, a universe of light. More bubbles fled from his lungs as he stared. Was he drowning? Was he hallucinating? The terrible dread that filled *each particle of water and mist that had been soaking into his soul, evaporated. He stared ahead, as if the river water wasn't stinging his eyes and his lungs weren't exploding with pain. It was like seeing the Northern Lights. A dazzling array of colour against the night of the river. After a moment, heedless of the last bubbles of air escaping him, he saw something at the centre of the display. Something that glowed so brightly white he thought it might blind him, something that all the rest of the colours spread from.*

He breathed in water, and the cuffs clicked free. Beside him, Lucas Blake's body drifted away, past the colours and away into the darkness. Christopher reached forward, using the last of his energy to push himself towards the glittering light, wondering if this sudden absence of fear was all part of the hallucination. He was dying. He had to be. And maybe it wasn't so terrible, after all.

He grabbed for the light and was surprised to feel something real between his fingers. As he hung in the water, no air left in his lungs to force him to the surface, the colours swirled faster around him. In them he saw fish and eels darting this way and that, a river alive with life which was drawn, as he had been, to the magical brightness. He looked closer. A necklace. Beads with a pendant in the middle. Silver, like the metal plates he'd seen in the walls at West Minster. It was beautiful—

—the pendant flashed a crimson red and Christopher recoiled, sucked in a second lungful of water as it burned his palm. The colours winked out and he looked up to see a body in the water before him. The middle-aged man's eyes were wide, and his pony tail whipped around his neck. One cowboy boot had come free to reveal a bare foot. One arm floated up towards Christopher as he sank, as if to grab him and drag him deeper into his death. The boy let out a silent scream, kicked away, and the water finally overwhelmed him.

He must have thrown himself from the bridge. *The thought came to Christopher as he kicked away from the dead body, fighting the unconsciousness that was pulling at him in black waves at the edge of his vision as the current grabbed him. He threw* himself from the bridge for me. *Christopher's palm was locked around the hot metal, and ancient words filled his head as the last of his life ebbed from his body. He no longer struggled and as he surrendered to the river, he wondered at the strangeness of his dying thought.*

One shall die and one shall be born. It has ever been thus. *And then there was darkness.*

'One shall die and one shall be born. It has ever been thus.' The words hurt his raw throat and lungs, and his voice was so gravelly he didn't recognise it as his own. He swallowed and the strained muscles of his tongue and throat screamed. The Traders must have pumped a lot of water from his lungs when they'd hauled him out of the river. Surely he'd been dead? How long had he been in the water? He remembered the lights. The body. Poor Lucas Blake vanishing into the bleak Times for ever.

'What did he say?' It was the other man, who stood alongside Curran Tugg. Elbows – Christopher recognised his thickset body now. His voice was filled with awe.

'You heard him,' Curran Tugg said. 'You heard him as well as I did.'

'How could he know those words?'

They were talking as if he wasn't sitting right in front of them, and with trembling hands, still weak from his ordeal in the water, Christopher fastened the pendant around his neck. The metal felt immediately warm against his chest and calmness flooded through him. He took the cup from Curran Tugg and sipped cautiously.

'He couldn't,' Tugg answered. Christopher could feel the green eyes evaluating him. Curran Tugg had realised what Christopher himself had the moment he'd tied the pendant around his neck. School and his old life were over. Everything had changed, once again. A death for a birth. A passing of a gift. And he knew for sure that the Magus' words at West

Minster were true. He would die at thirty-eight and not before.

'But that can't be,' Elbows continued. 'Those words ... they're always the first words of ...'

'... a new seer.' Christopher finished the sentence for him and met his gaze steadily. There was a long pause as Curran Tugg stared at him.

'Well, let's hope you're better at it than the last one,' he said eventually with a sniff. 'He was one of yours as well. Or so I heard. A seer that refused to see.'

Christopher said nothing but he stood up, his legs steady, and looked over the boat's sturdy wooden side. He could see nothing through the thick mist, but he found the smell was no longer so foul, nor did it affect his mood. There was a fog in his mind, too. Things he knew that he couldn't know. He was the Seer – he knew it in his bones, even though the word was unfamiliar. He knew the man who had worn the pendant before him had come back to the Nowhere for this moment of transfer; to give this gift to him alone.

'In the river, though?' Elbows' unhappy muttering carried over the lapping of the water and pounding of oars. 'That's not right. The river's too powerful. A seer transfer in the Times. Can't be good.'

'Not our problem,' Curran Tugg answered. 'We'll get him back to Fowkes. The boy's lucky to be alive.'

Christopher touched the pendant that hung at his neck as if it had been there forever. He didn't think luck had anything to do with his survival. Fate, perhaps. But not luck.

THREE

Alex Currie-Clark didn't look down as Jarvis and Hector Allbright, another of the Aged Knights, undressed him. Even with his suddenly weak vision, he had no desire to face his new body yet.

'That's it,' Allbright said, taking Alex's trousers off to be replaced by stripy pyjamas, just like those Allbright was wearing. 'I know you feel all out of sorts, but you'll get used to it.' His milky eyes met Alex's and he could see a strength in there. 'We don't have much choice.' As he allowed the men to dress him, he wondered if he'd come across Hector Allbright before. Had they passed in the corridors of Orrery House? There weren't that many of the Aged still up and about – most sank into a comatose state as the years passed. There hadn't been an Ageing for a while. Not until today, at least.

He looked at Hector Allbright's wrinkled face and sagging jowls. He was shorter than Alex and stockier, with a small paunch visible under his dressing gown. He didn't ring any bells but Alex realised, with dismay, that the elderly had all looked the same to him. They had seemed a lifetime away, and now here he was with his personal timeline folded in on itself. A small sob escaped him, and he was ashamed of it.

'Let it out,' Allbright said, standing back as Jarvis leaned in to rearrange his pillows. 'You've got to. Otherwise it'll fester like a wound that refuses to heal and make you bitter. I've seen it, and old and bitter isn't a combination that suits anyone.' He nodded towards the small black moleskin notebook and the tin of mints on the side. 'The mints will keep you alert. We don't know why, but they do.'

'What's the book for?' Alex asked.

Hector Allbright smiled a little. 'It's for your memories. For all the magic that happens between the Somewhere and the Nowhere. You write it down for the records. In your voice rather than the voice of History.'

Alex almost laughed. That was a joke. A bad one. 'I doubt I'll need a whole notebook. I must be the shortest-lived Knight there's ever been.'

'You're still a Knight, son,' Hector Allbright said. 'Until the end. There's always a chance of a reversal too.' The last sentence was delivered too wistfully for Alex to believe Allbright had any faith in it.

'I'll take it from here, Mr Allbright,' Jarvis said.

'Right you are.' He nodded at Alex. 'I'll pop back in shortly. We can talk if you'd like.'

Alex didn't answer, but it seemed Allbright hadn't expected him to; he was already shuffling back out into the corridor. The door closed, and Alex stood shakily to allow Jarvis to pull back the covers and let him climb in. When the bed was ready, he sank gratefully into the soft mattress. He shivered slightly as Jarvis carefully pulled the layers of duck down duvet and blankets up to his neck and realised something else. He'd always been sweltering in Orrery House, where the heating was always set to some tropical temperature, and yet now he felt as if there was a draught creeping through the house from the December cold outside. Was that part of the Ageing too, this coldness?

'You'll find you're coldest now,' Jarvis said, as if reading his mind. Or maybe it was because he'd done this so many times before. 'And you'll probably sleep most of today. By tomorrow you will be feeling much better. The first day is always the worst.' He smiled, and Alex was surprised by the kindness in it. He'd never really *seen* Jarvis before. He was just – well – *Jarvis*. The butler. Impersonal, professional and somewhat remote.

'I'll bring you up a cup of tea and a mince pie.'

'Thank you.' The stranger's voice that came out of his mouth made him want to cry all over again.

'What brought you back so urgently?' Jarvis asked, as he pulled the curtains closed to block out the new day. 'Is there anything I should do to assist you?'

'No,' Alex said, his voice slurring slightly. Sleep was claiming him, a thick, confused sleep that had already half-convinced him it was all a terrible dream, that he was safe in the Knights' headquarters in the Nowhere. 'It was something Fin wanted to talk to Ted about,' he mumbled. 'Something he figured out.' His eyes drifted shut.

'Really? He always was a bright boy. What did he figure out?' Jarvis' voice came from miles away, pulling Alex back from the blissful oblivion of sleep.

'Mr Currie-Clark?' Jarvis' voice was sharper. 'What has the boy figured out?'

Alex frowned slightly. Why couldn't Jarvis just leave him to rest? The bed was so soft and the covers ...

'What does he want to tell Mr Merryweather?'

'A traitor,' Alex mumbled, barely aware of his own words. 'He knows who the traitor is.' His head lolled to one side, and within a moment he was snoring.

'A traitor?' Ted said. 'Do you mean Simeon Soames?'

'What? No. No I don't mean him.' Fin frowned, suddenly confused. 'Why would I mean him?' He looked from Ted to Harper Jones, who was leaning against the rack of books to Ted's left and staring at the floor, and then back to Ted. Why would they think Soames was a traitor?

'Simeon went to the palace to see if Arnold-Mather was there,' Ted said. ''E never came back.'

'The Rage must've got him,' Harper said. 'Or Arnold-Mather and his men killed him. Either way, he's lost to us.' Under his blond hair, the Knight's eyes had darkened. 'We should have given Christopher's potion to Cardrew or Freddie.'

'Easy, son.' Ted slapped his arm. ''E might be dead, for all we know. Don't tarnish 'is name yet.'

'Let's hope he *is* dead.' Freddie Wise appeared on the narrow gantry ahead of them. 'Terrible as that sounds. If he's alive and the Rage has turned him then Arnold-Mather has a lot of information about us at his fingertips.' He peered at Harper over his bifocals. 'And you, young man, should be careful before you harbour hatred so quickly. None of us is immune to the lure of wickedness. Evil often comes with an appearance of strength and we all like to think strength in our leaders will keep us safe. Simeon had a bad time when he Aged. He was lucky he didn't go completely mad. So whatever has happened, don't hate him. If the Rage has got him then I should imagine he hates himself.'

'I know,' Harper said. 'It's just been a very long night and we've lost too many good people.' His shoulders slumped slightly and the natural quiet of the library was filled with a heavier silence, one weighed down by grief. Fin felt a stab inside as he thought of their losses: Tova, the Prince Regent, Lucas Blake, and Christopher. The last went right to his heart. And he ached for the loss of Anaïs and Joe, who, although not dead, were still gone – one lost to madness and one become an enemy.

'Yes, we have,' Freddie Wise said quietly. 'And we must not let them be lost in vain.'

'It's not Simeon Soames I'm talking about,' Finmere said, taking a deep breath and knowing he was about to strike another blow to Ted's heart. 'It's Jarvis.'

Ted visibly recoiled as if he'd been punched, and all the gathered men turned to stare at Fin as if waiting for him to laugh and tell them it was just a stupid not-very-funny joke he'd made up. Fin met each of their gazes in turn, not knowing what more he could say.

'We've found something!'

The voice cut through the stunned quiet and Cardrew Cutler's face appeared around the edge of a rack of books several feet away. 'Well, I say we. I mean the librarian. She's quite a woman.' He paused. 'What is it? What did I say?'

Ted had paled. Neither he nor Freddie Wise nor Harper looked at Cutler, who might as well have been invisible. 'Jarvis?' Ted swore. 'Can't be. Not Jarvis.'

'Mr Arnold-Mather knows too much about our plans. I don't believe Judge Brown would have given him details about people and places, but Arnold-Mather still managed to make an alliance with St John Golden.' Fin spoke quickly, as if that could somehow lessen the butler's betrayal. 'And even after Golden was trapped in the Incarcerator mirror Christopher's dad still knew what happening and where Joe was and how to get to him.'

'But ... Jarvis?' Cardrew Cutler had come forward, whatever he'd found momentarily forgotten. 'What makes you think it's him? Maybe it's one of the new Knights.'

'I've been going over everyone in my head,' Fin said. 'He's the only one it can be. The new Knights have been too busy doing what they're told. They haven't had time to make a phone call, let alone anything else, and none of them know stuff like you guys or Fowkes does. The thing about Jarvis is that he hears *everything*.'

'It's true,' Freddie Wise said softly. 'Jarvis serves us coffee in the Oval Room and we barely notice he's there when we're talking.'

'He's *everywhere*,' Fin said. 'No one ever pays him any attention. It's like he's invisible. It's part of his job.'

'But Jarvis has been with Orrery House for years. Twenty? Thirty maybe?' Cutler said. 'He's one of us.'

'No,' Fin said, surprised at the firmness in his voice. Was that him or Baxter? 'I don't think he is.'

'It can't be true,' Ted said. His face was pale and in the bright strip lighting of the library the lines on his face seemed deeper. He looked old. "Ow many traitors can there be? And 'ow could we not know?'

'Fin's right, though,' Harper Jones said. 'It is the only logical explanation. We've got to at least entertain it, however little we like it.'

'I agree.' Freddie Wise nodded. He squeezed Ted's shoulder. 'We're at war, old friend. Yesterday's allies can become today's enemies in the blink of an eye. You can't blame yourself.'

'But what did we ever do to 'im?' Ted shook his head. 'What did we do to make 'im turn on us?'

'I don't think people betray others because of something that is *done* to them. It's because of something they *want* or because of something they perceive.' Freddie Wise leaned on his walking stick but his back was straight and strong. 'If Jarvis was unhappy then he could have spoken to us. He didn't. It was his choice. There is no blame at your door, Ted Merryweather, nor at Harlequin's. Just you remember that. War brings out the worst in some people, and the one coming with this storm is going to be a battle like nothing we've seen.'

'Is Jarvis still at Orrery House?' Harper Jones asked.

'Yes.' Fin swallowed hard and steadied himself for the breaking of more bad news. 'I left him putting Alex Currie-Clark to bed.' His throat closed slightly around the next words. 'Alex Aged.'

A hard silence fell, broken only by gasps. 'Poor sod,' Harper Jones said eventually and Fin saw dark shadows flit over his face. 'Poor bloody sod.'

'Does Jarvis know you suspect him?' Freddie Wise asked, his face grim.

'No,' Fin said. 'With Alex ... with the Ageing I don't think he would have noticed anything with me. I was trying to be normal. As normal as I could be.'

'We should still get back,' Ted said. 'I don't like the thought of him there without us.'

'You need to see this first,' Cardrew Cutler said, signalling them forward as he turned and hurried along the narrow metal gantry between the shelves. 'We've found something. It's about that crack in the table.'

'Jarvis can wait a little longer,' Freddie Wise said. 'In essence this news changes nothing, except that we are more informed. There's no one at the house who can tell him anything, and Fowkes knows we're here.' His cane tapped on the gantry as he headed after Cutler, and the rest of the group followed.

They took the narrow stairs in single file and eventually came to a reading room that looked more like a snug, slightly tired drawing room than anywhere in the libraries that Fin was used to, at Eastfields or even St Martin's. The table lamps were lit, bathing the room in a warm golden glow, and on each of three large desks several books lay open as well as scribbled in notebooks and pencils. On the floor, screwed up balls of paper surrounded the small wastepaper bins where someone – Cardrew Cutler probably – had thrown them from one desk or another, and missed.

The librarian, a woman with mousy hair and glasses whose dark frames looked too heavy for her small features and delicate figure, looked up. She had been jotting something down from one of the larger volumes.

'Esme is ever so good at all this,' Cardrew Cutler said proudly. 'We'd get nowhere without her. She found all these books, you know. Every one of them had been hidden in a coded subsection of the library. We could have searched for years and not found them.'

'That's why we have a librarian,' Freddie Wise said, and smiled at Esme.

'Oh dear,' she muttered, blushing slightly. The words sounded like a nervous habit rather than an exclamation that there was something wrong. 'All libraries have systems. These books are just arranged in a slightly more complex system than the rest. That part is quite simple. The codes they're written in, however, are more complicated. But we're getting there.' She flashed Cutler a sudden, tight smile and Fin realised that her blush was from both nervousness and excitement.

'Yes, we are,' Cutler agreed. He was beaming at her and Fin saw an echoing flush of excitement in his sagging cheeks. It was weird. How old was Cardrew Cutler, really? Under the Ageing? 'She's teaching me,' Cutler continued. 'It's quite fascinating.'

'You're a natural,' the librarian said, pushing her glasses back up on her nose and turning a slightly brighter shade of pink.

'What exactly have you found?' Harper Jones asked.

'Well ... oh dear,' Esme said, as Cutler nodded her on. 'It's not all that good, I'm afraid.'

'Nothing is, at the moment,' Freddie Wise said. 'But we still need to know.'

The librarian coughed a little and then took a deep breath. 'The table and the map beneath are representations of all the worlds. More than that, really. They're somehow linked to the nature of existence itself, and that's how we can see current activity on them. If the map shows the worlds, then the table itself represents the universe.'

'Go on,' Ted said.

'If the surface of the table has a crack in it, that means all the worlds have been fundamentally damaged. The universe itself is in danger.'

'So what 'appens if the crack keeps getting bigger?'

The librarian's delicate shoulders shrugged a little and her eyes widened. 'Eventually all the worlds would collapse into themselves. It would be like a black hole. An implosion.' Her words were barely more than a whisper. 'Everything would cease to exist.'

'When?' Freddie Wise asked.

'From what we can make out, and from what Cardrew has told me about the current state of the table, I would guess we have a hundred years or so. But the larger the crack grows the harder it will be to close.'

'And eventually,' Cardrew Cutler added, 'there will come a point of no return.'

'Is this happening because Joe has the stories?' Fin asked.

'It can't be.' Harper shook his head. 'Not just because of that, anyway.' He looked at the others. 'Do you remember when Simeon first noticed the hairline crack? That was after Joe had two of the stories but before he took the rest.' Fin flinched slightly when he heard the word *took*. It made what Joe had done sound so *intentional*. He refused to believe that this was Joe's fault. Not really.

'And it got dramatically bigger about two hours ago,' Freddie Wise said thoughtfully. 'That was a long time after Joe became the Storyholder. This must be something else.'

'We'll keep looking for an explanation,' Cardrew Cutler said, 'but it seems to me Arnold-Mather and Joe have done something, we just don't know about yet. And I doubt *they* realise the potential consequences. Not even Arnold-Mather can be that mad.'

Fin wasn't so sure. Cardrew Cutler hadn't seen what was happening in the Nowhere. Maybe a hundred years away was far enough away for Arnold-Mather to risk. He took a deep breath. Or perhaps not. Arnold-Mather probably thought if he looked hard enough he'd find a way to cheat death.

'Time will tell,' Ted said. 'You keep lookin' in them books. All the answers is in the books, either 'ere or there.'

Esme and Cardrew Cutler both nodded and then grinned shyly at each other. If the world was really about to end then it didn't seem to be bothering those two that much. Fin looked at the massive tomes and slim volumes that were the focus of their work. It was funny; most of the time he thought books were pretty boring. Factual ones, anyway. Now here they were, and the fate of everything depended on what the books could tell them.

A sudden blast of ice cold wind made him shiver and he turned in time to see a few flakes of sparkling black snow melt drift on to the carpet and melt, leaving damp smears behind.

With a deft flick of his sword, Fowkes closed the doorway between the worlds behind him, shutting off the black and white view of a cold, snowy morning in that other London.

'Something's happened,' Fowkes said.

'What now?' Harper Jones spoke for all of them as weight sagged even heavier into the collective shoulders of the group. Fin stared at Fowkes who suddenly smiled. It was a strange sight amidst their grief, especially from Fowkes after Tova's death. Still, it was heart-warming. *Almost like the Fowkes of the old days.* The thought came out of nowhere and killed Fin's rising spirits. Because it wasn't his thought – it was Baxter's. He pushed it away. He was Finmere Tingewick Smith. Adam Baxter was dead.

'Curran Tugg and the Traders are back from the South. They've got someone with them.' Fowkes looked at Fin. 'It's Christopher.' His smile grew wider. 'He's not dead.'

FOUR

By the time dawn became morning, the train of carriages and wagons had reached the crumbling eastern edge of the city. The eerie silence that surrounded them was broken only by the rattling of wheels and clattering of hooves and the occasional shout as Simeon Soames directed them this way or that, his horse moving up and down the ranks as he kept them all together.

Joe, his head still throbbing with all the pressure of so many stories, found that he was comforted by Simeon Soames' presence. He was a link to everything they had both left behind, and occasionally Joe would peer out as the blond Knight passed the narrow carriage window and they would catch each other's eye. Joe was sure he saw a reflection of his own thoughts in the man's expression. *How did we come to this? What are we doing here?* They were bound together in their betrayal, and although that feeling sat in the pit of his stomach and made him constantly queasy, he still felt better when Soames was near.

The straightness of the wooden seat, covered only with the thinnest of padding, and the constant bumps and jolts from the uneven road, were making his back ache. Joe wished for the stones back, just for a minute or so, just to allow him to fall asleep. It had been a beautiful, empty, colourless sleep. The kind of sleep he'd taken for granted only a few months ago when life had been simple: Eastfields, football and surviving the Brickman Estate. His heart ached again. It was Christmas Day and the only present he wanted was for things to be as they had been. He should have given Tova the stories. He should have. Even as he thought it, however, a small voice inside rebelled and held tight to the cargo he carried. The stories were his. They had wanted *him*, Joe Manning, not Tova or any of the others. He was special. *He* was the Storyholder. The voice made him tired and, as the carriage jolted over another pothole, he pulled slightly away from the dozing man sharing the carriage with him, even though his thighs were starting to numb with the cold.

He peered out through the tatty curtain and let the cold air sting his face. The glittering black snow was falling steadily now. He stared, mesmerised, unable to decide if it was beautiful or terrible and realised that perhaps some things were both. The Five Eternal Stories were both. He'd learned that quickly enough. He slipped his hand outside and let the snow melt on his fingers, the black smearing across his brown fingers. It was like dry ice, damp for a moment and then gone, leaving an ash-like residue behind. He wiped it away. The flakes didn't hold his story – he was merely one strand in it – this black snow was all part of Mr Arnold-Mather's tale. Right now, Joe decided, all the worlds were bit-part players in Mr Arnold-Mather's story.

Something scampered alongside the carriage and Joe looked down to see the creatures that used to be people scuttling along the road. They were weaving in and out of the horses, easily keeping pace without tiring, always drawn to him. Their clothes hung muddy and forgotten from their bodies, and black tongues stretched from mouths half-hidden by long, damp, dark hair. Their red eyes glowed though, shining like rotten jewels embedded in their pale faces. His Army of the Mad. He shivered slightly, as much from his revulsion at their adoration as from the cold.

Up ahead someone called the procession to a halt and, without waiting for permission, Joe opened the door and climbed down, eager to stretch his stiff legs. Behind him someone, maybe Edgar Blacken with his badly burned face, was waking Arnold-Mather and it was moments before the former Minister was striding to the front.

Joe followed him, a few feet behind and with four of the mad scurrying around him. He flashed them a look and they pulled away slightly, allowing Simeon Soames to fall into step beside him. It was a strange sight they faced. The wall that encased the city was barely more than knee-high rubble in places, non-existent in others and, on the London side, there was a small group of higgledy-piggledy stone buildings with smoke rising in tired streams from makeshift chimneys. It was almost an independent village, this far from the hustle and bustle of the Circus and the Boroughs and the building looked almost medieval … although, when men emerged warily from them, they wore trousers and flat caps in various shades of beige as if they'd stepped from the pages of a 1920s photograph album.

Beyond the remnants of the wall lay the marshes, a vast stretch of soggy, dangerous ground that Joe doubted, even on a sunny day, would ever look anything less than forbidding. As it was, in the gloomy light and with the black snow falling, the slick wetness with straggly patches of grass thrusting through here and there looked like desolation itself. Perhaps that was why the Future Blocks, bursting up from the ground at the far side of the marshland, appeared even more shocking that they might otherwise.

A vast dome sat on top of a large rock outcrop, surrounded by four buildings that, while not high enough to be skyscrapers, were still taller than anything else Joe had seen in the Nowhere. They were constructed from gleaming metals and clean glass panels, but it wasn't the buildings that took his breath away so much as the colours that shone upwards from them. Bright yellows and pinks and blues blurred together in a wonderful smear against the sky, like a rainbow haze or the lights from a distant funfair.

'And these people are ...?' Mr Arnold-Mather had stopped in front of the gathering villagers who huddled together as the mad scampered around them. They looked terrified and Joe didn't blame them. Terrified had become a near-constant state for him since the Prince Regent was executed – an event he'd come to think of as *the point of no return*, from which his destiny had been sealed. He saw a little boy's curious face appear in one of the doorways for a moment before the child was hastily yanked back inside.

'Rice-growers and marsh farmers,' Edgar Blacken said.

'At least we won't starve as we take control,' Arnold-Mather said, smiling tightly. He examined the small group. 'And you all have families, yes?' For a moment the men said nothing, until several palace guardsmen stepped forward with their swords raised. There was a grudging muttering of acknow-ledgement.

'Good. I shall expect your allegiance.' Arnold-Mather turned with a grand sweep of his coat. 'Do you see that boy there?'

Joe felt all eyes turn his way and more of the mad closed in on him. The men nodded.

'He's the Storyholder. Your Storyholder. And the Future Blocks are where he wishes to make his home.'

There were more mutterings. Joe tried to shut them out and stared instead at the beautiful buildings in the distance.

'They're quite something, aren't they?' Simeon Soames said, quietly.

'Does anyone live there?' Joe was glad of the Knight's conversation. It almost stopped him hearing Edgar Blacken explaining how the path through the marshes moved and only the rice-growers knew how to find it. That in itself wasn't so bad – it was hearing Arnold-Mather's light tone as he laid out the horrific things he would do if the locals didn't oblige him.

'No, I don't think so.' Simeon Soames also had his eyes firmly on the distant dome. 'The Knights sometimes went there, I know that much. St John Golden did a long time ago, when the buildings first appeared, because the Regent wanted a report on them.'

'Appeared?'

'Yes. Most of the places in the Nowhere have grown from odds and ends of stuff falling between the worlds, but some buildings' – he looked down at Joe and for a moment it was almost like nothing had changed for either of them, and they were just waiting for Fin or Fowkes to show up – 'like the St Paul's that arrived in flames and has never been able to be mended, they just show up. There tends to be something special, something different, about those places.'

Joe didn't say anything, but he felt the vibrations inside him. The Knight was right. There *was* something special about the dome.

'Some of the rice growers tried living there for a while. It would have made sense for them. They could travel that far without getting woozy, and none of the better housing they'd tried building over here would stay up, but they just couldn't settle there. They said it felt unnatural. Then a few of the Knights suggested that it might make a better base than the House of Charter's Square. It owes so much of its design to the O2 and Canary Wharf – it's almost more of the Somewhere than the Nowhere. So they tried for a few days. I wasn't there, but the Knights who were said stuff *worked*; like computers needing no charge, and mobile phones getting some weird signal that allowed all the boys to call each other … but they couldn't stay either. Golden said it was too far from the city centre and the Knights were supposed to be there to help in emergencies, but the rest said they left because it felt *wrong*. As if they weren't supposed to be there.'

His quiet words trailed off and he frowned slightly. 'It's as if it's been waiting.'

'What for?' Joe asked. He knew the answer, though, even before Simeon Soames said it.

'The right occupant, I suppose.'

Once again, Joe's stomach twisted in knots. Had the Future Blocks been waiting for them? Had he ever really had a choice or was this all Fate, his path laid out for him? He stared at the dome and the sky above it, and his breath hitched slightly. 'Is it just me,' he asked, 'or are the colours changing?'

Somewhere ahead, a child started to cry.

FIVE

The small group had gathered in the kitchen, and were sipping hot tea and coffee as Mrs Baker added more wood to the roaring fire in the grate. Outside, Jack Ditch's team of urchins kept a lookout in case of any sudden attacks, but the Nowhere streets were desolate and unnaturally quiet. Most people had shut themselves away behind locked doors and were peering out at the black snow. The Rage was passing, and although no one was foolish enough to think the fighting was over, it seemed there was some respite for now. The earlier skirmish had clearly been a decoy to keep the Knights occupied as Arnold-Mather left the palace, which had been looted and damaged in the dying embers of the night's Rage. Arnold-Mather and his guarded convoy of wagons and carriages had been seen heading towards the east of the city and so, for now, those in the House of Charter's Square allowed themselves a breath of relief and some time to gather their thoughts.

'We need to find a different base over here other than this house,' Benjamin Wakley said. 'Maybe two or three. There's no point in being a sitting target.'

'Agreed,' Fowkes said. 'Savjani, can you help with that?'

The clothcrafter nodded. 'Of course.'

'That bastard'll 'ave spies too, soon enough,' Jack Ditch muttered. He was sitting on the edge of the rough wooden table and taking long sips from a cup, while thoughtfully rubbing his scarred ear between his thick fingers. Fin was pretty sure he was drinking something stronger than coffee. 'The Rage'll 'ave changed people, that much is for sure,' Ditch continued. 'It's going to be tough knowing who to trust from now on. Even among my own. In times like this there's always them that will turn on a coin.'

'No honour among thieves?' Fowkes asked.

'Not thieves nor Knights, Andrew Fowkes,' Ditch replied and the two men nodded at each other sagely.

'Something like that.'

'He won't come for us yet.' The voice was soft but filled with something that wasn't quite authority, but was equally commanding. 'He'll build his citadel first. His *kingdom*.' Christopher, sitting on the chair closest to the fire, was bathed in a golden glow from the flames, making it look almost as if a halo shone around him. It was the first time anyone had suggested Arnold-Mather was the Dark King of the Prophecy and just hearing it said aloud made Finmere shiver. The Prophecy bound them all together; him, Joe, Christopher and *Baxter*. It was hard to deny that it was coming to pass. The rest of those gathered around the table all stared at Christopher with expressions of wary awe

Christopher, the schoolboy mimic who had entertained all the boys at St Martin's with his sharp impersonations of teachers and celebrities alike, had become someone who could silence a room of grown men. He'd always been less afraid to speak up than Fin or Joe, having a natural confidence that came with his posh background, but this was something different. There was a stillness about him that hadn't been there before, a certainty, but despite it Fin doubted his friend could have changed all that much. He wished everyone else would sod off for a while and just leave him, Mona and Christopher alone. They'd hugged and smiled when Fin had come back with Fowkes but the rest had all been here and they hadn't been able to chill and be themselves.

As the conversation started up again, Fowkes directed the

Wakley twins to go with Elbows to scout out where Arnold-Mather had taken Joe and the rest of his followers, Fin's mind drifted. He couldn't help it. He was tired and too much had happened over the past twenty-four hours for him to concentrate on anything for long. With Christopher's return the atmosphere had become a strange mixture of joy and sadness. It was almost as if his surprise survival was a reminder of all their losses. Lucas Blake's bright smile flashed in Fin's mind and his stomach turned at the thought of the Knight drowning in that awful river. He looked again at Christopher and the strange pendant that now hung around his neck. Why had Lucas Blake drowned when Christopher hadn't? Maybe he had that question the wrong way around. How had Christopher survived? The mist alone would surely have been enough to drive him mad, let alone being submerged in the River Times itself. *Mad.* The word rang like a bell in his head.

'Where's George Porter?' he asked, cutting across the talking men.

'Who?' Jack Ditch frowned.

'He's the one who's been attacking people and changing them,' Fowkes said. 'I'd forgotten about him. He went into Clarke's Well, and somehow he came back with some kind of infection.'

'We sent him to the dead world and he brought death back with him,' Christopher said.

'They're not dead!' Fin was adamant, remembering Anaïs' bright ice-white hair, that would now be black and lank. 'They're changed, not dead.'

'I wasn't talking about them.' Christopher smiled softly, a sad expression that made Fin feel he was looking at a stranger. He didn't like it at all. It was bad enough that Joe had been damaged by the stories, without Christopher changing too.

'The White Tower emptied during the Rage, that's what people 'ave been saying.' Jack Ditch drained his cup. 'They went to the palace.'

'Oh no.' Mona sat bolt upright, her face paling. 'I sent a message there about George Porter. For the Regent. I said we thought he was going to West Minster, but the Regent wouldn't have got it.' Tears flooded to her eyes, but she shook them away with a flick of her purple hair. 'Arnold-Mather would have.'

There was a long pause. 'Maybe he ignored it,' a stocky blond man said. He was Kent Jasper, one of the new Knights Fin didn't really know.

'Maybe.' Fowkes didn't sound confident. Justin Arnold-Mather was a thorough man – he'd shown that already. If something was important enough to send a message to the Regent about it, then he probably wouldn't have just let it go.

'Hopefully Porter wasn't there,' Henry Wakley said.

'I've never seen London so quiet.' Jack Ditch had wandered over to the window and was staring out. His face was grim. 'The Rage might 'ave done its worst and moved on, but it's left its mark behind.' His eyes glanced left and right along the street. 'This kind of silence only comes from fear.' He glanced back at Fowkes and then Curran Tugg. 'You know what this means, don't you?'

'It's the Prophecy,' Curran Tugg said. 'It's coming to pass. That's all that could shake the city like this.' His swarthy face darkened. 'It's the only thing that could make the Gypsies kill Lucas Blake and try to kill you.'

Fin's stomach squirmed again as eyes in the room darted his way for a split second. *When life and death are bound in one, the balance of all will come undone.*

Those were the words he saw echoed in their concerned glances. Whatever had happened to Christopher in the river, and however much Joe had changed because of the stories, none of it could be as weird as Finmere Tingewick Smith's beginnings – no mother giving birth to him, he'd been created by dark magic from the dead bones of a Knight. It still felt like he was talking about a stranger, in his head. It made

40

him feel like a stranger, and if he felt that way about *himself,* how did everyone else feel about him? Fowkes, especially?

Mitesh Savjani stroked his dark pointed beard and looked at Christopher. 'We should take the Seer to his house. It's been closed up long enough.'

'What house?' Fowkes asked, his question echoed in the confused expressions around the room.

'It was Arthur Mulligan's house,' Savjani said. 'Before he left. He inherited it from the Seer before him, and now Christopher has inherited it from him.'

'You're right,' Jack Ditch said. 'That place has been closed up too long. We need to show folks we 'ave a seer again. Give 'em some 'ope.' He paused. 'Because, by my dead mother's eyes, we all need a bit of that.'

SIX

As meeting places went, it wasn't one that could be confusing. There was only one working sewer lamp left in the City of London and it sat in Carting Lane, just off the Strand next to the Savoy Hotel, where it constantly gave out its dirty yellow glow.

Levi Dodge leaned against it and waited patiently. His long coat served to keep him warm as well as hide the sword that hung at his side. He was early. That was fine. He wasn't a man who suffered from impatience and he enjoyed the quiet – even this unusual quiet that filled London. He didn't think about it much, but then he wasn't a man with much imagination. He simply did as he was told. He shifted his body weight to stop the sword rubbing against his hip. The sword, taken from Joe, was something else he didn't think about. Simeon Soames had shown him how to use it – although making it work was still a very hit and miss affair for Dodge – and he had no qualms when he stepped through the cut open doorway, no more than when using the one in the House of Detention. He didn't dislike Simeon Soames for his fear of travelling, but nor did he understand it. There were too many uncontrollable variables in life as far as Levi Dodge was concerned. There was no point in being afraid of them.

He checked his watch. At precisely two minutes to ten, Jarvis came around the corner and hurried over. At first, Dodge couldn't make out what was so different about him, but as the thin middle-aged man drew closer, he realised

42

Jarvis wasn't wearing his butler's garb and was carrying a small suitcase. He looked quite different in the beige trousers and long jacket. Less impressive. Older.

'They know,' Jarvis hissed. His thin face was pinched, all the animation he hid while moving silently through the corridors of Orrery House suddenly set free in his expression. 'The boy, Finmere. He's figured it out somehow.'

'Are you sure?' Levi Dodge hadn't moved from his spot.

'Yes, I'm sure.' Jarvis put the suitcase down and pulled a packet of cigarettes from his pocket and lit one. 'You have to take me with you. I can't go back to Orrery House. God only knows what they'll do to me.'

For a long moment, Levi Dodge said nothing, and then he nodded. He thought for a second about simply running Jarvis through with the concealed sword, but the boss might have other plans for him. Dodge didn't think so – after all, Jarvis had now outgrown his usefulness and this wasn't a charity. The decision, however, wasn't hers to make, and he could kill Jarvis as easily in the Nowhere as he could here. Or they could add him to the army of the mad. That thought came last. For a man who was rarely unsettled by wickedness, the mad did leave Levi Dodge a little disconcerted. Not that it showed. And not that he allowed himself to indulge his worries.

'I have something to do first,' he said eventually. 'Then we'll go.' He saw a flicker of both relief and excitement in Jarvis' eyes. Perhaps he, too, had wondered if he'd have any value now his treachery was known.

'There's a pub down off Sheep Street. The Star and Garter.' Levi Dodge pulled a key from his pocket and handed it to Jarvis. 'There's a house with a black door next to it. Let yourself in and wait for us there.'

'Us?' Jarvis said. Levi Dodge turned his back on the ex-butler and walked away without answering.

*

After leaving Jarvis, Levi Dodge walked through London's empty streets towards Tower Bridge, keeping one eye peeled for taxis. He'd walk the whole way if he had to, but he'd need a car to bring him back. Plus, the air was turning bitter, cooling instead of warming as Christmas Day morning passed. The mist held tiny shards of ice in it that stung his face and lungs. Somewhere in the distance he could hear a choir singing a melancholy carol, but their voices were lacklustre. No church bells were ringing out yet. Without realising it, Levi Dodge picked up his pace.

Finally, a black cab chugged along the Embankment and he leapt inside. He gave the driver directions and sat back against the leather, sinking into the comfort of the warm air blasting from the vents. 'I'll need you to wait for me,' he said.

'Right you are, guv'nor,' the driver answered cheerfully. 'So long as you know it's double fare today.'

Levi Dodge nodded.

'Then I'll wait as long as you like.'

She'd answered within two minutes of his knocking; a bustling rotund bundle of earthy warmth and energy wearing a bright purple dress and matching shoes. Her perfume, something lavender and vanilla, wafted out at him, carried on the heat from inside the small flat. For a moment, Levi Dodge thought he would very much like to go inside and sit on what would no doubt be a small, inexpensive sofa in a spotless but friendly lounge. He blinked the thought away. Levi Dodge did not trouble himself with the softer side of life, nor with imagining of things that couldn't come to pass. Levi Dodge followed orders, just like he'd always done, and slowly, very slowly, he built up his nest egg so that when he decided the time had come for him to disappear into the shadows, he could do so very comfortably indeed. The problem he faced was that he saw nothing but shadows when he looked to a

44

future without work. Still, the money was there. That was all that mattered.

'Mrs Manning?' he asked. He tried to instil some kind of emotion into his naturally monotone voice.

'That's right. Are you collecting?' Her voice was smooth like honey but her eyes were sharp. 'I'm just about to go to church.'

'No.' He took off his Bowler hat, exposing his balding skull to the cold. 'It's about your son, Joe.'

A widening of the eyes. 'Joe? Is he okay?'

'He should be fine,' Levi Dodge said, 'but he's got suspected appendicitis. The doctor's coming, but we thought perhaps you'd like to ...?'

Mrs Manning had already disappeared to grab her coat and bag, turning off light switches as she went, a sudden flurry of activity. Seconds later she was with him in the freezing cold on the narrow walkway that led to the stairs and down to the courtyard of the Brickman Estate. 'Come on, then,' she said, bustling past the cheap Santas and flickering lights that decorated the windows of the rows of flats.

'Of course,' Levi Dodge said. 'I have a cab waiting. You'll be with your son in no time.'

He slid his hand deep in his right-hand pocket and touched the syringe. He'd had to guess the dosage, but Mrs Manning wasn't a small woman and he was glad he'd erred on the side of caution. He'd wait until they were out of the taxi and just inside the house before injecting her. She'd be suspicious by then, but he could manage her. He wondered if anyone had ever travelled between the worlds while unconscious before and if it would have any effect. As he closed the taxi door behind them, he also wondered why he was doing so much wondering lately. Was it an effect of the Nowhere? Was all this talk of stories and prophecy doing something to his mind?

This was no time to develop an imagination, he thought,

as he caught a glimpse of an old lady hunched over her walking stick hobbling slowly down the street, a small bag of presents clutched in one hand. Three boys in hoodies strolled behind her, but they were catching up. Levi Dodge caught the expression on one of their faces as the cab rushed past them. It was full of malicious intent, an expression he'd seen before. He firmly shut the old lady and her fate from his mind, and concentrated on Mrs Manning beside him.

SEVEN

'This is the Seer's house?' Fowkes stared. 'Why have I never seen this place before?' He wasn't the only one looking at the building with a certain amount of puzzlement.

'Maybe you have,' Christopher said. 'Maybe you just looked at it side-on and didn't see it. This is the most anorexic house I've ever seen.' Mona and Fin exchanged a happy glance. That sounded much more like *their* Christopher. Fin looked at the building again. Christopher had a point. From the front, the house was a large five-storey building with impressive steps that led up to a solid front door with two wide windows. When you looked at it from the side, however, it only went back about six or eight feet. It was the thinnest house Fin had ever seen.

'Did they run out of bricks or something?' he asked, as they came back round to the front. Although the strange house was detached, there was a row of Georgian houses set a little way behind it, and a few to its right where space allowed.

'At least I don't live in a slum,' Christopher said. The house stood at a diagonal rather than in curved rows like the others, making its thinness even more obvious. 'And at least I have glass,' he finished, looking at the windows that glinted, even with the heavy wooden shutters closed behind them. 'That puts me one step ahead of the Knights' place already. And in the coming weather,' he glanced up at the falling dark snow that smeared the pale steps as it landed, 'I think a home with good draught exclusion might be a necessity.' Fowkes and

Savjani stared at him and after a second Mona did too. There was something in their faces and Christopher rolled his eyes. 'Calm down, that wasn't me "seeing",' he said. 'That was just common bloody sense. It's obvious the Black Tempest is coming, isn't it?' He pointed at the sky. 'I mean, we've all grasped that, haven't we? Doesn't take a genius.' He looked back at the front door before muttering, 'I don't even know how to *see*, anyway.'

'Oh good,' Fowkes said. 'So, we'll go from a Seer who refused to See to one who can't.'

'He didn't say he couldn't, old friend.' Savjani patted Fowkes on the back and climbed the steps to stand beside Christopher. 'He just said he didn't know how.' The tailor smiled widely, his dark eyes twinkling. 'A seer in the Nowhere again. This is truly a moment of light in the darkness.'

Christopher shuffled uncomfortably and Fin understood it. It seemed that he and both his best friends were having to get used to people looking at them strangely.

'Let's get inside,' Fowkes said, breaking the moment. 'It's bloody freezing out here.'

'Who's got the key?' Christopher asked.

'You have,' Savjani said.

'No I—' Christopher frowned for a moment and then his denial drifted away as one hand went to the pendant hanging around his neck. He unclasped it and looked at the door again. There was a small indentation right in the middle of the gargoyle knocker. Slowly, he pressed the strange silver token into it. For a second, it shone with all the colours of mother-of-pearl.

Locks clicked and whirred in a flurry of activity and then fell silent. With the pendant hanging around his neck again, Christopher reached for the large gold doorknob and turned. The door swung open.

*

48

The house had been locked up for so many decades that it was almost as cold inside as it was out, but as soon as Fowkes flicked the first light switch pipes started to grumble into life in the walls around them, firing the veins of the building back into life now that they had someone to tend to again.

'Wow,' Christopher said. 'Somehow I thought it would be bigger on the inside.'

Fin followed his friend, letting him explore the narrow rooms first. There was a small sitting room with a grate for a fire and beyond that a study and then a kitchen and downstairs toilet. All very practical, Fin thought, and couldn't help but feel mildly disappointed. He wasn't sure what he'd been expecting, but an ordinary house wasn't it. As Mona started opening the shutters to let in what little natural light the day offered, Christopher led the way up a spiral staircase to the next floor, Fowkes and Savjani following right behind him.

The light switch on the wall did nothing but, in the gloom, Fowkes spotted gas lamps at uniform spaces against the wall, and turned their knobs to fill the room with a warm yellow glow.

'Blimey,' Fin breathed. No one moved as they took in their surroundings. The ground floor was clearly designed for visitors, Fin concluded, whereas this first floor was something else, something more. A collector's den. The walls had been knocked through, so a single room ran the length of the house with a small flight of stairs at one end leading up to the next level. Between them and that staircase was a treasure trove of strange bits and pieces, some laid out on small square tables with chairs in front of them, others hanging from the walls, and some items placed on upturned crates. One of them, bright orange, said 'Sainsbury's' on it. Fowkes crouched beside it. 'I guess all this was brought here by Arthur Mulligan. I didn't take him for a hoarder.'

Christopher moved carefully between the tables, picking up the strange items he found on them. One held a crystal ball, another some patterned cards, and on a third several candles of different shapes and sizes that had dripped different coloured wax all over a bread board, as if they had been tilted over it while burning. There were dark stones, buckets of liquids, mirrors, all placed carefully in the cramped space.

'All of this,' Savjani breathed, 'all of this is about seeing. Different ways to see.'

Christopher had stopped at the far wall, staring at a large machine. It looked like a cross between a pinball machine and a jukebox. 'How the hell did he get that here?' Fowkes muttered.

'What is it?' Fin said. He went to stand beside Christopher and stared at it. The bright red paint was chipped in places revealing touches of rust beneath, but the yellow and gold that spelled the word ZOLTAR! across the top was still bright and untouched by dust or grime. A model of a man filled the space behind the glass. He had dark, angry eyes, a turban on his head, and one hand rested on a white ball.

'He looks a little like me,' Savjani said, stroking his pointed beard that was nearly a match to the man's painted black one.

'But less friendly,' Fin said.

Christopher wiped the top of the machine with his sleeve. 'It's a fortune telling machine,' he said. 'See?' He pointed to the large coin slot at the side. 'You put the money in there.'

Fin leaned in to take a closer look. 'It doesn't tell you how much to put in. That's a bit strange.'

'And what do those buttons do?' Mona squeezed between the boys, pointing at the row of buttons below the glass case. 'What are the symbols on them?'

'The zodiac,' Fin said.

'The what?'

'Here's the money,' Christopher said, tipping some large coins out of a jar that had been balanced on top of the machine. They were thick and made of something a little

50

like gold but with swirls of other metallic colours running through them. He frowned slightly. 'It's warm.'

Fin took one from him. 'No, it isn't.' The metal was cold, exactly as he would expect it to be after sitting in a jar in a disused house for years.

'It is to me.' Christopher tipped the coins back, and Fin noticed that those he'd touched glowed somewhat brighter than the rest.

'This isn't from your world?' Savjani held a coin out to Fowkes who shook his head. 'Nor from here,' Savjani mused. 'Perhaps it came from the South. Magi money of old.' He slipped the coin back in the jar. 'I think maybe this machine is not quite so ordinary as it seems.'

'Try it!' Fin said, eager to see what it would do.

'No.' Christopher shook his head. 'Maybe later.' He looked around at the wealth of strangeness that filled the room and suddenly he was the new, quieter, thoughtful Christopher again. 'He was fascinated by *seeing*, wasn't he? He collected all this, not any of the Seers before him. I can feel it.'

'For someone who refused to *see*, he clearly wanted to understand it, I'll give you that,' Fowkes said.

'If I can't figure out how to See with all this to help me then I might as well just give up.'

'Every seer is different.' Savjani smiled, his manicured fingers interlaced and resting on his belly. 'You will find your own path.' He clapped his hands together. 'And now for the rest of the house? This floor is not for us, I think.' He ushered them towards the stairs and Fin found he was glad to leave the first floor behind. It was just one more reminder of how this adventure was changing them all for good.

Thankfully, the rest of the house was more normal. There was another sitting room, more comfy this time, and a small kitchenette and then on the fourth floor, the bedroom and bathroom, both large, airy and with bright white electric

51

lighting which offered a sense of modernity that the lower floors lacked.

'Look at this,' Christopher said, holding up a framed black and white picture. Three young men in sharp black suits and with slicked-back hair grinned out at them. Fin stared at it. Two of the faces looked almost familiar, but he couldn't quite place them.

'Bloody hell,' Fowkes said. 'That's Ted Merryweather and Harlequin Brown, on either side of Arthur.'

Fin stared at it. They all looked so young and happy. Was that really Ted? And the judge? Was this what time did to people? He looked at Christopher's troubled expression and wondered if maybe the changes happened on the inside first. But then, what did he know? He wasn't even a proper person. He was made from the soul of a dead man. The thought, as always, made him feel slightly sick.

Christopher turned away from the picture and started opening up the shutters. Fin went to help him. He didn't want to look into the past. It made him think too much about who he was. At least the photos were from before Fowkes' and Baxter's times. He wasn't sure he was ready to see a picture of Baxter yet. He wasn't sure he'd *ever* be ready for that.

The grey daylight barely added to the brightness from the spotlights above, and the snow, falling heavier, caught against the glass and began to black out the windows. It wasn't the weather that caught both boys' attention, however. It was the view. It might be some distance away, but the central window directly faced the Dome of the Future Blocks.

Feet thumped up the stairs and Mona appeared, breathless and flushed, in the doorway. 'How long have we been here? Half an hour? Someone's just delivered a hamper of food and drink. They knocked on the door but when I got there they'd gone. How strange is that?'

'It's as it should be.' Savjani smiled at his daughter. 'The word that the Seer has returned will spread. It will rally the good and make them stronger in their hearts for the dark days that might be coming. This is a good sign; a generous action on the eve of the tempest. It bodes well for us, after all we have lost to the darkness.'

'Isn't it strange,' Christopher whispered, staring through the window, the tailor's words clearly not touching his thoughts, 'how the house has been built at an angle so that it directly faces that Dome? None of the other houses do, just this one.' His soft words dampened the moment and the others joined the two boys and stared out of the glass. 'How long has the house been here?' he asked.

'Long before the Dome arrived,' Savjani said. 'I don't know how old it is.'

'And yet somehow it knew,' Christopher continued. 'As if it was waiting. As if it knew this moment would come. Father and son facing each other from opposite sides of the city. From opposite sides of everything that means anything.'

'They might not have gone there,' Fin said. 'We don't know for sure.'

'Where else would he go? He's there.'

Fin didn't argue. Whereas the Future Blocks had always seemed like something bright and fascinating on the horizon, now the Dome looked ominous against the angry backdrop of the sky.

'Look,' Mona breathed, finally saying what they were all thinking. 'The lights are changing colours.' It was true.

If there had been any doubt as to where Arnold-Mather and Joe had taken their army, it was gone now.

EIGHT

A few watery streaks of the original colours that had hung, like the Northern Lights, above the Dome of the Future Blocks were just visible if you strained your eyes hard enough, but most had merged into a watery pink hue streaked with black snow.

Elbows tugged Henry Wakley down lower, so his face was pressed into the cold hard mound of earth they were hidden behind. To his left Henry's twin, Benjamin, was fiddling at his belt for his binoculars. 'It's not exactly crowded in this part of the city, is it?' Benjamin offered Elbows a set of small regulation army binoculars but the trader shook his head and took his own spyglass from within his leather jacket.

The three men settled, lying quietly on their fronts, only their glasses visible over the edge of the earth. Although Arnold-Mather and his train of followers were more than a hundred feet away, the binoculars brought them in close. Out on the marshes beyond the crumbling city wall, a group of palace guard, with a few of the mad alongside them, were slowly following two of the locals. They were all heading towards the Dome.

'There's Soames,' Henry said. 'Beside Joe.' The ex-Knight and the teenage boy were sitting on a section of the wall while Arnold-Mather talked to a man who might have been handsome if it weren't for the terrible weeping burn that had destroyed one side of his face. 'Why aren't they headed over there? Surely they'd want to reach safety first? Let someone else bring up the rear?'

'The path moves every two hours,' Elbows said. 'The marsh farmers and rice-growers know how to see the changes coming and read the new way through. But it takes years to learn to track the shifts in the earth.'

'So he's sending them first in case it's a trap?' Benjamin didn't lower his glasses.

'Aye.'

'So he leads from the rear,' Henry added. 'Like the arse he is.'

The other two men looked at him.

'What?' He smiled and it was almost infectious, but a sudden shriek from below caught their attention, cutting any shared humour dead.

A group of people were being dragged through the village by guardsmen who threw them down at Arnold-Mather's feet. It was a family; a short, stocky man, a slim woman and a boy of six or seven. The sobbing woman had been carrying a bundle whose contents were now spread across the filthy ground; a smattering of ornaments, a flash of jewellery and a teddy bear, all tangled up in clothes.

'We weren't leaving,' the man said, despite the evidence to the contrary. 'We really weren't. We wouldn't.'

Simeon Soames joined Arnold-Mather, but Joe remained against the wall, his head down.

'We don't want any trouble,' the woman sobbed, holding her frightened son close. 'I just wanted to see my sister. I just wanted to ... we don't want to be part of anything. We just want to—'

'Oh, do be quiet,' Arnold-Mather said, his voice sharp in the silent, icy morning. 'You're giving me a headache.' He looked at the rest of the villagers who stood in tight groups well away from the three on the ground, as if they feared they could somehow catch their guilt.

'Is this the sort of loyalty your Storyholder can expect?' he boomed at them, projecting his voice in a way no doubt honed during Prime Minister's questions and parliamentary debates. 'That as soon as you think his back is turned, you'll try to run?' He laughed. 'Where will you run to? Don't you see the snow falling? Don't you understand his power?' He nodded to one of the guardsmen who hauled the father to his feet. 'Shall I show you how this kind of loyalty is rewarded?' He muttered something to the man with the burned face who waved a covered cart over. He tore the cloth away to reveal a man curled up in a ball in the centre of a cage. Joe, against the wall, at the centre of everything and yet forgotten for a moment, hunched further over as if he'd rather reduce himself to nothing than watch.

'Who is that?' Benjamin whispered, watching the burned man.

'Don't know him.' Elbows shrugged. 'One of yours?'

Arnold-Mather smiled at the man held between the two guardsmen. 'Tell, me traitor, who do you value more? Your wife or your son?'

'What? I don't ...' The man's face crumpled as his wife sobbed louder.

'It's a simple question. If you had to choose one to keep safe, which would it be? The boy or his mother?'

A terrible hush fell in the village, only the woman's sobbing cutting through it, carried on the occasional sigh of the rising wind.

'You can't make me ... you can't ... how could I ...' The man's voice was weak, appalled at the situation that had been presented to him.

'If you don't choose, I'll choose for you.'

On the ground the woman and the child hugged each other. Finally the man muttered something. The burned man moved quickly, pulling the woman away from the child and dragging her towards the cage.

'No! No ... no!' she called out, the words a stream of snot and panic as she struggled helplessly against the strong arms. 'Not me! No, not me! Please!'

Her son ran for his father but was swept up in a guardsman's arms. The cage door opened and the woman was thrust inside.

'What's happening?' Henry whispered. 'I can't see.' Below, the burned man stood in their direct line of vision.

'I'm going down there.' Benjamin braced to move, but Elbows pulled him back.

'There is nothing you can do down there except die,' he growled. 'What do you think? You think you can grab them and take them to your world?' The trader kept his grip tight on the young Knight's arm. 'You can't. They will cut you down before you can open a doorway.' He glanced at the figures below. 'This is their fate. You can't change it.'

'Look,' Henry breathed, his eyes pressed into his binoculars. 'Look at her.'

Benjamin relaxed in Elbows' grip and they returned their focus to the people in the distance. Whatever the man in the cage had done to the woman, it was changing her. Her hair was turning black and falling free around her shoulders, and all they could do was watch in horror.

'The mad,' Benjamin said. 'He's turned her into one of the mad.'

'And now the boy,' Arnold-Mather said. 'I didn't say that I would save one, I only asked which you would choose.' The man screamed as the child was flung into the cage only to emerge moments later, already changing. Arnold-Mather waited until the transformations were complete and then spoke softly to the burned man, who took his dagger out and slit the broken man's throat. He tumbled to the ground, his blood vanishing into the black snow beneath his trembling body. Finally, he lay still, his eyes open wide and staring up at the unfriendly sky. The creatures who had so recently been his family didn't even glance his way as they scampered towards Joe. The teenager kicked them away.

Arnold-Mather turned to the assembled villagers. 'I think we understand each other now?' he said with a soft smile. 'But just in case more of you get any ideas about leaving, I shall take your children with me to the Dome.'

There was a ripple of cries and hushes from the rice-growers and marsh farmers as they clung tightly to their children.

'They will be safe with me, as long as you do as I tell you. I *will* have your loyalty, one way or another.'

'Sir!' A man called over from the gap in the wall. 'They've made it to the Dome! We should go.'

As Arnold-Mather, Joe and the caged man started their procession across the marshes, the village children in tow, Elbows and the Wakley twins crept to their horses and started the journey back to the heart of the city. None of them spoke for a long time. The sheer cruelty and heartlessness of the man who controlled the Storyholder shocked even Benjamin Wakley, who'd seen plenty of violence during his time in the army. This was different, though, and all three men knew it.

As the buildings grew more cramped and the paths became streets and roads, they paused and turned to look at the Future Blocks behind them.

'He made it across the marshes, then,' Benjamin said quietly. The other two didn't have to ask how he knew. The answer was clear. Through the black snowfall they could see the brooding crimson red glow from the Dome. There was nothing pale about it now. It was the colour of blood or, more, as if the fires of hell themselves were burning in the Future Blocks. Perhaps they were.

NINE

Fin sniffed hard as the combination of cold air and the heat from his hand-held welding torch made his nose run. His legs had numbed two hatches back, and his jeans were soaked to the knees, where the wet snow had crept up through the fabric from the ground. Still, he wasn't complaining. It was good to be doing something useful. He glanced over at Fowkes, who was hunched over the other side of the heavy metal doorway, sealing up the last few inches of the hatch. It was weird to be hanging out with Fowkes, just the two of them. Since the revelations in the House of Real Truths they'd tried to stay normal, which meant Fowkes growling at everything Fin said, but it was impossible.

'I think that one's pretty sealed up, don't you?' Fin said, sitting back on his heels. 'How many more to go?'

They'd left Christopher to get adjusted to his new home, and Mona and her father had gone to see which of the Borough Guard remained at their posts across the city, while Fowkes, Fin and the traders had agreed to seal up the hatches leading from the Lost Rivers below using Anaïs' map. Fin had seen how much the decision had hurt Curran Tugg – to finally accept that the Gypsy Traders had become victims of the Rage – but allowing them to roam freely over the city after what they'd done to Christopher and Lucas Blake would be foolhardy. If all the over ground exits – the ones on the map at least – were covered then they could only come out from their secret underground burrows via the river.

In all the confusion after Traitor's Gate, there was no certainty that Francois Manot had returned to his home: he might still be out on the water. But several of Curran Tugg's men were out there too; and while most of them wanted to find Arnold-Mather, it was a matter of pride for the Traders to bring the Gypsy Trader leader to justice.

'This is killing my back,' Fin said as he stretched. 'And I've got really bad pins and needles in my legs.'

'You're getting old.' Fowkes smiled. 'Although I can't actually feel my legs, so I'm definitely older.'

Fin smiled back, but the friendliness between them was awkward. He wanted to say something about Tova and all the pain Fowkes must be feeling, but he couldn't find the words. He wasn't sure he knew how to express his thoughts anyway. In fact, he wasn't even sure they were *his* thoughts. Maybe all the good stuff, the kindness in him, was really Baxter? Maybe without Baxter he'd be one of those standing with Arnold-Mather? They'd all seen the sky darken to crimson – it was no longer just conjecture where Joe was. Would Fin be standing beneath that awful red glow without Baxter inside him? *No,* he told himself silently as he got to his feet and shook out his legs, *Without Baxter you'd be nothing. No cardboard box, no blanket, no ring. Not even an ordinary baby.* He felt as inconsequential as the drifting snow around him. A living ghost.

'You all right?' Fowkes asked, his dark eyes troubled.

'Yeah.' Fin nodded. 'Yeah, just hard not to think too much, you know.'

'I know.' Fowkes nodded. 'I've spent a lot of years thinking too much.' He paused. 'Not that it did me a lot of good. Nor Tova.' He looked up at the sky. 'It's your actions, not your thoughts, that really count. What you can live with doing, and what you can't.' His eyes had fallen to rest on the tip of a building in the distance. It was the Old Bailey House of Real Truths, the distinctive shape clear in the higgledy-piggledy London skyline. Fin stared for a moment too. His heart ached thinking about Tova's death, the woman who had created him and, like Fowkes, he harboured a kernel of anger at her for leaving them in this mess. For making them face their truths without her.

'If she'd had the stories, she'd never have done it,' Fowkes said softly. 'Or if she'd had time to adjust to not having them. She was strong. Don't let her final act become the sum of all she was.'

Fin shuffled his feet awkwardly, feeling very much like a sixteen-year-old and not at all like a dead man in a boy's body. His skin flushed.

'Where to next?' he asked, wanting to change the subject before Fowkes could mention Baxter. 'How many more have we got to do?' They'd split the job with some of the Traders and Jack Ditch's boys, little teams of welders spread out across the city.

'What?' Fowkes snapped out of his momentary reverie.

'Where to next? I want to get these done and get some dry clothes on.'

'I'm not sure, I think we're going to ...' Fowkes' words drifted into silence and his eyes narrowed slightly. 'What the ...?'

'Fowkes?' Fin asked.

The Knight pointed in reply. 'Look.'

Fin turned. A building, only the top of which was visible, was starting to glow. A beautiful, golden colour from the windows like sunshine through storm clouds. After a moment even the bricks shimmered with light. Fin stared, open-mouthed, as the brightness grew. All around them came the sound of locks being hesitantly pulled back as people emerged from the safety of their homes. They stood in doorways and allowed themselves cautious smiles that didn't quite eradicate the fear from their nervous faces, but pushed it to the edges for a moment. Fin wasn't sure if he was imagining it, but it even seemed that the snow was falling less thickly and that the air had warmed a little, taking the biting edge from the icy wind.

'Is that ...' he frowned slightly, '... is that Christopher's house?' He turned and glanced back at the Dome, which glowed a brooding red in such contrast with the joyful light that shone like a slice of sunshine in the gloom.

'Yes,' Fowkes said. 'Yes it is. He's doing it. He's really doing it.'

'Doing what?' Fin asked, although the answer was coming at him on the breeze from every whispering doorway.

'He's seeing,' Fowkes replied. 'He's *seeing*!'

TEN

Christopher wasn't aware of the light flooding from his house or the sudden warmth that throbbed from the walls, dispelling the final hints of chill they held from the years being closed up and forgotten. He had no idea that the building was surging with life and joy and purpose. He stared at the Zoltar machine, his eyes unfocused. On the other side of the glass, the model's eyes burned red and its mouth was open at the hinges. The white ball beneath the plastic palm had turned black, as if all of space were contained within it.

Christopher wasn't aware of any of it. He hadn't been aware of much since deciding to slide a coin from the jar into the slot. His fingers had itched for it in a way that they hadn't when he looked at all the other objects on the tables around the large second floor room. The Zoltar machine might have just been one of many collector's items for Arthur Mulligan, but it called to Christopher. He found it was always in the corner of his eye. So, finally, when the others had left, he'd taken a coin, a deep breath, and rolled it in. Lights had come on inside the glass as the machine whirred into life, highlighting the angry torso it held. The bulbs in Zoltar's eyes sparked into life and his jaw dropped open. When the deep rumbling laugh had come from inside its works somewhere, Christopher had been disappointed. It was just a tacky fairground gimmick, after all.

But he'd leaned forward, his hands touching the edges of the console holding the strange zodiac buttons, and everything had changed. Electricity surged through his palms to the very core of him and then back down and into the machine. He stared at the ball under the mannequin's hand. It was changing. The white was turning into a mist within the sphere, a fog that danced and twisted into something darker. It drew him in until there was nothing else ... nothing but ...

Cold and dark. Hard earth beneath his feet. Chill, empty air that holds no ghosts of fire or laughter. Things scamper past. This is their home. The sun doesn't shine here. There is only the dark and the cold. If a God exists then he long ago turned his back on those who dwell here and this place has become a horror. Dead and yet not dead. Unnatural.

The last world. The ninth of nine.

He hears sobbing, the human sound so out of place here. The creatures that scurry around in the darkness do not speak, do not eat, do not die of old age. They simply exist. They have been here for so long they have forgotten what they were before.

Christopher, there and yet not there, looks at the man who huddles behind a boulder at the edge of the dark snake of the river. His heart aches slightly at the man's terror. He remembers the well. He remembers how they pushed him down it. How far did he fall to reach the ninth world? Is time the same here? How long has he been here? One of the creatures lies at his feet and the sobbing muttering man disembowels it with his golden sword. He strips meat from its pale body and eats, sobbing and gagging. Christopher doesn't want to watch. He doesn't want to see this. He turns to face the river, barely visible in the constant night. Along its edge shapes and shadows lunge at him and he realises they are pieces of wreckage. The rotten corpses of boats and tugs and an entire washed-up civilisation. His eyes widen.

Time runs backwards so fast he can't keep track. The images are a blur, but they get brighter and warmer until suddenly they stop. He gasps for breath. The air is hot, not stiflingly so, but pleasant. Mediterranean. The river glitters in the sunshine and all around him people wander this way and that through the market stalls laden with cheeses and wines and bread. Boats chug through the water. Children laugh as they dart around their mothers' legs. This is a happy place. Peaceful, clean and civilised.

Time rolls forward again. How many years? Hundreds? A thousand? The market is gone, replaced by houses. He stands in a narrow cobbled street. The sun still shines, but he hears no laughter. Coughs and splutters come from within the houses and many of the doors are marked with red symbols. The few people that do scurry through the streets hold masks over their faces. Sickness is here. Death is here.

He shifts. He's in a laboratory. Men and women sit hunched over microscopes and test tubes. They are all tired. Dark circles ring their eyes and their movements have the slightly jittery edge of those who haven't slept for far too long. They are almost defeated.

Later. The same laboratory. Laughter, smiles, celebrations. A vaccine. A cure! The world can be saved. Lines of ordinary people taking their turns to be inoculated against the feverish death that has come for them all. The sick and the healthy, all are eager for cure or prevention. They've seen the death. The rot under the fingernails. The marbling whiteness of the skin as iron escapes the body. The redness of the eyes and the terrible rotting black of the tongue just before death.

There is laughter in the streets again, for a while. People are healthy. The terrible plague that threatened to destroy them all has passed. They celebrate.

For a while all is well.

Time shifts. Not so very far, this time. Christopher can see the changes as they flash by.

They got it wrong. People are changing. Everyone is changing. What should have immunised has infected, but not with disease. They are becoming something else, something which carries traits of the disease but has a life of its own. At first there is panic, but that only lasts as long as the sense of self does.

The city, the world, falls quiet as the population hides away to

65

transform. A few people, those who failed to be injected out of fear or by chance, wander the streets in a daze. Some throw themselves from buildings or into the river. Others, in fear, fight. Most fall sick and die. And eventually, the people emerge from their houses, only they are not people any more. Their eyes are red and dart this way and that in their pale faces. Their fingernails are crowned in black. They function on instinct, scampering over the buildings and through the river. They do not eat. They do not die. Their world turns for too many years and the buildings slowly crumble.

Eventually the sun dies, and darkness reigns. The creatures, the once smiling, people of the world, live on. Until one day, the man arrives, a man from the first world, thrown down a well in the second. He is there a long time. He cries. He wanders. He drinks the river water. When he is near starving and half-mad he kills and eats the first creature, smashing its skull with a rock and hacking through the tough skin to find the flesh. And time passes. He forgets who he is. Sometimes his tongue grows long and his eyes blaze red, but it never lasts. He never quite becomes one of the ninth world creatures, but at times he is something that is close.

When he is awake he wanders aimlessly. He has forgotten light. He has forgotten why he has the sword that hangs at his side. To drown out the endless silence he mutters unintelligible words to himself until his throat is hoarse. In his saner moments, he thinks perhaps he should throw himself into the strip of the river and sink. He keeps walking.

Finally, in all the darkness, he sees something bright. A tiny stone, embedded in the earth. Against all the laws of nature it shines like a star trapped in the dead ground. He cries and falls to his knees, scrabbling at it until his fingers bleed. He must get it out. He must. It's been so very long since he's seen anything other than shadows and shapes and darkness. The pebble sings to him. Eventually, he uses the sword. He knows the sword is special – although he can't remember why any more, he knows its blade is not like others.

He strikes the earth with it all the same. Over and over until

all his muscles ache and he's coated in sweat in the dry coldness
that is all the atmosphere left on the world. He grunts and yells
in frustration with each blow and in the shadows the creatures
draw near and watch. The blade sings as it shatters on his final
strike, sending shards of metal into the shadows. The man casts
the handle away, caring only about the small stone, now free from
its imprisonment in the rocks. He holds it tight and for the first
time in a long time he feels something close to warmth in his
bones. His energy is returning.

Returning.

That's what he needs to do. Return to the place almost forgot-
ten. The pebble is safe in his fist, and it is leading the way ...

Christopher leapt back a pace or two as the images abruptly
ended. He was sweating and he squinted against the light,
even though he had not been plunged into darkness. He
stared at the Zoltar machine. The lightbulbs in the dummy's
eyes had gone out and the ball beneath its hand had returned
to white, as if nothing had happened. But the air Christopher
breathed was thick with life, so different from the empty cold
he'd felt in his lungs only moments before. His heart raced.
He'd witnessed the past. He'd seen George Porter's experiences before he returned, and brought a plague with him,
there was no doubt of that. He ran downstairs.

Surely the Seer was supposed to see the future? That was
the point, wasn't it? Was this yet another thing he just
couldn't get right? He dismissed the thought as he opened
the door and stepped out into the snow. The *seeing* had been
true. It had been too powerful to be otherwise. He needed
to reach Ted or the Knights and share it with them. George
Porter had brought more than the madness back with him.
He'd brought that pebble. And somehow both things were of
great importance to the future of the Nowhere, and probably
the Somewhere too. He knew it.

ELEVEN

There were several things that Joe liked about the Future Blocks. They were warm and dry for a start, and there was something about their modernity that reminded him of home. Of the Gherkin building, he decided as the elevator hummed around him. He bet that inside the Gherkin it looked a lot like the Dome of the Future Blocks – all sleek and smooth and quietly efficient. He expected to hear high heels clicking on the floor as women in suits marched this way and that carrying folders of important stuff that someone like Joe would never understand.

In fact, Joe thought, as he stepped out of the lift at the lower level, it was natural that Mr Arnold-Mather felt so comfortable here. He'd been born to a life like this, what was surprising was how at home *he* felt. Boys from the Brickman Estate did not get to hang out in posh places like this. It wasn't part of their lives, whatever old Boggy Marsh tried to drum into them about working hard, and university opportunities and expanding your horizons. Still, he'd learned a lot in the past few weeks, and not for the first time he wondered if the stories had made him cleverer. They were changing him, he was sure of that.

Most of the people who had come with them were exploring the tall towers on either side of the Dome and making their homes there, wide-eyed and in awe at the futuristic nature of the buildings, while the guardsmen made the main dome, the new palace, secure. If any of them were worried by the deep red glow that hung above the building and stained the sky, they weren't showing it. Perhaps, like Mr Arnold-Mather, they saw it as a symbol of their power over the rest of the city. People only had to look at the sky to see who was running things now, or would be very soon.

Joe, however, wasn't so sure. Yes, he felt calmer in the Dome, and the heat and anger and noise in his head from the stories was definitely subdued – if not muted, like when he was holding the stones – but even that disturbed him. He paused by a large curved window, and looked out at the distant city.

'There's the shining building,' he said softly as Mr Arnold-Mather came alongside him. 'The one Simeon Soames pointed out. It's fading again.' In the distance the glowing building, as he thought of it, was indeed blending back into the grey background. For a while it had shone so brightly they had all stopped to stare. 'What was it, do you think?'

'We'll know soon enough. Edgar's asking around. Whatever it is, I doubt it can harm us.'

Joe sometimes wondered if Mr Arnold-Mather was in danger of becoming over-confident. He didn't know Fin and the Knights like Joe did. He didn't understand how brave and strong they were. His heart twinged slightly as he watched the black snow falling outside. How could friends find themselves on such different sides? He still loved Fin, he knew that, but it didn't dampen his anger at them, and it didn't stop him *liking* being as important as Fin was. He liked, for once, that he had his own place in events. He wasn't Fin's sidekick any more. They *all* knew who Joe Manning was.

'It's beautiful, isn't it?' Mr Arnold-Mather said, his breath forming a spot of condensation on the glass that the functional heat of the building quickly dispelled. Joe knew he didn't mean the fading house in the distance, but the snow.

'Yes,' he said, 'it is.' And it was. There was something remarkably soothing about the perfect black flakes that glinted and glittered as they fell. He could watch it for hours. for a moment. 'But what does it mean? It's beautiful, but sad.'

'You're worrying again.' Mr Arnold-Mather squeezed his shoulder in what could have been a fatherly gesture but which gripped too tightly to be anything other than mildly threatening. 'Things won't always be so confrontational. Nothing worth having comes easily, and your old friends will soon realise that you're in charge now. They'll be kneeling at your feet before too long, trust me.' He gestured to the window. 'You're in charge of all of this. You're the new king. Doesn't it feel good?'

Joe wondered why, if he was in charge, he felt so much like a prisoner. He'd exchanged house arrest at the Old Bailey House of Real Truths under the watchful eyes of Fowkes and Tova, for Arnold-Mather and the Dome. Or had he? He looked around and felt the rush of the stories inside him. Things *were* different now. He was the Storyholder. It was easy to let Mr Arnold-Mather be in charge – he was good at it – but the power still lay with Joe. The politician would do well to remember that.

They turned away from the window and continued their quiet exploration of the strange structure until they had worked their way down to the lowest level where, at its heart, they found an empty circular room with only one thick door that was invisible until they approached it, and then swung open.

Inside, the man and the teenager stood in the centre and the door closed, its edges immediately blending into the wall around it, sealing them in. Arnold-Mather stepped towards it nervously.

'It'll open again,' Joe said, his voice deadened in the strange space.

'How can you be so sure?' Mr Arnold-Mather said, but his feet stopped where they were.

'It just will.' Joe wasn't entirely sure how he knew it, but he did. The stones and the stories could make a lot of things happen. *The stones.*

'It's quieter in here,' he said.

'That's because we're in a virtual tomb beneath the building,' Arnold-Mather muttered. 'Of course it's bloody quieter.' His eyes kept darting back to the door, and for the first time in their acquaintance Joe realised he was more relaxed than his forbidding mentor, who clearly didn't like the idea of being trapped down here.

'No, it's quiet like when I hold the stones. It's quiet in my head. It's like the room is helping me.'

'Really?' Arnold-Mather turned to look at him properly, his anxiety quashed by his curiosity.

'Yes, really.' Joe rolled his head around on his neck, easing all the tension that had been building up there.

'And now?' Arnold-Mather pulled the small pouch containing the stones from his pocket and handed them to Joe. As soon as the boy took them, the walls of the dome within the Dome hummed loudly, sending vibrations up through their feet. Joe's eyes widened, but Arnold-Mather grabbed the pouch back before he could speak.

'Well, well,' he said. 'That was interesting.'

'That felt ... I don't know how that felt,' Joe said. 'Weird?'

Arnold-Mather walked him back towards the wall and the door, as Joe had said it would, swung open.

'You carry on exploring. Or perhaps you might like to examine your quarters. If you need anything just ask Edgar or Simeon. I have a few things to do, but I think you need to rest. Tonight we'll have a late Christmas feast.' Arnold-Mather paused and smiled. 'And we'll have visitors!'

Joe turned back. 'Visitors? Who?'

'You'll have to wait and see. Now off you go, you look tired.'

Joe was tired. He hadn't realised it until he'd come out of the circular room, but now he felt as if he could sleep for a week. And the noise was back in his head. But visitors? His heart leapt a little with excitement. Who? He wondered if by visitors, Mr Arnold-Mather actually meant prisoners they'd captured, but he found he didn't really care much either way. Familiar faces, that's what made his pulse race. Maybe there would be a Christmas, after all.

Justin Arnold-Mather waited until Joe had vanished from view before looking back at the circular room. He stepped close enough for the door to open, and he peered through. It was the engine room. Of course it was. Whatever power the Future Blocks had been running on must have come from somewhere deep in the ground in the marshes – perhaps from the mysterious River Times itself – but that was simply a reserve power. Now it was running on Joe, and the boy didn't even realise it. No wonder he felt calmer here. The building was absorbing his energy. That's why the sky had changed colour. Arnold-Mather needed to find a way to enhance and then transfer that power. To feed it to himself, if that was at all possible. He stepped back to allow the door to close and vanish again. Of course it was possible. Anything was possible. His fingers toyed with the pouch in his pocket. But first there was the question of the stones. What had Joe said about them earlier? They were 'part of the one stone'?

There was someone he needed to talk to, but first he had to see if the valets had discovered anything in their books.

TWELVE

George Porter, still in his cage, had been stored in a locked room with three guards outside – a room only Arnold-Mather had the key to. If Porter got free it wouldn't be long before the Knights tracked him down, and although they wouldn't be able to use his 'gift' to their advantage – it was clear that the mad followed Joe – his loss would be a blow to Arnold-Mather's new regime. As had been proven with the marsh farmers, George Porter, whatever he had become, was a very useful weapon of terror. And why kill your enemies when you could turn them into mindless slaves instead?

This afternoon, however, it wasn't that particular ability that interested Arnold-Mather. It was information. The valets had found something in the book he held tucked under his arm, and he needed Porter to confirm the truth of it. His heart raced. He wasn't a man prone to fits of excitement, but if what the valets had found was true then he was about to discover a secondary source of power to match the one he already had in Joe – maybe even exceed it.

He could feel sweat damp in his armpits. Despite the warmth of the Dome he'd continued to wear the long black coat he'd taken from the palace. He needed to find a thinner replacement, but for now this made him feel and look regal, and it impressed the people of the Nowhere who had followed him after the Rage. And so it, and he, should. He was evidently the dark king of the Prophecy. The boy Joe Manning was simply his puppet.

He allowed himself a tight smile as he stepped into the darkened room and waited for the guards to close the door. This was fate and prophecy all rolled into one. And to think that the PM had been about to expel him from the Cabinet. There might be a surprise in store for that man if all continued to go according to plan. Not that Arnold-Mather much cared for the Somewhere any more. It was a past life. His future lay in the Nowhere.

The shadowy shape in the cage shuffled forwards and pale fingers wrapped around the bars, disembodied for a moment before Porter's wan face appeared behind them. His eyes, sunken into dark hollows, were flecked with desperate hope. He licked his lips, his darting tongue pink and very human.

'You've got them with you, haven't you?' he said, his mouth and nose pressed hard into the gap between the bars. 'I can feel them.'

Arnold-Mather pulled the small pouch from his pocket and held it up. 'These?'

In the cage, Porter whimpered, a sound more animal than human, and he clung harder to the metal, one slim hand stretching out through the bars, pleading. 'Please ... please ... just for a moment ...'

'Maybe.' Arnold-Mather dangled the pouch just out of Porter's reach. 'But only if you answer my questions.' The proximity of the object of his desire brought on a fresh bout of salivating and mewling from Porter.

Part of the one stone. That was what Joe Manning had said. He hadn't known what it had meant, not until the valets had come running to him fifteen minutes ago with the book. Now he needed it confirmed. He tipped the two stones into his hand, one much smaller than the second chunkier piece, but both the same pale colour. His palm tingled with pleasurable warmth. Arnold-Mather knew he wasn't immune to their pull either, but he had no intention of becoming addicted to them the way Porter had. He'd find a safe place for them soon enough. Just as soon as he knew what they were.

'You took this one,' he held up the larger piece, 'from the tip of the spire at West Minster, I'm told.'

'Yes ... Yes ... I did.' Porter nodded vigorously, his bloodshot eyes never lifting from his prize. His words were becoming sibilant. Perhaps his excitement was bringing on his physical changes, or perhaps time was making him more monster than man.

'How did you know it was there?' he asked.

Porter frowned, as if trying to grasp a wriggly eel of memory that was determined to slip away. 'I just knew,' he said eventually. 'The other one led me there. The one that kept me warm.'

Arnold-Mather looked down at the smaller of the two stones, a tiny inconsequential thing. 'And where did you find the first one?' He held it out and let Porter's greedy fingers brush against it for a few seconds. The man's whole body trembled with ecstasy. He immediately calmed, and whatever changes might have been coming over him ceased.

'It shone in the dark. It called to me.'

'Where did it shine?'

'The sword broke, but I got it out.' Porter's eyes had glazed over slightly. Arnold-Mather drew closer, crouching so that he was level with the caged man. 'But where, Porter? Where was it?'

'In the other place,' Porter shuddered, his eyes darkening. 'It was cold. Empty.'

'Where was this place? Here? Was it in the Nowhere, or in the Somewhere?'

Porter gave his head a tiny shake. 'It was so far away. It took me so long to get back. The stone brought me.' He paused. 'So far away I thought I'd be there forever. Another world.'

With the words he'd been waiting for finally spoken, Arnold-Mather smiled. Excitement surged through his veins. So the book was right. He turned suddenly and left Porter howling in his cage, his lust for the stones denied, and strode back towards the large room at the centre of the Dome that he had made his command post. He needed to act now, and fast. Everything was coming together perfectly.

THIRTEEN

It was late afternoon on Christmas Day when they gathered in the Oval Room at Orrery House, all those who had come from the cold of the Nowhere stripping down to their T-shirts to cope with the sweltering heat of the familiar building.

'You're seeing the past?' Cardrew Cutler frowned at Christopher from his seat across the table. 'That's a bit off, isn't it? Are you sure you're doing it right? Maybe try facing the other way or something. See if that helps?'

'Don't be ridiculous,' Freddie Wise cut in. 'There's only *seeing*. However it's done. You can't dictate these things.'

Fin thought Christopher looked remarkably calm as the two old men bickered around him.

'Well, it's hard to know, isn't it?' Cutler continued. 'It's not as if Arthur did a lot of it, even before he gave it all up.'

'But *seeing* the past, it just don't seem right,' Ted said. 'How can the past 'elp us? What's to be gained from it?'

'Everything, sometimes,' Fowkes said from his place at the head of the table. 'Our present and future are born from our past.' There was a sombre pain in his words.

'Why don't you all just hush up and let the boy talk,' Mrs Baker said as she bustled around them, filling up tea and coffee cups. It was strange to see her in Jarvis' place – even though Fin had revealed the butler's treachery he still had difficulty believing Jarvis had been spying on them. It was even stranger to think that only a couple of months ago Mrs Baker had been the landlady of the boarding house he stayed in during his years at Eastfields. Nothing in that life had been as it seemed, not for him anyway, and not for Christopher and Joe either. There had been a Prophecy waiting for them – *One plus one plus one is four.*

'So what did you see, Christopher?' Freddie Wise asked.

'George Porter,' Christopher said. Glances were exchanged around the room. The Wakley twins and Elbows had confirmed that Arnold-Mather had Porter and shared what they'd seen him do to the rice grower and his family. 'He was on a dead world,' Christopher continued. 'The ninth world.' He looked at Fowkes and then Fin. 'So we know where Clerke's Well leads now. The furthest of all the worlds. One you can't even see on the map.'

'A dead world?' Cardrew Cutler leaned forward.

'A cold world. Even the sun had burned out. By rights nothing should have lived, but there were creatures there. Things that had once been people, but had been changed by a virus, and a cure that was worse than the disease.'

'Like the mad?' Fin asked quietly.

'When they got sick they looked a little like the mad.' Christopher nodded. 'But only before they changed and the world died. Porter was eating them. That's probably how he got it, like he's half-infected and can still spread it.'

'At least the mad don't seem to be able to pass it on. Only Porter,' Fowkes said.

'They can't yet, anyway,' Christopher replied. All eyes turned to him, Fin's included. 'I can't help but feel that seeing the history of that world, when they were all alive and normal, was some kind of warning. That it would happen here, and in the Somewhere, if we didn't stop it. Otherwise, why would I See all that?' He paused. 'Unless it was about the stone.'

'Stone?' Freddie Wise said sharply.

'There was something about it. It shone in the darkness and George broke his sword to get it. The stone brought him back here.'

'A stone you say?' Cardrew Cutler asked. 'I'll speak to Esme. See if she can find anything.' He was on his feet quickly, whatever aches and pains his Ageing might have brought him forgotten in his eagerness to see the librarian.

'A broken stone.' Christopher's face clouded. 'A broken stone that wants to be whole. But must never be allowed to be. Don't ask me how I know that. I just do. I knew it when I saw it.'

'Esme will track it down somewhere,' Cardrew Cutler said, already opening the door. 'But she'll probably need help. I'll go and check ...' His words were lost as he disappeared into the corridor. The door clicked shut behind him.

Fin saw Fowkes look at Ted, who rolled his eyes, and then at Freddie Wise who merely shrugged. 'Old age has never been an impediment to love,' he said. 'And Cardrew's not all that old – not really.' He sipped his coffee. 'Now what about security?'

'We'll have to make the doorway safe,' Fowkes said. 'On both sides if possible. If we can't then we'll at least need lookouts. The doorway could be just as useful to us as to them if we need to get people over there without swords and training. We also need a new headquarters. Everyone in the Nowhere knows where our base is, and although we can see people coming it's not that easy to defend. We'll use Savjani's shop at the Circus for now, but his alliance with us isn't a secret. Arnold-Mather will send people there once he's settled in the Future Blocks.'

'The more established he becomes, the more afraid people will get and then it won't be *his* people you need to worry about, it'll be the ones around you. Spies. Ordinary citizens trying to make themselves safe by turning you in. Or trying to grab power for themselves. It's always the way, whichever world you're in.'

The voice belonged to an unfamiliar man shuffling into the room and helping his companion to a chair. 'We saw Cardrew mooning over the librarian so thought we'd join you.' He nodded at Fin and Christopher. 'I'm Hector Allbright. You know young Currie-Clark here.'

Fin nodded and tried to smile, but his heart hurt at the sight of the old man.

'He should be in bed,' Freddie Wise said softly. 'I'm surprised he's even awake. Everyone sleeps through the first day after the Ageing.'

'We can sleep when we're dead,' Alex Currie-Clark wheezed. 'There are more important things now.'

'If you want a safe and secure base for the Knights,' Allbright continued, landing with a heavy thump in his own chair, 'then it has to be over here.'

'Here?' Fowkes said. 'But we need a base *there*.'

'Why? We can still go back and forth from here, as you do now. They clearly have the base advantage in the Nowhere, so we need to make ours in the Somewhere. Why have a headquarters that they will find and attack easily? If they want to attack us, make the stakes higher. Make them risk Ageing too. Travelling adds another firewall to our defences. It'll thin out his volunteers. It makes sense.'

'We'll look like we're running away,' Fowkes growled.

'So?' Allbright said. 'We won't be. We can have safe houses over there – you have good people who can provide those. But the main base should be here.'

''E's right,' Ted said. 'We don't know how bad things are going to get, but we all know it ain't going to be good. We need you lot safe over 'ere.'

'I think it's a good idea,' Christopher cut in softly. 'But I won't be relocating. My house needs to stay unlocked. I need to stay there.'

'What?' Fin stared at his friend. 'But your dad—'

'My dad won't come for me.' Christopher cut him off. 'Not yet anyway, and I'm needed in the Nowhere.' He leaned forward. 'When I came out of the house today, just after I'd

80

seen everything I just told you, there were baskets and parcels several feet deep outside the front door. Food. Drink. Clothes. Far too much for me. It freaked me out, if I'm honest. I gave a lot of it away on my way to the Knights' house, to anyone who came out of their houses to see me. They were smiling. Not afraid; not in that moment anyway.' He looked around the table. 'I'm not on some crazy ego trip. It's not about me. It's about the Seer. They *need* the Seer. Our people do, at least. The ones not turned by the Rage, who are staying strong in the face of the coming tempest. If I leave the Nowhere and they find out, then they'll lose all hope. A seer leaving in a time of crisis? They'll all turn to my— turn to *him* ... because they'll have no one left – no Storyholder, no Regent, no Seer.'

'They'll still have the Knights,' Fin said, hating the thought of Christopher staying in that house. It was a landmark, an easy target for anyone. He'd thought his friend was dead once already – he didn't want to go through that grief again, especially not with Joe working against them.

'With all due respect, the Knights don't count. They're not part of the Nowhere.'

'Neither are you! You're from here!'

'I *was* from here,' Christopher said, his calm tone in complete contrast to Fin's indignant one. 'But only before I swallowed the river's water and she spat me out a seer. The Nowhere's where I belong now.' He glanced at the men around the table. 'And they all know it.'

As he looked at the grim determination on his friend's face, Fin felt something close to envy. He wished he knew where he belonged as clearly as Christopher did. 'I'll stay with you, then. If you think your house is safe.'

'I think my house is safe for me. I'm not sure how the place feels about visitors. You're better off with the Knights. You should stay with Fowkes.'

Fin wasn't sure if Christopher meant to make it sound like that's where Fin belonged or whether he was just being paranoid. *He* didn't belong with Fowkes – Baxter did. And he *wasn't* Baxter.

'How can you be so sure your father won't try to capture you?' Fowkes asked.

'I know him.'

'Oh dear Lord!' Freddie Wise exclaimed, standing up suddenly. 'Of course!' He was staring into space, utterly oblivious to the conversation going on around him.

'Freddie?' Ted said. 'You all right? Not 'aving a stroke I 'ope.'

'I'm fine. Yes ... no ... I'm fine but I'm not fine. A broken stone ... of course!' His eyes were bright. '*So long as the stone of Brutus is safe, so long shall London flourish,*' he said.

'What the hell are you talking about?' Fowkes asked.

'The stone. The London Stone. *Our* stone.' He clapped his hands, urging them out of their seats. 'We need to hurry. Fowkes, send Christopher back. If Arnold-Mather beats us to it, then god only knows what will happen and if the boy's right then the Nowhere will need him. We need to grab a cab. And quickly.'

FOURTEEN

Levi Dodge was nothing if not efficient. He was almost psychotically so. In fact, there had been one doctor who, after *that* incident when he'd been a child, had claimed that he was psychotic, but Levi Dodge knew otherwise. He knew he was just very, very good at getting things done.

He sniffed the cold London air. With Jarvis and a sedated Mrs Manning in tow, he'd gone back to the Nowhere and made his way to the Future Blocks ... just in time to be sent straight back by a very excitable Arnold-Mather who gave him very precise instructions. He'd remained impassive, but a small part of him wanted Arnold-Mather to send someone else. He would have quite liked to sit down with a cup of tea, or something stronger, for half an hour or so. He wanted to point out that he wasn't quite as young as he used to be. He didn't say either of these things, of course. He simply tipped his Bowler hat and got on with it. Complaining wasn't in either his nature or his job description. He was the man who *got things done* for Justin Arnold-Mather; he was the only man the former minister trusted implicitly. Who else could he send?

The preparations hadn't taken long. The cameras around Cannon Street tube station had been disabled, and now two palace guardsmen were nervously taking the blowtorches Levi Dodge had procured to the metal railings protecting the stone they were after. Despite the cold and the encroaching gloom, he could see the sweat on their brows, but wasn't sure if it was from the blast of flame, from fear, or because they'd travelled. Perhaps it was all three. Not that either of them had protested against their mission for long. A glimpse of George Porter's cage was a very effective persuasive technique. As it was, he'd kept the party small. Just him, the two guardsmen, Edgar Blacken and two of the mad, who now had small swords and daggers tucked into their belts as they scampered up and down the street, keeping watch.

He'd seen Blacken's reserve at arming the mad, but Arnold-Mather was right. The Army of the Mad was hardly an army if it didn't have any weapons. Their instructions had been to guard the stone, and thus far they were following their orders. Levi Dodge thought they showed a little more menace in the Somewhere than they had in the Future Blocks. Their red eyes were almost alert, and there was venom in each hiss. Perhaps their presence wasn't helping the guardsmen's nerves either. He looked down at the trolley at his feet. Still, at this rate, another ten minutes and they'd be done.

'This place smells bad,' Edgar Blacken muttered. 'Dirty. Greasy.' The burned man wasn't sweating, and hadn't required any extra persuasion to travel. Levi Dodge respected that, but there was a tightness in his jaw, and when the quiet was broken by the occasional rumble of a distant car, Blacken flinched slightly. He might have travelled without complaint, but he was still very aware he was in a different world. Levi Dodge sucked in a deep breath of cold air. It tasted of home to him. 'At least we don't have the stink of that river,' he answered.

'We're through,' one of the guardsmen said, looking round. Levi Dodge returned his attention to the job at hand. Just the glass to deal with and they'd be done.

'So, where are we going?' The cab had pulled away before they'd even closed the door, and Fin clung on as they jolted around the corner. 'What is the London Stone? Something from the Nowhere?' His sword clanged against Fowkes' as the grown man slid along the seat towards him before grabbing some purchase and steadying himself. On the other side of the taxi Freddie Wise remained remarkably still and kept his balance as if the car was barely moving.

'No, this is very much our stone. Legend claims it was part of an altar built by Brutus the Trojan, the founder of London. Some think it was a distance marker used by the Romans. A symbolic central point in the City of London, from which every distance in Roman Britain was calculated. Maybe it was, maybe it wasn't. All anyone knows for certain is that it's definitely ancient and can't be linked to any discernible purpose.' He didn't look at either Fin or Fowkes as he talked, but stared through the window into the darkening afternoon, tracking their progress through the empty streets.

'One of Queen Elizabeth I's advisers believed it had magical powers. He was quite obsessive about it.' He glanced over at Fin. 'And who knows, maybe he was right. There is *something* special about the London Stone, that can't be doubted.'

'What do you mean?' Fowkes asked.

'Simply that for such an ordinary hunk of rock to have been preserved and looked after for so many hundreds of years, there must be something special about it, even if that sense is unconscious and we can't account for it.'

'So where is it now?' Fin asked. 'A museum?'

'I'd be happier if it was. Museums are harder to get into. The stone sits in the same place it has since it was discovered; it's opposite Cannon Street tube. It's part of the wall of a shop. Just above pavement level. You've probably walked past it a thousand times and never noticed. Like most Londoners.'

'It's never been moved?' Fowkes said.

'No. Perhaps on some level people are wary of moving it. Maybe there is something in the old proverb after all. And if there is, we'd better get there fast.'

'The old proverb?'

'"So long as the stone of Brutus is safe, so shall London flourish."'

Fin swallowed hard. It sounded far too much like the Prophecy to him. And the problem with sayings that started 'so long as' was the implication that one day that would cease to be the case. It wasn't lost on Fowkes or Freddie Wise either and they all sat in a tense and uncomfortable silence after that. Finally, the cab screeched round the last corner.

'Oh no,' Freddie Wise said, as he gazed at the street ahead. 'Hurry! Hurry! We must stop them!'

The old man moved fast, pressing away from the seat with his cane and shoving the door open. Fin followed as Fowkes leapt out the other side.

'Hey!' Fowkes shouted. 'Hey! Stop!'

Fin's heart was in his mouth. Up ahead, two men were lifting a large pale stone, struggling and straining to get it onto a low trolley. Beside them stood a man in a suit and Bowler hat, and another who at first looked Hollywood handsome but when he turned towards them revealed the other side of his face, burned and melted beyond recognition.

Freddie Wise was stumbling along the pavement as fast as he could. 'We must stop them!'

As one, Fin and Fowkes drew their swords, and Fin felt the power from the metal surge through him. The man in the Bowler hat drew his own sword and, in the gloom, Fin saw the stone glint at its hilt. Jade green, just like the stone in his ring. Baxter's sword. He was using Baxter's sword! Rage filled him, and Fin raced ahead, Fowkes sprinting at his side.

The two struggling men had finally got the stone onto the trolley, just as Baxter's sword began cutting open a doorway.

'Wait, Freddie!' Fowkes cried out as the old man threw himself towards the man with the Bowler hat. The doorway disappeared for a moment, but the burned man pushed Wise away with a rough shove, sending the old man sprawling onto the pavement.

'No!' Fin yelled and leapt forward. His eyes met the burned man's, who almost smiled and then whistled. Two creatures leapt out of the falling night, hissing and both pulling at the short swords tucking into their belts. One headed for Fowkes, blocking his path to the stone, and the other shrieked as it launched itself towards the helpless Freddie Wise, who, lying on the pavement, batted weakly at it with his cane.

The man with the Bowler hat was opening the doorway again. More clumsily than any Knight, but he was still managing it, the black and white image on the other side slowly unfolding. Figures were waiting there, and one of them was Simeon Soames. As Fin's eyes met his across the worlds he was sure he saw guilt in the Knight's expression before he stepped out of view.

Fin's face heated as he stared at the jewelled sword. *His* sword. No, Baxter's sword.

'Stop them, Fin!' Freddie Wise wheezed. 'They mustn't take the stone! They mustn't . . .' His words were cut off as the mad attacking him gripped his throat with one pale hand, the other trying to stab at Freddie with the steel blade raised high above his head. Fin stared. The black fingernails were digging into the old man's sagging skin, and although Freddie Wise was using both hands to hold the knife at bay, he wasn't strong enough and it was moving steadily closer.

Fin glanced from Freddie to Fowkes, who was battling the second mad, the small creature a whirling mass of black hair and pale skin, and then to the men desperately hauling the stone towards the opening to the Nowhere. If he tried to stop them, then Freddie Wise would die. He was certain of it. Fowkes had his hands full, and Wise only had a few moments before he'd either pass out or be stabbed. Fin did the only thing he could do. Turning away from the stone, he let out a roar and kicked out hard at the creature, who shrieked and fell away from Wise.

Fin raised his sword ready for the onslaught. Behind him,

Freddie Wise gasped for air and tried to crawl towards the stone, but Fin had no time to heed his desperate words. The mad attacked and it came fast, hissing and snarling with every strike of its blade. Fin's body moved on instinct, his own sword countering each blow as they twisted and turned on the London street in a parody of some kind of waltz. Sometimes he and Fowkes switched places as the four figures battled, and at others they were back to back. His mind was calm, but his heart raced until, finally, his sword found its mark and slid sickeningly into the mad's body.

The creature slumped to the ground and, as Fin watched, its hair darkened to a light brown and the face adjusted until it looked human. It wasn't Anaïs. Just some man he didn't know. The relief thumped into his belly like a punch. He turned to look at Fowkes who also stood over a dead man, again, no one he recognised.

'Poor bastards,' Fowkes muttered. 'Poor sodding bastards.'

Fin looked down at his own sword, thick blood smeared across its blade. 'These swords aren't meant for killing,' he said softly. The last time he'd carried a sword that had been used in violence it had been Judge Harlequin Brown's blood that stained it – killed by rogue Knights with his own sword. Somehow this fresh death on the metal damaged the Judge's memory.

'Well, sometimes the rules change,' Fowkes said. 'Sometimes you have no choice.'

Fin looked at the man on the ground. The man he'd killed. Suddenly, he felt sick. How had he even done it? He didn't know how to use a sword. Not like this. Most days he still found it heavy to carry, let alone to whirl around his head and use properly in a fight. He'd killed a man. Even if it was one of the mad, it wasn't this man's fault. And now he was dead. He felt Fowkes grip his shoulder. 'You had no choice,' the Knight said. 'Neither of us did.' Fin nodded and swallowed hard, forcing some moisture into his dry mouth.

'You fought really well,' Fowkes said, his voice melancholy and his eyes thoughtful. Fin turned away. He knew what the Commander was thinking – that it was Baxter who had wielded the sword, not Fin. Fin also knew he was probably right. He was born of a dead man, and it was the dead man that had done the fighting. So why did he still feel like he'd killed a man, he wondered? If Baxter had held the sword then why couldn't he, whoever and wherever he was, have the guilt? Why couldn't he just bugger off entirely?

'Oh no ...' Freddie Wise stood staring at the space where the doorway to the Nowhere had been. 'Oh no. This is all my fault. I shouldn't have come with you. I should have stayed behind. I thought I could help. For a moment I thought I was a young man.' His normally sharp, calm voice was little more than a whisper. 'They have the stone.' Distant thunder rumbled overhead and the street lights flickered. Fin looked up, filled with a terrible sense of foreboding.

'The Black Tempest is coming,' Fowkes said softly, his own eyes turned upwards. 'I can feel it.'

And as his words faded into the quiet night, the first heavy flakes of snow began to fall.

FIFTEEN

Joe had barely eaten a thing. His full plate of delicious turkey, sausages, roast potatoes and all kinds of other delights coated in a thick swirl of gravy sat untouched on his plate. Across the table, his mother hadn't touched hers either, but that was probably less the shock of seeing him and the Nowhere and more the sedatives that were clearly still in her system. She looked at him occasionally and made a slight exclamation, as if surprised to see him there – as if all this were just a dream.

Mr Arnold-Mather said drugging her had been necessary for the trip and Joe had been so happy to see her that he'd not cared at first, but now they were seated around the table, like some mockery of a family, he found he cared a lot. For a start, why should he be on this side with Jarvis' lip-smacking eating while Arnold-Mather was sitting next to her? He didn't like the way Christopher's father looked at his mother either.

'Whassa matter, Joe?' Mrs Manning slurred at him. 'Not eating? Not like you.' 'Not' and 'like' blurred into one and she sounded drunk. She didn't sound like his mum at all. His head started to throb as the stories raged in response to his growing anger. He'd quickly learned that in order to keep them manageable and quiet, he had to stay completely calm and let nothing faze him. That was easier said than done, so most of the time his head was filled with pain and the noise of the colours inside him, each holding millions of tiny stories all demanding his attention. He'd never been very good at being calm, even back when all he cared about was football and hearing the last school bell of the day.

'Yes, come on, lad.' Mr Arnold-Mather grinned at him. 'Eat up.'

'I've got a headache,' he mumbled. His gravy was starting to congeal. Normally he wolfed down a Christmas dinner and had two or three helpings; this year it felt as though one mouthful would make him throw up. This wasn't a Christmas dinner. Not really. It just looked like one. Joe wasn't sure what it was.

'If I'd known I'd see you, I'd have brought your presents.' His mum smiled for a moment and then her brow furrowed. 'The man said you were sick. You're not sick, are you?'

'No, Mum,' Joe muttered. He wished his mum could just go home. Why had Arnold-Mather brought her here? He looked at the man's glittering eyes. And what was he so excited about this evening? Joe stared down at his plate again and tried to block out the sense that his skull was exploding from the inside. Why didn't he understand anything that was going on around him?

'Why did he say my boy was sick?' Mrs Manning looked at Justin Arnold-Mather. 'That man with the hat ...'

The far door opened, and Joe looked up to see Levi Dodge and Simeon Soames come in.

'Him.' Mrs Manning's eyes widened again. 'Him. He told me my boy was sick ... and we got a taxi, and then ...' her words faded slightly. 'And then there was him.' She nodded at Jarvis who was shovelling another forkful of meat into his mouth. '... and then I was here. How did I get here?'

'Well?' Mr Arnold-Mather was on his feet. 'Did we succeed?'

Levi Dodge nodded curtly. 'We did.'

'Excellent!' Mr Arnold-Mather threw his napkin down on the table in delight. 'Excellent!' He turned to Joe. 'Come with me, young man. I think I have something for that headache of yours.'

91

'Where are we going?' Jarvis looked up. 'Is it something important?'

'You stay here and keep Mrs Manning company, there's a good chap.' Arnold-Mather barely glanced at the ex-butler and Joe was sure he saw a flicker of discontent in Jarvis' expression. Had he really thought he'd come over to the Nowhere and suddenly be important? Joe almost laughed. Or cried. Or both. Were any of them important? He left his untouched food and followed Christopher's dad.

'Don't be long, Joe,' Mrs Manning slurred after him. 'You have to do your homework.'

Joe's heart flinched but he didn't look back as he joined Simeon Soames and Levi Dodge. The latter was staring into the dining room, his face impassive. 'Did you drug her again?' he said eventually.

'I thought it was necessary,' Arnold-Mather said. 'Just for now.' He swept past them, leading the way towards the lift. 'Now let's see if we can make this a Christmas to remember.' He clapped his hands, and Joe exchanged a glance with Simeon Soames before they did as they always did, and followed him. It was a moment before Joe realised that Levi Dodge wasn't with them. The man in the Bowler hat was still staring into the dining room. Finally, he pulled the doors shut and caught the others up. He wouldn't meet Joe's quizzical gaze, and then the lift doors opened and they journeyed silently down into the heart of the Dome.

In the basement – the only word Joe could think of to describe the sub-level below the marshes from which the Dome sprang up – the pain in his head eased, even as George Porter's wails and sobs became audible.

'Please ... Please ... just let me ... please ...' His drifting words chased after them as they strode towards the wall with no door. As they grew closer, the pressure in Joe's head eased some more. He remembered feeling quieter in the room, but not like this. What had changed? The door swung open as they approached and, catching a glimpse of what lay inside, Joe's eyes widened and his pace picked up.

It was a stone. Much larger than those that Arnold-Mather kept in the pouch, more like a boulder, its edges rough, but it was the same creamy colour as the others. Joe's skin tingled. They stood around it, silent for a moment.

'It's ...' he started. 'It's like the others ... isn't it?' He lifted his hand to touch it. 'It's part of the one stone.' The final words came from somewhere in the heart of the stories that filled him. This stone was part of their story, their DNA, so intrinsically linked that he couldn't quite understand it.

'Yes.' Arnold-Mather nodded. 'Yes, I think it is.' He gripped Joe's wrist before his fingers could reach the surface of the rock. 'Can you feel its power? I think I can, but that's only because I'm holding these.' He pulled the pouch free from his pocket. Even cased as they were in cloth, an electric tingle ran through Joe. 'You see,' Mr Arnold-Mather said, so softly that Joe doubted that Simeon Soames or Levi Dodge, who were standing a few feet away, could hear, 'I'm wondering if the stones help share the power. Shall we find out?'

Joe's eyes widened, and his soul felt torn. The stones were so right and at the same time the stones were wrong. This amount of energy in one place was *wrong*. 'The stones *are* the power,' he muttered, as Arnold-Mather released his hand and then tumbled the two stones into his palm. Arnold-Mather gripped his wrist.

'No, Joe. *You* are the power. The stones are something else. Let's find out what, shall we?'

Joe looked down at the rocks he held. His mind was calm again, a cool stream of water after the raging heat. How could it be bad to feel calm? If this was what the two small stones did, then what could three do? How much better would he feel then?

He leaned forward, with one in each hand, to press each small stone into the surface of the boulder.

Everything changed. Light danced behind his eyes as warmth and brightness rushed in a tidal wave up his arms. On some small level, he was aware of the building trembling around him, and a wind whipping up into a hurricane that tore around the room at the heart of which stood he, and the stones and Arnold-Mather. The building shook. The wind roared. The stories expanded inside him, and expanded and expanded.

'I can see everything!' he shouted. 'I can touch everything!' It was beautiful. It was terrible. It was too much.

With a whoop of glee, Arnold-Mather thrust his own hands against the surface. His eyes shone like black pools and Joe felt that darkness creeping up through him like burning tar. He gasped, sucking in dry, almost empty air. Arnold-Mather was contaminating everything. He was *influencing* everything. 'No, no—' He tried to tear his hands away, but Arnold-Mather held them down.

'So much power!' Arnold-Mather shouted over the roar of the wind. 'Magic, Joe! It's magic!'

'It's too much!' As the tearing wind that had pressed Simeon Soames and Levi Dodge into the circular walls closed in on them, Joe had to scream to be heard. The air blasted his face. 'It's too much!' Pressure was building in his head again; his eardrums felt as if they might burst. His whole body felt as if it might burst.

'Something's happening!' Arnold-Mather laughed maniacally. 'Something's happening! Can't you feel it?'

Joe looked at the madman opposite him and for a moment the lost Joe, the football-playing Joe of Eastfields Comprehensive, the Joe that was buried so deep inside him that he'd thought him dead, that Joe wondered if he could push all that power back and into Arnold-Mather and kill him with it.

And then the wind suddenly dropped, and Joe felt all the power of the universe surge through him.

SIXTEEN

Christopher hadn't moved from the window since he'd returned from the Somewhere. He'd thought the Nowhere was where he needed to be, but as soon as he'd crossed the threshold of his house it had become a certainty. Just like this strange angular building was now *his* house, he knew he had to be here. His father and his fate had always been here. As if the Nowhere was in their blood, somehow. It was like something he could almost see. Maybe he should try harder, See whatever he could, but he sensed it wasn't that important. Things were what they were. People changed. All of them had changed, and no doubt there were still changes to come. It was the nature of life.

A sharp wind blew gusts of heavy black snow to beat against the glass like a flurry of bat wings, but Christopher's eyes stayed fixed on the distant Dome. The air of foreboding that had hung across the city since the Rage was now almost oppressive. Like the moments before a summer storm, he thought as he watched the coal red glow that darkened the horizon. A *storm. A tempest.*

In the distance the crimson red deepened and gave off a sudden burst of crackling electricity, glittering in the sky like sparkling firework embers against the night. But they didn't fade. If anything they grew brighter, hanging like stars for a moment before starting to move, circling in the air above the Dome. Deep in the earth, something rumbled, and gave a groan that sent shivers through the house and forced Christopher to grab the window sill to keep his balance. His teeth rattled with the awful vibrations. Surprised and fearful shouts from the street below were sucked by a frenzied wind. As the glittering lights in the distance whirled, London shook. Rubbish and debris in the roads was picked up and thrown angrily this way and that. Somewhere glass smashed, and no doubt the shards joined the mad dance in the sky too.

The lights danced lower and lower until they fell and coated the Dome in brightness for a moment before being drawn along its surface, forming a single line of light reaching from the centre of the Dome and up as far as Christopher could see. Outside, the wind suddenly dropped to nothing. Silence spread across the city as the buildings stilled. A million people held their breath, in one world for all the worlds, Christopher amongst them. He caught sight of his ghostly reflection between him and the thin line of light against red in the distance. His mouth was half-open. His eyes were wide. He looked like a schoolboy, not a seer.

His skin tingled. Whatever it was it wasn't over, he realised. It was only—

The world shook again. White pain shot through his head and he released the window ledge to clutch his temples. He might have screamed. He forced his eyes up. Black fire surged up the white light and shot up into the sky.

'No ...' Christopher whispered, even though he knew it was futile. 'No ...!'

The crack was so loud, its force so great, that it blew out the window and knocked him to the floor, smashing the wind from his lungs and leaving him curled up and gasping for air as he had on Curran Tugg's boat, soaking wet and stinking of the river. He lay there for a few moments as the world steadied itself. Finally, his ears ringing, he hauled himself to his feet, his legs shaking almost as hard as the building had moments earlier. There were small cuts on his face where the glass had hit him, but he barely noticed them. His breath sounded rough, loud and ragged, as he peered through the gaping space of the window.

For a long minute he couldn't take in what he was seeing, and then slowly a low moan built in his chest. As tears sprang to his eyes, he released it. He stared for a long, long time. Starting above the Dome, a long ragged cut ran across the sky, and through it Christopher could just make out the blackness of *nothing* threatening to tumble through and consume them all should the gap get any wider.

Tears trickled down his face.

And so it had begun.

It was quiet in Charterhouse Square. All the lights in Orrery House had gone out after the tremor that had rumbled through London, shaking the pavements and buildings just hard enough to stop any cars on the road this late on Christmas Day and to give anyone sitting at home pause. At first, Ted and Cardrew Cutler had thought a fuse had blown, but with a moan of 'God help us all,' from Freddie Wise the search for the fuse box was forgotten. Freddie, still hunched over and pale after his experience at Cannon Street, had been staring out of the window. When they glimpsed what he'd seen, the group – those fit and well enough to walk – had gone outside. It needed to be seen properly.

The temperature had dropped well below freezing in the space of a few minutes, but Fin barely felt the cold that burned his lungs with every breath. For a long time, no one spoke. The lights had failed across London, and as the day dipped into night it looked like a ghost city, long dead and forgotten, like the city Christopher had described from his vision. No doubt there were others like them, coming out of their front doors to see, but in the middle of the City of London on Christmas Day, residents were scarce, and the huddle of boy, Knight and old men stood alone in the expanding gloom. Not that anyone would be looking at street level. Fin was pretty sure that all eyes would be turned skyward in awe and dread.

Footsteps approached, there was the click of a lighter and the heady scent of a roll-up cigarette.

'That crack in the table's cover?' Ted said quietly. 'It's bigger now. Much bigger. It ain't wide, but it's long.' There was a pause. 'It looks exactly like that.'

Fin's eyes were fixed on the thin white line that cut across the sky, beginning in the east of the city and ending over their heads, as if someone had taken a thin white felt-tip and drawn jaggedly across the dusky sky.

'What is it?' Fin asked, finally, knowing that none of them had an answer.

'It's no good, I know that much,' Ted said, sucking hard on his cigarette. 'Got to be to do with those stones. And poor Joe. It's all the worlds in this now, Fin. That ain't never 'appened before.'

'The Somewhere is sturdy,' Fowkes said. 'Nothing should touch it. It's the first world.' They fell into silence, all staring at the sky. Sirens wailed in the distance. At some point they would have to go back inside, to plan and fight and try and find a way to put this right, but not now. At that moment, they just stood and stared.

'I'll tell you what it is,' Cardrew Cutler said at last, no hint of the usual warm merriment in his voice. 'It's the beginning.' He paused to take Ted's cigarette and puff on it a little before handing it back. 'It's the beginning of the end of everything.'

SEVENTEEN

*There had once been a stone. That's how the legends of the begin-
ning told it. One stone, in one uninhabitable world. There was too
much power for life to form, too much raw magic pulsing through
the one river. The air hummed with electricity and, as the millen-
nia passed, the pressure built and built ...*

*... and after eons the pressure became too much. The stone at
the heart of the world cracked. Its splitting shook the universe and
forced galaxies to realign in the wake of the tremendous surge of
energy. The one stone had become nine, which floated apart, each
drifting upwards until they hung in a line with vast swathes of
space between each one.*

*The stone tried to pull itself together, but now the force of its
own magic was keeping it apart. Instead, dust and earth and energy
rose to join each piece. The river, the lifeblood of the universe,
divided into sections, forming nine paths of water within which
life could grow. And so the worlds formed; nine layers of one world
held together by the stone and the river, held apart by the very
magic that had created them. As strange creatures claimed the first
world, where they would rule for the ages before man arrived, the
Magi were the first to walk from the water in the second world.
They found the stone and kept it safe. They knew, they'd learned
in the river of their birth, that the nine pieces of stone must never
be reunited. Doing so would mean the destruction of life itself in
an instant. The nine would explode in a blaze of energy that would
light space and time for an eternity. So after much debate, eventually they embedded the second world's stone high in their temple*

where no harm could come to it. They welcomed the arrival of men who tumbled through the cuts between the worlds. The worlds changed and grew and filled with bustling life. The stones passed into legend. Were forgotten. Even when they began to dream the Prophecy, a dream shared by generation upon generation of Magi, none thought of the stone.

They thought of the stone now. As the panels in the walls glowed and burned in the place of the Elders, as one they knew what had occurred. The silence of contemplation was broken as beads tumbled to the floor, clattering like tiny hailstones against the stone flags. The earth rippled with a boom that made even the Elders flinch as it shook the walls. Outside, they looked beyond the blazing, distant lights of the many citadels that had become their homes, and upwards to the sky.

It was ripped. It was slashed black against the night sky. There was nothing but the void beyond – not space, not the stars, simply destruction. The Magi muttered sacred words and incantations quietly under their breaths as they stared. The warm night air was tinted with a cold that didn't belong in the South. A coldness that was normally trapped in the mist on the river and sent back to the shores of the North.

'The Magi wait, the Magi See the unravelling of worlds, this our prophecy.' The words hung unspoken on the desert air. The unravelling of worlds, that was what the rip in the sky held.

'We must protect the South.'

'We must protect the North.'

'We will do that by protecting the South.'

There was a long pause.

'There is magic there now. Too much. And no Magi to absorb it.'

'There are Magi.'

'Corrupted. Impure.'

Again a pause. More quiet, fearful mutterings. They thought of the men they had never met – travellers from the reflection of their world – and how their fates were all bound together. Bound in the stories and the river and the words long ago recorded on the map and in the Magi's heads and hearts.

'If only we could See the Prophecy's end.'

'There is no point to wishes we cannot fulfil.' One strong voice came from behind them. They did not turn, but as they listened to her their nerves calmed and they felt their inner balance somewhat restored. 'But we must man the towers. We must use magic to protect the citadels. We must be ready to put our differences aside and, if called on, to live or die side by side with those who banished us.' The voice paused. 'Perhaps it is time we embraced the corrupt and impure. The lost children of our forefathers.'

'And what of the boy?' The man's voice was as dry and old as the sands themselves. 'He who is life and death and beyond nature. The boy who does not belong in any world. The boy of Magic without Magic. The boy who should not exist.'

The woman let out a long sigh and the sand shifted as her breath reached it. She did not answer. She had no answer. The boy was a riddle as yet unsolved.

PART TWO

———◆———

The South

EIGHTEEN

Fin felt something was wrong when he first cut open the doorway. The warm tingle he had expected up his arm was more like an electric shock and, for a moment, the opening wobbled.

'You okay?' Fowkes asked.

'Just felt weird,' Fin said. 'Probably nothing.' They both stepped through into the Nowhere, leaving Orrery House in darkness, and the old Knights to scurry around with candles until the power came back on. Despite knowing how tired they both were, no one had fought Fin's suggestion that he and Fowkes head back at once. Harper Jones could guard Orrery House, but if even the Somewhere had been affected then things had to be bad in its sister world. They needed to bring their people to safety, and form a proper plan to take on Arnold-Mather.

It was only when the doorway closed behind them that the boy and the Knight realised how bad things might be. The air was icy, far colder than it had been only hours before, and frozen water droplets hung in the air. 'Look,' Fowkes said, pointing upwards. In the Somewhere the line across the sky had been thin and white – here it was a great black gash, the same shape but far wider and more menacing. Fin shivered. In the distance, he could see the red sky over the Dome of the Future Blocks, angry and bright. The power cut in his own London suddenly seemed almost inconsequential. Whatever had happened here was worse.

'What happened to the snow?' Fin muttered, the words coming out in a stream of frozen mist. He did up the last buttons of his coat, turned up his collar and tucked his chin into it, covering his already-stinging nose.

'I don't know,' Fowkes said. 'But at least we won't leave footprints. Let's get to the house. It's too quiet out here.' When they left the black snow had been falling steadily but now it had vanished. Everything was coated in a thick white frost. The Nowhere had become an icy blue landscape that glittered in the dusk. Icicles hung from the eaves of the houses around them and although the windows in this part of town were normally empty of glass and covered with thick drapes, Fin saw that most of them had been sealed up with some kind of cement instead. The Nowhere residents must have worked incredibly fast to fill in the windows since the Rage last night.

Their feet slipped clumsily this way and that as they hurried round the corner towards the House of Charter's Square, and then Fin gasped as the building came into sight. They both came to a standstill, the cold forgotten. The House of Charter's Square was nothing more than a blackened burnt-out shell, abandoned and ruined. Ice had formed on its husk, smothering the charcoal remains of the charred wood. The roof had collapsed, folding the remnants of the structure in on itself. But it wasn't the fate of the building that stole both Fin and Fowkes' breath and made them step closer together. It was the thing impaled in front of it.

The head.

Fin's heart raced and his stomach turned queasily. The head was on a spiked pole driven into the ground before the house. The eyes had rolled back and the mouth was open in anguish. The skin, rotten in places, was blue and frozen open in death and the skin of the man's neck hung in ragged edges. But still, in the instant he saw it Fin recognised the distorted, horrified face. It was the new Knight he'd barely spoken to: Kent Jasper.

'We have to get out of here,' Fowkes whispered. A pale strip of yellow light shone from a house on the corner as a shutter was opened a fraction. 'We're being watched.'

'But, what— How ...?' Fin couldn't take his eyes from the dead man. When had this happened? *What* had happened here? Christopher. Mona. His heart tightened as he thought of his friends. If this had been done to a Knight, then what might have happened to them?

'Not now.' Fowkes grabbed his arm and pulled him away, keeping them close to the walls and in as much shadow as possible. Neither of them spoke as they scurried along the edges of the buildings. More shadowy faces appeared in windows and doorways, eyes following them as they passed, and Fin had the feeling it was more than just curious residents. As well as the crunching of their own feet on the ice, he could hear lighter, faster footsteps. He glanced up to the roof line but could see nothing. Maybe it was just his imagination, which had also planted the eerie thought that Kent Jasper's eyes had rolled all the way around in his head and were now staring after them, full of anger and blame. He took a step closer to Fowkes, the tops of his ears burning with more than just the cold.

Night was falling quickly which at least offered them more cover, but the city remained dark, no friendly lights glowing from the shops or flats above. He glanced at the sky again, where the midnight gash stood out against the ordinary darkness, an ominous unnatural tear. What could have happened to make everyone so afraid so quickly?

They skirted the square and hurried towards the side door of the Old Bailey House of Real Truths, Fowkes forcing the frozen door open and then glancing around to check they hadn't been seen, before following Fin inside.

The hallway was bright, the lights in the walls glowing

even though their glass had been smashed, and Fin flinched slightly after the oppressive darkness outside. At least it was warm, although he wondered at that too. But then, the Old Bailey was a special place with a strength that came from the building itself rather than the people who inhabited it. He'd felt that the first time Fowkes had brought him here, and he'd felt it again when he'd learned his own, awful truth. He made an effort not to look at the bottom step of the curved staircase as Fowkes ran up the steps and then reappeared, shrugging, moments later. 'The flat's wrecked, and empty. And freezing. One of the windows is broken and the ice has crept inside.'

'What's going on?' Fin asked, and followed the Knight to the central chamber. Fowkes pushed the heavy doors open, neither he nor Fin having anything to fear from the truth any more. They stood in the doorway for several seconds before slowly stepping inside. Fin's mouth fell open as his feet crunched across the broken glass that covered the floor. The Truth Chamber had been destroyed. Wrecked. Utterly smashed. One set of high shelves had tilted forward until it had come to rest on the next, knocking it over to the next and so forth, like a row of half-tipped dominoes propped up by the high walls around them. Their contents, the precious truth vials themselves, lay shattered beneath their feet.

'Where's the liquid? Where are the Archivers?' Fin asked quietly, his words echoing eerily in the room. The albino men might have run away, but would the coloured truths have simply evaporated when the containers had broken? He had no idea what the liquid inside had actually been, but surely it should still be coating the floor? 'Why would anyone do this?'

'I was wondering more who *could* do this,' Fowkes said. 'No one comes in here. You know that.'

'The mad did it.'

The voice made them jump, and both Fin and Fowkes drew their swords as they spun round. Henry Wakley stood

108

in the doorway, three of Jack Ditch's urchins with him. None of them smiled as they stepped forward, and Henry's eyes were narrowed and suspicious. There were dark rings beneath them and none of his easy charm twinkled in their blue. That wasn't all that had changed, although it took Fin a moment to notice it. He wasn't wearing his cloak, but instead had on thick trousers and a top under a heavy overcoat. Henry didn't look like a Knight at all. 'They don't come here so much now. But they did at the beginning.'

'Henry?' Fowkes asked. 'What the hell's going on?'

'Is it you? Is it really you?'

Fowkes frowned. 'Of course it's me. What's the matter? You look like you've seen a ghost.'

For the first time Henry Wakley showed a hint of the cheeky twin he used to be, a smile cracking hesitantly on his face. He grabbed Fowkes, both hands squeezing his shoulders and then turned and did the same to Fin. 'You have no idea ... you have no idea ...'

'Look,' one of the street kids pointed at Fin's sword. 'Look. It's still bright. It's still golden.'

'I don't understand—' Fowkes started, but Wakley cut him off.

'We need to get you both to the Seer's house. Before night falls completely.' They froze as a series of bloodthirsty howls and yelps cut through the silence.

'What was that?' Fin whispered, his blood suddenly cold in his veins.

'They're out early,' one of the boys said.

'Something's drawn them out.'

'What?' Fin said, but the children and Wakley muttered a conversation around them as if he and Fowkes didn't exist.

'Maybe the swords, maybe they can feel it?'

'If they cut through—'

'Don't be stupid—'

'But they came somehow—'

'We need to go.' Wakley's voice was firm. 'That's not a patrol, that's a pack. They're probably not alone either.' He nodded at the smallest boy, who took the lead. 'You know the route, Jester. Get us there safe.'

Fin glanced at Fowkes, who grabbed Wakley's arm as he led them away. 'But what ... ?'

'Questions can wait.' The young Knight paused and then gave his half-smile again. 'But it's bloody good to see you, boss. It really is.' With that, they were back out into the freezing night, Fin working hard to keep his footing as he followed the others' sure tread on the icy ground.

The route was unexpected. Instead of keeping to the main roads, the small party nipped in and out of side streets, pausing to knock here and there on a door. It was a soft coded tap, after which the residents would cautiously open up and then hurry the group through to the back and let them out again. Very few words were spoken; arms were squeezed instead, as if the mad would hear even the slightest word of care as they sneaked through the darkened houses. Fin kept quiet. The howls that cut through the frozen air seemed to come from further away than they had, but they still made Fin tremble to his bones. If Henry Wakley and Ditch's boys were staying quiet, then he would too.

They moved like this for about half an hour, far longer than the journey should have taken, and by the time they reached the last house Fin was quite disoriented. How many Boroughs had they passed through? Why weren't Jack Ditch's boys feeling the effects of the Travelling? If they weren't Traders then they should all be exhausted. No one moved around much in the Nowhere. That was just how it was. But now it looked like that had changed. There was too much to think about and his hands and feet were numb and his face stinging. He was just relieved that the freezing air was dry, too dry maybe, but at least he wasn't soaked to the skin from snow. It was hard to want to do much other than keep moving when he was so cold, and he let the thoughts drift away for now. Something major had happened while they'd been away, that was for sure. He was just going to have to wait to find out what.

Instead of going to the back door and out into the road again, the group followed an elderly man and the small yellow glow of his candle down into the cellar of the house. It was a large, solid brick Georgian building, but the downstairs rooms they'd passed through were half-empty and the fireplaces were unlit. The old man was wrapped in several cardigans and was wearing fingerless gloves. Fin thought the house might look affluent, but its owner certainly wasn't.

In the cellar the man stood back as Henry Wakley sought out a hidden lever on the dusty floor, and he stared first at Fin and then at Fowkes. 'They've come from your world, haven't they?' he said eventually, as Henry pulled up a trapdoor. 'They've come to help us.'

Ditch's boys scrambled into the hole in the ground first, and moments later a light glowed from the pit. Henry smiled at the old man and Fin saw genuine affection pass between them. 'Perhaps there is hope, after all,' Henry said.

The old man's eyes glittered with tears and he muttered something Fin couldn't quite catch under his breath. Fin wanted to talk to him, to understand, but Henry grabbed his arm and suddenly he was climbing down the rope ladder into a tunnel beneath the house.

As they trotted along the rough passageway, Fin had to watch his head here and there, but Henry and Fowkes were stooping the whole way. Wooden props were wedged against the wall every few feet and struts ran across the low, uneven ceiling. Fin had to fight his rising claustrophobic panic by taking deep breaths and reminding himself that the mad were hunting them in the streets outside. They were safer in this makeshift tunnel, risking its collapse, than they were outside. He glanced sideways. There were newer pieces of wood alongside the old, signs of repairs. Who used this tunnel? How long had it been here? Here and there other dark tunnels joined the one they were following. How many tunnels were there? How did anyone know which tunnel they were meant to be in? Eventually, with a tremendous sigh of relief, he reached the other end and they all waited until a hatch opened, flooding the gloom with light, allowing them to climb out.

The first thing Fin noticed was the warmth. It was a wave of heat that made him shiver the cold away, the kind of heat he'd only ever felt in Orrery House ... although this heat felt more natural. It was as if it were the temperature the building *liked* to be and had settled on. The second thing he noticed was Christopher, staring at him from the other side of the room. The Seer's house. Of course. They'd finally made it. He grinned at Christopher as Jester and a smaller boy closed the trapdoor and replaced the rug, hiding all evidence of how they'd arrived.

'That's really cool! When did you find the passageway?'

Christopher wasn't smiling. He was just staring at Fin and Fowkes, his expression almost disbelieving as Henry went to stand beside him. 'What?' Fin asked. 'Why are you looking at us like that?'

'We didn't find the passageway,' Christopher said eventually. 'We built it.'

'What?' Fin said. 'I don't get it. How could you ... ?'

'What the hell is going on here?' Fowkes growled.

'I'm not sure,' Christopher said 'What happened back there? In the Somewhere? After I left?'

'We went to Cannon Street,' Fowkes said, 'to where the London Stone was. Arnold-Mather had beaten us to it. We fought them but they escaped back here, taking the stone with them.'

'And then?'

'We went back to Orrery House. The tempest was coming, the weather had changed. Snow was falling.' Fowkes' voice was soft as the flakes themselves and his dark eyes were thoughtful. Fin's eyes darted from the Knight to his school friend and back again. They had both grasped something that he was still missing. What was it? 'Then an hour or so later, something happened. Something terrible. The power failed. The crack in the table got longer in an instant, and then, when we went outside, we saw the tear in the sky.'

'But not like here,' Fin cut in. 'Here it's wide and black – there it's white and thin. Like a long, jagged scratch in the sky.'

'And then?' Christopher asked.

'Then we came here.'

Wakley sucked air through his teeth and the street boys muttered and cursed in shock.

'What?' Fin asked. 'What's going on? Why's everything so weird?'

'I think we all need a drink,' Christopher said, and Henry Wakley poured them all a small glass of what looked like thick, red wine from a decanter hidden in a writing desk against the wall. He gave a glass to Christopher first and then to Fowkes, before looking back for Christopher's nod to give a glass to Fin. So Christopher got to say when Fin had a drink now? What was that all about? Fin took a sip, and let the liquid thaw his insides as the heat from the house was thawing him from outside.

'How long was it between the crack appearing in the sky and you came back here?'

'Roughly?' Fowkes asked.

Christopher half-smiled. 'Roughly will do.'

'Forty-five minutes? Maybe less?'

'We came back pretty much straight away,' Fin added. 'We were worried about you.'

'I knew it!' Henry Wakley exclaimed with a grin that almost matched the one Fin had grown used to. 'I knew there'd be a reason! I knew they wouldn't have just left us!'

'Left you?' Fin said. 'What are you on about?'

'How long has it been here?' Fowkes asked softly. 'How long have you waited for us?'

Christopher sipped his wine before he answered. 'Eight years, Andrew Fowkes. It's been eight long years.'

'But ...' Fin said, his head spinning; *the ice, the head on the spike, the tunnel, the fear, now it makes sense.* 'But it can't have been. You look exactly the same.' He looked at Henry Wakley. 'All of you do.'

'Time passes. No one ages,' Henry Wakley said. 'Not that we can see. But if it's been less than an hour back there, then perhaps that's why.'

Back there. Not home. *There.* Fin felt dizzy. Eight years. He couldn't get his head around it.

'Time's become a funny thing,' Christopher said. '*Things* still change and age. It must have still been black snow when you were here last, not this awful ice. We thought perhaps the crack had broken time.' He looked at Fin and smiled. 'Some of us thought the crack had broken the first world. That you were all gone. In our darkest moments some wondered if perhaps you had seen what happened here and abandoned us. I didn't believe it. Neither did Mona. Nor Henry.'

'Mona? How is—'

'Why didn't you come back?' Fowkes cut in. 'Why wait for us?'

Henry drew his sword from where it was hidden within the folds of his coat and sweaters. For a moment, Fin didn't recognise it at all. Where it had shone gold and brilliant when Henry had cut open his first doorway in St Paul's Cathedral, now it was the colour of rough steel, cold and grey. The stone in the pommel was clear with no hint of colour at all. It was a dead thing, and Fin gripped the hilt of his own sword more tightly as his heart ached for all the empty sword represented.

'It happened when the sky cracked,' Henry said. 'I almost *felt* it happen. Like something being sucked out of me. None of the swords work any more. Not ours, not theirs. We tried the doorway, of course. So did they. But it had sealed up as if it had never been there. Is it open at your end?'

'It's only been forty-five minutes,' Fowkes said, leaning back against the arm of a chair. 'I don't think anyone has checked. But if it's closed here, I don't see how it could be open there.'

'But your swords still work!' Wakley smiled. 'The battle's not over yet.'

Fowkes drew the weapon and they all stared at the glinting gold. 'I should have been here,' he muttered. 'Eight years?' He looked up again at the young Knight. 'When did they get Kent Jasper?'

'Four years ago,' Christopher said. 'He was a good Knight.'

'We should take his head down. Why have you left it out there?'

'It's supposed to be a warning to us and those who stand with us. If we take it down then there will be repercussions – and it'll be the ordinary people who suffer. We've learned that the hard way. Kent Jasper is dead. He can't suffer any more.'

'We should get you out of here,' Fowkes said. 'Get you home and rested.'

Both Christopher and Wakley shook their heads. 'We won't leave. Not with the Nowhere like this. We can't leave our people here,' Wakley said. 'What if we couldn't get back?'

'Aside from that, the mad are out in force tonight. Perhaps the Dark King has felt your arrival and sent them out. Hunting for the first doorway to open in almost a decade. He'll want your swords.'

'The Dark King?' Fin said. 'You mean Joe?'

'No.' Christopher almost laughed. 'Not Joe. My father.'

NINETEEN

'My lord, the spies are coming back.' Edgar Blacken was standing by the window in the large room that had, over the years, become Justin Arnold-Mather's throne room, filled with the finest furniture that the Nowhere's London and the dead regent's palace had to offer. Their colours had grown richer, and the wood darker as they'd settled into the strange, magical electricity of the Dark King's domain. Most furnishings eventually assumed a black or reddish hue and, in this room in particular, nothing ever appeared light or bright. Arnold-Mather didn't mind. He'd always preferred a more traditional look, and his sumptuous surroundings reminded him of everything Parliament – the little he remembered of it – could have been. It was funny how that old life had simply faded away. The Somewhere itself seemed to have disappeared. Until tonight, that was.

He hauled himself to his feet and made his way over to join Blacken. Although no one around him appeared to age or change, he knew that wasn't the case for himself. He hadn't aged as such, but he had changed. His skin was rough and swarthy. His eyebrows were heavier and hung like hoods over his suspicious eyes, and he was thicker in his torso than he had been. His spine curved slightly, as if the power that had surged through Joe and into him all those years ago had taken its toll on his body. It was a small price to pay for the electricity that crackled in his fingertips and the dark magic that itched beneath the surface of his skin. No one thought

116

for a moment that he was anything but all-powerful, despite the way he shuffled slightly under the extra weight he carried and the gold and jewellery he draped himself in. He was the Dark King, the Prophecy come alive. He ruled the Nowhere with a grip of iron and his subjects bowed to his every request. Until today, his focus had been on how to attack the South again but now, with the flurry of energy that had rippled through the building and made the walls shimmer white for a moment, the Somewhere, so long forgotten, had reared its ugly head.

'I'm not seeing any unusual prisoners,' Blacken muttered. Arnold-Mather grunted, displeased, and looked down at the guardsmen riding in, the mad scampering and howling around them, always on guard should anyone be foolish enough to attack. The marshes and the area around the Future Blocks, and the Dome in particular, had also changed since Arnold-Mather first claimed them as his base. Now there were walkways and gangplanks and sentry towers, all built on the shifting land. Many had died during the construction, sucked screaming into the boggy earth below, but eventually he had bent the land to his will and the platforms remained where he wanted them. Fires burned on the tips of poles below, the golden light a contrast with the red that covered everything around the Dome.

'Something shifted tonight. I felt it. A tear in the city. It made the boy scream. He said it was swords. Golden swords. But there are no swords like that here. Someone's come from the Somewhere.' He avoided using the word *Knights*. Walls had ears and despite his servants' constant assurances of loyalty, a rumour like that would spread like wildfire through the city. If Knights had returned from the Somewhere, he wanted to hear the rumour and know it to be true, not wonder if it was a rumour that had started in his own home. He looked at Blacken. 'I trust we still have people watching the Seer's house?'

'Yes.' Blacken nodded. 'They've seen nothing unusual.' He hesitated for a moment and then added, 'I still think we should do something about him. Bring him here, at least. You know the rebels flock to him. I don't understand why you leave him out there.'

'That's because you don't understand people.' Arnold-Mather smiled, aware that his side teeth, now black but not rotten, glinted like coal as he did. 'We need him to provide hope if we're to make our *fear* truly effective. And, anyway, he hasn't done us any harm yet.' In the distance the city lay like an icy wasteland, small streams of smoke rising here and there from houses as night fell. It was past curfew and there would be no one about but his patrols.

'Where's Simeon Soames?' he asked. He'd had no cause to doubt the blond ex-Knight, but there was still something slightly distant about the commander of the army that irked Arnold-Mather.

'Out beyond the city walls with the young ones. Scouting. There are areas out there where the ground isn't so hard. He thinks perhaps we could grow crops there.'

'Perhaps,' Arnold-Mather said, bored by the suggestion. He wanted them to discover golden material like that of the Knights' swords, or come back with the other ores that glinted in the crumbling remains of West Minster. Food, pleasurable as it was, wasn't a necessity. People weren't ageing and people weren't hungry. He only ate because he enjoyed the sensation, not because he needed to, and the rest of the people – those with access to food, at least – were the same. It made them feel normal, that was all.

The door at the far end of the room opened and two guardsmen dragged a middle-aged woman in, wearing a rough coat and thick boots. Her hair hung loose around her face.

'You caught her out after curfew?' Arnold-Mather asked the guard.

'Yes, sir. This one and a few others.'

118

'You,' the woman hissed and then spat at Arnold-Mather's feet. 'Look what you've done to us. You suck our heat from the ground and leave us mired in ice. We're frozen in time. London hums with *wrong* magic and the Storyholder is never seen. You won't break us, though. There will always be someone to fight you.'

Justin Arnold-Mather stared coolly into her angry eyes and then flicked his wrist. His fingers sparkled as if red glitter was spilling from their tips. In the corner of the room a cloth fell away from the gilded cage it had covered. George Porter, curled up inside, moaned. The woman was still shouting at Arnold-Mather as the guards flung her inside. Thankfully, she stopped very quickly. He noticed that Edgar Blacken didn't watch and that surprised him. When had he started to get queasy at the sight of George creating the mad?

'Take the rest to the palace,' he said quietly. 'They will not be so lucky.'

Simeon Soames' mood had soured as soon as he and the pack of young ones were back within the old walls of the city. Not that there was much to bring them cheer further north. The ground was still hard, and the ice was thick in most places, but they had found one or two areas of old crop land that were muddy and some small pools that had somehow evaded the grip of the constant winter. About a mile out, there had been one small tree standing, leaves shivering, in the cold.

They'd stared at it for a long time, the youngs with wonder at the fragile green spines, and Simeon Soames with an ache in his heart. 'What is it?' Number Seven had asked breathlessly. 'A Christmas tree,' he'd answered. They didn't know what Christmas was, and for most, they hadn't seen a tree that was anything but frozen spindly skeleton limbs, but they didn't ask more questions. It was as if they feared they might spoil the moment.

Simeon had let them stare at it for a while, despite the cold that dug beneath his heavy coat and made him shiver. For all the magic that now filled the land there was very little left that was magical, and the young ones saw the least magic of all, living as they did somewhere between pets and prisoners. He'd let them stare at the tree while he gazed at the vague shapes beyond the hills in the distance. He looked that way a lot these days. At first he had seen nothing but emptiness out there but then, the first time he'd come this far as dusk was falling, he'd caught a twinkle of lights or a glint of glass on the brow of a distant hill. He'd since become fascinated by it. Once he'd left the night patrols to ride towards it, and had been convinced there was a faint glow in the sky, coming from the hidden valley. There was a city there, he was sure of it. A city that knew nothing of London and its troubles. He'd wondered if the river wound through its core and if there was a mist over it. He'd wondered a lot.

Simeon nodded at a guardsman as he led the youngs onto the marsh walkways. They no longer looked sideways at their old homes – that urge had been beaten out of them in the early years – but Simeon knew the marsh farmers, locked within those frozen huts and ramshackle cottages, peered through their darkened windows and ached for their lost children.

'Do you think one day you'll just keep riding?'

The group had fallen into a subdued silence as they approached the entrance to the Dome and Number Four's soft voice almost made Simeon jump. His horse whinnied beneath him and he looked down at the walking girl. 'I don't know what you mean.'

'Yes you do.' She kept her voice down and her eyes ahead, as did Simeon. Her hair, blonde like his, poked out from under her rough woollen hat and the edges curled around it. She sniffed and wiped her nose with the back of her small hand. Number Four had been eight when they'd taken her from her parents. She'd now been eight for a very long time. 'The valley. The one with the lights.'

Simeon's heart fluttered. He wasn't mad. There were lights. There *was* a city. 'That's why you take us out here just before curfew. So you can see it.'

'You're mistaken,' he said, climbing down from his horse and handing the reins to the waiting boy. He undid his heavy coat and his skin tingled as he waited for the doors to slide open. This close to the Dome the air was warm and the ground had never frozen. The marsh farmers and rice-growers could still work, harvesting food that no one particularly wanted to eat. The horses and livestock kept in the nearby blocks were healthy and those who lived within the blocks and the Dome that made up the Dark King's citadel did not have to fear the icy cold, chilblains or frostbite during the worst times. With each passing year more of the people of London trickled across the walkways, their spirits broken and seeking protection. It should have made Simeon glad, but he never took pleasure in it. He had chosen his side, but he couldn't bring himself to think of it as the *right* side. He was a paradox. He thought of the lights in the valley. 'There are no lights in the valley,' he said.

'I wouldn't blame you,' she said softly. 'If you did ride away. Just so you know.'

As the doors opened, he looked down and she was looking up at him. 'I will not ride away,' he said. He could see in her wise, sad, forever child eyes that she didn't believe him.

The hot air in the open base of the Dome was filled with a hundred smells; laundry, smelting, roasting pig. While Joe and the stones might be the engine that powered the Dome and the Dark King himself, this vast open space was the human engine that powered the citadel. As they turned away and headed for the higher levels, Simeon envied those who sweated and toiled to keep the Dome clean, fed and armed. They could almost, if they thought hard enough about it, pretend that nothing had changed.

*

He should have taken the young ones straight down to their cells, but instead they went to the furthest stairs and climbed to the fourth floor. The cells on the lower ground floor were rarely guarded these days, no more than a cursory check was made on the young ones, and somehow they had become his responsibility. It was a responsibility he didn't mind. There was something about the young ones that reminded him of the Knights. They looked at him with a loyalty he didn't deserve.

Mrs Manning was waiting for them at the door to her vast quarters and she smiled as she counted all eleven of them in and then bustled around as they headed off for baths and hot chocolates and fresh clothes. 'I've made you a new game to take to your bedrooms with you,' she said. 'It's called Snakes and Ladders!' She held up two carefully painted boards of squares and the curious children crowded round. 'Baths first! Then I'll show you how to play.'

Simeon poured them both a glass of wine as she shooed them off. What had started as a one-off three years ago had become a routine and he hadn't felt any need to tell Arnold-Mather about it. The young ones were no real concern of the king's – in many ways he should have returned them to their families once his grip on London was firm, but that would have been an act of compassion and the Dark King was not known for such an emotion. Anyway, Simeon allowed the children to visit as much for Mrs Manning's sake as for their own. It brought her eyes to life.

'We found a Christmas tree about a mile out,' he said as he handed her a glass. 'They loved it.'

'I think I've had enough of Christmas,' she said. 'It's been Christmas for too long.' Her full face, built for humour and life, was at odds with the sad smile she often wore. If the years had taken their toll on her body, he wondered how she would look now. Thin? Grey? Probably.

'There was a pig roasting downstairs.'

'He'll want my company at dinner tonight, then.' Her voice was empty. 'I suppose it's been a while. I can ask him about Joe. Maybe he'll let me see him...' her words drifted off. 'Where is Mr Dodge?' she asked.

'At the palace.'

'I don't envy him the work he does there,' she said. 'Do you?'

'No,' Simeon Soames said, wondering at Mrs Manning's interest in the Dark King's henchman. It wasn't the first time she'd asked after him on these secret visits. 'No, I don't.'

They stood by the window and looked out at the frozen city. The uneven skyline glittered with white ice and everywhere to the right of the misty snake of the river was tinted blue in the night, apart from the small defiant glow of yellow from the Seer's house.

'It's quite beautiful in some ways, isn't it?' she said. 'Beautiful and terrible.' Simeon Soames didn't answer. He was thinking of the valley of light.

TWENTY

The roof tiles were not only slippery but very cold, and after thirty minutes of lying on them Mona's body was aching with the chill. She could never get used to the constant winter that coated the city. Four years ago her father had created a new, fine weave of woollen fabric designed to use the body's own heat to keep out the cold. It helped, but although she wore three layers of it under her black leather jumpsuit, there was only so long you could stay immobile before the cold would win.

She raised the looking glasses again, careful not to let the cold metal touch her skin, and peered at the grounds of the palace a few hundred feet away. The mad, as usual, stayed close to the railings ready to leap over the spikes and watched the city as several guards marched up and down inside the gates, pausing at the burning oil drums to warm themselves before moving on. Three gallows stood in the centre of the yard, bodies still hanging from them after the executions that had taken place just before dusk. They would remain there until the next day when the executioner, in all her finery, would make the next three beaten and broken prisoners bring them down and cut their heads off to be shoved on the spikes that lined the palace walls. When that was done, they would climb the wooden steps, the nooses would go around their own necks and it would be their turn to swing.

Mona was there every day, hidden in the crowds, watching. Christopher had given up trying to stop her, but one or two of Ditch's boys would come along and keep an eye out for any spies who might recognise her. They never did. They were all too busy watching men and women dying, and Mona hated herself a little bit for the relief she felt every time the people who emerged from the palace were strangers.

She sniffed, her nose stinging in the bitter cold, and turned the glasses towards the building itself. It was always gloomy looking, the shutters closed over the vast windows or heavy curtains drawn, but solitary lights flickered here and there as guards moved along the cells, checking on the prisoners who were allowed to look through barred windows at a freedom they would never have again.

Levi Dodge had gone in an hour before with a cartload of new prisoners, and Mona's stomach turned at the thought of the terror, and probably pain, they would now be experiencing. Alexander Palace, once the Prince Regent's home, was now the most feared place in London after the Dome itself. No one who was taken in ever came out again, unless they were taken to the Dark King and added to the army of the mad. In the silence of these new London nights the inmates' tortured screams were carried across the city by the icy wind, like the pitiful wails of ghosts. Mona knew she wasn't alone in wishing the screamers would die when she heard those sounds, for their own poor sakes rather than anyone else's.

She stiffened as the main doors of the palace opened and fresh guards emerged to switch shifts with those outside. When the time came, this was the moment when they would strike. All they needed was a way to distract the mad and lure them from their grotesque positions, wrapped around the spikes and railings which bore the disembodied heads of dead rebels. Arnold-Mather would like to add hers to the collection, centre stage, she was sure.

A low whistle cut through the night and she jumped, the eyeglass nearly slipping from her gloved hands. The whistle came again, three low notes, and she slithered sideways to her rope, coiled at the edge of the roof, and peered over. There was a small figure on the pavement below, only visible in the gloom by the flash of his eyes.

'Jester?' she whispered.

'You've got to get back to the Seer's 'ouse. Right away.'

Mona's stomach flipped again. 'Why? What's happened?' She gripped the rope and slid down expertly.

'Can't say,' Jester grinned. 'Just got to get everyone back.'

'Everyone?' With a precise flick of her wrist she sent a ripple up the rope, freeing the hook at the top to tumble into her waiting hands. 'We never have everyone together. You know the rules.'

'This is special.' The boy's eyes were sparkling. 'Trust me. Where's Curran Tugg?'

'The Red Lion, I think. That's his base for tonight.' She'd barely whispered the words before the boy scarpered into the shadows. Her heart thumped and her chilled insides warmed. Whatever had happened, it wasn't a bad thing. She glanced back over her shoulder at the palace and whispered, 'Night, Dad,' into the cold air before heading into the tunnels.

Mitesh Savjani kept his head lowered as Levi Dodge and the Lieutenant of the Guard made their way down the long corridor of cages and makeshift prison cells that had once been an elegant palace hallway. He knew it was Levi Dodge. The sound of those heels clicking softly on the marble was recognised by every inmates but there were few, if any, who had been there as long as Savjani and his companion. Savjani knew that Dodge's tread was slightly heavier on his left foot than his right and that his gait was slightly shorter than average. It was surprising what you noticed about a sound when it carried with it life or death.

The feet stopped, somewhere out of sight, and a heavy chain of keys rattled before a lock was turned. 'No ...' the weak voice was filled with disbelief, 'no, not me ... not me

... I didn't do anything!' Feet scuffed as the unfortunate man was dragged from his cell. 'I'm just a baker! But ... no ... no ...!' The words dissolved into a sob as the prisoner was half-carried, half-dragged past Savjani's cell, but the tailor didn't look up. He tugged strands of his long, matted black hair over his face and pulled his knees in to make himself smaller in his cold, filthy corner. He wondered how much he already resembled the mad. He was a far cry from his former, impeccably presented self, still wearing, as he was, the ragged disguise that he'd been captured in.

The feet stopped outside his cell and his heart froze with fear, not for himself, but for what he might reveal were he tortured. The names and places he might give up. Everyone gave names in the end; names of innocent neighbours and friends. Family, even. Anything to make them stop. He heard the screams every night. He didn't blame them; he didn't know if he could bear up under that pressure. He was, after all, just a tailor.

'What about this one? He's overdue.' The lieutenant spoke as if Savjani wasn't even there. 'Him and the bloke next to him. They've been here too long. Bloody, filthy tramps. Maybe we should send them for the mad.' He spat on the ground after the final words. The torch he carried was warm and bright and Savjani ached to look at it, but kept his head down during the endless pause as Levi Dodge decided his future. Eventually he couldn't help but look up, and for a long moment Dodge stared right into his eyes.

'No,' the Bowler-hatted man said, 'not these two.'

'All right, then. You're the boss.'

They moved on, the tailor forgotten.

It was only after the Nightwalk was done and the unlucky three had been taken away to whatever awaited them on the floor below that the tailor slowly uncurled and climbed to his feet. He pressed his face to the bars on his right. 'We live to fight another day, my friend,' he whispered.

127

'That we do.' Jack Ditch's reply was soft in the darkness. 'But I'm starting to wonder at our luck, ain't you? If this was cards, we'd 'ave been thrown out of the 'ouse for cheatin'.'

Savjani said nothing. The same thought had occurred to him too often recently. For not one but both of them to have survived the two years since their capture was incredibly unlikely. He hadn't said anything to Ditch, because he couldn't explain it, but he was sure – and became surer with each Nightwalk that passed them by – that somehow Levi Dodge knew who they were and, stranger still, was choosing to spare them. Savjani didn't understand it, but he didn't think that Dodge's motives could be good. How could they be? He was the Dark King's man, and Savjani knew a soldier when he saw one.

'Maybe they're saving the best till last, eh?' Jack Ditch said and then laughed a little before the sound became a hacking wet cough. It was a cough that came more frequently in the night. He may not have changed outwardly, but the constant cold and damp was taking its toll on the old criminal.

A few minutes later the screams started and, outside, as if the pain in those awful sounds excited them, the mad clinging to the railings began to howl as well.

TWENTY-ONE

On the first floor of the Seer's house the Zoltar machine still stood against one wall, but the rest of the fortune-telling equipment had been cleared away and a thick wooden table now stood at the centre of the large space. 'Shouldn't we stay downstairs near the tunnels, in case we need to use them?'

'They won't attack us here,' Christopher said.

'How can you be so sure?' From what Fin had seen of the new Nowhere, Arnold-Mather had a firm grip on London.

'He hasn't yet, and why would he now? He doesn't know you're here. Not for sure. Anyway, it's not so easy to get in. The house has its own protection.' Christopher didn't elaborate and Fin didn't ask more. There was enough to get his head round. Like Christopher technically being twenty-four for a start, even though he looked exactly the same. Fin had been back an hour or so now. Was that merely the blink of an eye at home? The room was filling up, piles of coats being tossed into corners as people enjoyed the warmth of the house. With each fresh arrival, Fin got more accustomed to the stares of disbelief or cries of joy before being crushed in one bear hug or another. Even Benjamin Wakley, the more reserved of the twins, had squeezed him hard and laughed while declaring their return a miracle. The air buzzed with excitement and Fin glanced sideways every now and then to catch his own slightly dazed expression reflected on Fowkes' face.

'Your wife is back!' one of the boys called up from the

lower floor, just seconds before Mona appeared taking the stairs two at a time, her purple hair bright against her black outfit. 'Fin?' she said. 'Is it really you?' Then she was on him, hugging him harder than any of the grown men had. 'Did he say your wife?' Fin asked Christopher over her shoulder.

'Eight years is a long time.'

'That is too weird. You're *married*?' Christopher blushed slightly in answer, a hint of the boy he'd been only a couple of hours before as far as Fin was concerned. Mona darted away to hug Fowkes, who didn't exactly hug her back but didn't push her away either. Fin watched her. She looked exactly the same. But she and Christopher were married? Despite the fact that they'd had to endure years here he still felt a twinge of envy. Anaïs was gone. One of the army of the mad for almost a decade, if she was still alive at all. Once again Fin, or Baxter or whoever he really was, felt entirely alone.

The wooden shutters were locked tight against the windows and, combined with the slightly unnatural damp heat that grew as people gathered, Fin felt as if he were in the bowels of an old ship trapped in Antarctic ice. The arriving men's faces glowed from the cold outside, and even Curran Tugg, the hardy leader of the Traders, wore a heavy coat instead of the leather jacket Fin associated with him and pulled off thick gloves in order to shake Fowkes' hand. The Commander of the Knights had been sombre ever since Christopher had told them about Savjani's capture. Fin knew why, too. Fowkes would believe he'd let yet another friend down. First Baxter, now Savjani.

'Show us your swords,' Benjamin Wakley said when the room settled. 'Please.' Fin pulled his free, as did Fowkes, and both blades shone golden and bright. Small gasps and mutters rose in the warm air. 'They're not fading,' Henry said. 'I feared they would, but they're not.'

'So why did ours stop working?' It was one of the new Knights Fin didn't know. Not so new any more.

'It must have been the power surge.' Benjamin ran one fingertip along the edge of Fin's sword. 'When the crack in the sky opened and time stopped. It must have been like an electrical surge, only magical. It knocked the swords out. Only these ones weren't there.'

'Maybe if we get your swords back to the Somewhere they'll work again?' Fin suggested.

'No,' Benjamin said. 'They're dead. It'll take more than that.'

'We should still get some of you back to Orrery House,' Fowkes said. 'You've done enough.'

'No.' Christopher spoke for them all. 'No one can go to the Somewhere. Not yet. For now, the fight is here. We've all heard the mad tonight. They're out in force, excited. They felt the magic, the doorway opening. And if they felt it, then *he* will have done too.' He looked calmly at Fowkes. 'If you open another doorway now, then he *will* come and we're not ready for him. Even if we all escaped to the Somewhere, he still has plenty of prisoners. He'd make them pay the price.'

'And if we didn't make it, if he got hold of one of your double-edged swords,' Benjamin said, 'then he would get to our London. Imagine what damage he could do there.'

'Imagine the mad in the Somewhere,' Henry said softly.

'He wants to expand,' Curran Tugg said. 'We know that from his attempts to take the South. If he could reach to the Somewhere—'

'Some days,' Mr Harvey from the Red Lion cut in, 'I miss the travelling sickness. If people still got so tired and weak from moving around, he would find it much harder to motivate his people, even with the mad.'

'People can move between Boroughs now?' Fowkes asked. 'The way we and the Traders can?'

'Yes. not that we get to travel much, not without the tunnels. Between the patrols and the curfews and the Borough identity cards, no one wants to get caught in the wrong zone.'

131

'It's what happened to my dad,' Mona said. 'Luckily, he and Jack Ditch were using false papers. They wouldn't have known who he was. I hope not, anyway.'

'We'll get him back.' Christopher squeezed her hand.

'If we can seize the palace,' Benjamin said, 'then the people might rise up and fight with us.'

They began talking over and around Fin in quick bursts of conversation, and he couldn't keep up. He felt completely lost and lagged behind the debate picking up the occasional scrap of information where he could.

'So our plan was to make a base in the Somewhere. We can't do that now. And given the time that has passed here, Arnold-Mather has a much greater hold on the Nowhere than anyone at home suspects,' Fowkes said eventually, cutting across the intense chatter. 'We need a new plan. If we can't go back then what can we do here? Attack the Dome? Maybe we could get inside—'

'You have to go south,' Christopher interrupted. 'Across the river.'

'It's not possible,' Tugg said. 'The Times barrier is up.'

'The what?' Fin asked.

'A wall of old magic, put up by the South to protect itself from invasion. Keeping what it can of all this madness out. No one can get through. We've tried, and we know the Dark King has too.'

'We have to try again,' Christopher said. 'Magic to fight magic; we need the Magi's help. Time hasn't stopped, even if it feels like it has. This endlessness can't go on forever. It's like a pressure is slowly building up, and I know I'm not the only one feeling it. The worlds will be destroyed – all of them – if we don't stop it. Exactly as the Prophecy says.' He looked around the room. 'They might let Fin pass. He's our last hope.'

There was a long moment of hushed silence at Christopher's words. At the thought that all of their battles were

132

inconsequential to the physics at work in the universe around them. The wheels that Arnold-Mather had set in motion.

'Why me?' Fin asked eventually. 'I'll go if you want me to,' he said, even though his mouth dried at the thought of the mist and the drowning sorrows it held, 'but why would they let me in?'

'You're the boy in their Prophecy.' Christopher's eyes were sad. 'Some of us have been touched by magic – had our lives changed by it – but you, Fin, you were *made* by magic. You're the boy who doesn't belong.'

Christopher's words were honest, but they struck Fin like blows. The boy who didn't belong. Was that really him?

'Fowkes should go with you.'

The commander looked up. 'I've only just made it here. I won't leave my men now. It's dangerous—'

'The world has changed,' Benjamin cut in. 'You don't know how it works here anymore. We can hold the fort, but Fin will need you with him.'

'And the swords will be safer if you take them South,' Henry added.

'It won't be easy,' Christopher said. 'We don't know the situation there, and even the Traders have never ventured beyond the docks. It's unknown territory. And the Magi may still want their revenge.'

Fin looked at Fowkes. The Knight drew his sword and held it high. 'Let us be ready!' he growled. Smiles rippled around the room as each Knight drew his dulled blade and matched him.

'Let us be ready!' the Knights cried.

TWENTY-TWO

They had said their emotional farewells at the Seer's house and left through the tunnels – the Wakley twins coming with them as an escort – and it had been agreed that Curran Tugg would go south with them. The small group finally emerged in the last house, one of the very few still inhabited at the desolate edge of the Borough of West Minster. In silence, they crept into the freezing London dawn, where the grey sky merged into the whiteness of the mist and the icy ground, and the black rip above them stood out against it all, defiant against nature.

They moved slowly, following the river but never straying too close to it, not because of the mist but because the river Traders might be out there somewhere. Even though they might not be able to see the boats, who knew how much those on the water could see or hear of the shore. Finally they passed the broken cathedral of the Magi, West Minster itself. Fin stared, his mouth dropping open and breath rushing out in steam as he realised how glorious it must once have been. How were they ever going to persuade the Magi to help them, after this had been done to their Cathedral?

'Why isn't it guarded?' Fin whispered.

'Old magic,' Benjamin Wakley answered. 'He doesn't like being reminded of it. Patrols of the mad come down from time to time. Anyone found hiding here gets thrown straight in the river.'

'I can't help but say it feels strange,' Curran Tugg muttered, as they reached the start of West Minster Bridge. 'Crossing the river on foot.'

'It's the safest way,' Henry said. 'Francois Manot's men are out on the water with their traps and their nets.'

'I know,' the Trader leader said. 'And that still makes my heart burn, even after all these years. The Times belongs to the Traders, not the Gypsies.'

'One day you'll have it back,' Benjamin said. 'If this mission goes well.'

As the men talked, Fin stared at the curving stone bridge that led into the mist, waiting patiently for them to cross it. It was beautiful and terrifying, like so much he'd encountered since the moment he'd first seen a double-edged sword – the same one he now carried – buried deep in the chest of Harlequin Brown. He thought of the old judge. He couldn't let him down. Not now. Not ever.

'Be careful. It may be guarded. Gypsy Traders or the mad. Arnold-Mather might be watching in case the Magi decide to lower the barrier and come north. They built this bridge. If they decided to attack us it's reasonable to assume they'd use it.'

'If only they had when this all started,' Fowkes said. 'Then maybe you'd have been spared these past eight years.'

'If we're going,' Curran Tugg said, 'then let's go.' Fin nodded, but his legs were trembling underneath him, and not entirely from the cold. The mist was waiting for them, and any waiting mad were the least they had to fear. Curran Tugg stepped between him and Fowkes. 'Take my hands.'

'What?' Fowkes stared at him. 'What for?'

'Because the mist won't touch me, but I won't be able to see you if you wander off when it gets inside your heads. And it will get inside your head, Andrew Fowkes, because that's what the mist does. I know you, remember? Your days of drinking and gambling and the Crookeries. There are dark places in your head and the mist loves those.' He turned to

Fin. 'And as for you, boy, who knows what the mist will do to you?'

'I'm sure those words are very comforting,' Henry Wakley cut in with a smile. He winked at Fin and Fin could have hugged him for it. 'You just remember what an adventure all this is, Finmere Tingewick Smith. Everything's exactly as it's meant to be. And we're here waiting for you.'

Fin smiled. He hoped he did anyway. He turned away from the twins and slipped his hand into Curran Tugg's. The Trader's palm was rough and calloused as it tightened round his soft one. It felt safe though even as the cold nipped at his fingertips.

'Let's go,' Fowkes said. Fin took a long, deep breath, and then they walked into the mist.

Joe was too hot. He was always too hot, even stripped down to a T-shirt and shorts. He lay completely still on the bed that had been his home since the London Stone had been brought into the Dome. He should never have touched it. He should never have let Arnold-Mather touch it. Now they were locked in some eternal power transfer, the stones and the Dark King using him like a conduit to let the magic flow.

His mum was talking and he wished he could turn his head and at least smile at her for her effort, but he didn't have the energy. The weight of the universe pinned him to the bed. He couldn't leave the room without screaming. Without the deadening power of this room and the stones, the pain of the magic and the knowledge of everything he carried inside was excruciating. He wanted to go outside, he really wanted to, just to show Christopher's dad that it was him, it was Joe, who really had the power … but he found that it was something he would do *another* day.

He wasn't listening to his mum's words, but the gentle tone of her voice was soothing. If he tried really hard he could almost imagine that he was back at home in the Brickman

Estate, and none of this had happened. He kept his eyes shut. Inside, he could feel the universe slowly tearing as if it were his own skin.

The door opened. Footsteps. Short gait.

'Is it time already?' his mum asked and he hated how sad she sounded and he hated himself for her even being here.

'If you stay too long the boss feels the change.' It was Mr Dodge. It was always Mr Dodge that came to end his mother's visits.

'Thank you, anyway,' she said. There was a long pause and he heard her get to her feet and walk slowly towards the door. 'Do you think he can still hear me?'

'I think he can hear everything,' Levi Dodge answered, and a moment later, they were gone. Only then did one solitary tear break free from beneath Joe's dark eyelid and slide down his face.

Fin had lost all sense of time. If it had frozen in the Nowhere, then he was sure it was stretching on West Minster Bridge. Time and the bridge had become one entity, leading them on for what seemed like eternity. The dawn was silent and although Fin knew the water was still lapping beneath him, all he could hear was his own ragged breathing. His palm sweated in Curran Tugg's dry one. Was it warmer here, stuck between North and South?

From nowhere, a sob built in his chest and a sudden wave of despair hit him. They would be here forever. He knew it. Stuck walking through the stinking, choking mist that scorched like hot tar in his lungs.

'How long have we been walking?' Fowkes asked. He sounded strange and the mist had such a firm grip on them that Fin couldn't even see him on Tugg's left side.

'Not long, Andrew Fowkes,' Tugg said. 'Only ten minutes or so. About the same until we reach the middle, I should reckon.'

'Ten minutes?' Fin asked, a sob escaping with the words. 'Is that all? And we've got another half an hour of *this*?'

'Feels like forever,' Fowkes said. 'It *has* been forever.'

'Just ten minutes,' the Trader repeated. 'Whatever you're feeling, it's not real. It's just the Times up to her tricks. She's playing with you, that's all. It's her way.'

'You have no idea what I'm feeling,' Fin said. Right then he hated Curran Tugg, for whom the mist was just a mist and the eternity they were stuck in was just ten minutes walking. What could he understand about anything? 'If you love the river so much maybe we should throw you over the side.' The words startled him, all the more when he realised how much he meant them. Tugg said nothing, just squeezed his hand more tightly. Fin tried to think of Henry Wakley and his cheeky smile and that wink. Somehow, though, whenever he got a grip on the image in his mind, the smile turned into a sneer. He didn't like it. The image drifted away and he didn't chase it. They fell into silence and Fin's feet kept trudging forwards because they didn't know where else to go. There was no back. There was only forwards.

A long time later the crying started. It came out of the mist, long and low and soft. Fin's heart squeezed. 'Tova?' Fowkes said. 'Is that you?' The three of them froze for a moment and then Tugg pulled them onwards. It *was* Tova. Fin knew it.

'Help me. You never helped me,' Tova said. A dark shape darted towards him through the thick white. 'Jump.' The whisper came right into his ear. He gasped. 'Jump for me,' Tova said. 'I did it. It's so easy. You just fall. You fall forever.'

'No,' Fin said. 'No, no, no.'

'Whatever you're hearing, son, it's not real.' Curran Tugg's voice sounded distant, his voice much thinner than the dead woman's in his ear.

'It's your fault I jumped,' Tova continued, sounding very real indeed to Fin. He was sure he could feel her cold, dead breath on his face. The mist was her breath. She was the mist.

138

'You watched me fall. I want to watch you fall. Dare, dare, *double*dare.'

Fin was crying. He could feel the hot tears on his face and he veered to his left, his body trying to head towards the wall. The edge. She wanted him to jump; it was either fall or keep going endlessly forward. Whatever waited below had to be better than walking forever through the mist. Maybe the bridge was where truth really lived, not trapped in the beautiful vials of the House of Real Truths. This was the stark reality. The end was all that waited for anyone. The journey didn't matter. Nothing mattered.

'Jump ...' Tova whispered, harsh and impatient. 'Jump!'

'No,' Fin repeated stubbornly. 'No, *no.*'

'I wasn't ready!' Another voice called from the mist. Lost and terrified. Lucas Blake. 'I wasn't ready, let us *not* be ready, I wasn't ready. It's so cold.'

Fowkes shouted something at him; a yell and a sob and a word, all blended into one despairing sound, and then, standing firmly between them, Curran Tugg began to sing a sea shanty, his voice low and sweet and out of place amid the calling dead. Fin tried to focus on it, but the earthy, hearty sound was lost. It wasn't enough. Not to keep them moving. Fin had a feeling he and Fowkes would pull the man in two if he held onto their hands for too long. He tugged harder to his left, trying to wrest his hand free. For now the Trader held on, but Fin knew he couldn't last.

'*Jump ...*'

'*I wasn't ready, Fowkes, I wasn't ready!*'

More dead swarmed in the swampy air ahead of them, more unformed voices and whispers becoming audible. Who next? The Prince Regent? Judge Harlequin Brown? How many more could come to blame them?

'Jump ...' Tova whispered, a whisper of breath against his ear. 'It's so easy.'

It would be easy too. For everything to be finished and

done with. Maybe that would make the world better. He was the boy who didn't belong, after all. Even Christopher, his best friend, had said it.

Curran Tugg's song came to an abrupt halt as he wrestled to keep hold of Fowkes. In their struggle he let go of Fin's hand, and suddenly he felt free, as if he could simply drift away. He looked at the fighting men as if they were part of a dream. They didn't mean anything. They weren't real. Tova was real. Jumping was real.

'No.' Fin surprised himself by saying the word. It had come from his own mouth, but it wasn't his voice. 'No,' it said again. His skin tingled. Light sparkled at the corner of his eyes. He was warm, truly warm for the first time since returning to the Nowhere. He looked up and the mist was just mist, wet and empty. The voices were gone. His ears hummed. He looked back at Tugg and Fowkes. The Trader was strong but Fowkes was deep in the river's grip.

Fin's feet moved purposefully, and with a different gait to his usual one. His stride was longer and more relaxed. He glanced again at the mist. There were flecks of rainbow colours in it that he hadn't seen before. It was beautiful. This wasn't how he'd seen the mist. Whose eyes were he seeing through? Before he knew it, he had reached the fighting men and he grabbed Fowkes' wrist.

'No,' he said again. He felt the warmth run through his palm into the man. 'This is not who you are. This is not who we are.'

Fowkes stared, the fight falling away from him. 'Your eyes,' he said eventually, his voice full of wonder. 'They're *his* eyes.'

'What's this?' Curran Tugg said. For the first time since they'd stepped onto the bridge it was the Trader who sounded afraid. 'This ain't natural.'

'It's natural for me,' Fin – the voice speaking from Fin – said. He drew his sword. 'There's two of them just ahead.' He spoke quietly, but with confidence. 'I can hear them moving.

The mad. We must be near the Barrier. We need to be quick.'

Fowkes was trembling, but he pulled his sword. 'What will be, will be,' he said softly.

'What will be, will be,' Baxter, within Fin, answered. Fin withdrew, and let the Knight have control. He didn't really have much choice. For the first time he felt at peace having Baxter inside him. He didn't struggle, he let the world go dark and drifted.

When he returned he was panting hard and warm blood had run from the sword onto his hand. He stared at it, shocked, as mist and sweat mixed on his forehead and his thick winter clothes clung to his body. Two men lay motionless in front of him, both with bloody slashes all over their bodies as if they had died in a frenzy of battle. They were so ordinary looking now that the mad had left them. Just people. To his relief neither of them was Anaïs. His shoulders aching from activity he couldn't remember, Fin lowered his sword. How long had he been gone? Minutes? It could have been hours for all he knew.

'What happened?' he asked, his voice once again his own.

'You tell us, boy.' Curran Tugg made no pretence of disguising his sudden wariness. 'Never seen anything like it. Not here, not in the harbours of the South.'

'Baxter,' Fowkes said. 'You were Baxter.' Fin looked down at the sword in his hand and then at the ring on his finger. The two that didn't match. His stomach twisted. 'He's gone now.' Had he gone, though? Where did Baxter end and he begin? Although, at least, if the fight had proved anything, it was that he and Baxter were separate, even if they were both in his body. He hoped it proved that anyway.

'Whatever it was,' Curran Tugg said, 'we need to move on. You're not clear of the mist yet.' He reached down and grabbed one of the dead men under the armpits. 'Get his feet, Andrew Fowkes.'

141

'What are you doing with them?' Fin asked.

'We can't leave them here. They'll rot. And there's enough to disturb the mind here already. Better to feed the river with them. Our blood is her blood, and the eels will be grateful.'

The mist was silent, and after they tipped the first man over the wall there was a long pause and then a muffled splash. Fin leaned over the side but couldn't see the surface. He had no idea how far the bridge was above the water. There was a second splash. 'Feed well, my friend,' Tugg muttered. 'From life, make life.'

Fin stared at something in front of him, just beyond the Knight and Curran Tugg. The mist must have thinned, as if perhaps the river was grateful for their offering, because suddenly Fin could see a wall of golden light glinting here and there in the clear patches. 'Look,' he breathed, 'Is that it? The barrier?'

Fowkes and Tugg turned and the three walked forwards until they were barely a foot from the rippling golden wall. 'That's it,' Tugg said.

'It looks like water,' Fowkes muttered. 'Liquid gold.' He reached out his hand to touch the surface, but Tugg held him back. 'I wouldn't,' he said. 'Things that look so pretty generally ain't.'

Fin tilted his head back. 'How far up does it go?'

'No one knows. But it doesn't matter. Climbing it is no option. If we're getting through then it has to be another way.'

'So how?' Fowkes asked. 'I'm not seeing a doorway.'

A doorway. Fin lifted his sword slightly and then wiped the blood from it with his sleeve while muttering a quiet apology to the poor dead men now in the river. The blade glinted. 'Look,' he said, 'it's exactly the same colour as the barrier.' He held it up in front of the wall and it was hard to see the difference between them.

'Makes sense,' Curran Tugg said, nodding. 'The Magi made

the swords, the river made the Magi, and the Magi and the river made the Times Barrier.'

Fin looked at the sword and dead Baxter's ring and then the wall. 'And magic made me,' he said softly. He stepped closer to the shimmering brightness. 'I'm Finmere Tingewick Smith,' he whispered to it. 'The boy who doesn't belong. I'm where life and death is bound in one. Let me in.' He lifted the sword and touched it to the surface and where they met a bright white light burst out, making Fowkes and Tugg flinch. Fin didn't though, the heat surging up his arm kept him in place. A section of the golden barrier melted back and an archway appeared. Fin gasped. He wasn't the only one. 'Go through,' he said. 'Go through quickly.' His arm was trembling from the pressure and as soon as he'd followed the men in and stepped across, the barrier closed behind them.

They were in the South.

TWENTY-THREE

Christopher waited until the drums that beat in time with the procession were nearly at the end of the street before he stepped outside. Mona, Jester and some of Jack Ditch's boys had hidden in the tunnels below the house, and the Wakley twins had gone, as was usual on procession days, to scout around the Dome for any weaknesses they'd missed. Christopher was never happy with their going together – the Knights were too valuable a resource to risk losing both at once – but they were brothers, twins, and he couldn't have stopped them even if he tried. He might be the Seer, but there was only so much he could do.

The air was at its arctic coldest in these moments after dawn, but every citizen had still shuffled outside and their muted cheers and muffled applause filled the frozen air. Christopher did not cheer as the carriage rumbled towards him, and nor did he wear a coat. When those in the streets bowed their heads Christopher kept his held high. Someone was watching, and he might be a man trapped in a boy's body but he was still the Seer. He represented hope, the light in the darkness. He sucked in a lungful of icy air and fought a shiver. All the Prophecy and fate aside, he'd never backed down to his dad before and he wasn't going to start now.

A heavily jewelled hand appeared through the carriage window and the steady procession drew to a halt at Christopher's front door. The mounted guards who surrounded it pulled back a little, their faces impassive, as he came down the steps from his house. The curtain on the carriage window opened and Arnold-Mather leaned forward. His father looked old – more than old – corrupted, as if every evil deed he committed had etched itself on his hunched physique. Did he even realise, Christopher wondered, how the magic was taking its toll on him? They stared at each other like strangers; father and son, Dark King and Seer.

Arnold-Mather stared at him for a long moment before running his tongue over his blackened teeth. 'Join me,' he said eventually. The words came as no surprise. The procession didn't always stop at the house, but when it did their barbed conversations always ran the same way.

'Never,' Christopher replied. Horses shuffled and whinnied around them, eager to keep moving and get back to the warmth of their stables.

'More and more are, you know.' Arnold-Mather bit into a peach and the juice dribbled down his chin. He didn't wipe it away. 'Everyone will eventually.'

'Not me,' Christopher replied.

'Hmm.' Arnold-Mather stared into the distance for a second as if weighing up the truth of this before bringing his gaze sharply back to his son. 'I had a strange feeling in the night that perhaps your friends might have returned. The boy, Finmere.'

'Not so far as I know.' Christopher maintained his steady gaze.

'Strange. Half an hour ago, the Gypsy Traders reported they'd felt something on the river. Nothing was pulled up in the nets, but there was a momentary change in the water. Nothing you know anything about, I take it?'

Christopher kept his face steady. Even the slightest twitch could give him away. Beneath the heavy eyebrows and hooded lids, his father's eyes were sharp and seeking out any hint of secrecy.

'Everything is strange these days,' Christopher said. 'Why

145

should the river be any different?' He looked up to see the mad scuttling along the rooftops. The lottery of the mad. If they paused and thumped hard on the roof, yowling their madness, then those inside would be taken to the palace. No one ever left the palace. Today it seemed the mad were remaining mercifully silent. Maybe they felt something unusual around them too. His father was still watching him.

'You can come in and look if you want,' Christopher said. 'There's no one inside.'

'No.' Arnold-Mather's eyes darkened slightly as he glanced towards the door. 'You're always being watched. I know there's no one in there.' He didn't trust the house, that was for sure, and Christopher didn't blame him. The house had very little time for anyone but the Seer. It also had its own magic, which no doubt the Dark King didn't trust should he and his dark magic enter.

'You'll join me eventually,' he said, rapping on the side of the carriage. 'You'll have no choice.'

Christopher said nothing, but moved back onto the steps of the house. He waited until the procession and the mad on the roofs had moved on to the beat of the drums, and then he went back into the warmth. So, there had been a disturbance on the river? That could only mean one thing, he was sure of it. Fin and Fowkes had made it through the barrier. He grinned and his eyes sparkled. For the first time in almost a decade he felt a bit like the Christopher of old.

Levi Dodge had stayed in the shadows while his boss, the Dark King, had spoken with the Seer. Even when there weren't any shadows, Levi Dodge felt he lived in them, ones created of his own making. That was his role. Through his window he could see Simeon Soames riding alongside them; the General of this new army. His face too was impassive. It was an expression that came naturally to Levi Dodge, but he doubted it was as easy for the ex-Knight.

'I take it you've had no luck locating the fat tailor?' Arnold-Mather asked. He'd leaned back in his seat, his body hidden by a swathe of furs, but his eyes glittered like the black snow that had heralded this new age all those years ago. 'If we get him, we can lure that daughter of his out. She leads the rebels. We get her, we get everyone.'

'We haven't found him yet,' Levi Dodge said. 'But we will.'

'Look harder.'

Levi Dodge didn't need to look up to feel Simeon Soames' eyes on him. Just as he never needed to look closely into *that* cell to know who was curled up in the corner. He pushed the thought away. There had once been simply orders and actions and a healthy bank account. Now he had orders and inactions and secrets that he no longer understood even though they were his own. How much longer could he keep the tailor hidden, he wondered, as the mad began to howl and stamp on a passing building. Screams filled the air as the residents were hauled out and thrown into the cart behind protesting their innocence – probably because they were innocent.

As long as he could, he concluded, settling back into the shadows. As long as he could.

TWENTY-FOUR

Where the mist on the northern side of the bridge had been cold and damp, in the south it was humid and clung to the skin. No ghosts called out, but strange creatures seemed to exist in it, and here and there Fin caught glimpses of large wings and sharp teeth. The three of them drew closer together as they walked and, despite the heat, kept their heavy coats on for fear of sharp talons grabbing them and tearing their flesh. None did, and after twenty minutes – which passed normally – the mist began to thin.

'Listen,' Fowkes said. Human sounds, the hustle and bustle of a busy city, were filling the silence. People called to each other, wheels rattled, there were a thousand indistinct sounds all vying for space in the air.

'Welcome to the South,' Curran Tugg said quietly as they finally left the mist and stepped into the bright, hot sunlight on the river bank.

The sun was right behind the group of men waiting for them and Fin squinted slightly as he stared. Most were armed, pointing swords and spears in their direction, their bodies still and tensed for attack. Fin put his hands up slowly, which did nothing to put them at ease, but then a stocky figure pushed through them, breaking the moment.

'That's Curran Tugg, as I live and breathe! Curran Tugg, I say! North Trader.'

'It is, for sure.' Tugg stepped forward and Fin and Fowkes followed in his wake. 'Is that you, Master Theaker?'

'It is, for sure,' the man repeated. His skin was as dark as the tanned leather of a blacksmith's apron and he wore a navy blue light cotton jacket with a thin shirt beneath. He held his hand out to shake Tugg's and Fin saw a red heart tattooed on the back of it. The same emblem was embroidered on his sleeve although, on the jacket pocket beneath the words 'Master of the Harbour' the heart was joined by the other three suits: clubs, diamonds and spades.

'All these years and you look exactly the same,' Master Theaker said, studying Tugg.

'Things aren't good in the North,' Tugg said softly. 'Everyone looks the same.'

Theaker's eyes widened slightly. Over his shoulder, Fin could see the soldiers had edged forward. They all shared Theaker's dark skin tone but their eyes were warier and they weren't showing any sign of lowering their weapons.

'We wondered,' Theaker said. He glanced up to the black slash that hung in the sky. 'Here time still moves, but more lazily than before. The Magi have protected us.'

'It's the Magi we've come to see,' Fin said. 'We need their help.' The soldiers' swords rose slightly higher.

'I'm Andrew Fowkes.' Fowkes held out his hand. 'Commander of the Knights of Nowhere. I'm not sure what you know of us, but I am only here for the good of all the worlds. This is Finmere Tingewick Smith, the boy from the Magi's prophecy. The Times Barrier let him through. Let that show the good faith between us.'

Theaker stared at Fowkes for a moment, and then looked back at Tugg. 'Likes a speech does he, this one?' He grinned, and slapped Fowkes on the arm. 'We trust the wall, my friend. But more than that, I trust Curran Tugg.' He clapped his hands together. 'Now, we must go. They're waiting for you.'

'Who's waiting?' Fin asked. 'The Magi?'

'No doubt them too, out in the middle of nothing, but for now I mean the four Kings of the citadels. They've been

149

waiting for you. The Magi warned them travellers might come. They want to see who the wall let through.'

Fin glanced back. On the northern side the Magi's barrier hadn't been visible through the thick mist, but here it glittered like fairy lights, charging the air around it with sparks of electricity. It was beautiful, Fin thought, really beautiful, and he felt a wave of sadness for the Magi who had been exiled across the bridge all those hundreds of years ago. Then he turned and faced the streets of the South, and his mission.

Theaker and the soldiers walked at a quick pace, and Fin fell over his feet a couple of times, his eyes utterly distracted from his path. The baking heat of the South wasn't the only difference between it and its sister London in the North. From the river came sounds of boats and fishermen singing, strange exotic tunes Fin didn't recognise, and as they wove their way through the narrow streets lined with sandy-coloured houses and street stalls, Fin could see brightly coloured domes and minarets glinting in the sunlight. He tugged his coat off, enjoying the dry heat after the icy cold that gripped the North. It was hard to believe they were barely a mile apart. He looked up at Curran Tugg. 'This place is amazing,' he said.

'Yes, it is, boy.' The Trader nodded. 'I've never come beyond the Harbour Master's zone before. Never been allowed into the heart of the city. All Trading is done at the river bank.'

'Look,' Fin said. A man sat on his haunches at the side of a building, a wooden flute in his hands. He was thin and old and his eyes were sunk so far into his face they were merely dark glitters, but his fingers moved swiftly. As he forced out a series of strange, harsh notes, Fin's eyes fell to the basket that sat on the sandy earth in front of the old man.

'Is he a snake-charmer?' Fin asked. The old man looked up, his lost eyes twinkling, and then Fin gasped. A glittering, scaly head emerged from the basket, a transparent creature that had no substance but slowly unfurled into a ghostly dragon, sparks of colour flying from its shimmering edges.

Two small children ran from a dwelling opposite and paused, giggling, beside Fin, who was aware that a few feet away the soldiers and the harbour master had stopped and were waiting for him. They could wait a moment or so longer. One of the children reached out and touched the hovering dragon's slowly flapping wing. The whole illusion rippled slightly and then as the old man picked up the tune the creature breathed a burst of fire before dissolving into a dust of colour that evaporated as the two children grabbed for it.

Curran Tugg flipped a coin at the man and then pulled Fin towards the impatient group. 'What was that?' Fin asked. 'Was that magic?'

The harbour master stared at him blankly and then burst into laughter. 'Open your eyes, boy. Look! We might not be the Magi, but since the wall went up we all have a little magic in the citadels.' He snapped his fingers and a flame emerged above his palm. He blew it out and winked. Fin's mouth fell open. His feet stumbled forward but his eyes were everywhere. A woman holding a basket of washing leaned out of a second floor window and then, while still talking to a child beside her, casually tossed the clothes out. Instead of falling they spread out along an invisible line that stopped at the building opposite. The woman turned away and went inside as if the clothes hanging on nothing was the most normal thing in the world.

With each corner they rounded there was more magic. Children giggling as they turned each other's hair different colours; a man selling bread whose cart rolled along beside him with nothing pulling it; more charmers of mythical creatures. Fin wasn't sure whether the joy of it all made him want to laugh or cry. The South was clearly a happy place, so different from the North. Even the people looked different.

'What are all the marks on your hands?' he asked. 'You've got the heart. I saw that little girl back there had a club on hers. What are they?'

'Houses, my boy,' Theaker said, holding out his hand. 'I'm of the House of Hearts. She's of Clubs. Each house has different tribes from the old days and we each have a different king. Each king commands a citadel.'

'So how do you know which you're part of?' Fin asked. 'Is it where you're born? Like the Boroughs?'

'No.' Theaker laughed again. 'I've heard many stories of the strange Northern people who can't move around their city. Can't quite get my head round it myself. Here, we go where we please, within reason. The mark,' he held his brown hand under Fin's nose again, 'is what you're born with. Sometimes families all stay in the same House, sometimes not. It only really matters in times of war. And we haven't had one of those for a long, long time.'

The streets widened into a boulevard lined with strange trees whose vast, thick green rubber leaves filled the air with the scent of something not quite lemon and not quite orange.

'Green Witch trees,' the harbour master said. 'This is the only place they grow. Their oil is the base for every expensive perfume sold in all the cities.' At the far end was a magnificent palace, only half visible behind the golden fence. At each corner of the building was a large golden dome, topped with one of the four suits, a heart, a spade, a diamond and a club, all made in silver.

'Green Witch Palace. Otherwise known as the palace of the four kings of the citadels. But that's a bit of a mouthful.' He grinned proudly. 'Quite something, isn't it? Bet your dandy Prince Regent's place in the North isn't like this, is it?'

'The Prince Regent's dead,' Fin said, still staring at the exotic palace. 'And he wasn't a dandy.'

'Right. Sorry. I didn't ... you only know what you hear, and I guess times change.'

'That they do,' Curran Tugg added. 'That they do.'

'Let's go and see these kings then,' Fowkes muttered. 'We don't have time to dally and if they're anything like the

Prince Regent I guess nothing ever goes simply when you want something.'

The harbour master laughed again, and slapped Fowkes on the shoulder. 'You're not wrong, my friend. You're not wrong.'

It was cool inside the palace and servants shuffled about here wearing thin cotton trousers and red or black shirts embroidered with their appropriate suit, either barefoot or wearing thin sandals. Fin's own feet were sweating and throbbing in his trainers from the heat and he wished he could take them off. The odour of cheesy feet was probably no way to meet the leaders of the South, though. He figured not even the smell from the Green Witch trees outside would overpower his current sock situation.

Although most of the corridors were neutral, here and there he would see a heart on a door or a club over an archway. They must be for that king's servants only. It seemed a very strange way to live but, in that respect, the Southern Nowhere was proving no different to the North. It was all very strange if he thought too much about it.

Finally they reached a set of large double doors shaped in a strange arch, exactly the way Fin imagined doorways to be in the hot dusty Arab and eastern countries of the Somewhere. Above it, engraved in silver, gold and a strange metal that shone like mother-of-pearl, were the words 'Full Deck'. Fin looked up at Fowkes who shrugged slightly. 'You think a pack of cards landed this side of the river once?' Fin asked quietly.

'Who knows?' Fowkes answered. 'Maybe we got our cards from *them*.' The doors opened and, with his heart racing, Fin stepped inside.

The first thing he noticed was that the kings were all fat. Each one was crammed into his gilded throne, rolls of flesh oozing out between the arms, the seat and wherever else it could find some release. Behind each throne stood two servants, their heads bowed and their hands resting on the back of the jewelled seats. Only when he looked closely did Fin realise the thrones were on wheels. Were the kings wheeled everywhere? No wonder they were so fat.

As if to prove his point the four kings, who had been facing each other from each of the four compass points, laid out on an ornate circle in the floor, were wheeled into a line to face Fin and Fowkes. The harbour master had hung back behind them slightly and stood with his head bowed. Fin lowered his head slightly too, but not so far that he couldn't peer up. Unlike Theaker and the rest of the population, who wore their house on the back of their hands, the kings' marks were on their foreheads. Jewels glittered at the edges and each king wore his long hair pulled back into a tight ponytail so that the symbol was clear. Their silken robes were all covered with designs made up of their own suits.

'So, these are the travellers from the North?' The voice was high and squeaky, more suited to a child than a grown man. 'How very exciting!'

'Oh, Diamond, you find everything exciting. Perhaps the Magi's barrier is failing? Have you thought about that? Perhaps this awful sky is about to tear for good?' The layers of fat squeezed through the gaps of his chair wobbled as the man spoke. 'Not every excitement is a good one.'

'Oh, Spade,' Heart leaned forward and threw a wink at Fin as he spoke. 'You always see the worst in every situation. The barrier is fine. The citadels are safe.'

'But we can't ignore the sky!'

'It's the North's problem.' Club glowered. 'Let them solve it.'

'Um, if I could speak,' Fin said, after swallowing hard. 'I think it's everyone's problem. The North, the South, the Somewhere and all the other worlds.' The four kings stared at him. 'Don't you?'

'And who might you be, coming in here and interrupting

our divine interactions?' Spade's eyes narrowed. 'People have been cast into the sands for less.'

'I told you,' Fowkes said quietly. 'Royal egos are a pain in the arse. And here we've got four of them.'

Despite his nerves, Fin giggled slightly. 'Egos or arses?'

It was the Knight's turn to snort a quiet laugh. 'We'll have to wait and see.'

'What?' Diamond said. 'What are you laughing at?'

'Your ridiculous voice, no doubt,' Spade replied, and Club sniggered.

'I can't help my voice, I can't! And you're very childish! Always—'

'Quiet, please!' Heart cut in. 'My Royal Flush commands the Houses this cycle. So please, brothers, be silent and let the boy speak.' He smiled again, his fat cheeks squeezing to accommodate the expression. 'Go on.'

'I'm Finmere Tingewick Smith. This is Andrew Fowkes, Commander of the Knights of Nowhere, and Curran Tugg is the leader of the Traders.'

'I can vouch for him,' Theaker cut in, before shuffling backwards again. 'He's known and respected.'

'We've come to seek help from the Magi. Things in the North are bad. Time has stopped. The Dark King has risen and—'

'But who are *you*?' Heart said.

'I'm ... I'm ...'

'He's the boy from the Magi's prophecy,' Fowkes said. 'Born out of magic from the bones of a dead man.'

'"When life and death are bound in one",' Fin said. 'That line was about me.'

'Yes. I note you didn't recite the second half,' Spade muttered. 'The bit about bringing about the end of all the worlds.'

'That's not exactly what the Prophecy says though, is it?' Heart cut in. 'It merely states that when he comes to exist, these things shall come to pass. You can't blame the boy for

155

existing, can you? From what I can see, he seems intent on saving the worlds rather than destroying them. Wouldn't you agree?'

'Just because he doesn't intend it, that doesn't mean he's not going to do it,' Club said.

'He has a point,' Diamond squeaked. 'But at the same time, the North clearly needs our help. Perhaps it's time we tried to bridge our problems, for want of a better word.'

'The North's problems are their own,' Club said. 'We need to protect ourselves. The Magi know best and they've chosen to keep the North out.'

'Not these three though,' Diamond countered. 'These three are very definitely here. Oh, it's so confusing! What to do for the best?'

'How do you ever get anything done?' Fin asked, his bewilderment at the backwards and forwards chatter between the kings getting the better of his nerves. 'Are you like this all the time?'

'When we see each other then, sadly, yes.' Heart sighed. 'It can be thoroughly exhausting.'

'Thankfully most of the law-making was done by our fore-fathers,' Spade added. 'And we have the Magi's wisdom on hand.'

'As the Magi saw fit to let us through their barrier, then perhaps you should see fit to let us see the Magi,' Fowkes said. 'Surely whether they help us or not should be their decision.'

'Yes,' said Heart. 'The traveller is right. This is Magi busi-ness, not Southern business.'

'Surely the two are interlinked?' Club said.

'My Flush, my decision.' There was a finality to Heart's tone that set the others muttering and grumbling, but no one interrupted him. 'The Magi have withdrawn to the Temple of Nowhere in the middle of Nothing. I believe they are meditating in order to keep the barrier strong. You should leave first thing in the morning, and you shall take two of the finest men of each suit with you. After that, your fate rests with the Magi.'

'All our fates are with them,' Fin said.

'Yes.' Heart nodded. 'I do believe you are right.'

Without any farewell pleasantries Heart clapped his hands twice and all four chairs were turned to face the other way. The four kings clapped their hands twice again, in unison, and were wheeled to four separate doors through which they vanished.

'Well, that's that then,' Fowkes said. 'Now I suppose we find somewhere to rest and wait for these men to find us in the morning.' He turned to face the courtier who had led them, but he remained where he'd positioned himself at the door.

'I believe our business here is concluded,' Curran Tugg said. 'If you would see us out.'

'They can stay with me and the missus,' Master Theaker said. 'We'll look after them at the Harbour House.'

The servant remained where he was, staring directly ahead until a door opened behind them and the group turned to find King Heart waddling towards them. He could only have taken a few steps, but he was breathing heavily and sweat was already forming on his forehead. The servant opened the door and disappeared, leaving them alone with the king.

'Where's your chair?' Fin asked. It was clear the man wasn't used to moving under his own steam. 'Shouldn't you sit down?'

'If I use the chair then my brothers will know where I am,' Heart wheezed. 'The chairs are like that.' His jowls shook as he spoke and it took all Fin's effort not to stare. 'And they mustn't hear this.'

'Is there a problem?' Fowkes asked.

'You must leave today, not in the morning. If you go immediately then you have a chance of surviving the sand.' He spoke in a breathless rush. 'I know Club. He wants no part of the problems in the North. He thinks if we ignore it, it will go away, and if we interfere we will bring doom down on our own heads.'

'Cheerful soul,' Fowkes said.

'But that's crazy. It's clear that whatever's happening is affecting the South too,' Fin said.

'He has no children.' Heart shrugged. 'He cares only for his own safety.'

Theaker made a harrumphing sound. 'Clubs are always selfish. You can spot 'em before you see their House. They have a look in their eyes.'

'They're the tribes of the disparate, perhaps,' Heart agreed before continuing. 'He'll send assassins after you in the morning and you'll never make it to the temple. His assassins are the best. He won't expect you to leave today, though. None of my brothers will.'

'I'm not surprised,' Theaker said. 'Only a fool would go into the Middle of Nothing at this time of day. The sun's too far gone.'

'What's the Middle of Nothing?' Fin asked.

'And why would only fools go there now?' Fowkes added.

'It's the desert beyond the boundaries of the citadels. The Magi have their temple a day's walk directly south.'

'Why does the sun matter?' Curran Tugg said.

'The sands shift at dusk. The wind takes them and whirls them into a storm. It will take your skin from your bones if you're exposed.'

'They can't make it to the Temple of Nowhere before dusk.' Theaker shook his head. 'It's foolhardy to suggest it.'

'It's the only way,' Heart said. 'I'll send good men with you. They'll know where to find caves should you run out of time.'

'Caves?' Whatever deference the harbour master might have had for his king was fast disappearing. 'They'll hardly find refuge in the caves, will they? Frying pans and fires come to mind!'

'What's wrong with the caves?' Fowkes asked in a tone that said *why can't anything just be easy?* Fin could identify with that. Why couldn't the Magi have just been waiting for them at the riverside?

'The Outcasts, that's what,' Theaker said.

'We don't have prisons here,' Heart said. 'We don't need them. We have the Middle of Nothing. Criminals are simply exiled from the citadels. Their House is burned from their hand and then they are taken to the city's edge where their magic fades. We watch them walk into the sands and then the gates are locked. What happens to them after that ... well.' He shrugged, sending his jowls wobbling again. 'It's up to fate.'

'They die, I should imagine,' Fin said, his eyes wide. 'The sand must kill them.'

'The sand or the other Outcasts,' Theaker muttered. 'Most die, this is true. But some survive. They find caves to hide in when the sands blow. They live on what they can find. Sand eels if they can catch them. But new Outcasts are easier prey. As are the weakest among their own numbers.'

'They eat people?' Fin asked, agog.

'So the stories say,' Theaker said. 'When people are desperate to survive they'll do pretty much anything, I reckon.'

'Aye,' Curran Tugg said, 'there's wisdom in that.'

'But that's horrible,' Fin said. He looked at Heart. How could the fat man who'd winked at him and helped them be capable of such meanness? 'What kind of criminals are exiled?'

'All kinds, of course. There is only crime, not types of crime.' He looked at Fin as if he were mad.

'So, if someone steals a loaf of bread they are exiled from citadels, the same as if they kill someone?' Suddenly the South wasn't sounding quite so friendly. 'But that's horrible. And what if someone's innocent and only convicted by mistake?'

The king frowned, not in anger but puzzlement. 'What strange questions you ask, boy. Quite ridiculous. How could an innocent person be convicted?' He let out a short laugh as he thought about it. 'Quite ridiculous.'

'So, we have to watch out for the sand, criminals, cannibals and assassins, that's basically what you're saying?' Fowkes asked and the king nodded. 'That's what I thought. Great.'

'We'd better leave now then,' Tugg grumbled. 'If we don't want to be doomed from the outset.'

'That's what I've been trying to say!' Heart smiled. He rubbed his hands together. 'And now you must go. My men are waiting for you outside. And good luck!'

Fin had a feeling they were going to need it.

TWENTY-FIVE

'So, this is the Middle of Nothing,' Fin said, as the heavy gates clunked shut behind them, leaving them very much outside the citadels, hidden behind their impossibly high walls the colour of the desert. Because that's what the Middle of Nothing obviously was – a desert. The city streets had been warm, but out here, with only the endless sea of sand ahead, the heat was almost overpowering, and even the gusts of wind that came at them burned.

'She's breathing her first. We can't delay.' Heart had sent four swarthy men to accompany them, none of whom had spoken more than instructions to either Fin, Fowkes or Curran Tugg since gathering them up. The four men, dressed as they were in pale, sandy colours that covered them head to foot and with their faces of rough skin, looked as if they had been born from the desert itself. They also looked very worried. That combination worried Fin as he carefully checked his water canteen. It didn't seem like much for half a day in the desert.

They set off at almost a jogging pace, and they travelled in silence, ignoring any attempt at conversation from the travellers. Fowkes's main interruptions were focussed on why they were running at all when they could have used horses, and why were they moving left and right instead of going straight. Surely they needed the most speed if the sandstorms were coming? He got no answers though, and finally just fell silent. After a couple of hours, Fin was exhausted, and his throat was dry and felt coated in sand. His own and Fowkes' and Tugg's rough breathing was the only sound as they pressed forward. By the time the four soldiers signalled them to a halt, his legs felt like jelly. One man pulled out a leather-bound spyglass and peered at the dunes behind and around them.

'What are you looking for?' His curiosity overcame the pain the words caused on the sandpaper of his throat.

'The sun's heat is dying,' another soldier said. Fin couldn't feel any evidence but took the man's word for it. 'This is a dangerous time of day to be out,' the man continued. 'The sand eels will return to their nests to sleep, and the Outcasts will come out of their caves to hunt them.'

Fin glanced at Fowkes, bent over and panting, and could see his own thoughts reflected on the Knight's face. If the soldiers were going to tell them they needed to move faster then he didn't think he could. He wasn't sure he could move at all. They'd left their heavy winter coats behind but under the strange clothing that matched their guides, even his T-shirt felt too thick and his face was burning as much from exertion as from the terrible heat. He took a long drink of water from his canteen. No amount of football training could prepare anyone for this. Even Curran Tugg stayed silent, his broad shoulders sagging slightly as he sat back on his haunches.

The man with the spyglass stiffened, and signalled another to him and the pair talked quietly, taking turns to stare into the distance behind them. The other two joined them, and there was pointing and nodding.

'What is it? Fowkes asked. 'What have you seen?'

'Assassins.'

'All kings must think the same,' Curran Tugg groaned as he got up. He, Fin and Fowkes joined the soldiers. They stared at the undulating sand, and Fin didn't need the spyglass to make out the moving shapes in the distance. Where Fin and the group had moved in a zigzag pattern across the sands, whoever was following them was moving in a straight line.

'Are they on horses?' Fin asked as his eyes focused better. Men on horses. Coming in a straight line. His stomach flipped.

'I'm too old for this shit,' Fowkes muttered.

The soldiers ignored them and continued talking quietly.

'We'll never outrun them,' Curran Tugg said. 'Why don't we have horses?'

'Horses would have been good.' Fowkes stared at their pursuers.

'The land can hear the horses.' The man with the spyglass tucked it back in its holster. 'Their hooves are like a heartbeat in the ground.' He paused. 'We must keep moving.' No one in the group argued.

The soldiers kept the same pace and strange sideways movements and Fin couldn't help but keep glancing backwards. The assassins weren't galloping – he doubted they could in this heat – but they were pushing the horses as hard as they would go and were definitely gaining ground. 'Why aren't we going straight? Like them?' he whispered to Fowkes. The Knight glanced sideways at him. 'They know better than we do.' Fin hoped he was right. 'The question is,' Fowkes continued, casting a dark eye backwards, 'do they know better than *they* do?'

The answer came about ten minutes later in the form of a sudden cry that cut through the silent desert air. The group stopped as one, and turned to look behind them, as more screams and shouts and terrible high-pitched shrieking followed that first cry. Fin frowned, unsure of what he was seeing. It looked as if the assassins and their rides were drowning in the waves of sand, as if it had become an ocean and was swallowing them. A horse appeared suddenly, rearing, its head thrashing this way and that before collapsing and vanishing again. The screaming continued.

'What's happening to them?' Fin asked.

'Outcasts.' One soldier spat on the ground. As he spoke, a

163

series of victorious whoops came across the sand and three figures emerged, cheering, onto the sand. One was holding up a horse's head, and another a somewhat smaller object. All three were splattered in blood, and smeared more across their faces. Fin shivered, remembering Kent Jasper's frozen head on a pole outside the Knight's house. 'What happened?' he asked.

'The dunes can look flat but they are not,' the soldier said, keeping his eyes forward. 'This is why we came on the harder ground. The outcasts will have heard the horses and known these assassins didn't understand the Middle of Nothing. They wait in the dips with weapons. When the riders come, they fall in the dip.'

'They cut the horse's tendons first,' a second soldier continued. 'It cripples them. The men fall and then they kill them all.'

'That pack of Outcasts will eat well tonight.' The first picked up the thread. 'Club should have sent better men.' He looked up at the sky. 'We have an hour or so before the sun sets. Our dangers have not passed yet.'

'Why doesn't that surprise me?' Fowkes grumbled.

As they moved on, Fin tried very hard not to listen to the assassins' screams, but the Outcasts seemed intent on taking a long and painful time killing them.

The assassins' screams were long forgotten as the sky shifted from clear blue to an angry amber and purple against the ominous black of the scar cut through it. The desert itself had started its own series of wails and cries as if possessed by banshees. Maybe it was, Fin thought as he tucked his head into his chin against the sudden rising wind. Nothing in the Nowhere would surprise him any more. The soldiers muttered and one pulled several leathery items from the bag on his back. He handed one to Fin. It was heavy and waxed, like a fisherman's coat, and Fin couldn't believe that the man had carried them all this way across the hot sand.

The soldiers pulled them over their heads and the others did the same. It was a huge leather kaftan that came down below Fin's ankles, more like a dress than coat. He tugged the hood up and clipped the flaps across his face, leaving only the strip across his eyes uncovered. A pair of goggles soon rectified that. No one asked why they were covering up – the rising the wind and the way the sand was lifting like a mist around them provided all the answers they needed. Night was falling. The desert was coming alive.

The men with Fin had become indistinguishable from each other, so he asked his question of all of them. 'Will this protect us from the sand?' His words were loud in his head, as if he was wearing a diving suit. It was almost claustrophobic.

'No, it won't stop the sand,' the answer came. 'But it will slow it down. Buy us ten or fifteen minutes more.'

'And we'll need them,' another said. 'We must move faster.'

No one argued, and despite their aching legs and heavy kaftans, the group picked up the pace, running as best they could over the sand that shifted too swiftly beneath their feet. Now and then someone stumbled, quickly pulled up by the others, but not entirely steady on their feet. They moved in a huddle with their heads down as the winds battered at them from every direction, shards of sand in every gust battering at their suited bodies, unbalancing them with each blast. Despite having the larger bodies around him, Fin could barely breathe as he battled the rising tide of the sand. Because that's what the desert had become – an ocean that rose in waves, beating them with its spray. He squinted behind his goggles, concentrating on keeping one foot moving in front of the other. He could barely make out his trainers. The sky was darkening. The air screeched, and then the corner of his leather sleeve was ripped away as a spiral of sand tore through it and Fin gasped as he pulled his exposed fingers up into what remained of the fabric. They weren't going to make it. He could see the others struggling as the same happened to them. The sand would force them to their knees, tear through their clothes to the skin beneath and leave nothing but bones for the Outcasts to pick over when the sun rose again over the Middle of Nothing. Their flesh would be like dust in the air, gone forever. Another blast of wind hit him hard in the chest, knocking his breath from him and stripping away a layer of leather. *We aren't going to make it.* The sentence repeated itself over and over in his head as night enveloped them. *We aren't going to make it.*

'Look!' The cry was barely audible, and Fin wasn't sure whether he heard the word first or whether it filtered through to him after he realised the others had stopped. 'Look!'

He fought the wind and did as he was told. Through the swirling haze of sand that tore through the air, he could just see it. Tears stung his eyes and he heard himself cry out with relief, although the sound was lost beyond the heavy flaps of his kaftan. Strange metal circles, like those which had lined West Minster Bridge glowed from the near-invisible walls and minarets that rose like a ghost from the desert where the sand allowed a glimpse. It was the Temple of Nowhere. They'd found it.

The soldiers behind him pushed Fin back into motion. If they hadn't he thought he would have just stood there, staring, until the desert claimed him. A hand grabbed clumsily for his arm and gripped hard. It was Fowkes, Fin was sure of it. They staggered forward together, leaning into each other, forcing their way through the remaining hundred yards or so to the gates.

'Pull the cord!' someone behind them yelled. 'Pull the cord!'

Stumbling into the rough wall, Fin saw a thick golden rope that flew this way and that above his head. He grabbed for it with the hand whose sleeve had been torn away. Even with the protection the temple offered from the wind, he screamed as sand ripped at his skin like shards of blasted glass, but he gritted his teeth and held on to the rope.

'Pull it!' the voice called again. Someone thumped into the wall beside him, and another hand joined his. The back of his hand burned hot and he was sure he was bleeding as the sand continued to strip his skin away but, with a yell, he and the man beside him tugged down hard. Somewhere, over the raging storm, a bell rang out as clear and strong as if the sands held no sway over it. Fin yanked his hand back into the remainder of his sleeve and pressed himself against the doors. Two men closed in around him, and he knew, unidentifiable as they were, that it was Fowkes and Curran Tugg.

'A twister!' A voice came from somewhere close by in the sand. 'A twister. Run, Scober, run!' For the first time since they'd left the safety of the citadels, Fin heard fear in the soldier's voice. He peered through the gaps between the men's arms, and he saw it. A swirl of sand had been drawn up into a tower, yellow and red crackles of light at its core that could only come from some kind of electricity. It darted through the darkness, cutting this way and that as the wind took it. A dark shadow stumbled before it.

'Faster, Scober!' Three soldiers were now alongside Fin but the last, Scober, must have fallen as they'd run for the door and was still twenty feet away. Between the wind and the sand, twenty feet was too much. The twister was coming for him, and fast.

'Run!' Fin yelled, as the twister loomed up behind the running man. '*Run!*' The wind silenced his words as if they had been nothing more than a thought. And then the shadowy figure and the twister collided. A sudden scream filled the air and Fin stared in horror as Scober became the heart of a funnel of glittering sand and light. The leather garb was torn away in a second, fragments flying in every direction before being completely torn apart by the rest of the sandstorm waiting

167

like a hungry hyena for any scraps the twister discarded. His skin glowed in the strange lights, and much as he wanted to, Fin couldn't look away. The man's eyes went first, the soft skin bursting and the jelly sucked away in a moment; then the sand stripped his skin and flesh from his bones until all that stood in the centre was a bloody mess. A bloody, screaming mess who wouldn't die quickly enough.

The door behind them opened and Fin fell backwards, landing in a heap on a cool marble floor. The world shifted around him so suddenly that for a moment he thought perhaps a twister had grabbed him too, and only when the heavy doors were pushed shut again he heard his own heavy breathing, not the raging wind or Scober's awful dying screams, did he realise that they were safe. They were inside the Temple of Nowhere. They'd found the Magi.

TWENTY-SIX

Fin had averted his eyes as the novice carefully smoothed balm over his lacerated hand and wrist and then wrapped a bandage tightly round it. He didn't want to see how much of his skin was missing. It reminded him of Scober's screams as his body was torn apart. The lotion was cooling and turned the searing pain into a dull throb. Fin wondered if it had magical properties and was almost tempted to ask, but the weathered man in the robe and heavy jewellery hadn't answered a single one of his questions so far, and his throat hurt too much from the sand to keep trying.

When the bandaging was done, the Magi had led him silently back through the maze of unusually warm corridors and reunited him with Fowkes and Curran Tugg, who were eating and talking quietly between themselves.

'Where are the soldiers?' Fin asked after several spoonfuls of thick soup.

'They're sand soldiers,' Curran Tugg replied quietly. 'They have no interest in politics. They're the only people, other than the Magi and the Outcasts, who have any understanding of the desert.'

'What's beyond the desert?' Fin said, tearing into a piece of bread and forcing his aching throat to swallow it.

'Who knows?' Curran Tugg answered. 'Would you want to explore the sands? What if they never end?'

Fin thought he had a point. Right now, he'd be happy to never see the desert again. If the Magi had chosen this place to keep them safe then he figured they weren't stupid. The desert was their greatest defence – they didn't need soldiers or magic to keep people away. For a while the three ate in silence and, when they had finished, Fin peered around him. 'What happens now?'

'Now we wait,' Fowkes said. 'They know why we're here. They foretold it, after all. While you were getting bandaged we told them all we could. So, now we wait. While they decide whether to help us or not. And you need to get some sleep.'

Despite his protests, Fin found himself being led down a dusty stairwell into the living space below the temple. The floors had been lined with a combination of stone tiles and the strange metal, but the walls were still carved from the hard earth that existed far below the dunes above, and as the door shut behind him, leaving him with only the glow from the metal for light, Fin crawled into the bed he'd been given and pulled the covers tight even though the air was warm.

How was he supposed to sleep while surrounded by the terrible sand? How could he trust the walls of this underground bedroom after what had happened to Scober? He pulled his knees up under his chin, feeling very much younger than sixteen. His mind wandered, focusing on his friends in the freezing north who seemed so far away. What were Christopher and Joe thinking now? Were they as isolated as he was? How so much could have happened to them all so quickly? Would they ever get back to their old lives? He closed his burning eyes. Of course they wouldn't. They had been changed them too much. He'd be happy if they could just manage being friends in a safe world. Or worlds. To living normal lives in whatever normality they chose. He thought of the sandy walls around him. How was he supposed to sleep down here? He'd never ...

He thought at first it was drums beating, the drums on the river that had signalled the Gypsy Traders dragging Lucas

Blake and Christopher to the water, and he sat bolt upright in the narrow bed. He blinked rapidly, uncertain of his surroundings, and slowly, as the world settled, he realised it wasn't drums he was hearing at all. It was a gong being beaten slowly and steadily, somewhere above him. With no idea of the time or how long he'd been sleeping, he pushed the covers back and reached for his jeans, pulling them on quickly. The gong was a summons.

Dressed, he stepped into the corridor. The metal in the floor now glowed more blue than pink and he realised as he looked at the strange symbols carved into it, that it was the same metal that had lined the sides of West Minster Bridge. He shouldn't be surprised, but he was. Until now, the Magi's role in the Nowhere's history had just been a legend. Now that he was here, among them, the truth of it was coming home to him. They were a long banished race – how on earth could he expect them to help?

'Good, you're up.'

Fin looked up to see Fowkes joining him from a room further along. 'What time is it?' Fin asked.

'It's dawn.' Fowkes walked quickly and the last vestiges of sleep left Fin as he struggled to keep up. 'They must have reached a decision.'

With a sense of something between dread and excitement growing in the pit of his stomach, Fin followed Fowkes up the stairs.

A hushed silence filled the main temple hall and none of the gathered Magi looked up from their seats as Fowkes and Fin joined Curran Tugg before the gathering. Fin stared at them though. There was something sacred about the atmosphere in the hall, dimly lit as it was by the large candles that sat in the dusty walls, and the strange pearlescent glow that came from the metal panels embedded between them. It was a room filled with a shared belief – that was the only way Fin could describe it. Men in red and yellow robes sat, heads

171

down and focused, worrying at strings of beads as they muttered strange words.

'What now?' he whispered.

Just as he spoke, a doorway appeared in the wall at the front of the hall and a line of men in red filed into the room. They formed a semicircle before the gathering and paused, the strange metal amulets at their throats glowing pink and blue. Fin, Fowkes and Tugg stood at their centre, and Fin's eyes were drawn to those necklaces. They reminded him of the one Christopher now wore, the Seer's necklace, the one that was the only key to the Seer's house. How far into the Nowhere did the Magi's influence stretch, even after all this time?

The gong, hidden somewhere out of sight, beat faster and Fin found his heart doing the same. The strange door in the wall was still open. Who were they waiting for?

A figure appeared in the doorway. Fin's mouth dropped open.

'A woman ...' he said breathlessly.

'Ten out of ten for observation,' Fowkes muttered back. They didn't look at each other. Why would they? Not when *she* was in front of them. Tova had been beautiful. Anaïs had been beautiful. But this woman, standing so tall in the strange doorway, was something entirely different. Her hair was a deep red and it fell in thick waves down over her shoulders. Her dress was entirely white, with a metal belt around her waist that shared the same colours as the amulets by the Elders wore, and the metal inlays around the world, but her belt glowed far more brightly, glittering like a band of stars. Her skin, unlike those weather-beaten dark skinned men of the South, whether soldiers or Magi, was pale and soft and her lips were full and pink.

She stepped towards them and the door behind her vanished back into the wall, the small candle at its centre shimmering brightly as if it hadn't moved at all.

172

She was tall, taller than Fowkes, and there was a strength in her stride as she took her place in the silent semicircle. The hall had fallen to a hush as she'd entered.

'The Queen of the Magi,' Curran Tugg whispered. 'I always believed she was a legend.'

The gong stopped, and its lingering echo vibrated around the building. Fin stared at the Queen of the Magi. She wasn't young, she wasn't old. She was ... he struggled to find the word. Ethereal, maybe? Her eyes were a sharp blue, but the edges were flecked with a purple so bright that, even from several feet away and about a foot lower in height, Fin could clearly make the colour out. She was *magical*, that was the right word. It was the only way to describe her.

The Elders bowed their heads as she reached the three strangers at the heart of their semicircle. Fin couldn't meet her gaze and dropped his eyes. This wasn't like meeting the Prince Regent all those months ago – or even like meeting Arnold-Mather at his London club. This woman had real power. Power that hummed around her like electricity.

'With the wisdom of the Elders, and the passion of our hearts, the Magi have reached their decision.' Her voice was like a plucked harp, ringing out in clear notes across the hall. 'I have made my decision,' she added more softly, for the ears of those closest to her. Fin swallowed hard. This was it. Could the Magi forgive their awful treatment in the past and help depose Justin Arnold-Mather, the Dark King? Or was the North to be left to fight alone, most probably in vain?

'All the worlds hang in the balance. The skies tell us that. Misused magic has been at work. We are in the heart of the Prophecy given so long ago as a warning to the two worlds. But we, the Magi, are as blind to that vision's end as those to whom it was given. There are no answers here. We are all united in the darkness.' For a moment there was silence, before she continued. 'We will help you. The Magi, the first people of all the worlds, will join you to restore the balance, or we will go with you into the abyss which others have brought upon us. This is my decision.'

Fin's heart leapt, and he looked up to see her smiling at him. 'So you'll come to the North with us? That's brilliant!'

'No.' She shook her head. 'I shall come to the Somewhere – the first world. We will leave immediately.'

'But we can't ... we ...' Fin's head was filled with the memory of the cold that surrounded Christopher and the Wakley twins and Mona and her dad and so many others. They were waiting. They were ...

'But we can't,' Fowkes said. 'Time has become different between the worlds. A few minutes in ours could be years in the North.'

'There is simply time,' the Queen said, as if those four words made everything clear. 'I must go to the Somewhere.'

'I'll return to the North,' Curran Tugg said. 'I'll bypass the citadel and wait with the others for your return.' His swarthy hand squeezed Fin's shoulder. 'However long that will be, we shall wait with new hope.'

'I will bring ten of the Magi with me, of different ranks. Their skills will be required in your world, and often,' her dazzling eyes rested once again on Fin for a moment, 'those among us with the least experience can often see what those jaded by experience can't.' Fin felt himself flushing under her gaze. She'd be disappointed when she realised he was just a teenager who had an uncanny knack of getting his friends into trouble. The boy who didn't belong. He gritted his teeth. There was no time for bitterness now. It would be no help. If they didn't win the battle against Arnold-Mather then they would all be destroyed and the strangeness of his unnatural birth would be just one more piece of dust in space. It was a grim thought.

For the first time since their arrival in the temple, the Magi were suddenly animated and the room hummed with

174

excitement. They clearly hadn't known in advance that their queen would help, or take some of them with her, and now there was a palpable tension as they waited to find out who would get to travel. Fin remembered the thrill of facing the doorway beneath the House of Detention. He hadn't known – none of them could have known – what would be waiting for them on the other side. They'd called it an *adventure*. He was about to tell himself how wrong he'd been, when he looked once again at the temple where he was stood, and at the men and Magi around him, and he stopped. It *had* been an adventure. It was still an adventure. Probably the greatest one he'd ever have. Yes, it was dangerous and, yes, the stakes couldn't be higher, but wasn't that the best kind of adventure? His skin tingled and he remembered his experiences on the bridge. When he had been half him and half Baxter. Were these Baxter's thoughts or his own? Maybe it didn't matter. Maybe all that mattered was the truth. Life was an adventure. *This* was an adventure.

The Magi travelled light and it was scarely twenty minutes before they were ready to cut their way through to Orrery House. Fin hugged Curran Tugg. The trader smiled, a rare expression for him. 'I'll see you when I see you,' he said gruffly. Sadness must have showed on both Fin and Fowkes' faces, because Tugg shook his head and slapped Fowkes hard on the arm. 'The length of time does not matter. We will still be here. This,' he gestured at the Magi around him, 'this is a good thing. The North will be ready and waiting for your return. You have my word.'

Fowkes raised his sword and then Fin turned his back on the Temple of Nowhere. It was time to go back to Orrery House and pray that the Magi could help them fight Justin Arnold-Mather. All the worlds depended on it.

TWENTY-SEVEN

'Fin?' Ted stared, his eyes bright in the candle light. 'What are you doing back so ...' His words drifted off as the Queen of the Magi and her entourage followed Fin through the doorway.

'Well, I'll be ...' Cardrew Cutler pushed his glasses further up his nose and leaned forward in his chair. 'Look at that, Freddie, look at that. It's the—'

'Magi.' Fin finished for him. 'How long have we been gone?'

'You only just left.' Freddie Wise hobbled closer to them, leaning heavily on his walking stick. He looked tired, the theft of the London Stone weighing on him more heavily than old age ever could. 'But I'm presuming that for you, that isn't the case.'

'It's a long story,' Fowkes said. 'One that we don't have the time to tell.'

'Intriguing,' Freddie said. 'May I introduce myself? Freddie Wise. It's an honour to meet you. A shame about the circumstances.'

The Queen nodded. 'It is an honour to meet one of the legendary Knights of Nowhere.'

'I'm afraid our honour is a tad tarnished of late.' Cardrew hurried forward and shook the woman's hand vigorously. 'But we hope to restore it.'

'We hope for the restoration of many things,' Freddie said.

Despite Cardrew's enthusiastic greeting, it was Freddie who

held the Queen's attention. Fin couldn't quite figure out why. But then, he was still struggling with the whole man/woman grown up thing at the moment. Christopher and Mona were married, Cardrew Cutler had gone all funny over the librarian and now the Queen of the Magi and Freddie Wise were looking at each other as if they shared a private, untold secret.

'The Magi have said they'll help us fight Arnold-Mather,' he said. 'They say the answers lie in our world. But we have to act quickly. Things are awful back there. Time's gone all funny.'

'So, what can we do to 'elp, ma'am?' Ted lit the last candle. 'We've got people out in the city, the cabbies and the like, and we can get you anywhere you need to go.'

'I presume you don't have time for any refreshments?' Freddie Wise said.

'Perhaps afterwards.' The Queen smiled.

'Yes, afterwards,' Fin cut in. 'They need our help *now*.'

'Where's Harper Jones?' Fowkes asked.

'Guarding the front door. There's some looting going on out there tonight,' Ted said. 'It's bad air, that's what it is. The black storm 'as stretched its fingers over 'ere and it's trying to get a grip.'

'My people will be manning their towers to check we are safe. I must find the one here and speak with them.' The Queen moved through the room towards the door. 'The boy, Finmere, is right. We must move quickly.' She turned her brilliant smile towards him. 'But he must also remember that we should not act in too much haste. For haste leads to errors and we most certainly have no time for those.' She looked at the huddled group of Magi that loitered close to where the doorway had been. Fin could see the confusion and fear in their eyes. For the first time they looked just like people and he warmed to them. They were the stuff of myths and stories, but perhaps that was how Fin and the Knights appeared to them.

'I shall leave my Magi here. They will need maps of your city. Preferably old ones, the older the better.'

'We can do that,' Cardrew said. 'Our librarian, Esme, she can help ... in fact I can help her ...' His voice trailed away, and Fin was sure that if the lights were working he'd see the old man blushing.

'Then I shall charge you with that task,' she said.

'The tower here?' Fowkes asked. 'I don't know where you mean.'

'There was a travelling man many, many years ago,' the Queen said softly. 'He was a man of vision.'

'A Knight?' Freddie Wise asked.

'No. But he travelled all the same. He was a friend of the Magi. He liked to build things, not destroy them. A rare trait amongst men. I called him the Birdman, not only for his name but for his soaring imagination. The tower, like the church that is so important to you Knights, is of his design.'

'Wren,' Freddie Wise said. 'Sir Christopher Wren.'

''E travelled?' Ted said. 'Who'd 'ave thought, eh?'

'There are eighty-nine Wren buildings in London,' Freddie Wise said. 'Some restored after the blitz, some lost, and some possibly not his at all. More than that, many of them have towers. This could take us a while.'

'It will be standing alone,' the Queen said.

'But still,' Freddie continued, 'We're going to have to ...'

'Pudding Lane – the Monument,' Cardrew cut in. 'That's one of Wren's. And it looks like a sort of tower too.'

'Then that's where we shall go.'

It was strange driving through London in darkness. It was a city that for Fin was always full of noise and light. When he'd boarded at Mrs Baker's house while at Eastfields the streets outside were always busy, even at two in the morning. London didn't stop. It didn't shut up, and it was never dark. That was part of what London was all about. Until tonight,

Fin decided, staring out of the cab window. Tonight, as the black snow fell, everything was different. With the exception of a glimpse here and there of small groups of people skulking in the shadows and breaking windows, the city was quiet. Not sleeping but silent, as if its soul had been sucked into the darkness. He didn't look up at the thin white line cutting across the sky. Maybe they'd all end up sucked into the darkness.

'You travel well,' Fowkes said to the Queen as the taxi drove past Cannon Street Tube, painfully familiar after their attempt to save the London Stone. 'I expected at least one or two of your party to suffer some after-effects.'

'We're the first people. There is Magi blood in all the worlds, which aids our travelling, surely you know that? It's not something many of my kind are proud of, that we have weakened our blood with yours, but it is the truth. It's why some people are better at travelling than others. They have our blood.' She sighed and looked out at the dark, freezing city. 'And this first world is so full of magic. It has always drawn us to it.'

'The Magi have been here before?' Fin asked.

'Of course. How do you think our forefathers saw the coming of the Dark King so clearly? The Prophecy was borne on the flow of the river. The river is all our lifeblood, but it was the Magi's first. And the Dark King, your Justin Arnold-Mather, he is as much one of us as one of you, I fear.'

'Wait.' Fin turned in his seat, the world beyond the window forgotten. 'He's a Magi?'

'Partly, yes. He wields dark magic too easily to be purely a man.'

'So that means ...'

'... Christopher's got Magi blood too.' Fowkes finished the sentence. 'That's why he could become the new Seer?'

'The Seers are always a mix of two worlds. Born in this, with Magi blood.' She smiled softly at Fin, as if all that they faced were nothing. 'You see? You are not alone in having a destiny. You can't carry their fates on your shoulders. You never brought your friends to this.'

'I didn't ...' Fin started. 'I don't—'

'Yes, you do. It's in your eyes.' She leaned back in her seat. 'You can't be responsible for others' choices. Sometimes they have no choice at all. Fate will have her say.'

'Well, I wish she'd bloody well stay out of it,' Fowkes grumbled, and the Queen burst into a sudden laugh.

'Oh, I have missed you Somewhere men. It's been a very long time.'

As she climbed out of the taxi, Fin was tempted to ask the Queen just how old she actually was but, as Curran Tugg had said, there were some answers you didn't need, and he figured that asking any woman her age wasn't polite – asking the Queen of the Magi was probably downright rude.

The cold bit sharply at his nose and ears and his bandaged arm throbbed as he followed Fowkes and the Queen over to the metal rails guarding the Monument. It rose two hundred feet above them; a single column that looked almost Roman to Fin. He couldn't even remember seeing it before and, once again, he was surprised by the number of secrets his London had to offer, how much history went unnoticed. Or perhaps it was just that the places that were linked to the *other* London made themselves a little less visible to those around them. The Queen led them around the large square base. 'Look,' she said, as she pointed out the inscriptions on three of the sides. 'Stories. Always stories. Where there are stories there is power. Remember that.'

'How are we going to get in?' Fowkes asked, his eyes on the locked metal gates and the door beyond. His voice was gruff, stories and the Storyholder no doubt always linked in his mind. Fin, knowing his own pain over losing Anaïs, couldn't imagine what the Knight was feeling. It was hard to remember that, new as this adventure was to him, Fowkes had been living it for years before Fin had even been born – if you could call it being born. In fact, Fin's entire life was simply part of Fowkes' adventure and he wondered if that was finally taking its toll.

'Magic, of course,' the Queen said, joining them at the railings. 'Magic recognises magic.' She pushed the gate. 'See? No locks.' Fin had been expecting some kind of sparks or something, but the gate and the door beyond simply weren't locked. Maybe magic wasn't quite as books and films had made him believe. Maybe it was something more natural than that. Still, he decided, following her inside, unlocking doors with a touch was pretty cool.

The narrow column was simply a house for the spiral staircase that led upwards as far as Fin could see.

'This should warm us up,' Fowkes muttered as, following the Queen, they started to climb. They kept a relatively brisk pace and by the time they reached the top both Fowkes and Fin were flushed and out of breath, but the Queen of the Magi seemed untouched by the exertion. Somehow Fin wasn't surprised. Maybe he wasn't the only one who wasn't entirely normal out of the three of them. Maybe in the Nowhere abnormal was the norm. Somehow that thought made him feel a little better about his own origins.

They came out onto the narrow viewing deck and for a moment Fin's head swam. Two hundred feet up was higher than he'd expected. The space between the wall and the grille was barely two or three feet and he couldn't help but feel that even with the cage that stretched from the floor up above his head, he might still fall.

'Don't look down,' Fowkes said. 'This is no worse than the gantries at the Crookeries, and you managed them all right.'

'This is higher than the gantries,' Fin muttered.

'Yes, but it's a hell of a lot safer. So it balances out.'

The Queen wrapped her fingers around the grille and took a deep breath. She stared out into the London night across the black strip of the River Times towards the South.

'What's she doing?' Fin whispered. The air around them suddenly felt warmer, heat radiating from the elegant woman as she concentrated.

'Your guess is as good as mine,' Fowkes said, stepping closer to her. Fin followed. As with everything that had led him to this moment, his curiosity outweighed his fear and he let his own hands touch the metal. It was warm. Whatever she was doing, it was working. Beneath his feet he could feel a slight vibration running through the column, tiny at first, the building slowly waking up to its forgotten purpose, and then stronger, building like the thrum of an engine, smooth and powerful.

'Look,' Fowkes said.

In the distance, far to the south of the city, a small yellow light began to glow, standing out against the darkened city like a sun. As it did, a similar glow spread across the viewing deck. Fin glanced up at the golden decoration at the top of the Monument above his head.

'No, you look,' he said, pointing upwards. The golden orb was blazing, the small metal prongs that extended from its surface now lost in a blur of light. 'What's happening?'

'The towers are awake,' the Queen answered. 'They're folding the city between them.'

'Folding the ... ?' Fin looked again at the yellow light in the distance. Projecting from it was a circle of white like the beam of a torch in the darkness. It was getting larger and closer.

'Surely everyone can see this?' Fowkes said. 'London's in a blackout. This place is going to be surrounded in minutes.'

'They can't see it,' she said, keeping her eyes on the brightness drawing closer to them. 'We're out of normal space now.'

'We're what?' Fin said. The yellow glow above them turned white as the viewing tower sent out its own beam of light, rushing out to meet the one coming towards them.

182

'It's just magic, Fin,' Fowkes said, the awe in his voice belying his casual words. 'It's magic at work. Go with it.'

They stood side by side as the two lights connected and an image appeared before them. Of another tower, far away. Two Magi standing on a viewing deck in bright sunshine. Behind them Fin could see the domes that littered the skyline of the citadels of the South. His mouth dropped open. He didn't even try to close it.

'All is well,' the Queen said, and the two men nodded and bowed. 'Keep the towers manned. When we are ready, you will know.'

'We will not leave,' one of the Magi answered. His voice was clear but it tinkled lightly, as if somewhere music was being added to his words. Was that how the Queen sounded to them?

'Let us be ready,' the Queen said.

'Let us be ready,' the Magi replied in unison. The Queen released the metal guard and in an instant the image, the light and the golden glow was gone. They were back on the deck in the freezing darkness. Fin felt giddy with the change and grabbed Fowkes' arm to steady himself. The Knight was staring at the Queen. 'Let us be ready?' he said. 'But that's ... that's what the Knights say. That's ...'

'Where did you think it came from?' the Queen said. 'Words and stories have power from the ages. The Magi came first. Our words are your words. Our stories are your stories. Sometimes our paths have crossed and no one remembers, but the words still exist.' She clapped her hands together. 'And now we must find the lines, if we are to have any chance of saving the worlds.'

'Um, what lines?' Fin asked. 'What do you mean?' The Queen didn't answer, but instead turned away. Fin and Fowkes watched as she strode back towards the stairs.

'Sometimes,' Fowkes muttered, 'I wish people would just speak bloody plainly.'

'Where would be the fun in that?' Fin answered.

'Oh, don't you bloody start.' Fowkes moved to follow her. 'If we get out of this alive, I'm taking up drinking again. Properly. It made life so much easier.'

TWENTY-EIGHT

They had left the Oval Room and retreated to the more cosy downstairs drawing room where the fire in the grate blazed merrily and did much to dispel the darkness that surrounded them, even if it made the house almost unbearably hot. For Ted and Harper Jones at least. The others, gathered in that semicircle of light – Freddie Wise, Cardrew Cutler, Hector Allbright and Alex Currie-Clark – all kept their thick cardigans on and buttoned up. The Aged felt the cold. Ted was quite surprised that young Currie-Clark was still awake. The first few days after Ageing were never good. It was quite a testament to the boy's strength. Mrs Baker came in, carefully carrying a tray of strong coffee, and once again Ted's stomach turned at the thought of Jarvis' betrayal of them. What had the Knights come to when they could no longer trust their own to be loyal?

'I can't imagine it,' Cardrew Cutler said, slurping his coffee. 'All those years passed in the Nowhere.'

'In the time it'll take you to drink that coffee, another year will have passed for those poor buggers,' Hector Allbright added.

'Time's a funny thing,' Ted said.

There was a long pause before Freddie Wise leaned forward, the leather of the old Chesterfield armchair creaking beneath him. 'It's terrible in some ways, perhaps not in others.'

The group turned to face the old man, and Ted realised that, subconsciously at least, they had all been waiting for him to speak. Freddie Wise had quietly taken over from Harlequin Brown in many ways. He was certainly living up to his name.

''Ow do you mean?'

'Horrendous as it might be for those trapped in it, it gives us an advantage. None of their swords work, so Arnold-Mather hasn't been able to come here, and even if he got hold of one of ours and sent his people to attack, he couldn't come himself. As we've learned, barely an hour here amounts to almost a decade there. He can't be gone for that long.' He swallowed a mouthful of coffee, his thoughtful eyes focused on the fire. 'We also don't know if this time difference is constant. Maybe the next time they go back there will be no change, or twenty years' difference. However, what we *do* know, and this is important, is that it's a false time. It's the first sign of the terrible fate that could well come to the universe, yes, but it's not real. It's frozen.'

'But that's the most awful part, surely?' Currie-Clark said.

'No. It could be a lot worse. This frozen moment is saving our people; they're not ageing. Imagine if they were stuck in this strange time differential for two or three hours here, our people there would have aged dramatically—'

'Not as dramatically as some of us.' Hector Allbright snorted.

'True, but enough to slow them down. If we left them for a full day ...' He shrugged. He didn't need to finish the sentence. It was clear to them all. More than a few hours, if time weren't frozen, and all their people in the Nowhere would be dead.

'But as Fowkes and Fin tell it, they've all remained exactly the same age as when the crack in the sky appeared. In a sense, so long as they're safe, it doesn't matter how long it takes us to find a weapon to use against Arnold-Mather. They'll still be there, ready to fight.'

'But what 'appens to 'em when we put time right again?' Ted asked. His brain was starting to ache.

'I guess we'll see when we get there.' Harper Jones smiled at him from his spot behind Freddie Wise's chair. 'They'll either age suddenly or they won't.'

'Let's hope they don't,' Alex Currie-Clark wheezed. 'There's been too much ageing going on around here of late.'

'So what do we do now?' Ted asked. Again, all eyes turned to Freddie Wise. Ted was relieved. His place had always been as the General, the second in command, the man to be relied on – but he had never been cut out to be the thinker or the leader. Freddie Wise and Fowkes made a good, if unusual, combination. They were harder than Harlequin Brown had been, but then the Judge's chosen Commander of the Knights had turned against them all. This pairing was more damaged but sometimes, Ted thought, a little of life's damage could be good for inner strength. Whether Fowkes and Freddie realised it or not, what didn't kill them made them stronger. And they'd both been through enough over the years to make them very strong indeed.

'We send someone back, of course, if only briefly, to let them know that the Magi are here and working on a plan. We must ensure they have hope. We also need to know how things stand there.'

'I wonder how long they've been waiting already.' Cardrew Cutler said, and once again they fell into quiet, the passing moments measured out by the crackling of the cheerful Christmas fire.

187

TWENTY-NINE

Christopher stared through the top floor window of the Seer's house. He wasn't sure how many houses were burning, but it was twenty at least. Was that as many as the previous night? Perhaps. Perhaps even more. At least in the ice there was little chance of the fires spreading to the houses around them. A small mercy perhaps, but a mercy all the same.

He didn't know who had started the craze of painting symbols of swords with jewelled hilts on houses and on communal buildings, but the show of resistance had brought swift and vicious retribution from his father. Worse, this time he did not add his prisoners to the growing ranks of the mad but had opted for a far more visible punishment. Men and women hung naked from crosses along the freezing roads, guarded – until they died, sobbing and in agony – by the strange scuttling red-eyed creatures who had once lived and breathed and laughed alongside them. What was this dominion that he had created, Christopher wondered. Was this really what his father saw as an empire? The slow destruction of layers of worlds and the similar systematic, slow destruction of the people who inhabited them?

Despite their terrible cause, the fires drew his eyes with the bursts of colour that ate at the tired houses. The days had all become one long blast of dark grey as if the Nowhere was shifting into some kind of dusky half-life before night finally claimed them, and the yellows, oranges and red that currently filled patches of the sky were almost too bright against it. Christmas decorations, he thought, for this never-ending Christmas Day. He wondered if those whose homes now burned had even drawn the swords on their properties themselves. Debts were being settled in the cruellest ways; Mona and Ditch's boys had heard tales of people sneaking out and painting the symbol on the doors of neighbours they had grown to hate. Perhaps the constant ice and lack of hunger or thirst was making them all seek some kind of release in other, nastier, ways. He felt older than his years, whatever that was. Even though it had been five years since Curran Tugg had returned from the South, many still hoped that the Magi, Finmere and the Knights would come and fight with them against this terrible future. It was the only hope they had. Christopher, however, found it harder and harder to keep his strength up. It was the way they all looked to him that drained him. As if he was something special, as if he had *answers* for them. He barely had answers for himself. Sixteen and nearly thirty all rolled into one. And all the time he carried his father's guilt. He couldn't show fear or worry – he had no right to. He was supposed to be strong – the light to his father's dark. As the Seer he was supposed to provide answers, but all he saw were glimpses of the past that suggested possible futures. He waited with everyone else for Finmere Tingewick Smith. He knew his friend would come – he knew that in his core rather than because he was the Seer, but every year that passed without their arrival left him disappointed. It was hard to be everyone's 'hope' when your own was in danger of fading.

Everything hinged on Fin. It always had, even if his friend failed to accept it. Christopher had known it even before the Zoltar machine had begun repeatedly showing him the events of Finmere's birth. He'd known it from the moment he'd sneaked out of St Martin's all those years ago to follow his one-year-here-one-year-there friend into an adventure. There was something about Fin – something Fin had never

189

realised – that he brought out the truly *good* in people. It was a rare quality, as Christopher had learned over the long, cold years.

Black smoke rose from the fading fires, no doubt being doused with freezing water by his father's soldiers now that the houses were ruined to preserve them in ice as a warning to others, until such time as he decided to knock them down and build something new there. He didn't follow the cloud upwards. He had no desire to look at the dark crack in the sky that hung over their heads like an axe. He tried not to, anyway. It was too easy to imagine it was getting bigger when perhaps it wasn't, like the mole on his arm he'd convinced himself was changing back when he was twelve. And whether the crack changed or not didn't really matter anyway. The pressure was building up behind it – he could feel it. One day it would just explode and then there would be no more days for any of them.

The house could feel it too. It was weakening, its bright-ness diminishing against the growing gloom ... unless it was weakening because he was. The Seer and the house were always linked. Arthur Mulligan was stronger than he looked; he'd been able to walk away from it. Christopher wasn't sure that he could, however much he wanted to and however much future circumstances might demand that he should. Sometimes he ached for his old life at St Martin's, getting straight A's and playing the fool, hating porridge for breakfast and longing for his father to notice him. But that life would mean no Mona, and there was the sticking point. He couldn't imagine any kind of life without Mona.

'Get off me! Get *off* me!' As if she'd heard his thoughts, her voice cut through the silence and the trapdoor crashed against the floor two storeys down. The sound of a struggle rose to meet him as he ran for the stairs, his heart racing. Who was here? Who was with her? A male voice groaned in pain.

'Shit!' Henry Wakley exclaimed. 'You bit me!'

So it wasn't the mad or any of his father's soldiers finally finding their way in; it was two of their own trying to subdue his wife. He mentally wished the Wakley twins luck. He'd yet to manage to win a battle with her, and she claimed she loved him.

'What the hell is going on?' He stared at the scene in front of him. Benjamin was closing the trap door as Henry Wakley stood across the room with his arms wrapped round Mona.

'She ...' His grip must have weakened slightly on seeing Christopher and as he tried to speak she broke free, heading back towards the hatch. 'Stop her!' Henry said, and Christopher grabbed his wife, who struggled furiously against him for a moment and then burst into tears. The sight of the girl he loved sobbing was enough to make his own fear curl into a knot in his stomach. These weren't angry tears, they came straight from a broken heart. He'd heard enough of them from others over the past years to recognise them.

'Why did you make me come back here?' She turned her head from his chest and glared at Benjamin Wakley. 'I needed to help him! I could have ... I needed to ...' She dissolved into sobbing again.

Christopher looked at the twins, who – hardy as they both were – seemed exhausted. Benjamin had a red mark on one cheek which Christopher was sure was due to sharp contact with Mona's elbow, and Henry was rubbing his forearm where she'd bitten him.

'It's the palace,' Benjamin said. 'They're going to execute the prisoners.'

'All of them,' Henry added.

'What?' Christopher's blood chilled. 'How do you ...?'

'It was a rumour, from sources on the inside, yesterday. We haven't heard from them since. I think the palace has gone into lock-down.'

Henry sank into a chair. 'Simeon Soames' band of brats

have been out spreading the news. It's in retaliation against everyone who thinks they can stand against the Dark King. Apparently he intends to crush the rebellion for good.'

'Those sword symbols were brave,' Benjamin said, 'but foolish.'

'We could have helped them!' Mona said. 'All of them ... My father ...'

Benjamin, always the soldier, and the one Christopher trusted implicitly with anything tactical, shook his head at Christopher. 'There's no way we could have got in. The place is swarming with the mad.'

'I could get in!' Mona pushed away from Christopher as her pain turned to anger. 'I can get in anywhere.'

'It's guarded from all angles. Levi Dodge went in yesterday and since then all gates have been sealed. And there's no way in underground, we know that.'

'We just need a diversion,' Mona said. 'We still have time.' She turned to Christopher, her eyes blazing. 'You know I can get my father out. You know it – if we attack the palace, all of us, then some of us sneak through and find them.'

Christopher looked at the distraught woman who hadn't aged a day in years, but carried, like they all did, the scars and experiences of those frozen days on her soul. His heart broke for her.

'Please,' she said. 'You're the Seer. People will fight with you. You know they will. Maybe this is the impetus we need to attack.'

'We can't attack,' Benjamin said softly. 'We have to wait.'

'Wait?' Mona hissed. 'What for? The legendary Knights and Finmere Tingewick flaming Smith? Where are they when we need them? Drinking tea with their feet up in that precious house of theirs?'

'You know that's not true,' Christopher said. He reached for her but she pulled away.

'No, I don't.'

'I think they're using this to lure us out,' Henry said. The years might not have aged his face but they had taken their toll on his cheery good humour. There was a sadness in his eyes that had never been there before. Christopher wondered if they all had it. He knew Fin was fighting for them, wherever he was, but he also understood Mona's anger. It was hard not to feel some envy for those on the other side.

'Arnold-Mather,' Henry continued – they never said 'your father' to Christopher and for that he was always grateful – 'knows something is going on. There have been too many rumours of hope over the past years. The Traders are storytellers, it's part of their nature. Their tales of the South and the Magi will have reached him. He's going to want to wipe out a fight before it happens.'

'He's relying on our honour,' Benjamin said. 'He's relying on our refusing to let those people die, whatever the cost.'

'And we shouldn't!' Mona stormed towards the door.

'The house won't let you out,' Christopher said softly. 'I won't let it let you out.' She stopped mid-stride and turned to face him.

'What?'

'We have to think about all the worlds, Mona. If I thought there was even the slightest chance we could get in and save them, I'd say yes. But if Benjamin says there isn't, I have to trust him.' He paused, his throat tightening. 'I won't lose you like that. It would be suicide.'

'What do you know?' Her eyes turned to ice. 'You're just a Somewhere boy. None of you belong here. What is this? You're going to let them all die; you don't think it matters? Like father like son!' The words hit him like blows, but the last sentence was a knife in his heart. Would she ever forgive him for this?

'Look, Mona ...' He stepped forward, suddenly very much an awkward sixteen-year-old boy again, but before he could finish his sentence, a slight wind picked up in the room behind him. The house shivered with energy. He turned to see Fowkes stepping through a doorway from the black and white world beyond. They all stared, even Mona.

'Fin's with the Magi Queen,' he said. 'She has some kind of plan. You have to stay strong. We're coming.'

'When?' Mona snarled at him. 'Another five years? Ten? Whenever it is, it'll be too late.'

'What's happened?' Fowkes frowned. Christopher almost laughed at the question. Only someone who'd been gone for a few minutes could think they could answer that one easily. *We're all tired,* Christopher wanted to say. *We're all tired and cold and fed up of hiding and fighting and being surrounded by fear and pain.* He didn't, though. He let the Knights do the talking.

'Arnold-Mather is going to execute all his prisoners today. Retaliation against rebellion,' Henry said.

'We think Savjani and Jack Ditch are still in there.'

'We don't think,' Mona said. 'We *know.*' She turned to Fowkes. 'I want to rescue them. I'm sure I can. You could help me. He's your friend, your best friend, he's always been there for you. You won't let him die, will you? You know this city, Fowkes, you lived in the Crookeries for long enough. You'll help me, won't you? They won't let me go.'

'There's no way in,' Christopher cut in. 'It's heavily guarded. We can't fight them all.'

'You could cut your way in!' Mona retaliated. 'You've got a double-edged sword that works. You know the palace.'

Fowkes stared at the pleading girl, and Christopher couldn't read his dark eyes, but he could see the flinty hardness of them.

'Yes, I could,' he said. 'And then we'd both die alongside your father and he would never forgive me for that. We don't know where he is in there. We don't know how heavily guarded it is, but you can be sure the mad will be everywhere. And, as you all pointed out last time I was here, I don't understand this new Nowhere.' He nodded at the Wakley twins. 'But they do. If they say it's a suicide mission, then I believe them.'

'You're a bastard.'

'You're probably right. Most days I think I'm much, much worse than that. But I know your father, I know what he would want me to say now, and I honour him enough to make that call.'

'I hate you,' Mona said, tears filling her eyes again. 'I hate all of you!' She ran for the stairs and no one stopped her. There was nowhere for her to go and if she wanted to lie on their bed and cry herself out of her rage, then Christopher wouldn't stop her.

'She always was a brave, reckless thing,' Fowkes said. 'Keep her here until it's all over. Keep her here for as long as it takes her to get all the hate out.'

'Then we might have to keep her here until you get back,' Henry Wakley said, looking at the blooming bruise on his arm.

'We're working as fast as we can,' Fowkes said. 'We wanted you to know that. I hate –' his words drifted slightly '– I hate not being here and standing with you through all this. But we will be back, and we will win. None of this can be in vain.' He raised his sword again. 'I hope I haven't drawn too much unwanted attention your way by coming here. We just thought it was important you know.'

'You picked a good moment,' Benjamin said. 'All the attention is on the palace. The mad are preoccupied. Arnold-Mather might have picked something up – we have no real idea what he can sense or not – but the Seer's house seems to be somewhat protected against him.'

Fowkes nodded. They had very little else to say, and within moments he was gone, back to the Somewhere. Christopher stared at the empty space and feared his decision had torn his marriage apart. Benjamin Wakley's words echoed in his head. *You picked a good time.* He wondered if the Knight was even aware of the irony. He turned to see them both staring at him.

'Go back out there,' he said, forcing his mind back to the current, terrible situation. 'Mona won't be the only one feeling this way. Try and make the relatives of those inside see that they need to stay safe. We have a big battle coming. We're going to need as many with us as we can get. We can't afford a suicide mission now.'

By the time the Knights had left he'd gone back upstairs and stared out of the window again while Mona cried behind him. The fires in the houses were gone. He could still see them though, whenever he closed his eyes.

THIRTY

Levi Dodge's heels tapped against the marble floor of the palace. Where it had once shone bright it was now dull and dirty, like the rest of the vast building. Who cleaned a prison? No one apparently, and since the windows had been boarded over there was very little release for the pungent odours of human waste, sweat and fear that now filled the corridors like an invisible smog.

'Where shall we start, sir?' The Lieutenant of the Guard walked briskly beside him, impatience in every step. 'There's quite a lot to get through. Are we hanging? Or beheading? Beheading might be quicker. Messier, but quicker.' The excitement was clear in his voice, and Levi Dodge wondered when he had become so cruel. The man had started sitting in on the interrogations three years ago, when he'd had no call to. What had driven him to seek out others' pain? For Dodge's part, he found no pleasure in the suffering of others; it was simply a means to an end. For him, at least, that hadn't changed in all these frozen years.

Around them, the mad and the guards hurried here and there with ropes and chains to bind prisoners. On each floor their captives were calling out, asking for answers, all aware that something had changed, and that today might be the day they'd all been dreading. Dodge wouldn't put it past the guards to have spread word of the fate that awaited them all.

Although, perhaps, not quite all of them. 'I've told the guards to work their way up from the lowest levels,' he said. 'Simeon Soames is down there with them now.' He wanted the ex-Knight kept occupied and out of sight while he implemented his plan. There were only two men among Arnold-Mather's men who would think to stop and question Levi Dodge. One was Edgar Blacken, who was patrolling the front of the palace where the executions were about to start taking place, and the other was Simeon Soames. Both would be worthy adversaries should they take him on, and it was a complication he wanted to avoid.

They headed further into the heart of the prison and the foul stench thickened. 'I want you to come with me,' he said. 'I have a job for you.'

'Anything you say, Mr Dodge,' the lieutenant said. Levi Dodge kept his pace even and his head clear. He gripped the bottle in his pocket and started slowly unscrewing the lid with his expert fingers. His body was on automatic pilot. Even if he'd never spoken his intentions aloud to himself over the years, they had always been leading him to this moment. Otherwise, why had he let the little tailor live, allowed his boss to believe they'd never captured him? Dark times called for dark deeds, and Levi Dodge was discovering he could be as treacherous as the next man.

By the time he reached the right corridor on one of the highest levels they were in the heart of the gloom, only the occasional oil lamp sputtering against the walls, trying to shed some light beyond their dirty shells. Even though he and the lieutenant were alone in this section, he waited until they reached a patch of almost complete dark near the tailor's cell before he made his move. The man beside him was caught completely unawares by the cloth that covered his mouth and, although he struggled for longer than Dodge had expected, he finally went limp.

A pair of dark eyes peered at him through the bars of the cage, the quiet sounds of the struggle having drawn Savjani from his normal space, curled up in the corner.

198

'What is happening?' the tailor whispered as Dodge, dragging the unconscious lieutenant with one hand, unlocked the door. He glanced around to be sure no guards had appeared and then pulled the man inside. Savjani scuttled backwards slightly, wary clearly but no longer trying to hide his identity, as his eyes met Dodge's.

'You all right, mate?' A phlegmy voice came from the cage next door.

'You have to be quiet.' Dodge had no time for explanations. He looked at Savjani and then down at the Lieutenant of the Guard. It was a good match. Not perfect, but close enough. Who ever really looked at the prisoners anyway? 'Help me undress him,' he said. The tailor stared silently at him, uncomprehending.

'You need to swap clothes. And you need to do it quickly. Or you will die.' Still the tailor didn't move. 'Do you want to see your daughter again? I'm *rescuing* you.'

That was enough to make the clothcrafter move and he dropped to his knees, his fingers, still dextrous from working for so many years with cloth and needles, swiftly loosening his jailor's clothes. Within minutes, they were tugging Savjani's stinking rags onto the body.

'We must roll him around,' Dodge said. 'Make him dirty.' He looked at Savjani. 'And tuck all your hair into his hat. Your face can be washed; your hair will take longer to deal with.'

When they were done, they left the unconscious man curled in the corner. He was starting to stir, his arm twitching.

'We have to go.'

Savjani grabbed his arm. 'What is happening? Why now?'

'Later.'

'No.' The tailor refused to move. 'Now.'

'All the prisoners are being executed today.' Dodge moved again to the cell door.

'What?' It was the sickly voice from the next door cell again. 'All of 'em? All of us?'

'We have to go,' Dodge snapped. He wanted the guards to be dragging the lieutenant from the cell and down to the executioner before he was fully conscious and time, in its own frozen paradox, was ticking on.

'No, no ...' Savjani pulled him back. 'We have to take my friend. I cannot leave my friend.'

'We can't. One uniform. One man.' Levi Dodge looked through to the next cage, where a pair of eyes shone in the gloom. 'I'm sorry.'

'We can't—'

'Yes you can.' The voice was stronger now, gruff. Perhaps the voice of the man he'd once been. 'You go. You 'elp that girl of yours end all this mess. You tell 'er Jack Ditch always said she was a grafter. One of the best.' He paused, his breath rattling. 'Like 'er father. Who I've been proud to know.'

'But Jack ...'

'You know as well as 'im and me, I'm done for anyway. Even if I could get out of this prison, I doubt I can even walk in a straight line no more. And my lungs, well, they'd give me away as a wrong 'un before we ever got to the gates.' The two men gripped hands through the bars. 'Now you go, mate. And don't look back. I'm all right, I am. I've 'ad more adventures in my time than most men could wish for.' He grinned and a gold tooth flashed. 'To be 'onest, I ain't got much fight left in me. Rather go out this way than waste away in bed somewhere.'

'We have to go,' Levi Dodge repeated.

'It has been an honour, my friend,' Savjani whispered, his voice breaking.

'The 'onour's been all mine.' Jack Ditch gave the cloth-crafter a gentle shove towards the door. 'Oi,' he said. 'Dodge.'

Levi Dodge turned. 'Yes?'

'Send 'em up this way first, eh? I've never been very good at waiting. If something's going to be done, then let's get it done.'

Dodge nodded. Despite his natural coolness, he felt a sudden respect for the stranger in the cage. Whatever he had been in his past life, he was brave. You could tell so much out about a person by seeing how they faced their end. He locked the door and leaned into Savjani. 'Walk tall and keep muttering as if we are engaged in a private conversation,' he said. 'And do whatever I say.'

Halfway down to the next level, he sent some guards up to seize the two longest serving prisoners in the palace prison and have them executed first. He didn't pause to wonder if the Lieutenant of the Guard would be fully awake by the time they dragged him to the block. He presumed so, but his imagination was reluctant to stretch that far. He needed to focus on getting them out. The dying throes of the unfortunate guard were already in the past as far as he was concerned. A done deed. And the man had been responsible for a lot of unnecessary death. Levi Dodge would not waste grief on him. Instead he wondered what Mrs Manning would make of his actions when she heard the news.

Simeon Soames had left the youngs behind the palace with instructions to wait for him in the warmth of the old parade guard hut while he brought the prisoners up from the basement. He hadn't wanted them seeing this. To be honest, immune as he'd become to many of the cruelties of Arnold-Mather's regime, it was something he could live without seeing as well. There were approximately two hundred prisoners in the cages, maybe more, and he knew there was a long day of killing ahead. They'd bring them up in threes or fours, no more. This first wave would be the easiest. It would get much harder when those still captive accepted the reality of what was happening and panicked.

He stood back and supervised the first three men shuffling across the courtyard, letting the guards and the mad take over leading them to the block. Each man was tied to the next and they squinted, even in the awful gloomy daylight, after being trapped in darkness for so long. Maybe it was a blessing that they were weak and disoriented. Maybe death would seem like a release. Or perhaps he hoped that, to make himself feel better about the monster he had clearly become.

'Hold up!' One guard shouted, blocking the prisoners. 'We've got these two to do first. Mr Dodge's orders!'

The three prisoners shuffled to a halt and waited, no sense of relief or fear about them, although one had started to mutter quietly under his breath. If they kept them waiting for too long, tears would start. 'But he told me to start with the basement.'

'Must have changed his mind. He's the boss.' The guard shrugged. Soames looked towards the block where two men were climbing the stairs. One stood tall and strong while the other stumbled and fell, weak on his feet. He seemed confused. 'There's been a mistake,' he slurred, and Soames noticed the other man give his fellow prisoner a short sharp kick which sent him back to his knees and killed his words.

'Where is Mr Dodge?' he asked, a vague sense of disquiet in the pit of his stomach.

'Over there,' the guard nodded to the far corner of the palace grounds. 'With the Lieutenant.'

Soames looked. Levi Dodge's Bowler hat and squat figure were perfectly recognisable as he walked steadily towards one of the smaller gates. His pace was casual and he seemed to be deep in conversation with the Lieutenant of the Guard beside him, leaning close together. Or were they? Was the other man actually leaning into him for support? He looked back to the scaffold, at the two men waiting there for the executioner's blade. The first man, rough looking and barrel-chested, stared at the soldiers with fire blazing in his eyes. They were almost laughing eyes. Why would he be laughing?

'There's been a mistake,' the second man said again, his dark skin paling in fear. 'It was Mr Dodge ... he ... I'm the lieutenant ... you can't ...' His words were lost beneath the soldiers' catcalls.

Soames stared. Despite his rags, the man's hair was silky clean as he shook his head, looking this way and that for some support. His eyes were too clear and the dirt that covered him wasn't as ingrained as it was on the others. Soames looked back towards the side gate. Dodge and his companion had almost reached it. The day brightened as his mind raced. If that *was* the lieutenant at the block then who was Dodge taking out of the prison? Had he pulled the same trick his boss had with Joe and the Prince Regent? Was the wrong man about to be executed?

The man's sobbing and cries of innocence were getting louder, and Soames noticed a slight increase in Dodge's even pace. From the block the thickset man stared defiantly at him as, beside him, the Indian man struggled in vain to get down from the block.

Savjani.

The name hit him. That's who Dodge was escorting out of the prison. They'd had the tailor all this time and never even known it. He opened his mouth to tell Edgar Blacken to stop Levi Dodge but no words came out. He looked from the gate to the scaffold and back again.

'I told you! I'm not a prisoner! I'm the lieutenant! It's Levi Dodge! He's—'

'Do him first,' Soames heard himself call. 'Shut his god-damned whining up. And I mean *now*!'

The guards, unused to any outbursts from him, grabbed the man and pulled him towards the block, one delivering a hard punch to his face to shut him up. They forced him onto his knees and the axe man, under the watchful eye of the executioner, stepped forward. Soames didn't watch, but met the eye of the other prisoner. They shared a tiny, impercept-ible nod. There was a sickening thud as the lieutenant's head hit the wooden floor of the scaffold. Someone laughed.

Without looking at the gate, Simeon Soames turned and headed back towards the palace. He whistled as he walked, an old tune from a world and a life he'd almost forgotten he'd ever had, hoping drown out the second thump of a head and body being separated. It didn't work, and this time he flinched at the sound. He thought of the youngs who were becoming so immune to cruelty, and he thought of Levi Dodge, the quiet, mysterious henchman, and what he'd just done. He tried not to think of his own complicity in it.

It was two hours and more than a hundred executions later that Dodge's duplicity was finally discovered. The lieutenant, it appeared, had a tattoo on the inside of his forearm, and the guard in charge of storing the bodies until they could be burned (only heads were required for spikes, after all) had spotted it. Combined with a general unease about where the lieutenant and Levi Dodge had gone on such a busy day at the prison, it prompted even the thickest of the guards to put two and two together and the alarm went up. Two and a half hours later Simeon Soames and Edgar Blacken stood in front of the Dark King and quietly told him of his sidekick's treachery.

It seemed hot inside the Dome after standing in the freezing palace grounds and Soames noticed that a small line of sweat had burst out on Edgar Blacken's forehead, just above the twisted, scarred skin that covered half of his face. He wondered how much of that was from the heat, and how much was from fear. At least it showed the man was sane. A little fear, given the news they'd just delivered, was a healthy reaction to the situation. Jarvis the butler had made a quiet exit as they'd talked, and now they were done Simeon's own heart was racing. As much as he'd tried to push his complicity in Dodge's betrayal from his mind, it still lurked there and all he could hope was that Arnold-Mather's powers didn't extend to mind reading just yet.

'Levi Dodge?' The Dark King gripped the arm of the throne, his knuckles white against the bright jewels of his various rings. His eyes glowered under their heavy brows. His words were soft but full of disbelief and both Soames and Edgar Blacken took the slightest step backwards, knowing that the truth would hit at any minute now.

'Who was the prisoner?'

'We think it was Savjani, the clothcrafter,' Edgar Blacken said. 'The guards say they didn't know who he was. Picked him up years ago and thought he was a tramp.'

'Years?' Arnold-Mather's teeth were almost all black now, glinting as his mouth moved. 'No one survives in the palace for years.'

'It would appear this man,' Simeon Soames took pity on Edgar Blacken and took over, 'and his companion, who we now believe was the notorious criminal Jack Ditch, were constantly overlooked by Dodge. He never tortured or executed them, although Ditch did go to the scaffold this morning. With the Lieutenant of the Guard, as it transpires.' Even with the fear that raced through his veins, Soames found he was almost enjoying passing the news on. The Dark King was fallible, it seemed. Which meant that, perhaps, there was hope for all of them and for the future.

'He's had that man locked up for *years*?' Arnold-Mather hissed in a spray of saliva. 'He's known for *years*?' He pushed himself away from the throne and shuffled towards the window, his hunched and heavy figure swathed in a heavy fur coat. He was no longer recognisable as the smart-suited minister who had once graced the halls of Westminster back in the Somewhere London. Simeon Soames barely remembered what that man had looked like.

'Where is he now?' Arnold-Mather stared out at the gloom that coated his frozen empire.

'We don't know,' Simeon Soames said. 'The mad and the soldiers are hunting him.'

'I have a suggestion.' Blacken stepped forward slightly, despite the hesitation in his voice. 'I think we should search the Seer's house. Everyone knows about the Seer and Savjani's daughter. If Dodge has taken the clothcrafter anywhere, surely it would be there?'

The thought had struck Soames but he hadn't spoken it aloud and he had hoped that it wouldn't occur to Blacken so quickly. Another treacherous hope that he didn't want to question just yet. Were his old loyalties returning? He wasn't sure – he had come so far down this path that he knew there was no real way back – and he certainly never wanted to travel again. He couldn't risk the Aging. He wouldn't. But his dreams were filled with the city in the valley and the possibilities held within the lights that glowed there.

'He's always fought me,' Arnold-Mather said, staring out of the window. Soames didn't need to stand alongside him to see where his gaze fell. It would be resting on the Seer's house. Arnold-Mather spent far more time staring at it than was probably sane. 'Why has my son always fought me?'

The two soldiers stayed silent. The question wasn't addressed to them but simply breathed aloud from the hidden spot where it rotted inside their king.

'And now he has Levi Dodge? My faithful servant?' His voice was rising. Soames glanced at Blacken. The truth was sinking in, and Arnold-Mather was not a man to take any misstep well. Was this it for them? Were they about to become part of the army of the mad? Soames wondered, briefly, if that might be a better existence than the one they now had, when Blacken's hand gripped his arm.

'Look,' he whispered.

Red sparks glittered at the tips of Arnold-Mather's fingers and the air around them began to shimmer. Whatever this was, it wasn't good. Soames pulled Blacken backwards as the pressure in the room started to build, an invisible tornado whirling around the hunched figure staring through the vast windows. They had just reached the far wall, Soames frantically pulling open one of the large doors to shield them, when Arnold-Mather threw his head back and roared in fury, unleashing a wave of power and magic with the terrifying sound.

Even with the door protecting them, both men were thrown back against the wall by the blast. They curled into each other, turning their backs outwards and, above the roar of wind and rage, Soames heard the window shatter. A second, higher pitched scream filled the room, and Soames knew with a certainty that it was Joe, the poor schoolboy Storyholder, screaming all those floors below them as Arnold-Mather sucked more power through him.

He thought his ears might bleed. He thought his head might explode. But then, just as consciousness threatened to leave him, the wind and sound vanished as suddenly as they had arrived. They stayed where they were, curled up behind the door, for several minutes, waiting for the ringing in their ears to fade and their legs to steady. By the time they dragged themselves to their feet, Arnold-Mather was gone.

Blacken was the first to reach the window, his boots crunching on the broken glass. His mouth fell open as he gazed upwards. Soames said nothing when he joined him, letting the freezing night air cool his skin. There was nothing either of them could say.

Soames stared at the rip in the sky, now so much wider than it had been before, a hungry mouth leaning down to swallow them up into its bleak oblivion. They stood side by side for a long time, until the cold had set their jaws rattling and bitterly numbed their ears.

'Next time,' Soames said, eventually, 'my vote is that we don't tell him.'

He didn't wait for Blacken's reply, but instead left the burned man there and went in search of the youngs and Mrs Manning. She would need some comfort now.

PART THREE

Prophecy's End

THIRTY-ONE

The Magi, after much discussion and studying of maps, divided into pairs. Ted did his best to help them blend in, dressing them in clothes from the old boys' wardrobes. When he was finished, while they didn't exactly look street, they at least looked as if they belonged in the Somewhere. Only the Queen refused to change but Mrs Baker, with all her earthy wisdom, managed to bustle her into a thick woollen overcoat.

Two of the Magi had come with Fin and the Queen to St Paul's, and the others had gone to four other churches, picked out along a three-mile stretch of London: St Clement Danes at Aldwych and the Temple at Fleet Street to one side of them, and St Helen's at Bishopsgate and St Dunstan's at Stepney to the other. Cardrew, Freddie Wise, Fowkes and Harper Jones had gone with the other pairs, each group taking separate black cabs through the silent, icy streets.

Fin, the Queen of the Magi, and her two companions had just stepped onto the pavement when the ground shook, deep below their feet, and the sky gave a loud and ominous rumble. The small group glanced up, and Fin saw what looked like pink flickers and flashes of lightning crackling across the edges of the jagged white line that so proudly scored across the night sky. Firecrackers or giant sparklers were all he could think of, and just as he was being drawn into the unusual lights, a single deafening crack burst overhead causing the whole group, the Queen included, to flinch and cover their ears. In the ringing silence that followed, they all warily turned their eyes upwards.

The Queen gasped, the blush on her pale cheeks fading to a sickly hue and she rocked slightly, unsteady on her feet for a moment. The two Magi pulled their strings of beads from their ill-fitting trousers and immediately began worrying at them, running them between their dark fingers and muttering in a language Fin didn't understand.

The sky was a black shroud above them. The glittering pink lights that had illuminated it were gone and the thin white line didn't look discernibly different, but Fin could feel that something had changed. It was as if the air was denser, thicker in his lungs, and his ears felt as if they might pop.

'What is it?' he asked, as the Magi Queen regained her footing and strode towards the base of the cathedral. 'What's happened?'

Her face was grim in the darkness, no working lights to bathe them in artificial daylight that normally illuminated St Paul's. Tonight, the church that was so important to the Knights was simply another shadowed building drowning in the endless night.

'I don't know,' she answered. 'Something has happened in the Nowhere. He's drawing on more magic. And none of it for good. We need to work fast.'

'What do we have to do?'

'Stand there,' she said. They stood on the second step and, for a second, Fin wondered at the constant presence of second steps in his strange life. Baxter died on the second step in the House of Real Truths, he had been left on the second step of the Old Bailey, and here they were again, on the second step outside St Paul's.

'Magic must fight magic, and we don't have enough of it. He's drained the Nowhere of everything it has, sucking the land dry. It's an unnatural magic at work, drawn from pieces of stone that should never have been reunited. If we are to fight him, then we need to be stronger. We need to become dangerously strong, just like he is.'

'And St Paul's has magic?' Fin asked, his teeth chattering loudly. In the past minute or two, the temperature had dropped several degrees and the falling snow solidified into ice as it landed. Was the Somewhere going to freeze the way the Nowhere had? Had time shifted for them now? There were too many questions he didn't have answers for; the Magi Queen, at least, had one.

'The Ley line holds the magic.'

'Ley line? The lines you were talking about earlier?'

'Yes. They're powerful alignments of buildings which allow those who know how to, to access the magic they harness. There are several in your city, but the one that runs through these five churches is the most powerful.'

'Because of the churches? It's religion?' Fin figured he could cope with a lot, but if the Queen told him God was real then he might need to sit down.

'Religion or magic, what is the division? A belief in something you cannot see which can be used for good or evil?' She shrugged slightly. 'Your world chose one and forgot the other, and in our world the magic was always too strong to ignore. We had no need of stories of saviours – as much as we cherish a great story. We had the Five Stories and the Storyholder.'

'And the Prophecy,' Fin added softly.

'Yes, and that too.'

'What do we do now?' Fin said. 'How do you get the magic?' Somewhere in the distance he could hear a variety of whoops and howls, menacing in the silent city. A gang? He knew those noises – they were the ones the boys on the Brickman Estate would make when they were terrorising some poor old man, or getting ready to attack a rival gang. The darkness was bringing them out onto the streets and soon there would be looting and blood. The Rage might not have attacked the Somewhere in the same way that it had the Nowhere but

213

its echoes were here. The worlds were all linked, and those who had turned to Joe and the Dark King in the Nowhere had their equivalents in this London and their wickedness was now awoken, as if they could sense their natural leaders despite being so far away.

'The Magi will summon it at each of the points on the ley line's path and channel it to us, here at the centre point. We will do our best to hold it.' She looked down at Fin, her eyes thoughtful. 'And then, what will be will be.'

Hearing Baxter's words coming from this woman made Fin shiver slightly, as did the way she was looking at him. 'What do you mean, "we"?' he asked.

'Dark magic has been made by the union between the Storyholder and the Dark King. We will need another union to fight it.'

'Me and Baxter?' Fin's stomach twisted. Always Baxter. Did Fin even exist at all? The Queen shook her head and smiled before leaning forward and stroking his hair. Despite the freezing cold, her hand was warm.

'No. You and I, young Fin. You have spaces inside you, areas it seems neither you nor Baxter want to inhabit. Empty places that I can see in your eyes. We will fill them with magic and we shall lead the fight together.'

'I don't know anything about magic,' Fin said, and didn't like that he sounded slightly afraid. He'd seen Christopher after his pact with the Magi – how changed he'd been – what would happen to him?

'But magic knows you,' she answered. 'It made you.' Fin thought about that for a quiet minute as the noise from the group of howling yobs faded, chasing their prey. She was right. If anyone was going to put all this right, then it should be him. For himself, and for Baxter and for Tova, if not for anyone else.

'So if we're carrying the magic,' he said, as she studied the step beneath them, seeing something in the concrete that was invisible to Fin, 'then it'll be you and me who have to face Joe and Arnold-Mather?'

'Ultimately, yes. The ten I have brought have other tasks to perform, if we are to win.' She smiled at him again, and he was sure he saw a touch of sadness in it this time. 'And you forget, Finmere Tingewick Smith, that the Magi could never see the end of the Prophecy. We are as blind to all our fates as you are.' On each hand she wore eight jewelled rings and she took four off and handed them to Fin. 'Now put these on and do as I do.' The metal was warm and the rings were a perfect fit, even though he was sure his fingers were fatter than the Queen's, and where he had to squeeze two under his bandage the broken flesh stung. His hands tingled as the cold fled from them. Beside him, the Queen stretched her hands out in front of her with her palms facing down. Fin did the same.

'What now?' he said.

'Now we wait.'

The two Magi who had accompanied them crouched sideways on the step below, alongside the points over which Fin and the Queen's hands were stretched. They closed their eyes and rocked backwards and forwards on their heels as they began to chant. Their fingers worked at the beads they carried, each moving in synch with the other. Fin dragged his eyes away and stared ahead. His heart thumped. What was going to—

He gasped as heat rushed up from the ground in a sudden fierce rush that burned into the palms of his hands, and he had to use all his strength to keep them level against the force. It was like the desert wind that had torn his skin, but this heat was strong and good, and despite the pressure, it felt soothing on his lacerated skin. Was it healing under there? His eyes had closed as a reflex, but he opened them. The Queen was glowing next to him, a rainbow of colours

215

dancing from her skin, and her hair flew out behind her. He looked at his own hands and the lights that sparked from them, a glittering mass of brightness that left shadows behind his eyes when he blinked. The force was almost overwhelming as he felt the warmth working its way inside him. His skin tingled and he watched as the force of the energy stripped his bandage from his hand. He wasn't surprised to see his skin fresh and smooth beneath. This was magic. No, he thought, as he felt the rhythm of the earth and all the worlds resonate with his heartbeat, this wasn't magic. This was *power*. This was everything that made the universe work. Raw energy. Magic. Everything.

The further it reached inside him, the faster it raced to fill him up. He glanced sideways at the Queen and saw her head was turned his way, her eyes wide. How much was he glittering? How did he look?

'It recognises me,' he said, his words coming from somewhere beyond the rush of wind and power. Tova had made him from magic and now that magic was claiming him. His lungs screamed as more light and air rushed into him from the earth below, knocking his breath aside. 'I can't take it all!'

The Queen reached across and grabbed his hand. 'Yes, you can!'

'I can't! I ...'

And as soon as it had begun, the surge was over. Fin crumpled to the floor, sucking in lungfuls of cold, crisp air, and cooling his hands on the icy second step.

'Yes, you can,' The Queen whispered, as she knelt beside him and smiled. 'Yes, you can.'

THIRTY-TWO

Orrery House was still lit by candles when they got back. However close someone, somewhere might have been to fixing the capital's electricity, the second strange shift in the ground had put paid to that. Thankfully, the heating ran on gas and that still worked, so the old men, many comatose, remained warm in their beds. Those who were awake gathered, a sombre group, in the Oval Room and waited for the Magi and their escorts to filter back. Fowkes was with the last pair and as they shrugged off their coats he looked from the Queen to Fin and back again.

'Did it work?' he asked.

'Yes. We have the magic,' the Queen said.

'How will that affect our London?' Freddie Wise was pacing the room, leaning heavily on his walking stick. 'Will draining the magic have weakened our world?'

'No,' Fin said. 'We didn't steal it, it was given. It'll renew. Top itself up.' He didn't know how he knew the answer, he just did. He could feel it thumping in his veins. This new power was filling him, all those empty spaces he hadn't known he had, as like the Queen had said it would. 'The magic wants the balance restored just as much as the rest of us.'

'So what now?' Ted said.

'Now we go back.' Fowkes was already drawing his sword. 'And we fight.'

'This time he'll definitely feel us coming through,' Fin said. 'We have too much magic.'

'Then we'll have to move fast. And the Seer's house will give us some protection.' Fowkes cut through the candlelit air and opened a doorway, but Fin frowned when he looked through. Something was wrong at Christopher's house. The lights were off, and in the gloom it looked as if all the furniture had been tossed around. Smashed glass glinted on the floor. He glanced at Fowkes, who held one hand up to keep the Magi back for the moment, and then the two of them stepped through, Fin with his sword ready. For the first time he hoped that Baxter was ready too, just in case they came face to face with the mad or others of Arnold-Mather's army. He trusted the dead Knight's sword skills much more than his own.

The house, however, was empty, and filled with the kind of chill cold that only came when buildings had been abandoned for a long time. Fin's heart sunk. Where were Christopher and Mona? Had they run, or had they been taken?

'Go to the window,' Fowkes said quietly. 'But stay in the shadow. See if anyone's out there. We need to get the others through anyway.'

Fin did as he was told, and as the Magi stepped from one world to the other, he pressed himself against the damp wall and peered out at the city. He was shocked by what he saw. Several Boroughs had been razed to the ground and make-shift camps had been set up, looking like the refugee camps Fin had only ever seen on the news. Here and there, in the grey gloom which covered the whole city, patches of red light glowed upwards from the bases of statues. The stone and bronze figures didn't much resemble the man he'd first met at Grey's club back before his first trip to the Nowhere, but he knew the hulking shape had to be that of the Dark King. How long had they been away this time? Had Arnold-Mather damaged time further with whatever he'd done to shake both worlds? He looked up at the dark crack in the sky. It was definitely wider.

'What are they doing?' Fowkes said, and Fin turned to

look. The Magi and their Queen had all come through the doorway but Fowkes was staring at something on the other side that Fin couldn't quite make out. He squeezed through the small huddle and joined the Commander of the Knights. Two figures were coming through from the black and white on the other side: Alex Currie-Clark and Hector Allbright. He could vaguely see Ted trying to hold them back but the men threw themselves into the space between the worlds, leaving Fowkes with no choice but to keep the door open.

'—to help!' Currie-Clark finished whatever he'd been shouting at that other world as he tumbled, Allbright alongside him, to the dusty floor. Fin stared at them in surprise.

'What the hell do you think you're playing at?' Fowkes hissed, as he gestured back at Ted and Freddie Wise. 'You need to go back. You can't be here! This is no place for old men and you know that!'

'Look.' Fin could barely get the words out. '*Look*, Fowkes. Look at them.'

The two men on the floor pulled themselves to their feet, the double-edged swords they'd hidden in their long coats clanking as they did. On the other side of the doorway the small group came closer. Fin wondered how Alex Currie-Clark's hair looked from the Somewhere. Could they see how red and thick it was? Because it seemed to shine, even in the grim darkness of the Seer's broken house. The thin grey wisps were gone, as were his watery eyes and stooped back. It was simply Alex Currie-Clark again, exactly as he had been when he first climbed out of the black cab, tall and gangly and over-excited.

'What happened?' Fin breathed, even though the answer was obvious to all of them as they looked at the two changed men in front of them. Hector Allbright had a full head of blond hair and couldn't have been much over thirty-five, was solid without being fat, but still had the same cheeky smile. He looked down at himself in wonder and then slapped

Currie-Clark hard on the arm and laughed.

'That's never happened before,' Fowkes said, looking from one to the other. 'It's been tried and the Ageing never reverses. It just stays the same, or even gets worse.'

'It's all the magic,' the Queen said. 'There's too much of it here. It's finding uses for itself to relieve the pressure. Before it rips the universe to pieces, that is.'

Fin tugged at Fowkes' free arm and pointed through the doorway. Freddie Wise was holding up a piece of paper, a message written in thick marker pen: KEEP THE DOORWAY OPEN. Fowkes nodded and then Ted and Freddie Wise disappeared out of view.

'You're going to have to help me, Fin. I'm not sure how long I can hold it.'

Fin had his sword up in a second and had no doubt that he could keep the doorway open for as long as was needed. 'You two,' Fowkes continued, nodding at Currie-Clark and Allbright. 'You guard us. Take the Magi to look out with you. I want to know the moment anything moves near the house, okay?'

'What are they doing back there?' the Magi Queen asked, peering through at the empty Oval Room at Orrery House.

Fowkes smiled. It was a rare, real smile from the haunted Knight. 'They're getting us an army.' He winked at Fin. 'Arnold-Mather might have an army of the mad, but we're going to have an army of the Knights of Nowhere.'

It was the doorway opening that pulled Joe out of the fugue state he'd been trapped in for most of the endless days and years that passed in the Nowhere. It wasn't that he wasn't aware of what was around him, it was just that everything inside him was so much more consuming. And, of course, the closer he got to the surface of himself, the more he felt the pain. It had been bad – agony – before Arnold-Mather had raged and widened the tear in the sky, but that had been

220

nothing compared to the pain now. He'd never really stopped screaming. It was easier to lose himself in the nothing and everything that lived in his core, than to rise and face that excruciating pain.

However bad it was, he always heard his mother's words, if not entirely consciously. So he knew, for example, that Levi Dodge had gone and that the news gave his mother a mixture of heartache and pride. He knew she was there, beside him, when the ripple ran through his soul. A doorway opening. A doorway from an old world, bringing *so much magic* with it. It was like a jolt of electricity surging through him and his eyes flew open, wide open, for the first time in too long. He snapped his head towards his mother who reached for him, her mouth open wide, and he could see in her face, just in that instant, everything she didn't tell him about. Everything Arnold-Mather had put her through during the long, frozen years. He could also, in this brief moment of clarity, see himself for who he was – for what he had become.

He thought of Fin and Fowkes and everything that he had betrayed, in his childishness, and he focused hard on sealing all the magic he could within himself. To keep the shockwaves coming from the doorway from passing through him and into Arnold-Mather. Was he even capable of it? He closed his eyes again, ignoring his mother's sorrow and his own for hurting her. He'd been the cause of so much damage that their own pain was simply a grain of sand in the desert. One story among so many. The surge of magic rushed up inside him, from the connection between Joe and the stones and the stories, and flooded outwards along that other con-nection – the second, invisible umbilical cord – that had been forged between him and the Dark King so many years ago. Joe didn't think he could ever cut it – he thought the link might be so strong that if one of them died, so would the other – but he wondered if he could squeeze it for a second and stop Arnold-Mather from sensing the doorway. His heart raced, his first proper physical sensation in a long time. Because if he could do this once, then he could do it again.

He turned his thoughts inwards, and concentrated exactly as Tova, the dead Storyholder, had taught him to all that time ago.

The doorway had been open for at least an hour, by Fin's reckoning, as the last of the old men came through. Although Fowkes was sweating with the effort, they'd managed to keep it open, the combination of adrenaline and the magic stored inside Fin seeing them through. The broken room was filled with Knights, many of whom had been Aged for decades, and although they were shocked and surprised and overwhelmed, they were still pulling on the shirts and trousers and swords they had been pushed through the doorway with. Slapping each other on the back and smiling, Freddie Wise, who didn't seem that much younger than he had been before, but no longer needed his walking stick, moved among them, giving them a brief account of what had brought them to this. Somewhere in the melee, Cardrew Cutler was doing the same ... but, Fin realised, he had no idea which of the men he was.

He and Fowkes nodded through the doorway to Ted and Harper Jackson and then closed the tear between the worlds.

'Why has no one found us yet?' Fowkes asked. 'They must have felt it.'

'And where are Christopher and Mona? And the Wakley twins? He couldn't have got them all, could he?' Fin didn't need to clarify who 'he' was.

'Where would they have gone?'

Fin looked around him at the mess. 'If they'd seen someone coming, then they'd have used the tunnels to get out.'

'Unless he'd found out about the tunnels,' Fowkes said, as the two of them fought their way through the crowd to the hatch.

'Christopher would have left us a message.' Fin peered at

the undersides of the furniture. 'He knew we would come back, and he knew we would come back here.'

'The door isn't damaged.' Fowkes pulled back the rug and fiddled for the hidden latch and then pulled the hidden hatch up, its edges almost indistinguishable from the wooden flooring that housed it. Icy darkness loomed below. Whether or not the tunnels had been discovered, it seemed no one thought they were worth guarding any more. Neither Christopher and Mona's people nor Arnold-Mather's. There were no flickering lamps below, just a rush of cold air. As he looked away, something caught his eye on the back of the wooden hatch. He frowned and peered closer. Something had been scribbled there in tiny writing. Christopher's scrawled handwriting. Exactly as unreadable as it had been in school.

'Wait,' Fin said. Fowkes had been reaching to close the hatch and he stopped him, leaning forward until the words were just visible in the gloom. 'He's left us a message,' Fin said. 'Look. "The stories no one wants to hear." It's from Christopher. It's his writing.'

'What does it mean? What stories no one wants to hear?'

'You should know this, Andrew Fowkes. Both of you should.' Fin turned to see Freddie Wise and the Magi Queen standing behind them.

'So what it is, Freddie, if you're so clever?' Fowkes asked with a grin.

'The Old Bailey House of Real Truths. The place filled with stories no one wants to hear.'

'Of course.' Fowkes' smile dissolved at the thought, and Fin felt the same strange heaviness in his soul. They had both faced truths there, and neither had liked what they'd learned. 'Of course,' Fowkes repeated.

'Hey,' someone called softly from somewhere by the window. 'Hey, come and look at this.'

The Knights had spread themselves through the building, guarding the various entrances and watching from the windows as calmly as if they had simply passed from one room to another in Orrery House. Fin felt a surge of pride just to be among them.

'Over there,' said the dark-haired young man who had summoned them. 'It looks like some kind of procession.' Even as he pointed out the moving line in the distance, Fin heard the faintest echo of drums cutting through the quiet. He shivered. He remembered the drums when Lucas Blake died in the river, when he'd thought Christopher was dead. What were they beating for now?

'Whatever it is, we should take advantage of the distraction and get to the House of Real Truths,' Fowkes said. 'Now we're here, we need to see if there's anyone left to fight with us.'

THIRTY-THREE

The ground was hard with black ice, even though the soldiers had gone ahead with the mad to try and clear it a little. Every so often one of the horses lost its footing and stumbled, and since leaving the Dome the coach with the Dark King wrapped warmly inside had slid numerous times. Arnold-Mather hadn't seemed to notice. He was intent on his monthly display.

Behind the coach on his own faithful horse, who had become accustomed to the terrible conditions on all their trips into the Outlands beyond the city, Simeon Soames wondered what the King thought this would achieve. Did he really think, after all this time, that a parade would draw the rebels out? The massacre at the prison hadn't done it, and in the eight years since then, they had got much better at hiding. He wondered about that. Why were they hiding? They had Levi Dodge – who knew all the ways in and out of the Dome – and they also had brave men. Arnold-Mather might have convinced himself they were cowering in some rats' nest somewhere, frightened of getting caught, but Soames wasn't so sure. He didn't think they were in hiding at all. He thought perhaps they were waiting, and that was a completely different thing.

He pulled his coat tighter around his neck. Despite Number Six riding in the saddle in front of him – one of the youngs always forced into this ritual with him – they were providing each other with very little body warmth, and before they'd left he'd wrapped his sheepskin waistcoat around the thin ten-year-old boy, to wear under his coat. He didn't know if Edgar Blacken had seen, or would care if he had, but Soames had told the boy to make sure it didn't show. There was very little room for kindness, even among their own, and the youngs had always been something in-between, even though they could no longer remember their lives before this one. Other than him and Mrs Manning, no one cared about the youngs. They were merely a symbol of what this Dark King could and would do.

'He must really hate that man,' Number Six whispered.

Simeon looked at Benjamin Wakley, barefoot and dressed only in torn trousers, who stumbled and fell once again as the mad tugged him this way and that with the chains attached to the collar around his neck. His hands were tied tightly behind his back and his pale skin was almost invisible beneath the colourful bruises, some red and fresh and others the older, darker colour of rotting apples. His head was shorn of his thick blond hair and there were scars all over his skull. The Knight struggled to his feet again, his eyes focusing on nothing.

'Yes, I think he does,' Soames answered. Along the roadside, Edgar Blacken roused the crowd, most of whom had empty, sad eyes, to taunt and spit on the prisoner.

'Why?'

For Number Six it was always 'why?' no matter how many years passed. Number Six liked to think about things, to understand them. People, mostly. He'd been born into the wrong age, Soames decided. He would find very little to like in people's motives here. 'He hates him because he's a Knight of Nowhere and he stands against the King.'

Was that why Arnold-Mather hated Wakley? Or was it that the man wouldn't break, no matter what they did to him? By rights he should have been dead a long time ago, and Soames was pretty sure the Dark King was using his powers to keep the young Knight alive solely to torment him and humiliate him on these monthly trawls through the city.

'Do you hate him?' Number Six asked.

'No,' Soames said, and was surprised to find a lump forming in the back of his throat. 'No, I don't hate him at all.' Number Six froze slightly in front of him, even at that age knowing that to so openly disagree with Arnold-Mather was akin to treason.

'They say you used to be a Knight. That your sword is a Knight's sword.'

'That was a long time ago,' Soames said.

'So you should hate him more, surely?'

Soames said nothing. Maybe he should. Maybe he should hate Wakley for being everything he was supposed to be. But Wakley had never Aged. Wakley still had hope.

'You chose this side over theirs,' Number Six continued. There was no guile in his voice but his words stung Soames.

'Yes, yes I did,' was all he could manage as an answer.

'Why?' The boy didn't look round but continued to stare at the battered, freezing man being dragged on this endless promenade ... after which he would be locked away once more in a small dark room in the Dome. And there he would stay, and be beaten, until another month of Christmas Days had been crossed off the calendar.

'Always a why with you, Number Six,' Soames said. He didn't give an answer. He wasn't really sure he had one. The way he'd changed sides in the palace, so long ago, had surprised even him. What had it been? Fear? The Rage? Both? Or maybe he had always been destined to choose this side. Maybe he had never been good enough for the Knights of Nowhere. Maybe that's where the truth lay. It rang true in his heart. He looked again at Benjamin Wakley, staggering forwards on bleeding feet. Maybe he should hate him more.

*

In the abandoned warehouse down by the Traders' wharf, Curran Tugg's men momentarily paused in their work as the drums beat louder.

'One day, he'll get bored and finally kill the poor bastard,' someone muttered.

'Or turn him. Soon there'll be more mad in the city than normal folk,' Elbows said.

The drums in the street were matched by another beat, coming from the misty river where Francois Manot and his Gypsies guarded the shoreline. The Traders' faces hardened.

'I've forgotten what the water feels like,' one said.

'We'll never get out there again.'

'We're sitting in this freezing dive building boats for a war that'll never come.'

'Don't you say that.' Curran Tugg got up from his seat by the window and turned on his men. 'Don't you ever let me hear you say that. There's a battle coming, you trust me on that, and I won't have the Traders shamed by being unprepared. I want boats ready to launch all along the river at a moment's notice.'

His men stared at him. 'It's been too many years,' Elbows said, 'since you came back from the South.'

'Thirteen,' someone grumbled.

'Unlucky for some.'

'Maybe it'll be lucky for us. We've been unlucky long enough.'

'I told you,' Tugg said. 'Time's different over there. We've got to have faith.'

'Yeah, right. And while we have faith, we'll just wait to get caught and killed for making boats that are never going to be used.'

Tugg stared at his men. He could understand their frustration. They lived for travelling and the water and telling tales of the South in smoky bars with a woman on their knee and a pint of ale in their hand. This life of hiding wasn't for them.

As was he, they were being ground down by the endless cold and gloom and the constant threat from the crack in the sky above them. At least he had met the Magi Queen. He had heard Fowkes' and Fin's promise to return. Yet even he, sometimes, felt his hope drifting away.

The Seer was in hiding. Something in the city had broken when the mad had wrecked his house after they'd finally forced their way in. None of them had realised how much they'd looked to that golden building as a symbol of goodness in these dark times and even though the Seer was still very much alive, knowing that wasn't the same as being able to glance to his house, a bright light in a dull skyline, and feel that things might change.

'So, what do you suggest we do?' he said, after a long pause. 'Give up? Walk out of here and snivel at the Dark King's feet? Sit in our houses at night and wonder when the knock on the door is coming and we'll be dragged away for no reason?' He paced up the line where they were polishing the finished hull. 'Or do we stay here and make ready? Keep our pride? Do I believe the Magi Queen will return? Yes, I do. Do I know when? No. Maybe we'll have fifty years to wait. But I for one will wait them out if it means I have a chance to reclaim our river from Manot.'

Mutterings of approval ran around the room. Traders were nothing if not proud and he knew it stung, every day, that the Gypsy Traders had control of their water.

'And if it looks as if the sky is about to tear in two and they still haven't returned? Then I want to be able to sail out and die on the water. In a sturdy boat I can be proud of.'

Outside the drums beat louder, as if Francois Manot could hear his words and was mocking him, or challenging him. Either way, it worked. Tugg watched as his men's backs straightened and they found their fire again. No one would leave. The boats would be built. He looked out of the window

229

at the mist, though, and he willed the boy and the Magi Queen to hurry back to them.

The attic floor was musty and the wood rough and damp beneath their knees as Levi Dodge, Mitesh Savjani and Henry Wakley peered cautiously over the edge of the eaves window at the passing procession.

'He's still alive,' Savjani said, 'and he still has some fight in his belly. You can see it.'

'He's more bruised than he was last month.' Henry spoke softly. 'And look at his feet. He's leaving a trail of blood on the ice.'

'Your brother has survived many years of this. He can survive more,' Savjani said. To his right, Levi Dodge said nothing. This didn't surprise the clothcrafter. He had learned that Dodge was a man of few words, but that hadn't stopped him developing a fondness and respect for him. Still waters ran deep and even though he was sure many among their number couldn't bring themselves to trust Dodge, Savjani was not one of them. Levi Dodge would die for them if called upon to do so, he was sure of it.

'Maybe we could do something,' Henry said. There was no longer a twinkle of laughter in his eyes. There hadn't been in the four years since Benjamin had been captured. 'I could take Soames out. He's got one of those kids with him, and he'll get in his way, make him slower. Maybe the crowd would help.'

Savjani squeezed his arm. 'When I was in the palace, you and your brother, you were wise. You wouldn't let my Mona try to save me. Not even when they were going to execute me.'

Henry turned to look at him, eyes heavy with pain and guilt. 'I know, but we—'

'No, my friend.' Savjani shook his head. 'I am not chastising you. You did the right thing. Had you let Mona come, she would have died. I would never have forgiven you. Any

230

of you.' He looked down at the procession that was passing. 'If I were to let you go down there, you would not save your brother. At best you would be captured yourself, and at worst you would be killed or turned into one of those poor mad creatures. Your brother would not forgive me. He wouldn't forgive any of us. And I certainly wouldn't forgive myself.' Below them, Simeon Soames and the Dark King's carriage passed out of sight and people scurried back into their houses, seeking warmth and at least a pretence of safety.

'Your brother is still alive. Let us just rejoice in the knowledge of that.' After a moment, Henry Wakley nodded.

'We need to go.' Levi Dodge finally spoke. 'While they're all distracted. We should be back before night falls. It's not safe in the dark.'

Savjani understood what the Bowler-hatted man meant, but as they moved from house to house through the eaves, he wondered if there was anywhere safe left at all.

THIRTY-FOUR

They had left the recovered Knights at the Seer's house, and Freddie, Fin, Fowkes and the Magi Queen had gone alone to the House of Real Truths to see what waited for them there. The streets were quiet and not so much as a curtain twitched as they trotted along the icy roads, staying close to the walls for cover, although in truth the evening gloom providing plenty of protection. As yet there was no sound of the mad scampering along the rooftops. Perhaps whatever procession had passed had tired them. Whatever the cause, Fin wasn't complaining.

They were nearly at the side door to the imposing building in the middle of the square when Fowkes pulled them back. 'Look.'

Fin squinted through the gloom. Three figures were making their way across the courtyard, moving fast and huddled together. 'Is that Henry Wakley?' he asked. 'And Savjani? He's out of prison?' He was about to step forward to greet them when Fowkes roughly pulled him back. 'Don't! You see who's with them?'

Fin looked again as the figures came closer. He couldn't make out the man's face, but the outline of the hat was clear. A Bowler hat. Levi Dodge? What were Henry Wakley and Savjani doing with him?

'Maybe they're become traitors,' Fowkes said, and Fin stared at him. How could he think that? How could he think that of Savjani?

232

'Not everyone is like Jarvis and Simeon Soames,' Freddie Wise said. 'Those are good men.'

'I'll believe it when I hear it from them.' Fowkes had his sword drawn, and Fin pulled his own. He didn't believe for one second that Savjani would have turned to Arnold-Mather's side, but he would stand by Fowkes. Freddie Wise and the Magi Queen pressed themselves into the wall behind Fowkes and Fin and when the three appeared in the doorway, Fowkes had his sword at Levi Dodge's neck before Henry Wakley had even drawn his. Fin held his own up as a warning and hoped he wouldn't have to use it. His hand was shaking and he'd drop the thing at the simplest provocation. He certainly couldn't imagine stabbing any of these people with it.

'I wouldn't if I was you, son.' Fowkes glanced at Henry Wakley who was reaching for his own sword. 'They didn't make me Commander of the Knights because of my charming personality.'

'Fowkes?' Savjani said, and his face broke into a grin. 'You're back!'

'What are you doing with him?' He tilted his head towards Levi Dodge who, very sensibly, had frozen in the doorway.

'He saved me!' The tailor reached one hand up to push the sword away. 'He's with us now. He has been for a long time, my friend.'

'It's true,' Henry Wakley said. 'Why do you think we're here at the Old Bailey? Did you find Christopher's message?'

'I think perhaps we should get inside. Before it's fully night.' Levi Dodge finally spoke although he still remained perfectly still, very much aware of the blade at his throat. 'We can resolve this there, one way or another.'

'He may have a point,' Freddie Wise said.

'One funny move –' Fowkes kept his eyes firmly on Dodge '– and I won't hesitate.'

Mitesh Savjani slid between them and pushed open the side door and nodded the small group in.

The hallway was dark – Fin was glad not to see that second step again – and Savjani led them down the side corridor, past the vast central chamber, and into a smaller side room. A gas light flickered against a wall, and Savjani turned it off and on again three times. A small door that Fin hadn't even noticed swung open and one of Jack Ditch's kids, Jester, peered round.

'You're back. We were getting worried ...' His eyes widened as he saw Fin and the others. 'Bloody 'ell! I don't believe it! They're back!' He grinned, stunned and beside himself to see them. 'Come on, then!'

Fowkes finally put his sword away and the four followed the others down a short staircase and into a well lit set of rooms below.

'What is this place?' Fin said. The room they stood in was lined with truth vials, but instead of the bright colours Fin remembered, these were filled with clear liquid.

'The Archivers' chambers.' Christopher's voice came from behind him. 'Those are the as yet undiscovered truths.'

'Christopher!' Fin turned to see his friend smiling at him from a doorway into another room. A small figure rushed at him and suddenly Mona was hugging him hard. 'Oh Fin, it's been such a long time. I've missed you.'

Over her shoulder Fin saw Christopher flinch slightly at Mona's affectionate display. What had happened since they'd been gone?

'How long has it been this time?' Fowkes asked. It was the next question in Fin's head.

'Thirteen years,' Christopher said. Looking at him, it was hard to believe. He looked just the same as he had the first time they crossed into the Nowhere. For a moment they were sombre, and then Fin grinned. 'We should get the others, now we know it's safe.'

'What others?' Henry Wakley asked.

'Wait and see. Just wait and see!'

234

Maybe it wasn't wise to have them all in one place, but it was the only way to formulate their plans, and as the Traders and Jack Ditch's men and boys arrived they all moved upstairs into the wrecked Truth Chamber where there was more space. They placed guards on the roof and the doors, but the streets outside were mercifully quiet. Apparently, the mad were not so keen on this part of town – as if even though the vials were smashed, the truths still lingered, and the mad did not want to face them. It was that, or Arnold-Mather didn't think anyone would be so stupid as to use the old building as a base. Fin thought it was probably the former since all of the buildings around the Old Bailey were also abandoned, the residents having moved away, perhaps not wanting to be near the building that symbolised everything the Nowhere had once been.

They ate and laughed and celebrated for a while, even the Magi joining in, but as night enveloped them a serious silence fell and they began to plan in earnest. Fin listened as the others talked, feeling very much younger than everyone else in the room. How old was Christopher now? In his thirties? It was hard to take in. For Christopher, their schoolboy friendship was more than half a lifetime ago, whereas for Fin it was still on-going.

When the time to attack came, the Traders would take to the rivers and fight the Gypsies on the water. The Knights would split up and attack Arnold-Mather's twin bases at the palace and the White Tower. Fin, Fowkes, Christopher, Mona and the Magi Queen would go to the Dome, and find Joe and Justin Arnold-Mather. But first, they needed to draw his army out. They needed to let him – and the rest of the Nowhere – know that they were here, armed with magic, and ready to fight. People would join them, Savjani was sure of it. All those who had lost relatives and loved ones over the years were yearning to fight back, but until now even a thought of rebellion had been almost suicidal.

'So how are we going to do that?' Fowkes asked. 'Christopher's house?'

'No.' the Magi Queen shook her head and raised her chin proudly. 'West Minster. The home of the Magi. We can bring that building to life again and make it shine like a beacon, as it did in the stories of old. Then I shall send them on a procession through the streets. We will show the people that the Magi and the Knights are back.'

'We can plan a route with good get-out points,' Mona said. 'Houses that lead to the tunnels, if needed.'

Glasses rose in a silent toast. So this was it. Fin felt the power bubbling under his skin. They were finally going to face Arnold-Mather. He wondered if he was the only one who had a small knot of fear tied firmly in the pit of his stomach.

THIRTY-FIVE

Fin wasn't sure how much he or anyone else slept that night, but he dozed in fits and bursts, and it seemed he'd only just laid down to sleep in the old Archivers' chambers when he was shaken awake again. It was still black outside but the air in the old building held the cold, crisp chill of morning. He shivered as he joined the quiet throng in the Truth Chamber and sought out the few faces he recognised. It was strange to think he must have shaved the Aged faces of the men who now looked like strangers. The atmosphere had changed as the hours passed, and where there had been a sense of devil-may-care excitement the night before, there was now a layer of tension in the room as people huddled together in small groups talking quietly about what lay ahead.

Outside, men stood in corners watching the streets, but thus far they had been lucky. Fin thought it was strange that Arnold-Mather and Joe hadn't felt all the new magic that had entered the Nowhere. Especially given the way the mad had come for them last time they'd cut through, from the presence of the swords alone. Was the Dark King losing his power? He shook the thought away. That was a dangerous way to think. They could take no chances.

Henry Wakley left with the Magi, a few Knights and some of Jack Ditch's boys about half an hour before dawn broke, giving them time to get to the wreck of West Minster before daylight. The rest watched them go, and Fin stood by Christopher and Mona but said nothing. This had started as his adventure, but now the Nowhere was far more his friends' world than it had ever been his. He was afraid that anything he said would sound crass and patronising so he sipped a mug of hot coffee someone passed him and quietly wished them well. Ditch's boys looked surprisingly alert despite having been busy for several hours already. They'd been daubing slogans on walls across London, declaring that the Knights and the Magi had come to fight the Dark King, and that Londoners everywhere should prepare to stand and fight. When they were revealed by daylight the Magi would have either done what they set out to, or not. And if not, then a few slogans on the walls would be the least of their worries.

'Are you ready, Finmere? Christopher?'

Fin turned to see the Magi Queen standing just behind them.

'As ready as I can be, without really knowing what I'm ready for,' Fin answered. He meant it seriously, but Cardrew Cutler and Freddie Wise both snorted with laughter as they passed him to brief another group. The reversal of the Ageing had filled the Knights with energy and good humour, which Fin thought they might need before the day was out.

'They're not taking this very seriously,' he muttered. The Queen's eyebrow arched.

'Of course they are. Those who are bravest often laugh when faced with the gravest danger.' She paused. 'And they would rather die here as Knights than die dribbling in wheel-chairs in that overheated house.'

'Lucas Blake joked until the very end,' Christopher said softly. He stared ahead, lost in a moment that, for him, was so many years in the past. 'He died like a Knight. The Queen is right. Laughter can make you brave. We should all remem-ber that.' He looked at Fin. 'If you can't laugh in the face of danger, then what were all those films we watched as kids about? Indiana Jones?'

238

'You hate Indiana Jones,' Fin said, but he couldn't stop the smile growing on his face.

'True, but the rest of you loved him. I was more of a James Bond man.'

'They both got the girls.'

'Yes, they did.' Christopher cast a glance at Mona. 'Didn't always work out well for Bond, though.'

'Ditch's boys know how to access the tunnels.' Mona spoke as if she hadn't heard a word exchanged between the two boys. 'They'll act as runners letting those co-ordinating from here know what's going on out there.'

'They all loved him though,' Fin continued to Christopher. He wasn't sure exactly what they were talking about any more, but he didn't like seeing the pained expressions on both his friends' faces. Whatever the problem was between them, it was adult business, and as much as he might like to think he was one, he was still just sixteen. His friends had all gone and become old without him.

'Are you ready, Christopher?' the Queen asked, ignoring their conversation.

'I don't know why you need me,' he said. 'Surely I could be more use out on the streets than going to the Dome with you and Fin.'

'He's your father,' she answered. 'You know his weaknesses better than anyone.'

'That,' Christopher said, 'would imply that I know my father. And that would be a mistake.' Christopher suddenly seemed sixteen again. Perhaps some things never changed. Maybe he was lucky not to have proper parents. The sting in his gut told him his thought was a lie before it was even finished. He'd give anything to have been born normally and he'd wish that as long as he lived. He looked back at the gathered groups. Which, all things considered, might not be much longer.

*

239

It was still dark when Henry Wakley and the Magi reached West Minster, but the first streaks of dark blue were beginning to appear alongside the black crack in the sky. There had been a few mad out on the streets who had squealed and rushed towards Wakley and the men, but then veered away when the group came closer and the Magi become visible. They'd scuttled away in different directions as if the knights were suddenly forgotten. Henry had made the Magi cover all sides and after that they moved quickly. They saw no soldiers. Perhaps Arnold-Mather thought the mad were sufficient to patrol the city streets at night. Most nights he was probably right.

'What are they doing?'

The Knights had taken their places, as instructed by the Magi, at the borders of the land around West Minster, finding spots amongst the weeds that had broken the flagstones as they forced themselves up through the ground.

'I have no idea,' Henry said. 'Let them worry about that, and we'll keep our eyes open for anything coming the other way.' He turned his back on the cathedral and faced the gloomy city, stamping his feet a little to try and force some warmth into them. He would never get used to this cold.

'Sounds fine to me,' Elwood said. 'It's just good to be able to see again.'

'How long were you Aged?' Henry asked. He looked again at the man beside him. He looked older than Henry, maybe thirty or so, although the passing of years had come to mean very little while the world was frozen.

'1968. I was thirty-two. What does that make me? Seventy-six? Seventy-seven? Ageing or not I would have died of old age soon enough. But here I am, back in the Nowhere, just as I was on that last day.'

'Time can be a funny thing,' Henry said.

'Yes, it can.'

There was a lull in the conversation after that, and just as

Henry thought he should fill it a hot surge of air hit them from behind and both men stumbled forward.

'What the ... ?' He turned, automatically drawing his dull sword, and beside him Elwood's own shone brightly. The Knight might have been Aged a long time, but his reactions were good.

'Look at that,' Elwood breathed, perhaps more to himself than to Henry, who couldn't help but stare.

The building was repairing itself. There was no other way to put it. Stained glass refilled the windows, the heavy doors that hung from the broken hinges righted themselves. The walls sloughed off their cover of moss and ivy and the stones shone white beneath.

'Stand back,' Henry said. The earth beneath them rumbled with energy as it brought West Minster back to life and he was sure that whatever the Magi had done, it wouldn't stop with the building. He was right. The weeded forecourt rippled, starting at the doors and rushing outwards, and as the hump ran through the ground the slabs it left behind were whole and clean, the weeds sucked back into the earth below.

Henry and Elwood stood at the edge and watched until the ripple stopped. All around the building, the Knights and Jack Ditch's boys stared, wide-eyed at the transformation. What had been a wreck was now magnificent. The paving stones were inlaid with strange metals that, even in the gloom of the breaking dawn, glowed brightly, matching the shine which came from the building itself. Light shone through the stained glass making the patterns look like laser shows streaming from them.

Henry stepped forward, as did several others, just as the Magi appeared through the vast doors.

'Stop!' one shouted. 'The old traps are reactivated. We'll lead you in.' Henry signalled to the boys and men to hold their positions while he and the Magi planned where to place them most strategically. His wonder at what had just

241

happened would have to wait until later. Until *after*. If there was to be an after.

They didn't have to wait long for the soldiers to come, and from his place just beyond one of the repaired perimeter walls, Henry Wakley saw Edgar Blacken directing the fifteen men he'd brought with him. He'd expected more. How arrogant was Arnold-Mather? But then, how big would the glow from West Minster have been from the Dome, especially if he hadn't sensed all the fresh magic now loose in the city?

Behind him, the building glowed softly. It wasn't until the last of the soldiers had stepped through the gates and onto the courtyard that the first scream bit through the quiet. It wasn't alone for long. Heavy slabs flipped up as if they were made of polystyrene, and several men fell down onto the spikes that waited for them below. Henry glanced around to make sure his men were staying low as darts flew from the walls with pinpoint accuracy into the necks and eyes of those who were left standing. The only man left unscathed when the Knights and the boys re-emerged was Edgar Blacken, who was standing very still on one solid stone square, as those around him groaned and screamed. If there were men still alive in the pit below then they would die down there, and Henry found he was comfortable with that. The first fight of the battle was no place for mercy. Not if you wanted to win. He'd learned many things the hard way during his time in the Nowhere and, in some cases, he'd started to think like Benjamin.

'Your weapons, please.' He strode over to Blacken.

'What is this?' the burned man said, as he handed over his sword and dagger. 'What *is* this?'

Henry smiled as he saw the man's eyes widen when the Magi emerged from their building and stood in a line across its door. He nodded at the Knights who held up their golden swords, so different from his own dull one.

'You go back to your boss,' he said quietly. 'And you tell him to prepare. Because we're coming for him. And we won't stop until this is over. One way or another.'

'You're not going to kill me?'

'I'm not going to kill you *now*.'

Only after Blacken had stumbled away did the first of the curious Nowhere residents appear, drawn by the new life in the building their ancestors had so cruelly destroyed. They muttered and smiled and laughed and cried, and it warmed Henry's heart. He looked to his men and the Magi.

'Are you ready for our own parade?' He grinned, and for the first time since his brother had been captured it felt like a real smile.

THIRTY-SIX

The room visibly darkened as Justin Arnold-Mather stormed back and forth across it. One hand gripped the arm of a crimson leather chair as he passed, and it turned black in seconds.

'The Magi and the Knights?' he demanded for the third time since Edgar Blacken had returned. Not that he needed Blacken to confirm it again. Reports were already coming in of the procession through the streets rousing people from their houses and calling for them to join in the battle. From the window he could see a small crowd outside the Dome, those Londoners who had chosen his side and had come to join the fight. They looked weak though, and afraid, even from so great a distance. He could see it in their posture. They weren't on his side because they loved or supported him; they were here because they feared the repercussions if they fought him and lost.

Still, dread was a good motivator, and the Knights might find that most of the many residents would stay behind their locked doors rather than be seen to take a side.

'They're saying the Magi Queen is here,' Simeon Soames said. 'And the boy too, Finmere.'

'Has anyone seen them?'

Soames shrugged and Arnold-Mather suppressed the magic that tingled in his fingers with the urge to hurt him. There was something about the ex-Knight that was starting to grate on him. An unspoken disloyalty. This fondness he clearly had for the youngs. Right now, though, he was most irritated

244

by the look in Soames' eye that seemed to say, *why didn't you know? Why didn't you feel them arrive?* The questions worried him too. He *should* have felt it. He was linked to the stones and magic ran through his veins straight from the core of the universe, never mind the worlds. He and Joe felt every fluctuation in it, even more so since the crack in the sky had widened. So why hadn't he felt it now? What had changed? He didn't like it. Not at all.

'You make sure the Dome is secure.' He nodded at Soames. 'You,' he turned to Blacken, 'get the mad out on the streets.'

'The mad won't go near the Magi. They wouldn't even approach West Minster with us; wisely, as it turned out'

'But they will scare the population,' Arnold-Mather snarled. 'Just do it; don't question me. And get the army out of the garrisons. I want half sent here to fortify our stronghold. The rest should be on the streets with the mad, make a show of our strength.'

'Yes, my Lord.'

Neither man moved and his irritation boiled over. 'Well? What are you waiting for? Go!' They didn't need telling again. Only when he was alone did he slump back into his chair and let the trembling run through his limbs. At first he wasn't sure what it was, it had been so long since he'd felt it, but then when his mouth turned sour it became clear. He was afraid. He should have *known* that the Magi and the Knights were back. He should have felt it. He flexed his fingers. Red still glittered there, but there were fewer sparks. What was happening to his power? He could feel his link with the boy, just as he always had. Was it different for him too? Between them, had they drained the world of its energy? Was the crack about to open wide and pull them all in?

He gritted his teeth, loathing the lack of answers, and got to his feet. So, the Knights and the boy were coming for him, were they? Probably with his own traitorous son. Well, let them come. He was the Dark King and he would be ready for them.

'Albert,' Ida Harvey said as she peered through the small gap in the shutters. 'Albert! Come here. You'll never believe it.'

'Stay away from there.' Her husband shuffled out from the behind the bar that was rarely used, the Dark King had placed so many curfews on his subjects. The stools were still up on the tables, as they had been for days. As much as people needed a drink under this terrifying regime, no one wanted to be seen doing it publicly. Albert Harvey didn't blame them. 'We're supposed to keep our 'eads down, remember? Don't draw attention to ourselves? Can't 'ave them finding that mirror upstairs, can we?'

'Come and look,' Ida repeated, signalling him with one hand. 'I can't believe my eyes.' She threw him an exasperated glance. 'If you don't look, you'll miss it!'

Knowing when he was beaten, Albert joined her at the window. His eyes widened as he saw the line walking steadily and confidently in the middle of the road. Each of the pale-skinned and blind-eyed men carried a single brightly-coloured vial, creating a rainbow of colour between them.

'The Archivers? The Archivers are back?'

'It looks like it.' His wife smiled, her face full and happy for a moment, just like it used to be. Across the road Albert saw other people peering out from behind curtains and met their eyes. They hadn't spoken to the neighbours for a long time. People had slowly become more insular and no one wanted to risk a falling out that might lead to lethal payback at the hands of the mad. This time, however, the face in the window opposite smiled at him. He smiled back.

'Fetch me a knife, there's a love. One of the catering ones.'

Ida stared at him. 'What do you want a knife for?'

'I'm going out there. They're going to need an escort.' Ida looked at him silently for a long time and then nodded. There were some things worth risking your life for, as they had both learned a long time ago.

Out he went, into the cold air, the knife tucked in his belt. He fell into step a few feet away from one of the Archivers, glancing around for any of the mad or approaching soldiers. The street was silent, but seconds after he'd begun walking he heard another door close. He smiled at the man who came from the house opposite and fell into step on the other side of the Archivers. The man nodded back. Within ten minutes, they were ten men strong, with more joining them as they turned each corner.

For the first time in years, Albert Harvey felt proud to be a Nowhere man. And, more importantly, he felt hope burning in his chest.

'So, you want most of the men round at the back of the Dome?' The soldier's eyes narrowed. 'But that doesn't make sense.'

'We're getting reports that's the way they're going to attack.' Simeon Soames was impatient. His heart was racing and he had too much to get done in too short a space of time. 'If you want to question the King about his plans, then I can arrange that.'

'No, no.' The soldier shook his head. 'If that's what you think we should do, then that's what we'll do.'

'Good. So do it.'

From the corner of his eye, Soames could see Edgar Blacken walking towards them.

'Now,' he snapped, and the soldier scurried off. The last thing he needed was for Blacken to know where he'd sent the greater part of the army.

'The youngs have found something,' he said, as Blacken reached him.

'What?'

'You need to see it. I'm not sure what it is, but it's made

from that strange Magi metal.' He strode along the walkway, subtly forcing Blacken to walk with him. 'I've had them put it in one of the downstairs storerooms until we decide what to do with it.'

'We should show it to the boss,' Blacken said.

'I thought you should see it first. Then we can take it to him together.'

As they walked into the heat of the Dome, Simeon Soames undid his jacket. The dagger was hard against his back, tucked under his belt. His hands felt clammy. There was no going back if he went through with his plan.

'Down there.' He nodded Blacken along a quiet corridor. 'I didn't want anyone stumbling across it.' The central Dome of the Future Blocks was vast and filled with tiny rooms and annexes, many of which were empty, and the corridor Soames had chosen was rarely used. He pulled a key out of his pocket as they reached the shadowy far end.

'Is it a weapon of some kind?' Blacken asked, and for an awful moment, Soames thought he'd spotted the bulge in his back through his coat. 'Perhaps we can use it against the Magi, if it is,' Blacken finished.

'I have no idea what it is, Maybe.' The door swung open, and Blacken stepped inside. Soames followed him. 'It's under that blanket.' His mouth was dry but his palms were sweating. As Blacken leaned forward, Soames pulled the dagger free.

'But there's nothing—'

Soames moved fast before Blacken's confusion could turn to suspicion. He grabbed the man around the neck, straightened him up and thrust the dagger into his lower back, twisting it hard. He pulled it out and stabbed the man again, several times. He kept his mind on the lights in the valley while Blacken struggled against him and finally gasped his last breath. Soames stood back and let the body slump to the ground before hastily covering it with the blanket he'd placed there less than twenty minutes before. He looked down at where blood was already seeping through the material. Had Edgar Blacken been a friend? No, not really, but he had been a colleague of sorts, and despite its necessity, Soames felt sick at having killed him so brutally. More than that he was a traitor, again. He turned and left, locking the door behind him. It would be a long time before anyone thought to look in there for Edgar Blacken. Long enough for his purposes.

He moved fast as he headed up to the next level. Thankfully the news of the Magi and the Knights' arrival had most people rushing around, too concerned with their own orders to pay much attention to anyone else. There were only a few people who would think to question Simeon Soames anyway, and one of them was currently cooling in a store room. There was a guard outside the door, as he'd expected.

'I need to see the prisoner,' he said. 'And you need to report to your Lieutenant for your fighting orders.'

'But what about 'im? Shouldn't I guard 'im?'

'He won't need guarding once I've dealt with him.'

'Oh. Right. Do you want me to wait? Till it's done?'

'Just give me the keys and go,' Soames said. 'The day I need help dispatching one chained up man is the day I'll cut my own throat.'

'Fair point, sir.' The soldier handed over a loop of keys and hurried away.

Soames waited until he was gone before unlocking the door and going in. The youngs would be gathering at the side gate by the stables. He had ten minutes to get to them. Explanations would have to wait.

To give Benjamin Wakley his due he walked well, staying mainly upright and not hobbling too much as they passed through the laundry area. Soames grabbed a hat and coat for the Knight to cover his shaved head and bloody shirt, and they continued through the servants' quarters to the area that housed the horses and groomsmen. If anyone recognised

Wakley then they didn't show it, and Soames expected that most of those at work neither knew nor cared who he was. They lived a different life to the soldiers, rarely leaving the Future Blocks and staying out of the politics of the city.

'Where are we going?' Benjamin Wakley muttered as they headed for the stables.

'I'm getting you out of here. The Knights and the Magi are coming to fight.'

A few pairs of eyes peered over the top of a stall gate. The youngs were there already. Good.

'You changing sides again, Soames?'

The words stung. Even battered and bruised, Benjamin Wakley was more of a Knight that Simeon Soames had ever been.

'Something like that.' The stable gate swung open and the youngs flooded out, Number Two leading the horse. It was already saddled, just like he'd told them. They were good kids, or people, or whatever they were after all this time. He looked at their expectant faces turned towards him for answers. He would miss that. He would miss them. But maybe one day, if all went well, they'd see each other again.

'What are we doing?'

'Where are we going?'

'What do we need the horse for?'

'Isn't that …?'

The questions came in an excited babble and he held one hand up to hush them, the other keeping Benjamin Wakley on his feet.

'I'm taking you home.'

The questions stopped for a shocked second and then a second, higher-pitched wave hit him. *This was their home, what did he mean, they didn't understand …*

'There's no time for this. Trust me. If we stay here, they will kill me.'

The hushed silence was longer after that. A heavy silence,

one that carried dread and understanding in it. 'We're taking this man with us. He'll make sure you're safe.'

'Where will you be?' Number Four asked thoughtfully.

'Don't worry about me,' he said. 'I'll be fine.' He mounted his horse, and pulled the Knight up behind him. 'Now let's go.'

The soldiers had done as they'd been instructed and most were patrolling the rear of the Dome, well out of sight as Simeon Soames led the small group out across the marshes. If anyone thought his leaving with the youngs and a stranger was suspicious they wouldn't go to Arnold-Mather about it directly – they'd look for Edgar Blacken first, and they'd be looking for him for quite some time.

The air grew colder as they reached the end of the sturdy walkways that kept them safe from the shifting land, and the youngs huddled around the horse, doing a little to keep Benjamin Wakley warm. The youngs were hardy, he'd give them that. If there was a battle coming, then they had a good chance of surviving it. Especially with the Knights and their parents around them, and with their knowledge of the mad and the Dark King's troops, they would be well armed. He had to rely on that.

The marsh farmers' ramshackle houses hadn't changed at all, and although many of those who hadn't had children had moved into the city, the rest had remained in sight of the Dome. Arnold-Mather had long ceased to pay them any attention, and considered them no threat – which they weren't. They were broken people living for a glance from children who no longer remembered them. The houses weren't guarded and although the road to the Dome passed them by, the gates were half a kilometre away. Still, he was careful in his approach. If he was caught now, it would end badly for all of them.

'Come on,' he said, as the youngs straggled slightly behind, 'keep up.' He looked round. 'What's wrong with you?' They

251

stared at him, and then beyond him to the buildings whose the doors were opening as the marsh farmers crept cautiously outside. It was the closest they had been to their children in a long time. The women covered their mouths with their hands to hold back their sobs, and the men stood beside them, simply staring.

'Why can't we come with you?' Number Six said.

'Because I'm tired of your whys,' Soames said harshly, and watched the boy flinch. 'I'm tired of looking after you. I have things I want to do myself.'

The children, not the youngs to him anymore, but children, gazed at him dolefully.

'I don't believe you,' Number Four said. 'You love us.'

This time it was his turn to flinch.

'Mum?' It was Number Three who broke the spell. He'd moved forwards, away from the group, and he frowned and tilted his head as he stared at a thickset woman with deep auburn hair piled in an untidy bun on top of her head. She nodded vigorously and smiled through her tears.

'Samuel? My Sammy?' She gripped the arm of the man next to her. 'Tell me it's not a dream. Tell me it's my Sammy come home.'

Her husband was less convinced by Soames' sudden appearance and his dark eyes were full of questions. It was obvious where Number Three – Samuel – got all his whys from.

'He's home,' Simeon said. 'They're all home.' As Number Three and his mother embraced, the other women surged forward, scooping their shocked children into their arms and squeezing them until they couldn't breathe. The men stood by Simeon, who helped Benjamin Wakley dismount. 'Keep them hidden here for now. The Magi and the Knights are in the city. They're going to fight the Dark King. Fowkes will come here, I'm sure. When he gets here tell him that I've sent most of the soldiers around the back of the Dome, and Edgar Blacken won't be a problem. If you need to send messages

252

to anyone, then the children know their way around the soldiers' main routes. They can take unused back alleys. They won't get caught.'

He mounted his horse. He was glad the children were overwhelmed by the women and that he didn't have to say his goodbyes. That wouldn't be good for any of them. They had their families to get back to, and he had his own path to find.

'Good luck,' he said, before pulling his dull blade from his belt and handing it to Benjamin Wakley. 'It's a Knight's sword,' he said. 'And I'm no Knight.' Wakley nodded as he took it, and Soames' heart warmed to see a hint of respect there. Maybe there was hope for him after all.

As he rode away, he didn't look back. He skirted the Dome and took the long way to the Outlands, not wanting to be spotted by the guards he'd placed there. His hands were freezing on the reins by the time the lights in the valley came into view in the distance, and his face burned with the early signs of frostbite as the icy wind blasted across the open plains. But he knew he would make it. He knew there was a new life waiting for him in that unknown, distant city. And he would grasp it with both hands.

THIRTY-SEVEN

They didn't leave the Old Bailey House of Real Truths until everyone else had gone. Once the palace was secured the Knights would make it their base – it had been designed to be easily defended – but if they couldn't take it, then they would fall back here. Hopefully, that wouldn't happen.

After the crush of men who had filled it, Fin felt that the few of them left were standing on a ghost ship.

'Shall we get started now, then?' Fowkes asked. Fin wasn't the only one who felt uncomfortable there. For both of them, too much of their lives were wrapped up in the these bricks and mortar. 'They should all be in position.'

'Yes. It's time.' The Magi Queen drew herself up tall. 'Let us be ready.'

'Let us be ready,' Fin repeated, his voice small. He didn't feel very ready at all.

Outside the day was simply grey, all colour muted by the black ice below their feet and the gloomy sky above them. The Magi Queen stood between Fin and Fowkes, and Christopher and Mona stayed a step behind. Fin could see the Dome glowing red in the distance, like a beacon calling them to approach if they dared. He thought of Joe and Arnold-Mather waiting for them there. He felt the power throbbing in his veins, but he had no idea how he was supposed to use it.

'How will we fight him?' he asked.

'It's not about fighting him,' the Queen said. 'We need to

draw his magic from him. And we need to break the link.'

She spoke as if she was explaining clearly, but to Fin it was just more riddles. He sighed and his breath steamed in front of him. 'I'm not sure I quite understand.'

'Then let's hope that the magic understands for you.'

'Look,' Mona spoke behind them. 'Look! You can see West Minster from here. Look at it.'

The building far in the distance shone, its spires repaired and the strange metal plates that decorated the surface glittering despite the lack of sun.

'And look over there,' Fowkes said, as a small group of men and women appeared around the corner ahead. They were carrying assorted weapons, mainly knives and spears made from household objects.

'So, it's true,' one said. 'The Magi Queen is here. And the Knights of Nowhere.'

'It's true,' Fowkes answered.

'Go to the palace and the White Tower,' Christopher called to them. 'They will need you there.'

'And gather as many as you can,' Fin added. 'When the fighting's done there, join us at the Dome.'

The man grinned and nodded. 'You heard them!' he called to those with him. 'Let's get to the fight!'

'Aye!' They raised their weapons high, and turned.

Doors opened, just a crack at first, and then more and more people ventured out. Others ran back with stories of the Magi in the streets, of the mad avoiding them, and of the magical restoration of West Minster. Within ten minutes. They must have sent thirty men to join the fight, and there was a small crowd of women and children trailing behind them as they walked, smiling and laughing.

'Keep them back,' Fowkes said to Christopher. 'We don't want them getting hurt.'

'I've tried,' Mona said. 'They won't leave. They say they're guarding us.'

'They think we're some kind of saviours,' Fowkes muttered. 'I don't like it.'

'Maybe we are,' the Queen said. 'Have some faith.'

'The thing about being a saviour that's never appealed to me,' Fowkes said as he tried to shoo some of the curious children away, 'is that they have to die in order to save the world. It's in every film. Never mind religion.'

'I don't think you should worry.' The Queen smiled. 'It's the innocent who normally take that path. Those like you have to learn to live with their sins.'

Despite her good humour and Fowkes' wryness, their words chilled Fin. They both had a point. How was this going to end for any of them – especially him, Christopher and Joe? *When one plus one plus one is four.* They were part of the Prophecy. How much more could it ask from them?

By the time the messengers rode into the White Tower, Mitesh Savjani's feet were numb, and he was feeling vaguely queasy and despondent from the stench of the mist rolling off the river. He tried to stay focused. If Levi Dodge was feeling the same then he wasn't showing it. Not that he ever did. Over the years, Savjani had learned a lot from the quiet man who had rescued him from death. He was no longer just a fat clothcrafter who had once dreamed of being a Knight like his friends. He was a tactician now. The eye for detail he had brought to his work of old, Levi Dodge had taught him to apply to this guerrilla war they had been fighting for so long. He was patient. He planned. And he no longer wheezed if he ran up a flight of stairs. But, all the same, his feet shuffled slightly under him to try and keep them mobile whereas Levi Dodge remained perfectly still.

'Sometimes, my friend, I wonder if you are human at all,' he muttered.

'You wouldn't be the first,' Dodge replied. 'So perhaps you

all have a point.' He paused. 'But if you're asking if I'm cold, I'm bloody freezing.'

'Then you are forgiven for looking immune to it,' Savjani said, laughing a little. Levi Dodge was still restrained with the others, but his own good cheer had slowly worn the man down. Unlike many others, Savjani could forgive him for what he had once been. It had taken very little effort at all. When it came down to it, Dodge had left everything he knew behind and risked death at the hands of Ditch's boys, Tugg's men and the Wakley twins when he'd saved Savjani. He had renewed himself. That was good enough for Mitesh Savjani, and he had made it good enough for the rest. But Dodge did not have a friend among the others as he had in the clothcrafter. A strange pair they might seem, but friends they were. Firm friends.

He glanced at the men in the building opposite, some on the roof and some peering through the windows, ready to leap out when necessary. Somewhere inside, the owners were tied up in a cupboard. Savjani didn't feel any sympathy for them. They were lucky to be alive. Those who lived this close to the White Tower were all those who had grovelled to the Dark King the most. They ran the city for him and took their payment in privileges and fine possessions, most of which had once been stolen from others.

In the building he currently stood behind, the Knights had subdued the Mayor of the East and his fat wife. It hadn't taken much doing. Once the mad had been despatched by the Knights – deaths that he felt a great sadness over, for the mad were not themselves – the residents had been too soft to fight back. They hadn't been hardened the way Savjani had. They'd had no need to. But as the Knights had broken into their homes on the cusp of dawn, just as the city and the mad were at their calmest, it had been interesting to see those who had for so long taken pleasure from others' fears feeling some themselves.

From the top of the building across the street a light glinted three times, and Savjani held up his own pocket mirror to return the signal. Everyone was in place. There were men behind the Tower in the fields that hadn't been farmed for so very long, and there were more placed at the sides, ready to run out and cut off any soldiers who tried to get back inside the palace once they realised they were under attack.

Running footsteps from behind made him spin round, his sword drawn and his feet forgetting their numbness in that moment of need. His heart thumped. Could their own attack have been some kind of trap? A group of figures trotted towards them, the man in front signalling the rest to stick close to the walls.

'Who are they?' Dodge asked.

'Reinforcements.' Savjani smiled. 'The people are coming out to fight with us.'

One of the Knights crept over to them and they hunkered down in the shadows as he gave instructions. When the battle started any newcomers could be as loud as they liked, but for now they had to stay hidden and quiet.

At least there had been no sign of Edgar Blacken or Simeon Soames. As the Generals of the Dark King's army they did most of the thinking and watching. Had they been here, the new arrivals could well have been spotted and given the game away. As it was, from what he could make out, the guards on top of the White Tower were distracted by the cold and by whatever was going on within the grounds. Savjani hoped the bustle was the troops gathering, and preparing to take to the streets to track the Magi down.

Finally, the gates began to open.

'Let us be ready,' Savjani said quietly.

'Let us be ready,' Levi Dodge replied.

And the battle began.

*

It was an hour past dawn and the city was filled with life and sound as Fin continued his steady walk through London with the others. Cries and shouts rose up in the air as fights broke out in the streets and, over all of it, he could hear screams and the clash of weapons from the forces that were meeting at the palace and the White Tower. It sounded as if the whole city was at war, and maybe it was. The children and women who'd been following them had finally taken refuge in various buildings along the way, but many people still ran this way and that, pausing when coming face to face with each other, unsure which side they might be on. All the bustle was starting to make Fin dizzy.

Fowkes had turned to check the rear when the flash of dark hair dropping to the ground caught the corner of Fin's eye. One of the mad, red eyes wide and black tongue hanging out of its mouth while it hissed and snarled, leapt towards the Commander of the Knights. With no time to call out, Fin acted on instinct and grabbed its thin, pale arm to stop it reaching Fowkes.

The surge of power that poured out of him was immediate, his skin burning hot. He gasped, unable to let go, and the mad froze and whipped its head round to stare at him. Fin tried to speak, but couldn't. As soon as the magic had raced through his hand and into the creature he was gripping, something came back the other way. It was rancid and cold and felt like poison in his veins, a venomous spider bite full of anger and hate. His body shuddered and he felt it being absorbed into the well of power in the pit of his being, just as he finally broke away from the mad and doubled over, retching hard. He could still feel it inside him. Smaller, and tightly contained, but there. Dark magic. Black magic.

He coughed and spat out thick saliva, too little food in his stomach to let him vomit. The wave of nausea passed and he shivered and stood up. No one was looking at him. They were

259

all looking past him. 'Thanks for your concern, but I'm okay.'
He spat some more. 'I think.'

'You did that,' Mona breathed. 'You did that, Fin.'

'What?' His legs were still shaking slightly, and he turned
to see what the fuss was about. It was only then that he realised that the whole street had fallen silent. Where people had
been running, calling and shouting to each other, they now
stood still. And they were staring. He could see why.

The mad was no longer mad. A young woman, maybe
twenty years old, stood shivering in its place. She pulled her
ragged clothes around her body. Her eyes were blue and her
hair was blonde. She looked around her. 'What am I ... ? I was
going to pick up a new dress. For Alma's wedding. And then
... and then ...'

A middle aged woman hurried over, pulling off her thick
coat. 'Here, get that on you. Get yourself warm. Come on,
we'll get a nice cup of tea. Maybe with a shot of something
in it.' She darted a brisk look at a man a few feet away and
he joined them, putting his other arm around the girl. The
couple turned and stared at Fin for a moment over their
shoulders. He wasn't sure what he saw there: fear or hope.
Perhaps some of both. That's certainly what he was feeling.

'We can cure them,' he said. He looked at the Magi Queen.
'We can save the mad! Anaïs, all of them. Just by touching
them.'

'We need to drain the Dark King's power. We can't take all
of this,' she nodded in the direction of the disappearing girl,
'as well. There are too many.'

'But we have to. We have to help as many as we can. They
don't deserve this. Nobody does.'

'There will be a cost.'

'Then,' Fin drew himself up tall, 'we'll pay it.' He looked
at Fowkes. 'Won't we?' The Knight didn't look entirely convinced, but he nodded.

'Yes, Fin, we will. Prices need paying, that's for sure.'

Christopher and Mona both stared at him, and then looked at each other. It was the first time Fin had seen them do that since he'd returned this time. Whatever they had fallen out over, maybe it was passing. He hoped so.

'My father should pay the price for it really, shouldn't he? But somehow I doubt he will.' Christopher shrugged. 'Men like that never do.' He took Mona's hand and squeezed it tightly. She flinched, surprised for a moment, and then looked up at him. She still loved Christopher, Fin could see it.

'But Fin's right,' Christopher, the Seer, continued. 'We have to help them where we can. Whatever the cost.' He cast his eyes down, and Fin wondered exactly what his friend knew. He was the Seer after all, and although he drew his knowledge from the past, Ted was always going on about the past being the only way to predict the future. Could Christopher have seen even part of how this was going to turn out?

'Come on, then,' Christopher said, slapping Fin on the shoulder. 'Let's keep going. And save whoever you can.' Fin let the couple go ahead and then fell into step with the Queen and Fowkes. He watched Christopher's back. The way he held Mona's hand so tightly. Something was wrong. That slap had been over-enthusiastic. Too friendly. It filled Fin with an unhappy sense of unease.

Curran Tugg stood on the prow of his boat and watched as the Gypsy Trader vessel sank below the mist line and into the depths of the Times. Men called from the water, but he didn't pull them out. The eels would put them out of their misery soon enough, and his own Traders weren't faring well enough to start having mercy on the opposition. He felt as though they had been fighting for ever, rather than for an hour, or maybe two. His shoulders ached and sweat stuck his heavy clothes to his skin.

The boat rocked below him as they turned hard. 'That's it!' he called to Elbows. 'Get over to Nairn. He needs our help!'

The long years off the water had taken their toll on his men, who had forgotten the strange tug of the currents and how to navigate the mist by the varying hues of light and dark that tinted it. They were holding their own, just, but they were out of practice and, more than that, they'd never been fighting men. Not beyond an honest pub brawl. It didn't come naturally to them, even after all this time skulking around the streets of the city. This was a battle, not a raid, and Curran Tugg wished he had one of the Wakley twins with him to make any sudden decisions. They were soldiers at heart. They had the instinct. Curran Tugg was just a river man.

He peered into the mist around him, listening to the shouts and cries as men leapt from one boat to another in the attack. Thus far, he could see no flares from those boats holding position in front of the entrances to the underground rivers, and that was a relief. On each of those boats, one man's sole charge was to send up a flare if it looked as if they were about to be boarded. The defensive line in front of them, the line which Tugg was part of, must be keeping the Gypsy Traders out. For now. That was all they had to do – contain the Gypsy Traders on the river until whatever had to be done, was done. They would not reach the lost rivers and the network of entrances that were all over town. They would not be able to join that battle on the land. Curran Tugg would make sure of that. It was the one task he and his men had been given, and he would not disappoint the people relying on him.

'Whose river is this, men?' He raised his hailer and boomed the words into the fight.

'Ours!' The replies came from all around him, some louder than others, and some with a grunt as they fought, but strong all the same.

'Who owns this river?' He felt his own spirits rising again. He and his men, out on the river they loved, where they would protect the city they loved.

'The goddamned Traders!'

'Then own it!' His boat came alongside Nairn's which was half boarded by a sleek Gypsy vessel on the other side. Men fought, some with knives but most with their bare fists, the way they did best. Curran Tugg grinned and leapt aboard. Francois Manot would not have the river for much longer. Not if he could help it.

THIRTY-EIGHT

'The White Tower?' Cardrew Cutler asked. He might have been younger than he'd been in a long time, but to Freddie Wise his friend was the most tired he'd seen him in at least a decade. But then Freddie wasn't looking so great himself. He'd caught a glimpse of his reflection, and like Cardrew, he had splatters of blood all over him – thankfully none of their own – and his clothes were rumpled and ripped from all the fighting.

'Secure. For now, anyway.'

'Good. Where are Dodge and Savjani?'

'Co-ordinating the spread of men through the city. There are still some residents loyal to the King who are putting up some resistance.'

'They've got more energy than I have,' Cutler said, rubbing his face. 'My shoulders are killing me. I never thought of my sword as heavy until today.'

'You've done well,' Freddie said. He looked through the window at the barricades going up around the palace: Knights, Magi and ordinary people all working together. He almost smiled at the sight of Alex Currie-Clark's thick red hair as he co-ordinated the teams, but above them all the tear in the sky still yawned ominously. There was no time for celebrations yet.

'They're still fighting on the river,' Cutler said. 'But the Lost Rivers are safe. I've put some men inside the entrances, just in case. I think we can spare them, now that we've been joined by so many volunteers.' He got up wearily.

'Where are the mad?' he asked, frowning. 'Surely they should be attacking us too?'

'They pulled back. About an hour ago. They stopped attacking all across the city and headed back to the Dome.'

'What do you make of it?'

'I'm not sure. It's good for us, but maybe not so good for the others.' He turned away from the view. His eyes kept being drawn up to the scar of fate hanging over all their heads, and to the red glow of the Dome in the distance. 'We'll know one way or the other soon enough.' The Ageing might have left his body, but Freddie was feeling his years in every inch of his soul. 'We may have won our battles, but this war is out of our hands.'

Fin had been aware of the mad following them for most of the walk, but as they grew closer to the Dome their numbers seemed to have swelled. Every time he turned his head he caught a glimpse of black hair or red eyes peering around a corner or down from a roof before ducking out of sight. It wasn't aggression – it was curiosity, as if what he and the Magi Queen had done to the few that had come close enough to touch had sent echoes through all of them.

'Why don't they come closer?' As they moved from the edge of the city and towards the rambling ramshackle village that made up the marsh farmers' homes, the ice had softened beneath their feet to a muddy slush. It was still cold, but the freezing edge had gone from the air and they could move more quickly.

'Who knows?' Fowkes said. 'Maybe they're nervous. At least they're not attacking us. Let's hope it stays that way.'

Up ahead, a curtain was pulled back and a face peered out. A moment later the door opened, and several figures came out to greet them.

'Is that ... ?' Christopher started, before a joyful smile filled his face. 'It is! It's Benjamin Wakley!' He and Mona ran the short gap between them and embraced the Knight, who just about managed to stay on his feet.

'But how did you get out?' Mona asked. Fin and Fowkes hung back, both knowing that although they were part of the Knights, they were not part of this reunion. This was a different bond, a different life that had been shared; one that they couldn't possibly understand.

'Simeon Soames,' Benjamin said, and looked at Fowkes. 'He got me out. He said you would come here, and to tell you he sent most of the soldiers round to the back and that Edgar Blacken won't be a problem.' A few children had appeared and were loitering in doorways, hanging back slightly.

'What are they doing?' a girl of about eight said, and she pulled a small dagger from the back of her belt. She was staring at the crowd of the mad who scuttled here and there but remained fifty feet or so behind.

'Nothing,' Mona said. 'They're not doing any harm.'

The girl looked at her as if she was crazy. 'They're the mad.'

'They can be cured. Put your knife away.'

'Where's Soames now?' Fowkes asked. 'Back inside?'

'I don't know,' Benjamin answered. 'He got on his horse and left.'

'The city in the valley,' the little girl said. She looked sad, even as her mother came and wrapped an arm around her. 'He's gone to the lights. Maybe one day I'll go there too.'

'We need to get moving.' Fowkes looked along the road to the gates. 'We need to get inside. You sure you're up to this?'

Benjamin nodded. 'Definitely. There are some faces in there I'd like to see while I have a sword in my hand.'

'Be wary of your anger,' the Queen said. 'It'll feed his dark magic. You have to rise above it. Be a Knight.'

'She has a point,' Christopher said. 'Easy as that is for me to say.'

'We're coming too.'

266

Fin had completely forgotten about the children who had now gathered in a line beside Fowkes.

'No, you can't.' One woman rushed forward and grabbed at her child. 'You've just come back, you've just—'

'We know our way around the Dome,' the little girl said. 'You don't. You'll need us in there.'

'It'll make you look much less suspicious if the soldiers see you coming in with us,' another added. 'We go in and out all the time with Simeon.'

Fowkes stared at them. 'Stay close, then. And do exactly as you're told.'

And so the weeping marsh farmers once again watched their children march towards the Dome, surrounded by an escort of the mad.

There were barely forty men guarding the front gates of the Future Blocks when they arrived. The mad had pulled closer around the small group and although they still made Fin nervous, between them and the children, the soldiers didn't realise that they were face to face with the enemy until the gates were half-open. As Fowkes and Benjamin Wakley took on the strongest of them, Mona and Christopher pushed the doors fully open and Fin grabbed two of the mad. Once again the sensation turned from powerful heat to sickly cold as he drew the bad magic out of the creatures. This time, however, he was ready for it.

As the two middle-aged men stared at each other, and then at him, Fin knew he'd done enough. The mad surged forward, attacking the surprised soldiers, some leaping onto the backs of the men and slitting their throats with wild gestures. They hissed and snarled as the men tried, in vain, to get away.

'They've changed sides!' Mona said. 'They've changed sides!'

'Let's get inside.' Fowkes was already jogging along the damp walkway leading to the vast central dome ahead.

'Quickly! Before they change their minds.'

Fin and the others followed him, their pace swift and swords drawn. It was an unnecessary concern though. Fin had known it since the transfer of energy. He'd felt the mad and they'd felt him. They'd *remembered*. And they wanted to be themselves again. Those that survived, he promised silently, would. Anaïs and her ice-white hair was among them some-where. She had to be. She had to survive so he could find her.

Within the Dome it was warm and the walls thrummed with energy. Fin waited for it to resonate with the power in-side him, but this was different. He could feel the dark magic made by Joe, Arnold-Mather and the stones, but the power that drove the building was more natural. Something from within the rocks and metals far below. He wondered if the swords and the Times barrier drew on that same power. It was reassuring. At least the building itself couldn't work against them.

'This way,' a boy of about ten said. 'The next floor up. That's where *he* normally is.'

'Take our stairs,' a little girl added. 'There'll be fewer people there than in the lifts and on the main ones.'

They jogged down a long corridor, scarcely passing a soul along the way. Where was everyone? From outside came the screams of those being massacred by the mad, and when Fin glanced out he could see that some of the creatures were now headed to the other blocks around the Dome, filled with ordinary people and families who worked for the King as servants and cooks and stable boys. They ran from the build-ings, weaving this way and that. Fin froze for a second, before he noticed that the mad might be terrifying the men, women and children who fled, but they weren't attacking them. Only the soldiers. They were almost herding people onto the paths leading out of the marshes and back to the city.

'Come on, Fin.' Christopher was halfway up the first flight of stairs. 'Something's changing. I can feel it.'

Fin turned away from the window and picked up his pace. Christopher was right. It felt as if all the air in the world had been compressed into a tiny box and they were trapped inside. Was it the rip in the sky? Was it the pressure finally too much? Or had Arnold-Mather realised how close he was to losing everything and decided to destroy them all rather than give it up? Was he that crazy? Or did he not even realise he was doing it?

They found the throne room. It was filled with awful dark furniture and heavy fabrics scented with something that made Fin feel slightly sick, but there was no sign of Arnold-Mather.

'Shit.' Fowkes kicked at the earth. 'Where the hell is he?'

'He'll be where Joe is.' Fin looked up. 'With Joe and the stones.'

'*The stones ...*' The desperate, thin voice that echoed his words came from a dark corner of the room. '*I want to touch the stones ... just one of them ...*'

Benjamin Wakley pulled the heavy velvet throw down to reveal the metal cage. George Porter sat inside, curled up in a corner. When he saw them he gripped the bars, the black half-moons in his nails a stark contrast to the paleness of the rest of his skin. He was the same pallor as Benjamin, the unhealthy hue of someone who hasn't seen fresh air in too long.

'Where are they?' the Magi Queen asked.

'Tell us and we might let you touch one,' Mona added.

'We might let you *keep* one.'

Porter's eyes widened and he pressed his face into the bars. He stank of sickness, and it took all of Fin's effort not to step away in disgust. Porter probably wouldn't have noticed.

'I just want to ... It's been such a long time ...' As he spoke, his tongue started to grow, stretching out over the edge of his mouth and curling around one of the bars.

'He's changing,' Christopher said. 'We have to be quick.'

'Where are the stones? We will take you to them.' The

269

Queen's voice was like honey. 'But if you don't tell us, we can't help you.'

Porter was dribbling. Whatever sanity he might have had was gone. Fin looked over at Christopher and saw the same mix of pity and guilt on his face that Fin was feeling. They'd done this to Porter when they pushed him down Clerke's Well. He had been a bad Knight and, yes, he'd been about to attack Fowkes, but he hadn't deserved this.

'Maybe we can cure him, like we do the mad.' He was about to reach between the bars when the Magi Queen stopped him.

'We can't help him. He's the source. He's ill, not mad.'

'We can't leave him here,' Benjamin Wakley said. 'If he falls into the wrong hands ...'

'Maybe we should kill him.' Fowkes stared at the thing in the cage whose desperation for the stones was changing him into something not quite human, not quite mad. 'It might be a mercy.'

'No more killing,' Christopher said. 'One day there might be a way to help him.'

Fin looked at Porter. The man in the cage had sunk to his haunches, and his growing tongue unfurled between the bars. *'Blood,'* he hissed, his voice losing its human quality and becoming something other, *'I smell blood ...'* An echo of a memory rang in the back of Fin's head.

'I've seen him before,' he whispered.

'Yes, we pushed him down a well,' Mona said. 'Even I remember that, and it was a lot longer ago for me than it was for you.'

'No.' Fin was still staring at the tongue. 'I saw him like this. I heard him.' He looked up at Christopher. 'He was in the mirror prison. He was there when I went looking for Tova.'

'But that can't be ...' Benjamin Wakley said. 'He wasn't here then.'

'Time's a funny thing,' Fowkes said. 'And I imagine it's even stranger in that place.' He looked thoughtfully at the ex-Knight. 'That's where we'll put him then. In the mirror.'

'But where is it?' Christopher asked. 'My father has been hunting for it for years.'

'In The Red Lion.' Fowkes smiled. 'Disguised as a bedroom mirror in Ida and Albert's spare room.' He covered the cage again, ignoring the yowl from within. 'Always hide things in plain sight, boys. That's your lesson for today.'

On the other side of the room, something wooden creaked and the group turned as one to see the door of a heavy cupboard swing open and a thin figure scramble out. If he'd been trying to do it quietly, then he'd failed miserably.

'Jarvis!' Fin said. The old Orrery House butler, the traitor that had been in their midst for so long, paused and stared at them in horror before trying to make a run for the door. Fowkes cut him off easily.

'Well, well, well,' he said, holding his sword to Jarvis' throat as Benjamin Wakley grabbed his arms. 'Look who's here.'

'I haven't done anything.' Jarvis licked his lips nervously. 'I had no choice. It was all Arnold-Mather and Golden. They made me.'

'Stop snivelling and tell us where he is now. Where does he keep the boy and the stones?'

'I don't ... I don't—'

'If you don't know then there's no point keeping you alive.' Wakley tightened his grip making Jarvis flinch. 'And this really is no time to find yourself capable of loyalty.'

'Downstairs.' Jarvis slumped against the Knight. 'I can show you where.'

'Come on then.'

'So,' Christopher said. 'Downstairs.' His face had paled a little, and Fin wondered how his friend was feeling. They had become the Dark King and the Seer, but before that they were just Justin and Christopher Arnold-Mather; father and son. Now they were going to face each other, directly, as enemies. When they'd been at school Fin had so often envied

271

Christopher his home life. He now realised how misguided such jealousy had been. He only had his own life, strange as that had been, and he couldn't see the troubles in another, so why wish for someone else's lot? He left the Queen's side and went to stand with Christopher and Mona. They had started this adventure together and they would end it together. There was just one of them missing.

'Let's go and find Joe,' he said quietly, and then, with Mona in the middle, the three held hands and started to walk.

THIRTY-NINE

It was only when they'd followed their reluctant guide right into the bowels of the Dome that the Magi Queen showed the first signs of being affected by the stones and the excess magic. Sweat appeared on her otherwise impassive face, and she frowned slightly as she tried to keep her balance.

'It's just here,' Jarvis said, scurrying forward. 'There's no proper door. But you'll see. It opens.' Now that he'd betrayed his master he was giving it his all, as turncoats tended to do.

The building trembled slightly and the Queen leaned against the wall.

'Are you okay?' Fin asked. The question was redundant. She clearly wasn't okay.

'I can't go in there.' Her voice was weak, not much more than a whisper. 'There's too much energy. We'll tear the building apart. If not the entire city.'

'I don't understand ...'

'It's the stones. I didn't think ... the stones and the Magi Queen in one place. There will be too many pulls on the power. The stones might break further and then who knows what could happen.' She gripped Fin's hand in her icy, sweating palm. 'I will go and see to the mad. Cure them. I can do that.' She nodded at Jarvis and Benjamin Wakley. 'They can come with me. This is no battle for soldiers.' She pulled Fin closer. 'Only you can win this. You and your friends. But remember,' and she glanced towards Christopher, 'you must draw him out. Don't attack him. It's the only way.'

'Draw him out,' Fin repeated and she nodded, a small smile returning to her face.

'I have faith in you, Finmere Tingewick Smith.' Benjamin Wakley reached for her arm to support her. 'We all do.'

Somehow Fin found that thought made him even more nervous. But he returned her smile and he, Mona, Christopher and Fowkes watched her leave before turning back to the wall, where somewhere a door would open if they stepped any closer.

'Let us be ready,' Fowkes muttered.

'Let us be ready,' the teenagers responded. They stepped forwards united and the wall slid away.

After the first wave of heat, it was the noise that made Fin recoil. The air was filled with a loud crackling, as though hundreds of bangers were being thrown to the ground. The stones, in the middle of the circular room, were covered in a glittering white electricity that chased itself over their surfaces. On the other side of them, Joe lay in a narrow single bed, flat on his back, his eyes open but staring at the ceiling. Beside him, Justin Arnold-Mather, wearing a heavy fur coat which, combined with the heat in the room, would probably have made an ordinary person faint, was holding Mrs Manning tightly by the throat.

He hadn't seen the small group who had crept inside, and her pleading eyes darted towards Fin. Fowkes carefully drew his sword but stayed back. Fin left his tucked into his belt. The Magi Queen had been right. However this was going to be won, it wouldn't be with violence.

'Stop whatever it is you're doing or I'll kill her!' Arnold-Mather screeched over the crackling that battered their eardrums. 'You know I will! I'll peel her skin from her body!'

Joe didn't move, and Arnold-Mather's fingers sparkled red as he tightened his grip on Mrs Manning's throat, her mouth coming open and her tongue sticking out as she tried to breathe.

'Always such a big man,' Christopher said, stepping forward. Fin moved alongside him. 'Is that why Mum was always drunk by four? Having to put up with your bullying?'

Arnold-Mather spun round, surprised. It was obvious no one had spoken to him like this in years and the challenge surprised him. His mouth turned up in a sneer, revealing rows of glittering black teeth. 'Ah, the prodigal son returns.' He stepped forward, throwing Mrs Manning into the wall as he did. 'And you've brought your little friend too. How sweet.'

Mona ran around the stones to Joe, perching on the edge of the bed and taking his hand, while Fowkes scooped Mrs Manning up and half-carried her to the door. Arnold-Mather didn't look at them. His focus was entirely on the two boys. Fin barely recognised him. His eyes were narrow and tinged with insanity and his wickedness showed in the crooked curves of his spine that twisted his overweight body. He had become a monster in more ways than one.

Fin and Christopher took another step towards the stones, small and careful, keeping their eyes fixed on the Dark King. 'You weren't even that good a politician in the Somewhere,' Christopher continued. 'You must have seen what they said about you? Even I had. It was always in the papers. The "almost man" who so nearly had what it took ... but just didn't.' Christopher smiled. 'Bit like this really.'

'I would have shared it all with you.' Arnold-Mather mimicked their movements and came closer, now arm's length from the boys with the crackling stones between them. 'But you always were such an ungrateful little Mummy's boy.'

'Of course I was. She had all the balls in the family. She could have made it all the way – that's what your cronies used to say behind your back. She had all the brains. Almost man? I think they were being kind, don't you?'

Fin watched the heat building between the two. Draw him

275

out. That's exactly what they were doing. Arnold-Mather had barely noticed Fin was there. This was their moment. Fin delved inside himself for the energy he'd brought back from his own London. He looked from the large central stone to the smaller pieces. A piece of home. He silently willed it to recognise the magic he carried. He'd need all the help he could get.

'No one respects you,' Christopher continued. 'They might be afraid of you, but they'll never respect you.' He smiled. 'They respect me though. They admire *me*. They see everything that you don't have. You're a mockery of a king. Pathetic. Just couldn't do it quite right, could you? Like everything else.'

Arnold-Mather snapped as every father-and-son argument they'd ever had rose to the surface. A howl of rage built, coming slowly at first, but getting louder and finally he raised his hands, red sparks flying angrily from his fingertips.

'Now,' Christopher said, stepping aside and letting Fin take his place. Fin didn't hesitate. He knew exactly what he had to do. He reached out, grabbed Arnold-Mather's hands, and pulled them right over the electricity from the pale rocks between them. Whatever the King had been about to launch at his son, Fin pulled it from him, the dark magic flowing from the King's hands into his own. Fin gasped at the first rush of it but he didn't let go. He wouldn't let go. He would draw him out. He would draw it all out, until there was nothing left. He gritted his teeth. And it came ...

Joe's head burned in agony. It was so endlessly painful; preventing Arnold-Mather from accessing all of the magic, from holding the stories and from the crack in the universe that grew stronger and more insistent with every endless day. He wanted to shut down, to drift, to ignore it all. He wanted to forget who he was, if he was still anyone at all. His mother had been there, Arnold-Mather had been threatening her – he was aware of that – but then there had been nothing until he felt the cool hand grip his. It eased the pain. He hadn't felt anything like that, not in a long time, not since ...

He turned his heavy head and smiled at Mona. It was all so very clear to him now. Everything was as it should be, as it was always going to be. Behind her he could see Christopher and Fin, Fin's knuckles white as he held the Dark King's hands, both of their mouths open as the magic battled inside them. Maybe they were screaming. Joe wasn't sure. It was hard to hear anything beyond the constant noise in his head these days, the stones throbbing so loudly with his heartbeat. But from Christopher's expression, he thought they were.

He squeezed Mona's hand. He had to concentrate on her. Her hair started to lift slightly as a wind picked up in the room. He ignored it. He had his own important job to do. He and fate had been waiting for this.

'I have to put them somewhere safe,' he said. He barely recognised his own voice, it had been so long since he'd heard it. Was he really so young as he sounded? Still with that London accent? Tears pricked at his eyes.

'Don't try to speak.' Mona leaned in and stroked his head with her free hand. It felt good. It felt right. He held her hand tighter.

'I'm sorry,' he said.

Fin could barely breathe. His throat ached from screaming but it was all he could do to vent some of the pressure building inside him. His body trembled to his very core as he pulled more and more of the blackness inside him, and yet there was always more to come. Wind whipped at his face and, although his hand refused to let go – he would never let go, whatever the cost – he tore his gaze away from the blazing coals of Arnold-Mather's eyes as coloured lights caught the corner of his vision.

Joe. Mona. Five bright strands circled both of them, locking them together in their own private hurricane of colour, far more beautiful and full of wonder than that within which he and Arnold-Mather

277

stood. Red, green, blue, black and white. The stories leaving out of Joe and entering Mona. Why? Why was he doing that?

Fin screamed louder as the black energy suddenly flooded towards him, Arnold-Mather stumbling a little on the other side. The man's eyes widened and he tried to yank his hands away, but Fin wouldn't let go. He was choking on the darkness, on the distorted magic. It was overwhelming him, but he wouldn't let go. Joe was no longer the Storyholder. The connection between him, Arnold-Mather and the stones was no longer powerful. Beside him, Christopher was trying to fight past the ever-rising wind to reach to Joe and Mona on the small bed. He was shouting, yelling something, but Fin was past hearing it. He was past hearing anything. Bright spots formed at the corners of his eyes and he knew he was going to pass out. Pass out or die.

Just as he fell to his knees, dragging Arnold-Mather forward before his grip finally broke, a surge of power hit him from the other side of the room. He lay on the cool floor and tried to focus as his insides fractured and splintered beyond any repair. The world had fallen into silence. The stones no longer crackled. All he could hear, as the first wave of excruciating nausea hit him, was Christopher screaming, 'Where is she? Where is she?'

Mona was gone.

'Fin? Fin?' Fowkes grabbed him and, with Mrs Manning's help, pulled him into a sitting position. 'Talk to me, Fin.'

He opened his mouth and tried to say something, but he had nothing to say. Aside from that his tongue felt as if it was burning. Burning and melting and destroying itself.

'What's happening to him?' Fowkes shouted the question, and Fin's head lolled to one side as he tried to look around. A figure sat sobbing on the floor, and for a moment, through his blurring vision, Fin didn't recognise him. The Dark King had gone. That was simply Justin Arnold-Mather, Christopher's dad. Hopeless and pathetic.

'What did he do to me?' the man whined. 'What did he

do to me?' His teeth were no longer black, and the hump was gone. He was ordinary again.

'What did you do to him?' Fowkes shouted, pulling his sword. Fin raised his arm weakly and pulled the Knight's hand down. Unable to speak, he just shook his head. He knew what was happening. The magic was too much. One person was never meant to hold so much, and it was destroying him, burning him up in an effort to sustain itself. The dark and light magic were still fighting each other, but he had become the battleground and he would be destroyed before the balance could return. Dying. He was dying.

'No, no, no.' Christopher's face loomed over him. 'No, this isn't right. Fight it, Fin.'

He tried to smile, but thought he perhaps only managed some half-hearted lop-sided affair. It would have to do. It would have to be enough to show them he was okay with this.

'It's still there,' Joe said. 'The crack in the sky. It's still there. I can feel it. It was too strong.'

In the moment of silence that followed, Fin's heart broke. So it was all for nothing. All their struggles and sacrifices. He'd tried. They'd have to remember that, however long they had left. He'd tried his best. He closed his eyes and was surprised to find he wasn't afraid. What would be would be.

What will be, will be.

Fin barely heard the words before the heat that tore at him abated, coolness rushing back through his veins. His insides knitted back together as the dark magic fled from his body, pulled away into something new – someone new. *No,* Fin wanted to scream. *Not Arnold-Mather, not Joe. No, I won't give it back, I won't ...* His eyes flew open.

It wasn't Arnold-Mather. Or Joe. There was another figure in the room. A young man, wearing a Knight's trousers and shirt, was on his knees, coughing. He looked up. He tried to smile at Fin and then grimaced as pain wracked his body.

'Baxter?' Fowkes said. His face had paled, his eyes were wide. Fin watched as the Commander of the Knights moved slowly towards his long-dead friend. It was Baxter. Fin knew it. He could feel the clean spaces inside him, still gurgling with Somewhere magic, where Baxter had been. His core.

'The one and only,' Baxter said. 'Not back for long, though, I think.' He smiled again, as Fowkes knelt beside him, his own face twisted in remorse and sadness.

'I'm so sorry,' he whispered. 'I'm so, so sorry. I ...'

'It doesn't matter.' Baxter gripped his arm. 'It really doesn't. I'd do it again. And again.' He clenched his teeth as the dark magic relentlessly destroyed him. 'You're my best friend, Fowkesy. Always were, always will be. No regrets. No remorse.'

The two men were locked in a moment of their own history, a time before Fin and Christopher and Joe were even born. Time could be a funny thing, Fin thought, watching them, fascinated. A tragic thing. A strange thing.

'I wasn't good enough,' Fowkes said. 'You should have let them come upstairs.'

'You wouldn't have done the other way round.' Baxter slumped a little. 'And don't tell me you would, because you're a crap liar.' He smiled again, tired and wan. 'We had some adventures, though, didn't we?' His blue eyes sparkled with good humour, and dimples dented his cheeks under his short, spiked hair. He didn't look so very much older than Fin.

'Yes, we did. We had the best,' Fowkes said, his voice choking as he tried to smile back.

'We *were* the best,' Baxter said. 'We rocked.' He slid backwards, and Fowkes sat behind him, holding him against his chest, both staring outwards. 'We *lived*.'

Fin stared at them both; Fowkes so worn and world-weary, Baxter so young, and wondered if they'd still have chosen to become Knights, all those years ago, if they'd known it would come to this.

'Of course we would, Fin.' Baxter smiled at him, reading his expression – or his mind. 'Life is nothing without adventures. Challenges. Friendship. I would do it all again in a heartbeat. It was all so bright. So brilliant.' For the first time, the young Knight looked sad, aware how little time he had left, and how much living he could have done.

'You can hear my thoughts?' Fin asked.

'I'm you, you're me. We're different but the same.' His voice was getting weaker. 'Like brothers, maybe. Who knows? You know as much about it as I do. But look! You're still here – even without me inside you. I could have told you that you were worrying over nothing. You're Fin, and you always were.'

'I wish … I wish …' Fin didn't know what he wished. He wished Fowkes wasn't crying, he wished Baxter could get rid of the magic and live all the years he missed out on, he wished Tova were still alive, and he wished they could all laugh again.

'There will be laughter again, you know,' Baxter said. 'Tell him, Fowkes. There's always laughter. And smiles. Comes with the adventures and with the stories of the adventures. The memories of them. Make sure you grab yours, Finmere. Grab them well. Just like me and Fowkes did.'

The Commander of the Knights squeezed his friend harder. Baxter's breathing was laboured, and he jerked and twitched as the last moments came. He lifted one hand and weakly gripped Fowkes' arm.

'Goodbye, old friend. If you can do one thing for me,' he wheezed and gave one last smile, 'cheer the fuck up a bit, you miserable bastard.'

Fowkes hiccoughed a laugh through his tears, and, in that moment, Baxter was gone.

FORTY

The Magi Queen could barely stand as Benjamin Wakley helped her to the river's edge. His feet slipped on the rocks and sludge, and the mist curled in tendrils around his legs as he struggled to keep them both upright. If they fell he wasn't sure he'd have the strength to get them back to their feet again. He was weak from captivity and so far it had been a long day; adrenaline could only keep him going for so long. Especially here, by the water's edge.

He fought the dark revulsion that filled his head as he breathed in its rotten scent. He'd faced worse. All those years locked away and tortured. He could cope with a few minutes of mist. Still, he could feel it working its way inside him, making him relive his despair. He gritted his teeth. He had never broken before. He wouldn't now, when he was finally free. Instead, he focused on what she'd just done. What he'd seen her do.

With the soldiers gone the mad had flocked to her, coming so close that Wakley thought at first she might be crushed. He'd kept Jarvis close, which wasn't hard given how afraid he was of the mad, and the three of them had stood at the centre of the small circle until the Magi Queen held her hands out and the first of them had been touched. After that, it was endless. One by one, they'd crept a step forward and let her touch them, lifting their madness until they were just a throng of confused people, wondering where they were and how they'd come to be there, and she was on the verge of collapse. The strain had started to show after the first wave but she'd continued regardless, until she was pale and exhausted and each of those who had gathered was cured. She had fallen into his arms then, and as he left Jarvis under the guard of those who owed the Magi Queen their lives, she had whispered two words: 'The river.'

So, here they were. Ankle deep in sludge, with a foul mist trying to pull him down into sobbing suicide. Somewhere out there on the water Curran Tugg was battling Francois Manot, and beyond that lay the protected South, the Queen's homeland. It was hard to imagine anything existed beyond the bank of mist.

'I need to kneel,' the Queen whispered, from where her head rested on his chest. 'And then when I'm done, we'll need to move back out of the river quickly. For both our sakes. Can you do that?'

'Yes,' he answered. He could find any amount of energy if it meant getting away from the water. He lowered her down, her white dress soaking as she knelt on the sharp shingle. Unable to bear being any closer to the mist, he didn't crouch beside her but stood instead. He watched as she looked out at the river and beyond for a moment. A single tear ran down her pale face.

'Forgive me,' she whispered, before closing her eyes and dipping her fingers into the water.

Curran Tugg and Francois Manot were wrestling on the deck of Tugg's boat when they felt the water begin to roil beneath them. Tugg's arms ached from holding Manot's knife back, hovering precariously close to his throat, and as the water shifted beneath them, so did the balance between them. Tugg took his opportunity and rolled on top of the Gypsy Trader, pinning him down.

From somewhere on the river behind them, bloodcurdling screams cut through the mist and sounds of battle alike. Both

Trader leaders froze. That wasn't the sound of men fighting. That was the sound of something other, something terrible.

'What is that?' he asked. The screams were spreading. They might have started at the boats guarding the lost rivers, but they were getting closer.

'*Oh, my eyes! Get my eyes out, get my eyes out!*'

'*Make it stop, make it stop.*'

'*I can't ... I can't take it ...*'

'I don't know.' Manot had stopped struggling, and for the first time in the years since the Rage the two Traders looked at each other like sane men. River men. Men who shared an understanding of things that most others didn't. 'Something's wrong with the water. With the mist. There's something in it. Something stronger.'

Curran Tugg lowered his knife and held his hand out to Manot, pulling him to his feet. Whatever their differences had been, now they were both facing something new, something that threatened the water that was part of their blood. More screams and mutterings came, much closer this time and, with an ache in his heart, Tugg recognised Elbow's voice amongst those calling for help.

'Look,' Manot whispered. He was staring behind them, looking shocked and horrified.

Tugg turned. The mist, which had always been a thick white, was changing colour. Some patches were a sickly green, others a grey, and as the colours absorbed the white, the blanket covering the water was becoming denser. As it swallowed up the two boats behind theirs, one from each side, both leaders saw their men stop fighting. For a moment, there was only confusion on their faces, but then they began to scream and wail, some cutting at their own faces and arms as if that could somehow ease whatever inner terrors they were facing. The mist slowly swallowed them and they were lost from sight, becoming the wail of ghosts before that too ceased.

284

... and now the mist was heading for them. 'We need to turn around,' Manot said. 'If we move fast we could get to the middle before it. Maybe the barrier is down.'

Tugg watched the wall of insanity coming towards them. Something had happened on the shore, and he hoped that it was something good. He hoped that the battles were being won and this damage to his river would be healed.

'It'll hit us before we've even turned the boat around,' he said. 'You know that.'

Manot said nothing and as the truth of their situation dawned on them, both men remained quiet. The mist came for them, relentless. The cries and yells were fading, and Tugg wondered how many men were still alive. Or perhaps the mist was now so solid it absorbed their screams. He supposed he'd never find out.

'I love the water,' he said, a decision reached in his mind.

'Aye, so do I,' Manot concurred.

They looked at each other, Manot as blond as Tugg was dark, the two leaders of the river men, and no more words needed to be said. They smiled as they turned away from the monstrosity that was coming to for them and climbed up on the side of the boat, their legs steady despite the strange currents at work beneath them. Tugg nodded at Manot who nodded back, and then they dived as one.

Tugg was still smiling as the light faded, his beloved river pulled him down to its bed and the eels came to feed.

FORTY-ONE

'It's going to tear,' Joe said.

Fin was still staring at Baxter's dead body when Joe broke the silence. His head felt heavy when he turned round. 'What?'

'The sky,' Joe said. 'I can feel it. I'm still connected to it.' He pushed himself away from the small bed and hobbled unsteadily towards the stones. 'The rift needs to be healed. It can't do it on its own.'

'Joe?' Mrs Manning rushed to him. 'Joe, you're okay, you're …' Her words faded into a sob as she pulled him into her ample bosom. Fin watched as Joe let her hold him for a moment and then gently but firmly pushed her away.

'Everything's all right, Mum. I've just got something to do.'

He looked at Fowkes, a glance that Fin didn't quite understand, and then nodded. The Knight got to his feet and put his arms round her, pulling her away slightly. Joe raised his hands over the stones.

'Where's Mona?' Christopher said. 'What have you done with her?'

'I sent her South,' Joe said. 'She's fine. She's the Storyholder now. But I needed her safe until all this was over.' Although he didn't cry, Christopher's face crumpled as if something in his soul was breaking.

'It's okay,' Fin said. 'We can get her back. We'll just cut through to the South. I've been there now. I can see it.'

The Dome rumbled around them, the whole building

shaking, and from somewhere outside came a huge crack of thunder. Mrs Manning shrieked into Fowkes' chest. For the moment, Mona and the South were forgotten.

'What did you do?' Christopher looked at Justin Arnold-Mather who sat, his knees pulled up under his chin, trying to look invisible. 'What did you do?'

'Nothing,' his father answered. 'I don't know what's happening. Honestly. I don't have any magic any more. This can't be me.'

'It had already started,' Joe said. 'The universe was fracturing on the other side of the crack. It's gone so far it can't pull back.' He ran one hand over his short curls and for a moment it felt to Fin as if they were back in school at Eastfields with Joe trying to figure out how to get out of a detention in order to go to football practice on the cold October evenings.

'So that's it?' Fowkes said. 'Game over?'

'No.' Joe was staring at the stones. 'I think I can stop it. I can heal it.'

'How?' Fin asked.

'Don't you even think about doing anything stupid, young man,' Mrs Manning pushed herself away from Fowkes. 'You've done enough stupid things in your time, my boy. No more.' Her eyes were filling with tears.

'But this isn't stupid, Mum.'

'What are you going to do?' Fin's stomach tightened into a knot.

'The only thing that can be done,' Joe said. 'I'm going to save the universe.' He grinned, the same cheerful smile Fin had seen so many times before. 'I've seen it. I've had it in me for all these years. It was brilliant. Wonderful. Now I can be part of it. But without all the pain of being tied here.'

'No ... no—' Mrs Manning started, but Fowkes pulled her back, stronger this time and not letting her go.

'I love you, Mum,' he said. 'You're the best.' He looked at

Fin. 'Thanks for the adventures, Fin. Thanks for being my best mate.'

'What are you doing?' Fin said again, even though he knew that this was goodbye. 'You can't —'

'That's the thing. I can.' Joe's grin widened. 'And I was never going to play for Arsenal, was I? I might as well get to save the world.'

'I don't want you to go,' Fin said quietly.

'I won't be gone,' Joe said. 'I'll be *everywhere.*'

His hands reached out and touched the stones. For a moment his and Fin's eyes locked, blue on brown, sad on contented.

'See ya, Fin,' Joe whispered.

And then the room exploded in light.

FORTY-TWO

The sky was blue above them, and even though only a couple of hours had passed since the crack in the sky had healed, the ice was already melting.

'It's nice to be warm again,' Christopher said as they walked.

'Let's find Mona,' Fin said. 'We've got an hour before we have to be back at the Old Bailey. We can at least find out where she is.' Normally, the idea of travelling would fill him with joy and excitement, but after everything that had happened, he just felt empty. He wanted the friends he had left to be back with him. Fowkes had reconvened with the Knights at the palace, Arnold-Mather was securely guarded by Savjani and Levi Dodge, and George Porter was being placed in the mirror prison. The smallest piece of stone was being dropped back down the Clerke's Well, to its home in the ninth world. Fowkes and Henry Wakley were returning the London Stone while the rest of the Knights did a tour of the Nowhere's London to see how much damage had been done in the fighting. Everything was, at last, being returned to normal. He should feel happier about it, and perhaps soon he would. But for now, he was just tired and shell-shocked.

'It's a nice thought,' Christopher said. He didn't look at Fin. 'But we can't.'

'What do you mean?'

'Try it. Try and cut through to the South.'

Confused, Fin raised his sword. He thought of the side street with the washing hanging between the buildings in mid-air, held by nothing but magic. He could see it clearly. He sliced through the air, and a juddering numb shock ran through his arm. No doorway opened. He frowned and tried again. What was the matter? The swords were working. Fowkes had used his to take the stone back. All the same, no doorway opened and the strange jarring sensation, as if he'd banged his funny bone, got worse the harder he tried.

'I don't understand ...'

'Look,' Christopher said, and crossed to the other side of the street. He pointed down an alleyway. Fin's gaze followed. From where they stood, they could see the river.

'What's happened to it?' Fin asked. The mist was thick, foully coloured and oppressive, rising much higher than it had before. Even from a distance it made Fin shiver and he felt a dark worm of despair uncurling in his stomach.

'The Magi Queen put the madness in it. She had to. Otherwise it would have killed her.'

'Did you See this? Did you know?'

'No, but I saw what happened here *before* and I knew it would be important.' The sun shone bright and warm on them as Christopher spoke. 'The mist has never been natural. A long time ago, the river was just like ours. People worked on it, crossed back and forth, fished in it. Swam in it. When the Magi were banished and they crossed to the South, they put all their anger and hatred into the water. They didn't want to be tempted to use their dark magic so they got rid of it all and turned the mist into a barrier between the two sides. At first no one could cross but then, as it slowly dissipated, the river people like the Traders found they could travel on it without any effect. The mist had thinned. It would have continued thinning until one day everything was as it was before.'

'And now?' Fin asked.

'One day it will thin again, to a point where Knights and

Traders can cross it,' Christopher said softly. 'But not in our lifetime.'

On top of losing Joe, Fin wasn't sure he wanted to accept this fresh misery. 'So Mona is stuck there? She can't come home?'

'Mona and the stories are trapped there,' Christopher said, 'and the Magi Queen and her people are trapped here.' He sighed and closed his eyes in the sunshine for a long moment before rolling his head around on his neck. 'Perhaps there's a balance to it. It's time the South had the stories, and it's time the Nowhere and the Magi made their peace. Perhaps, as she's a queen already, we can persuade the North to offer her the empty throne. They could do a lot worse.'

'But ...' Fin's sense of loss over Mona was overwhelmed as he realised what Christopher must be feeling. 'But she's your wife. She's ...'

Christopher looked at him with a sad smile and Fin's words tailed off. What could he say? Nothing. Nothing that would be good enough. Christopher and Mona were never going to see each other again. He and Mona were never going to see each other again.

'Come on,' Christopher said, saving Fin from his awkwardness. 'Let's go.'

FORTY-THREE

The Knights had gathered back at the Old Bailey House of Real Truths to find the Archivers repairing the damage with the same silent diligence with which they cared for their truths.

'Where did they go?' Fin asked Fowkes.

'Who knows? Wherever they came from originally, I suppose.' He paused. 'Maybe Simeon Soames' city in the valley.'

They left the albinos to their work and went upstairs to the abandoned Storyholder's apartments. They would no longer be needed. Tova was gone, Joe was gone, and now Mona was lost, far away.

'There are always losses,' Fowkes said quietly, looking at the troubled expression on Fin's face. 'But you have to learn to celebrate the great sacrifices those people made. Focus on that. It's the only way to mourn them with respect.'

Looking at Christopher and Savjani, standing together in a far corner of the sitting room, Fin thought Fowkes made it sound easy. But still, both of them held their chins high and had dry eyes. He needed to match their strength, at least on the outside.

Henry Wakley held the doorway to the Somewhere open. He nodded to Levi Dodge, Mrs Manning and Freddie Wise, who had a cowed Justin Arnold-Mather and Jarvis beside him. 'You three go first. Then the rest of you.'

On the other side, Fin could make out Ted, Harper Jones and Esme the librarian. The lights were back on in the house, and there, as in the Nowhere, time had returned to normal. He watched as the first few stepped across and reappeared, and then finally Freddie Wise followed them. Cardrew Cutler had wormed his way to the front, as eager to see the librarian as she was to see him, when it became clear that something in the Somewhere wasn't quite right.

'Wait.' Fowkes placed his hand against Cardrew's chest, holding him back. Fin peered into the doorway. On the other side, Freddie Wise had collapsed. A wave of murmurs ran round the room as everyone tried to see, jostling past each other.

'What is it?' Benjamin Wakley asked, forcing his way through, with the Magi Queen at his side. She peered in.

'I thought this might happen,' she said softly.

'What?' Fowkes asked.

'It's the Ageing. It's returned. Worse this time.' She looked up at the Commander of the Knights. 'The balance has been restored. Everything is returned to its normal state. If your men return, they will go back to how they were, or worse.' She looked back at the black-and-white scene playing out on the other side, where Ted and Levi Dodge were trying to get the suddenly ancient man to his feet. In the background, Mrs Baker rushed to help, her hands over her mouth. 'Like with poor Freddie,' the Queen finished.

'You mean ... ?' Cardrew Cutler looked up at Esme, waiting for him on the other side. 'We can't go back?'

'Not if you want to stay as you are. If you wish to remain young, the Nowhere must be your home now.' She turned to look at the men. 'Perhaps it's time that we had Knights of Nowhere who lived here.'

The gathered men looked at each other, and after a moment began to nod and murmur their assent. Fin figured there were worse fates than to live in this magical city, and all of these Knights had lived through one of them. He looked back at Cardrew Cutler, who was staring forlornly through the doorway.

'She could come here?' Fin suggested nervously, and Cardrew looked at him and grinned before beckoning frantically to the woman who stood so close and yet a world away.

It was as she stepped through and landed, giggling, in Cardrew Cutler's arms, that Fin noticed something else was wrong. Red glittered in the black-and-white image of the Somewhere. There was never colour in the doorway images, only a sepia old movie look. What was ... *Arnold-Mather*. Fin's heart raced.

'Something's wrong. I didn't get all of the magic!' he cried. Harper Jones had collapsed to the floor, and the Oval Room, between his collapse and that of Freddie Wise, was now in chaos. The door was open and Christopher's dad had vanished.

'What?' Fowkes frowned.

'He kept some of the magic! He's getting away!' Without pausing to explain, Fin leapt through the doorway.

The heat hit him hard but he kept running, almost stumbling over Mrs Manning and Levi Dodge who, having got Freddie Wise into a chair, had now gone to help Harper Jones. *They love each other*, Fin thought out of nowhere, as he sprinted to the door. *They'll be okay.*

'He went downstairs, Fin love!' shouted Mrs Baker. 'Ted's gone after him!' She leaned back against the wall to let him pass. 'Hurry! Third floor I think! The secret room!'

Fin knew, even as he ran, that he was too late.

The corridor had been empty when Fin and Ted reached it, the wall and the alcove intact. The only clue that Arnold-Mather had escaped through the secret room was a splash of water from the flower vase darkening the white carpet beneath them. Christopher's father was gone.

Fowkes had joined them a few moments later, and had cursed angrily before returning to the Oval Room to rejoin the others. Was Arnold-Mather still a threat to them or the worlds? Fin didn't think so, and he was sure the others didn't either, but he didn't deserve to get away so easily. Not with everything he'd done. He and Ted stood on the stairs and watched as Mrs Baker led Freddie Wise to one of the bedrooms. The old man didn't look at them and exhaustion washed over Fin. Was this how victory was supposed to feel?

'Do you want to go in with them?' Ted asked, nodding towards the door that Fowkes was closing. Fin shook his head. With everything that had happened, he needed something else. Something familiar. There was also something niggling in the back of his mind – something to do with the secret room in the alcove – and he needed some peace to set it free.

'I need a cup of tea,' he said, eventually. 'What about you?'

They sat in the familiar warmth of the kitchen in the basement and Ted poured two mugs of tea from the teapot. They hadn't said much and that was fine with Fin. The tea was strong and sweet and, as he sipped it, he felt stronger. And in some ways suddenly much older, even though Baxter was gone. Whatever he was feeling, it was all him, whoever he was. The world wasn't going back to normal. Not really. It was just adjusting to the change. Christopher was the Seer and his life was in the Nowhere, even though Mona was lost to the South. He tried not to feel the sadness of that thought and instead remembered that so far as the Knights and the Nowhere were concerned, anything was possible. Maybe not today, or tomorrow, but who knew what adventure might come along and lead to a change for them.

'What about Christopher's mum?' The thought struck him suddenly. 'What will she be told?'

'That's something for Fowkes and Christopher to figure out between 'em, I guess,' Ted said. Fin nodded. There would always be a story – a sad one maybe – but a story all the same. That was how the worlds existed. Stories.

'Don't you want to talk to Fowkes?' Ted asked. He was watching Fin carefully. They'd come a long way since the days of birthday cakes with one candle in them. From one year here and one year there. The boy and the man were equals of sorts now. They understood each other.

'I don't think so,' Fin said. The itch in his head was growing. Joe was gone, to an existence that Fin couldn't even imagine, and there was only Fin left, back here in Orrery House. The three of them had spiralled to different lives or existences, and there was nothing that could bring it back to normal. This wasn't his destiny. He was sure of it. At first he'd thought he should find Anaïs and they could make a life together – and perhaps sometime in the future they would – but one kiss did not make a fate whatever books and movies had preached. Destinies were individual. He and Christopher and Joe had learned that. He'd thought that, once this adventure was over, that his fate would be with the Knights – but now he wasn't so sure. Life and the worlds didn't work like that. Maybe there was something else waiting for him. Being in the Somewhere felt wrong. And the Nowhere? That was Christopher's and the Magi Queen's for now, and he had a feeling that they were heading for a period of peace and prosperity. They'd earned it.

It was the secret room. It was bugging him. More than that. It was calling to him.

'Can we go upstairs again, Ted?' he said.

The old man looked at him for a second from behind his teacup and then nodded. 'Whatever you want, Fin, son,' he said.

Time could be a funny thing, Fin thought as they climbed the stairs and everything suddenly became clear to him. Judge Harlequin Brown had been right. It really could.

'I was too slow,' Ted said, as he stared at the wall. 'I was too old and too slow, Fin. 'Ow did 'e even know about this room? 'Ow?'

Fin stared at the alcove with the flowers in it. 'Jarvis must've told him about it, I guess.'

'The door was closing before I got here. 'Ow could he be so fast?'

'He kept a little bit of magic back, I think,' Fin said. 'It's not your fault.' He looked at the vase again. In his head, he heard a tune whistling: 'She'll be coming round the mountain when she comes.' 'And doors can always be opened again.'

He lifted the vase and placed it on the ground. The secret doorway swung open. Fin smiled. He started to quietly whistle 'Ten green bottles' and he and Ted ducked into the narrow corridor, staying hunched over until the room opened out. Unlike the last time Fin had seen it, the room was devoid of clutter. Empty. Unlived in. That didn't surprise Fin. In fact, it made him smile. Of course it wasn't lived in.

''e's gone,' Ted said, despondent. ''e could be anywhere by now.'

'He'll be somewhere,' Fin said as fate and destiny and adventure all slotted into place in front of him. 'I'll find him.'

'What do you mean? You'll find 'im?'

'This place.' Fin looked around at the room. 'I'll go wherever it takes me.'

'But you can't!' Ted said. 'You can't do that!'

'You don't get it, do you, Ted?' Fin grinned. He'd come full circle. '*I already have.*'

'I don't follow, Fin. What're you saying?'

'The judge knew.' Fin laughed a little to himself. 'On the night of my sixteenth birthday, when I found this room and the old man in it? When he came through that door and said "Finmere", it wasn't because he knew I'd wandered in here. He was already talking to me. To the old man.' The memory was so vivid. The old man being told off by the Judge for luring Fin in with the whistling. The ring and the sword. The twinkle in the old man's eye when he told Fin to ask Ted what his name might have been if he'd been abandoned on a different day. He knew so much about Fin. He *was* Fin.

'Time's a funny thing, Ted,' he said. 'You should know that.' Fin's heart was soaring. One day he'd see Judge Harlequin Brown again. One day he'd have filled this room with his own books and adventures. His feet itched to get to them. A boy who didn't belong in either world needed to follow his fate to all the other places that existed.

'If they find Anaïs alive,' he said, almost laughing at the thought of everything that lay ahead. Adventures. Just like Baxter had said, adventures needed to be grabbed. 'Tell her I'm thinking of her. Who knows, maybe one day I'll be able to come back for her, maybe she'll decide she likes travelling. Tell Christopher I'll find his dad. He won't cause trouble ever again.'

'But Fin ...' Ted's eyes were watering. 'You need to ... people will ... what about Fowkes?'

'There's no time to tell him.' Fin shook his head. 'Fowkes will understand. I need to follow Arnold-Mather now, before he gets too far ahead of me. And this isn't goodbye, Ted. Just keep moving those flowers. I'll be back one day.'

He shuffled the old man to the door.

'Wait,' Ted said, and rummaged in his pocket, pulling out his old battered cigarette tin. ''Ere. Take this. I want you to have it.'

Fin hugged the old nightwatchman, accepting the tin and relishing the scent of tobacco and aftershave that had been the one constant in his life. Holding the tin he took a step backwards, watching the wall close between them. He placed the cigarette tin on one of the empty shelves and smiled, before sitting down in the desk chair. The air trembled slightly and the room moved.

It was time for another adventure.

EPILOGUE

The stars twinkled over London and the air was crisp and cold. The city was beautiful, but Christopher Arnold-Mather, the Seer, barely saw his surroundings. This place was no longer his home and the city was not, and never had been, the purpose of his visit. His fingers were cold as he worked at the locks on the tall building that rose like a pillar high into the night sky. Finally they came free, and he began the long climb to the viewing platform at the top of Pudding Lane Monument.

In the heat of the South, the Storyholder stood at the top of the tower in the baking midday sun and waited, as she had four times a year for the ten years that had passed since the wondrous city had become her home. Her heart raced with excitement and pain, as it always did.

The towers sang to each other across the worlds, and the two lovers talked until dawn was breaking and night was falling.

Above them, the universe smiled.

ACKNOWLEDGEMENTS

First off, now that the story is done, I want to thank the people who were there on that walk round London that inspired it: Adrienne, Mike, Christopher and Jo – between us we've produced these three books and two babies since then! Not bad work!

Also, thanks as always to my agent, Veronique, and my editor Gillian Redfearn, and all the posse at Gollancz and Fierce Fiction. You all totally rock.